Isabel Allende

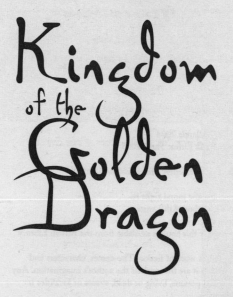

Kingdom of the Golden Dragon

Translated from the Spanish by
MARGARET SAYERS PEDEN

HARPER PERENNIAL

Harper Perennial
An imprint of HarperCollins*Publishers*
77–85 Fulham Palace Road
Hammersmith, London W6 8JB

www.harperperennial.co.uk

This edition published by Harper Perennial 2005

6

First published in Great Britain by Flamingo 2004

Copyright © Isabel A
PS section copyright (

PS™ is a trademark (

Isabel Allende asserts
be identified as the au

A catalogue record for

This novel is entirely
incidents portrayed in
resemblance to actual
entirely coincidental.

ISBN 0 00 717748 8

Typeset in Adobe Caslon

Printed and bound in Great Britain by Clays Ltd, St Ives plc

*For my friend Tabra Tunoa, tireless traveler,
who took me to the Himalayas and told me about
the Golden Dragon.*

Contents

CHAPTER ONE

The Land of Snow and Ice

❋

THE BUDDHIST MONK NAMED Tensing and his disciple, Prince Dil Bahadur, had been climbing in the high peaks north of the Himalayas for many days, a region of eternal ice where no one but a few lamas had ever ventured. Neither of the two was counting the hours, because time did not interest them. The calendar is a human invention; time does not exist on the spiritual level, the master had taught his student.

For them it was the crossing that was important; the prince was making it for the first time. The monk remembered having done it in a previous life, but those memories were rather blurred. They were following the markings on an ancient parchment, orienting themselves by the stars in a terrain where even in summer conditions were very harsh. The temperature of several degrees below zero was endurable only two months during the year, when ominous storms were not lashing the mountains.

Even beneath the sunny, cloudless skies, the cold

1

was intense. They were wearing rough wool tunics, and cloaks made from yak hide. Leather boots from the same animal covered their feet, with the long hair turned in and the outside weather-proofed with yak butter. The travelers placed each foot with care; one misstep on the ice and they could tumble hundreds of yards into the deep chasms that sliced through the mountains as if cleft by God's hatchet.

Luminous snowy peaks stood out against a sky of deep blue. The travelers moved at a slow pace, because at those heights there was very little oxygen. They rested frequently, so their lungs would become accustomed to the altitude. Their chests ached, as did their ears and their heads. They were suffering from nausea and fatigue, but neither of the two mentioned such bodily weakness, saving their breath in order to get the maximum benefit from each mouthful of air.

They were searching for rare plants found only in the Valley of the Yetis, plants essential in preparing medicinal lotions and balms. If they survived the dangers of this journey, they would consider themselves initiated, for their characters would be tempered like steel. Their will and courage would be put to the test many times during that climb. The disciple would need both will and courage to carry out the task that awaited him in life, which was why he had been given the name Dil Bahadur, "brave heart" in the language of the Forbidden Kingdom. The pilgrimage to the Valley of the Yetis was one of the last steps in the harsh training the prince had been undergoing for twelve years.

The youth did not know the true reason for their trek, which was much more important than the gathering of curative plants or his initiation as a lama, or superior being. His master could not reveal it to him, just as he could not speak to him of many other things. Tensing's role was to guide the prince during each stage of his long apprenticeship; he was charged with strengthening the young man's body and his character and cultivating his mind, testing the quality of his spirit again and again. Dil Bahadur would discover the reason for the journey to the Valley of the Yetis later, when he found himself before the fabled statue of the Golden Dragon.

On their backs, Tensing and Dil Bahadur were carrying bundles that contained the blankets, grain, and yak butter they would need to survive. Rolled around their waists were coils of yak-hair rope, which they used in climbing, and in one hand each grasped a long, strong walking staff, which they used for support, for defending themselves in case of attack, and for setting up their improvised tent at night. In places where experience had taught them that fresh snow often covered deep openings, they also used their staffs to test the depth and firmness of a surface before stepping onto it. Frequently they were forced to make long detours around fissures that couldn't be jumped over. Sometimes, to avoid going out of their way for hours, they laid one of the staffs across the crevasse, and only when they were sure it was firmly seated on either side did they dare step onto it and then leap to the other side— never more than one step, because the risk of plummeting into empty space was too big. They made such leaps without thinking, with their minds clear, trusting in physical skill, instinct, and luck, because if they stopped to weigh each move it would be impossible to make it. When the opening was wider than the length of the staff, they looped a rope around an overhanging rock, then one of them tied the other end of the rope around his waist, took a running start, and leaped, swinging back and forth like a pendulum until he reached the other side. The young disciple, who had great stamina and courage in the face of danger, always hesitated at the moment they were forced to use those methods.

The pair had come to such a chasm, and the lama was looking for the best place to cross. The youth briefly closed his eyes, sending a prayer skyward.

"Do you fear dying, Dil Bahadur?" Tensing inquired, smiling.

"No, honorable master. The moment of my death was written in my fate before my birth. I shall die when my work is finished in this reincarnation and my spirit is ready to fly, but I do fear breaking all my bones down there, and living," the youth replied, pointing to the impressive precipice yawning at their feet.

"That could, perhaps, present a problem," the lama conceded with good humor. "If you open your mind and heart, it will seem easier," he added.

"What would you do if I were to fall?"

"Should that occur, I would possibly have to think about it. For the moment, my thoughts are turned to other things."

"May I know what, master?"

"The beauty of the panorama," the lama replied, indicating the endless chain of mountains, the immaculate white of the snow, the brilliant sky.

"It is like the landscape of the moon," the youth observed.

"Possibly . . . What part of the moon have you

visited, Dil Bahadur?" the lama asked, hiding another smile.

"I have not traveled that far as yet, master, but I imagine it like this."

"On the moon, the sky is black and there are no mountains like these. There is no snow, either; everything is rock and ash-colored dust."

"Perhaps some day I shall be able to make an astral voyage to the moon, like my honorable master," the disciple conceded.

"Perhaps . . ."

After the lama positioned his staff, both took off their tunics and cloaks, which kept them from moving freely, and made four bundles of their belongings. The lama was built like an athlete. His shoulders and arms were pure muscle, his neck was as broad as a normal man's thigh, and his legs as thick as tree trunks. That formidable warrior's body contrasted markedly with his serene face, gentle eyes, and delicate—almost feminine—and always-smiling mouth. Tensing took the bundles one by one, built up momentum by rotating his arm like the vanes of a windmill, and tossed the bundles to the other side of the chasm.

"The fear is not real, Dil Bahadur; it is only in your mind, like all other things. Our thoughts form what we believe to be reality," he said.

"At this moment, my mind is creating a very deep crevasse, master," the prince murmured.

"And my mind is creating a very strong bridge," the lama replied.

He waved to the youth, who stood waiting in the snow, then took one step above the void, planting his right foot at the middle of the wood staff and a fraction of a second later throwing himself forward, reaching the other side with his left foot. Dil Bahadur imitated him with less grace and speed, but gave no sign of nervousness. The master noticed that his student's skin was gleaming with sweat. They quickly dressed and resumed walking.

"Is it much farther?" Dil Bahadur wanted to know.

"Possibly."

"Would it be imprudent, master, to request that you not always answer 'possibly'?"

"Perhaps it would." Tensing smiled, and after a pause added that, according to the instructions on the parchment, they were to continue north. The most difficult portion of their path lay ahead.

"Have you seen the Yetis, master?"

"They are like dragons, they shoot fire from their ears and they have four pairs of arms."

"Amazing!" the youth exclaimed.

"How many times have I told you not to believe everything you hear? Seek truth for yourself," the lama laughed.

"Master, we are not studying the teachings of Buddha, we are simply talking." The disciple sighed, annoyed.

"I have not seen the Yetis in this life, but I remember them from a previous one. We share common ancestors, and several thousand years ago they had a civilization almost as developed as our own, but now they are very primitive and of limited intelligence."

"What happened?"

"They are very aggressive. They killed each other and destroyed everything they had, including the land. The survivors fled to the peaks of the Himalayas and there their race began to decline. Now they are like animals," the lama explained.

"Are there many of them?"

"Everything is relative. They will seem to be many if they attack us and few if they are friendly. In any case, they do not live very long lives but they reproduce easily; therefore I suppose there will be a number of them in the valley. They live in an inaccessible region where no one can find them, but sometimes one of them ventures out in search of food and gets lost. That is possibly the source of the tracks attributed to the Abominable Snowman, as he is called," the lama put forward.

"Their footprints are enormous. They must be giants. Will they still be very aggressive?"

"You ask many questions for which there are no answers, Dil Bahadur," the master replied.

Tensing led his disciple through the mountain peaks, leaping chasms, scaling vertical faces, slipping along narrow paths cut into the rock. Occasionally they came across old hanging bridges, but they were in very poor condition and could be used only with great care. When there was wind or sleet, they looked for shelter and waited. Once a day they ate their *tsampa*, a mixture of toasted barley flour, dried herbs, yak butter, and salt. They found abundant water beneath the crust of ice. Young Dil Bahadur often had the impression that they were walking in circles, because the landscape looked the same, but he said nothing about his doubts: it would be discourteous to his master.

As evening fell, they looked for a sheltered place to spend the night. Sometimes it was nothing but a rift in which they could find comfort protected from the wind, other nights they might find a cave, but occasionally they had no choice but to sleep out in the open, barely shielded by their yak cloaks. Once they set up their austere camp, they sat facing the setting sun, legs crossed, and chanted the essential mantra of Buddha, repeating over and over *Om mani padme hum*—Hail, precious jewel in the heart of the lotus. The echo would repeat their prayer, multiplying it to infinity among the high peaks of the Himalayas.

During the day's march they gathered sticks and dried grasses, which they carried in their pouches for building the nightly fire and for cooking their food. After the evening meal, they meditated for an hour. During that time the cold left them stiff as ice statues, but they scarcely felt it. They were used to such immobility, which brought them calm and peace. In their Buddhist practices, master and student sat in absolute relaxation, but remained alert. They rid themselves of all the distractions and worries of the world, though they never forgot the suffering that existed everywhere.

After scaling mountains for several days and climbing the frozen heights, they came to Chenthan Dzong, the fortified monastery of the ancient lamas who had invented the form of hand-to-hand combat called Tao-shu. In the nineteenth century, the monastery had been destroyed by an earthquake and had to be abandoned. It was built of stone, brick, and wood, with more than a hundred rooms that seemed glued to the edge of an impressive cliff. For centuries the monastery had housed monks whose lives were dedicated to spiritual quest and to perfecting the martial arts.

The Tao-shu monks had originally been physicians with an exceptional knowledge of anatomy. In their practice they had identified vulnerable points of the body that were numbed or paralyzed when pressed, and they combined that knowledge with techniques of wrestling known in Asia. Their objective was to reach spiritual perfection through control of their own strength and emotions. Although they were invincible in hand-to-hand combat, they did not use the Tao-shu for violent ends, only as a physical and mental exercise. Similarly, they did not teach their art to just anyone, only to certain chosen men and women. Tensing had learned Tao-shu from those monks, and he had taught it to his disciple Dil Bahadur.

The earthquake, snow, ice, and the passage of time had eroded most of the building, but two wings were still standing, although they were in ruins. The travelers had reached the monastery by climbing a precipice so difficult and remote that no one had attempted it for more than half a century.

"Soon they will come to the monastery by air," Tensing observed.

"Do you believe, master, that they will discover the Valley of the Yetis from airplanes?" the prince inquired.

"Possibly."

"Imagine how much effort could have been saved. Before long we could have flown here."

"I hope that it will not be so. If they trap the Yetis, they will turn them into circus animals, or slaves," the lama said.

They went into Chenthan Dzong to rest and to spend the night in its shelter. Threadbare tapestries with religious images still hung on some of the walls, and they found cooking vessels and weapons the warrior monks who survived the earthquake had not been able to take with them. There were several representations of Buddha in varying postures, including an enormous statue of the Enlightened One lying prone on the ground. The gilt had cracked away, but the remainder of the statue was intact. Ice and blowing snow covered nearly everything, lending the ruins a particularly beautiful aspect, as if it were a crystal palace. Behind the building, an avalanche had created the only level surface in the area, a kind of courtyard about the size of a basketball court.

"Could an airplane land here, master?" asked Dil Bahadur, unable to disguise his fascination with the few modern apparatuses he knew.

"I know nothing of these things, Dil Bahadur. I have never seen an airplane land, but it seems to me that this space is very small, and besides, the mountains act like a funnel, drawing strong air currents."

In the kitchen they found pots and other iron implements, candles, charcoal, sticks for making a fire, and some grains preserved by the cold. There were also vessels for holding oil and a container of honey, which the prince had never seen. Tensing gave him a taste, and for the first time in his life the prince felt something sweet on his tongue. The surprise and the pleasure nearly knocked him off his feet. They built a fire for cooking and lighted candles before the statues, as a sign of respect. That night they would eat well and they would sleep beneath a roof: the occasion merited a special brief ceremony of thanks.

They were meditating in silence when they heard a low moan echoing through the ruins of the monastery. They opened their eyes just as a rare white tiger padded into the ruined room, a half-ton of muscle and white fur, the fiercest animal known to the world.

Telepathically, the prince received his master's command, and tried to obey, although his instinctive reaction had been to call on Tao-shu and leap up to defend himself. If he could get close enough to reach behind the cat's ears, he could paralyze it; he sat motionless, however, trying to breathe calmly so the beast would not pick up the scent of fear. The huge feline slowly advanced toward the monks. Despite the imminent danger in which he found himself, the prince could not help but admire the animal's extraordinary beauty. Its fur was a pale ivory with dark markings, and its blue eyes were the color of some of the glaciers in the Himalayas. It was an adult male, enormous, powerful, a perfect specimen.

Sitting in the lotus position with legs crossed and hands upon their knees, Tensing and Dil Bahadur watched the tiger move toward them. They both knew that if it was hungry, there was little possibility of stopping it. Their hope was that the animal had eaten, although it was not very likely that game was abundant in these barren solitudes. Tensing possessed uncommon psychic powers because he was a *tulku*, the reincarnation of a High Lama of antiquity. He concentrated that power like a beam to penetrate the beast's mind.

They felt the breath of the great cat on their faces, an exhalation of warm, fetid air escaping from its jaws.

Another terrible roar shook the air. The beast approached to within a few inches of the two, so close that they could feel the prick of its stiff whiskers. For several seconds, which seemed eternal, it circled around them, sniffing them and feinting with one enormous paw, but not menacing them. The master and his disciple sat absolutely motionless, leaving themselves open to warmth and compassion, displaying no fear or aggression, only empathy. Once the tiger's curiosity had been satisfied, it left with the same solemn dignity with which it had come.

"You see, Dil Bahadur, how sometimes calm is effective," was the lama's only comment. The prince was unable to answer because his voice had frozen in his breast.

Despite that unexpected visit, master and student decided to stay and spend the night in Chenthan Dzong, but they took the precaution of sleeping near a bonfire, and of keeping within reach a couple of lances they found among the weapons abandoned by the Tao-shu monks. The tiger did not return, but the next morning, when they continued their march, they saw its paw marks on the gleaming snow, and far away they heard its roars echoing among the peaks.

CHAPTER TWO

The Valley of the Yetis

✦

A FEW DAYS LATER, TENSING shouted jubilantly and pointed to a narrow canyon between two vertical faces of the mountain: two black walls polished by millions of years of ice and erosion. They entered the canyon with great caution, scrambling over loose rocks and avoiding deep holes. With each step they had to test the firmness of the terrain with their poles.

Tensing threw a stone into one of the openings, and it was so deep that they never heard it hit bottom. Overhead, the sky was barely visible as a blue ribbon stretching between gleaming walls of rock. They were surprised to hear a chorus of horrifying moans.

"It is fortunate, is it not, that we do not believe in ghosts or demons," commented the lama.

"Then maybe it is my imagination that is making me hear those wails?" the prince asked, his skin prickling with fright.

"Possibly the wind is blowing through here like air blowing through a trumpet."

They had progressed a good way when they were assaulted by the stench of rotten eggs.

"Sulfur," the master explained.

"I can't breathe," said Dil Bahadur, pinching his nostrils.

"Perhaps it is best to imagine you are smelling the perfume of flowers," Tensing suggested.

"'Of all fragrances,'" the prince recited, smiling, "'the sweetest is that of virtue.'"

"Imagine, then, that this is the sweet scent of virtue," the lama replied, laughing.

The pass was approximately a mile in length, but it took them two hours to travel that distance. In some places the passage was so narrow that they had to scoot sideways between the rocks, dizzied by the thin air, but they did not hesitate, because the parchment clearly indicated that there was a way out. They saw niches dug into the walls, which contained skulls and large piles of bones, some seemingly human.

"This must be the Yetis' cemetery," Dil Bahadur had commented.

A breath of moist, warm air, like nothing they had ever felt, announced the end of the canyon.

Tensing was the first to step out, followed closely by his disciple. When Dil Bahadur saw the landscape that lay before them, he thought he must be on another planet. If he hadn't been so weighed down by bodily fatigue, and if his stomach weren't churning from the stink of the sulfur, he would have thought he had made an astral journey.

"There it is: the Valley of the Yetis," the lama announced.

Before them stretched a volcanic mesa dotted with patches of harsh gray-green vegetation: dense shrubs and giant mushrooms of various shapes and colors were growing everywhere. They saw rushing streams and bubbling pools of water, strange rock formations, and tall columns of white smoke billowing from the ground. A delicate fog floated on the air, erasing shapes in the distance and giving the valley the look of a dreamscape. The visitors felt they had left reality behind, as if they had entered another dimension. After the intense cold of traveling through the mountains for so many days, that warm vapor was a true gift to the senses despite the lingering, nauseating odor that thankfully was less intense here than in the canyon.

"In olden days, certain lamas, carefully selected for their physical endurance and spiritual fortitude, made this journey once every twenty years to collect the medicinal plants that do not grow anywhere else," Tensing explained.

He said that in 1950 Tibet had been invaded by the Chinese, who destroyed more than six thousand monasteries and shut down the rest. Most of the lamas left to live in other countries, such as India and Nepal, carrying the teachings of Buddha into exile. Instead of snuffing out Buddhism, as the invading Chinese intended, the lamas accomplished exactly the opposite: they spread it throughout the world. Even so, much of the knowledge about medicine, as well as the lamas' psychic practices, was lost.

"The plants were dried, ground, and mixed with other ingredients. One gram of those powders may be more precious than all the world's gold, Dil Bahadur," his master told him.

"We can't carry many plants. Too bad we didn't bring a yak," the youth commented.

"Possibly a yak would not willingly have crossed these mountains; I do not see a yak keeping its footing with a staff, Dil Bahadur," said the master. "We will carry what we can."

They entered the mysterious valley, and after walking for a short time they saw something that resembled skeletons. The lama informed his disciple that they were the petrified bones of animals that roamed before the universal flood. He got down on all fours and began to search the ground until he found a dark rock with red spots.

"This is dragon excrement, Dil Bahadur. It has magical properties."

"I must not believe everything I hear, is that not true, master?" the youth replied.

"No, but perhaps in this case it is all right to believe me," the lama said, handing the specimen to his disciple.

The prince hesitated. The idea of touching that stone-hard blob did not appeal to him.

"It is petrified," laughed Tensing. "It can cure broken bones in only minutes. One pinch of this, ground and dissolved in rice alcohol, can transport you to any of the stars in the firmament."

The small specimen Tensing had discovered had an opening through which the lama passed a cord and hung it around Dil Bahadur's neck.

"This is like a shield; it has the power to deflect certain metals. Arrows, knives, and other cutting weapons cannot harm you."

The youth laughed. "Perhaps it will be an infected tooth, a slip on the ice, or being hit in the head by a rock that will kill me."

"We will all die; that is the one certainty, Dil Bahadur."

The lama and the prince made camp beside a warm fumarole, enveloped in its dense column of vapor and happy to spend a comfortable night for the first time in several days. They had made tea with the water from a nearby thermal spring. The water was boiling when it reached the surface, and as the bubbles cooled they turned a pale lavender. The geyser fed a steaming stream that had fleshy purple flowers growing along its banks.

The monk rarely slept, but he would sit for long periods in the lotus position with his eyes half-closed, resting and renewing his energy. He had the ability to remain absolutely motionless, with his mind controlling his breathing, his blood pressure, his heart rate, and his temperature, so that his body entered a state of hibernation. As quickly as he attained absolute rest, he could respond to an emergency, with all his powerful muscles primed to mount a defense. Dil Bahadur had tried for years to imitate him, without success. Exhausted, he fell asleep the moment his head touched the ground.

The prince awakened amid a chorus of terrifying

grunts. The instant he opened his eyes and saw what surrounded him, he sprang to his feet, nerves tingling, with his knees bent and arms extended in the attack position. The tranquil voice of the master stopped him just as he was preparing to strike a blow.

"Be calm. These are Yetis. Send them waves of warmth and compassion, as you did to the white tiger," the lama murmured.

They were encircled by a horde of repulsive creatures about four and a half feet tall, covered from head to toe in tangled, filthy white fur; their arms were long, and their short, bowed legs ended in enormous feet like a monkey's. Dil Bahadur could imagine that the tracks of those huge feet were the source of the legend about them. But then, to whom did the long bones and gigantic skulls they'd seen in the tunnel belong?

The small stature of the creatures in no way diminished their ferocious appearance. Their flat, hairy faces were almost human, but their expressions were bestial; their eyes were small and round, their ears pointed like a dog's, and their teeth were long and sharp. Between grunts, they extended dark purplish-blue tongues that curled at the tip, like a reptile's. Over their chests they wore blood-splattered breastplates that were tied at the shoulder and waist. They were brandishing menacing clubs and sharpened rocks, but despite their weapons and the fact that they greatly outnumbered the new-comers, they were keeping a prudent distance. It was beginning to grow light, and the early dawn, veiled in thick fog, lent a nightmarish tone to the scene.

Tensing got to his feet, slowly, in order not to pro-voke a reaction from their "welcoming committee." Compared to the giant lama, the Yetis seemed even more squat and misshapen. The master's aura had not changed color; it was still gold and white, which reflected his perfect serenity, while the flickering auras of most of the Yetis were dull, earth tones, indicating illness and fear.

The prince could guess why they had not been immediately attacked: the creatures seemed to be wait-ing for someone. In a few moments he saw a figure approaching that was much taller than the others, even though it seemed to be bowed by age. It was the same species as the Yetis, but much taller. If the creature had been able to stand up straight, it would have been as tall as Tensing, but in addition to great age it was deformed by a hump on its back that forced it to walk with its upper body parallel to the ground. Unlike the other Yetis, naked except for their long filthy hair and their breastplates, this female was adorned in necklaces of teeth and bone; she wore a moth-eaten cape of white-tiger skin and held a twisted staff in her hand.

The creature could not be called a woman, though her gender was female. She was not exactly an animal, but neither could she be called human. Her hair was very thin and had fallen out in patches, revealing a pink, scaly skin that looked like a rat's tail. She was covered by an impenetrable crust of grease, dried blood, mud, and filth that emitted a foul stench. Her fingernails were black claws, and her few remaining teeth were loose and danced in her jaws with every breath she drew. Green slime trickled from her nostrils, and her rheumy eyes shone through tufts of the bristly hair covering her face. As she walked toward the visitors, the Yetis moved back in deference. It was obvious that she was in command, apparently the queen or the priestess of the tribe.

Surprised, Dil Bahadur watched as his master knelt before this hideous creature, joined his hands before his face, and recited the traditional greeting of the Forbidden Kingdom.

"*Tampo kachi,*" he said.

"*Grr-ympr,*" she roared, spraying him with saliva.

On his knees, Tensing was at the level of the bent-over old woman, and thus able to look directly into her eyes. Dil Bahadur imitated the lama, even though in that posture he would not be able to defend himself against the Yetis, who continued to wave their clubs. Out of the corner of his eye, he calculated that there were ten or twelve gathered around them, and who knows how many more nearby.

The female chieftain uttered a series of sharp, guttural sounds that, when combined, seemed to be a kind of language. Dil Bahadur had the impression that he had heard it before, but he didn't know where. He could not understand a single word, even though the sounds were familiar. At once, the Yetis knelt in unison and touched their foreheads to the ground, though they did not put down their weapons, wavering between that ceremonious greeting and the impulse to club the two strangers to death.

The ancient female Yeti calmed the others as she repeated the grunt that sounded like *Grr-ympr*. The visitors assumed that that was her name. Tensing listened very closely and Dil Bahadur made an effort to capture on a telepathic level what those creatures were thinking, but their minds were a tangle of incomprehensible visions. He concentrated on what the sorceress was trying to communicate; she obviously was more evolved than the others. Several images took form in his brain. He saw hairy little animals like white rabbits shiver convulsively and then turn rigid. He saw corpses and burial places; he saw several Yetis rolling another toward a boiling fumarole; he saw blood, death, brutality, and terror.

"Be c-careful, master, they are v-very savage," the youth stammered.

"Possibly they are more frightened than we are, Dil Bahadur," the lama replied.

Grr-ympr gestured to the other Yetis, who finally lowered their clubs as she turned and walked away, gesturing to the prince and his master to follow. Flanked by the Yetis, they followed her past tall columns of steam and thermal waters to some natural openings in the volcanic soil. Along the way, they saw additional Yetis, all seated or lying down, none of whom made any sign of moving toward them.

Burning lava from some ancient volcanic eruption had frozen as it contacted ice and snow, but had continued to flow for some time beneath the surface. That was how the caves and underground tunnels in which the Yetis had made their dwellings had been formed. In places where the crust of lava had ruptured, a little light occasionally filtered in. Most of the caves were low and narrow, and Tensing did not enter those, though they maintained a pleasant temperature thanks to the memory of lava heat that remained in the walls and the warm waters of the fumaroles that flowed beneath them. In this way the Yetis protected themselves against the weather; otherwise it would have been impossible for them to endure the winter.

There were no objects of any kind in the caves, nothing but stinking hides, some with chunks of flesh still attached. With horror Dil Bahadur realized that some of the skins were those of the Yetis themselves, surely torn from dead bodies. The rest were hides of *chegnos*, animals unknown in the rest of the world, which the Yetis kept in corrals fenced with rock and snow. The *chegnos* were smaller than yaks and had curved horns like a ram's. The Yetis used their meat, fat, skin, and even their dried excrement, which served as fuel. Without those noble animals, which ate very little and endured even the lowest temperature, the Yetis could not survive.

"We will stay here a few days, Dil Bahadur. Try to learn the Yetis' language," said the lama.

"Why, master? We will never be called on to use it again."

"I won't, perhaps, but you will," Tensing replied.

Little by little they familiarized themselves with the sounds those creatures uttered. Using the words they had acquired, and reading Grr-ympr's mind, Tensing and Dil Bahadur learned of the tragedy of the creatures' existence: with every generation fewer offspring were being born, and of those, fewer were living. The fate of the adults was not much better. Each generation was physically smaller and weaker than the previous one; their life span had shortened dramatically, and only a few individuals had enough strength to perform the necessary tasks, such as herding the *chegnos*, collecting plants, and hunting for food. This was a punishment of the gods or demons that lived in these mountains, Grr-ympr assured them. She said that the Yetis had tried to appease them with offerings, but the deaths of several sacrificial victims, who had been torn asunder or thrown into the boiling water of the fumaroles, had not ended the divine curse.

Grr-ympr had lived for many years. Her authority lay in her memory and her experience, which no other Yeti possessed. The tribe believed that she had supernatural powers, and for two generations had hoped that she would make things right with the gods; her magic, however, had not lifted the spell and had not saved her people from approaching extinction. Grr-ympr recounted that she had appealed to the gods again and again, and now, finally, they had come: The moment she saw Tensing and Dil Bahadur, she had guessed who they were. And that was why the Yetis had not attacked them.

All this was communicated to the visitors from the mind of the greatly troubled, ancient Yeti.

"When these creatures learn that we are mere humans, not gods, I don't think they're going to be very happy," the prince observed.

"Possibly . . . but compared to them, and despite our infinite shortcomings, we are semi-gods," the lama smiled.

Grr-ympr could remember the time when the Yetis were tall and well built, and were protected by fur so thick that they could survive the elements in the cold-est and highest regions of the planet. The bones the visitors had seen in the canyon were those of their ancestors, the giant Yetis. They kept them there out of respect, although now no one but Grr-ympr could remember them. She had been a young female when the tribe discovered the valley of the hot springs, where the temperature was bearable and life less difficult because green things grew there, and in addition to the *chegnos* there were mice and goats to hunt.

The witch remembered having seen the gods one other time in her life, gods like Tensing and Dil Bahadur, who had come to the valley looking for plants. In exchange for the herbs and seeds they took away, they had left the Yetis valuable knowledge that greatly improved their lives. They had taught them to domesticate the *chegnos* and cook their meat, although now they seldom had energy enough to strike stones and make a fire. Any game they could catch they ate raw and, if they were starving, as a last resort they killed *chegnos* or ate the corpses of other Yetis. The lamas had also taught them to identify themselves by name. Grr-ympr meant "wise woman" in the Yeti tongue.

It had been a very long time since any god appeared in the valley, Grr-ympr informed them telepathically. Tensing calculated that for at least half a century, since China invaded Tibet, no expedition had come to look for medicinal plants. Now the Yetis were not living as long, and no one except the ancient sorceress had seen humans, but the legend of the enlightened lamas existed in their collective memory.

Tensing was seated in a cave larger than the others, the only one he could crawl into, a place undoubtedly used to hold something like a tribal council. Dil

Bahadur and Grr-ympr sat on either side of the lama, and gradually the other Yetis arrived, some so weak they could barely drag themselves across the ground. The ones that had met them with threatening stones and clubs were the warriors of that pathetic group. They stayed outside to stand guard, never for an instant putting down their weapons.

One by one the Yetis filed in, some twenty in total, not counting the dozen warriors. They were nearly all females, and, to judge by their hide and teeth, they seemed young, but very ill. Tensing examined each one, treating them with great respect in order not to frighten them. The last five were carrying babies, the tribe's only surviving offspring. They did not have the repugnant appearance of the adults; they looked like little, white, loose-jointed monkeys. They were limp; they couldn't hold up their heads or move their limbs; their eyes were shut tight and they were barely breathing.

Moved, Dil Bahadur saw that these creatures loved their children as much as any other mother. They held their babies in their arms tenderly, sniffed and licked them, snuggled them to their breasts to nurse them, and moaned with anguish when the infants did not react.

"It is very sad, master. They are dying," the youth observed.

"Life is filled with suffering. Our mission is to relieve it, Dil Bahadur," Tensing replied.

The light in the cave was so weak, and the odor so unbearable, that the lama motioned them all outside, where the tribe gathered again. Grr-ympr attempted a few steps of a healing dance around the sick babies, uttering chilling cries and making her bone-and-teeth necklaces clatter. The Yetis accompanied her with a chorus of moans.

Ignoring the uproar of wailing around him, Tensing bent over the children. Dil Bahadur watched his master's expression change, as it usually did when he was using his curative powers. The lama picked up one of the smallest babies, which fit comfortably in the palm of his hand, and examined it intently. Then he approached one of the mothers, making friendly gestures to calm her, and studied a few drops of her milk.

"What is happening to the children?" the prince asked.

"Possibly they are dying of hunger," said Tensing.

"Hunger? Their mothers aren't feeding them?"

Tensing pointed out that the Yetis' milk was a yellow, transparent liquid. Then he called the warriors, who did not want to respond until Grr-ympr grunted an order, and the lama examined them as well, paying particular attention to their purple tongues. The only one whose tongue was not that color was the ancient Grr-ympr. Her mouth was a dark, evil-smelling pit that did not invite close inspection, but Tensing was not a man to back away from unpleasantness.

"All the Yetis are undernourished except for Grr-ympr, whose only symptoms are those of advanced age. I calculate that she must be a hundred," the lama concluded.

"What has changed in the valley? Why don't they have enough food?" the prince asked.

"Perhaps they have food; they may simply be ill and not assimilating what they eat. The babies depend on their mother's milk, which is not rich enough to nourish them; it's like water, and that is why they are dying at the age of a few weeks or months. The adults have more resources because they eat meat and plants, but something has weakened them."

"Which is why they've been getting smaller and dying young," suggested Dil Bahadur.

"Possibly."

Dil Bahadur rolled his eyes; sometimes his master's vagueness made him crazy.

"This is a problem that has developed during the last two generations, because Grr-ympr remembers when the Yetis were as tall as she is. At this rate, they probably will disappear in a few years," said the prince.

"Possibly," the lama replied for the hundredth time; he was thinking about something else. He added, "Grr-ympr also could remember when they had moved to this valley. That may mean that there is something harmful here, something that is destroying the Yetis."

"That must be it! Can we save them, master?"

"Perhaps . . ."

The monk closed his eyes and prayed for a few minutes, asking for inspiration to resolve the problem and for humility to understand that the result was not in his hands. He would do the best he could, but he could not control life or death.

At the end of his short meditation, Tensing washed his hands, then went to one of the corrals. There he picked out a female *chegno* and milked it. He filled his bowl with warm, foaming milk, and carried it back to the infants. He wet a rag in the milk and placed it to the lips of one of the babies. At first the child did not react, but after a few seconds the smell of the milk stirred it; its lips opened, and it began weakly to suck the rag. The lama gestured to the mothers that they should imitate him.

It was a long and tedious process to teach the Yetis to milk the *chegnos* and to feed the babies drop by drop. The Yetis had a minimal capacity for reasoning, but they were able to learn by repetition. The master and the disciple spent the whole day on the project, and they saw the results that same night when three of the babies cried for the first time. The next day all five were crying, asking for milk, and soon they opened their eyes and were able to move.

Dil Bahadur felt as proud as if the solution had been his idea, but Tensing didn't stop there. He had to find an explanation. He studied everything the Yetis put in their mouths without coming upon the cause of their distress. Then he and his disciple themselves began to suffer stomach pains and vomit bile, although they had eaten only their usual *tsampa*. They hadn't tried the *chegno* meat the Yetis offered them, because they were vegetarians.

"What have we eaten that is different, Dil Bahadur—the one thing?" the master asked as he prepared a medicinal tea for their digestion.

"Nothing, master," the youth replied, pale as death.

"It has to be something," Tensing insisted.

"All we have eaten is our *tsampa*, not a bite of anything else . . ." the prince murmured.

Tensing passed the bowl with the tea to Dil Bahadur, who, doubled over with pain, put it to his lips. But he stopped short before he swallowed, spitting the liquid into the snow.

"The water, master! It's the hot water!"

Normally they boiled water or snow to prepare their *tsampa* and their tea, but in the valley they had been using the boiling water from one of the many thermal springs bubbling from the ground.

"That's what is poisoning the Yetis, master," the prince insisted.

They had seen them use the lavender-colored water from the thermal spring to make the soup of mushrooms, herbs, and purple flowers that served as the basis of their diet. Grr-ympr, however, had lost her appetite over the years, and every two or three days she ate only a little raw meat; when she was thirsty she stuffed handfuls of snow into her mouth. The thermal water—which obviously contained toxic minerals—was what they themselves had used to brew their tea. For the next few hours they avoided it completely, and the discomfort that had been tormenting them ended. To be certain that they had found the source of the problem, the next day Dil Bahadur brewed tea with the suspected water and drank it. He was soon vomiting, but happy to have proved his theory.

Practicing great patience, the lama and his disciple informed Grr-ympr that the lavender-colored water must be strictly prohibited, along with the purple flowers that grew on the banks of the stream. The thermal water could be used for bathing but not for drinking or preparing food, they told her. They didn't bother to explain that it contained harmful minerals, because the ancient Yeti would not have understood; it would be enough that the Yetis would honor her instructions. Grr-ympr made her task easy. She called her subjects together and notified them of a new law: Anyone who drank that water would be thrown into a fumarole. Understood? They all understood.

The tribe helped Tensing and Dil Bahadur collect the medicinal plants they needed. Throughout the week they stayed in the Valley of the Yetis, the visitors were able to watch the babies' health improve every day and see that the adults were growing stronger in direct ratio to how fast the purple faded from their tongues.

Grr-ympr personally accompanied the lama and his

disciple when the moment came to leave. She watched them start in the direction of the canyon they'd come through when they arrived. After some hesitation, because she feared revealing the Yeti's secrets even to these gods, she motioned that they should follow her in the opposite direction. For more than an hour the lama and the prince walked behind her along a narrow path that wove among the columns of vapor and pools of boiling water, leaving the primitive village of the Yetis behind.

The sorceress led them to the edge of the volcanic plain, pointed to an opening in the mountain, and told them that from time to time the Yetis used that pass to go out in search of food. Tensing understood what she was telling them: This was a shortcut in the form of a natural tunnel. The mysterious valley was much closer to civilization than anyone had supposed. The parchment Tensing carried with him indicated the only route known to the lamas, which was much longer and filled with many more obstacles, but no one knew of this secret pass. As he found its location on the parchment, Tensing realized that the tunnel descended straight down into the mountain and came out near Chenthan Dzong, the ruined monastery. This route would save them two-thirds of their original trek.

Grr-ympr bid them farewell in the only way she knew how to show affection: She licked their faces and hands until they were wet with saliva and mucus.

The instant the horrible priestess turned to start back, Dil Bahadur and Tensing rolled in the snow to cleanse themselves. The master was laughing, but the disciple was barely able to keep from throwing up.

"Our only consolation is that we will never see that fine lady again," the youth commented.

"*Never* is a long time, Dil Bahadur. Possibly life has a surprise in store for us," the lama replied, stepping with determination into the narrow tunnel.

CHAPTER THREE

Three Fabulous Eggs

❋

ON THE OTHER SIDE OF THE WORLD, Alexander Cold was arriving in New York, accompanied by his grandmother Kate. The sun of the Amazon had burned the American boy the color of wood. He wore his hair Indian-style: a bowl cut with a shaved circle on the crown of his head, and in that circle was a new scar. He had his filthy backpack over his shoulder, and he carried a bottle of milky liquid. Kate Cold, as tanned as her grandson, was dressed in her usual khaki shorts and mud-caked shoes. Her gray hair—which she herself cut without looking in the mirror—gave her the look of a Mohican that had just been rudely awakened. She was tired, but her eyes glittered behind broken glasses held together with tape. Her luggage consisted of a tube about six feet long and an assortment of bundles of uncommon shapes and sizes.

"Do you have anything to declare?" the immigration officer inquired, throwing a disapproving look at Alex's strange haircut and at his grandmother's general appearance.

It was five in the morning, and the man was as tired as the air passengers who had just flown in from Brazil.

"Nothing. We're reporters for *International Geographic*. All we're carrying is equipment for our work," Kate Cold replied.

"Fruit? Vegetables? Food?"

"Just this 'water of health' to cure my mother," said Alex, showing the man the bottle he had hand-carried throughout the trip.

"Pay no attention to him, officer, this boy has a big imagination," Kate interrupted.

"What is that?" the official asked, pointing to the tube.

"A blowgun."

"A what?"

"That's a kind of hollow cane the Indians of the Amazon use to shoot darts poisoned with . . ." Alexander started to explain before his grandmother silenced him with a kick.

The man was distracted and didn't ask any further questions, so he never learned about the quiver containing the darts or the gourd holding the deadly curare poison, which were wrapped in other bundles.

"Anything more?"

Alexander looked in the pockets of his jacket and pulled out three glass balls.

"What are those?"

"I believe they're diamonds," the boy said and immediately received another sharp kick from his grandmother.

"Diamonds. That's a good one! What have you been smoking, boy?" the official exclaimed, laughing out loud as he stamped their passports and waved them on.

When they opened the door of Kate's apartment in New York City, a blast of fetid air struck Kate and Alexander in the face. The writer clapped a hand to her head. It wasn't the first time she'd gone on a trip and left the garbage in the kitchen. They stumbled inside, holding their noses. While Kate organized their luggage, her grandson opened the windows and took charge of the garbage, which had already sprouted flora and fauna. When at last they succeeded in finding a place for the blowgun in the tiny apartment, Kate collapsed feet-out on the sofa, and sighed. She was afraid that she was beginning to feel the weight of her sixty-some years.

Alexander took the round stones from his jacket and put them on the table. His grandmother gave them an indifferent glance. They looked like those glass paperweights tourists buy.

"They *are* diamonds, Kate," the boy informed her.

"Right! And I'm Marilyn Monroe," the writer answered.

"Who?"

"Awghh," she groaned, horrified at the generational abyss that separated her from her grandson.

"That must be someone from your time," Alexander suggested.

"*This* is my time! This is more my time than yours. At least I don't live on another planet, the way you do," his grandmother grumbled.

"No, really, they're diamonds, Kate," Alexander insisted.

"Fine, Alexander, they're diamonds."

"Could you call me Jaguar? That's my totemic animal. The diamonds don't belong to us, Kate. They belong to the People of the Mist. I promised Nadia we would use them to protect the Indians."

"Yeah, yeah, yeah," she mumbled, paying no attention to her grandson.

"We can use these to finance the foundation you and

Professor Leblanc are planning to set up."

"I think that blow to your head shook a few screws loose, child," Kate replied, absentmindedly putting the crystal eggs into her jacket pocket.

In weeks to come, the writer would have reason to revise her opinion of her grandson.

Kate had the crystal eggs in her possession for two weeks, completely forgetting about them until she moved her jacket from a chair and one of the stones fell on her foot, crushing her toes. By that time her grandson, Alexander, was back at his parents' home in California. The writer limped around several days with bruised toes and the eggs in her pocket, sometimes unconsciously playing with them. One morning she went to get a cup of coffee at a shop on her block and left one of the "diamonds" on the table. The owner, an Italian she had known for more than twenty years, caught up with her at the next corner.

"Kate! You left this glass ball!" he shouted, tossing it to her over the heads of the other pedestrians.

She caught it and kept walking, with the thought that it was time to do something about those eggs. With no plan in mind, she headed for the street in midtown that was lined with jewelers' shops, where she found herself before the door of a store owned by an old love of hers, Isaac Rosenblat. Forty years before, they had been close to getting married, but Joseph Cold had come along and seduced Kate by playing his flute for her. Kate was sure that the flute was magic. Within a short time Joseph Cold had become one of the most famous musicians in the world. "The same flute my foolish grandson left somewhere in the Amazon," Kate thought, furious. She had given Alexander's ear a good twist when he lost his grandfather's magnificent instrument.

Isaac Rosenblat was a pillar of the Jewish community, rich, respected, and the father of six children. He was one of those easygoing people who fulfill their responsibilities with no fuss and whose soul is at peace, but when he saw Kate Cold walk into his shop he felt himself sinking into a morass of memories. In one instant he was again the shy young man who had loved this woman with the desperation of first love. In those days Kate had been a girl with porcelain skin and an untamed red mane; now she had more wrinkles than a parchment, and the gray hair she cut with scissors was standing up like straw in a broom.

"Kate! You haven't changed, my girl, I'd pick you out

in any crowd," he murmured with heartfelt emotion.

"Don't lie, you shameless old sweet-talker," she replied, feeling flattered despite herself and dropping her knapsack, which thudded to the floor like a sack of potatoes.

"You've come to tell me that you made a mistake and to ask me to forgive you for having left me with a broken heart, isn't that it?" the jeweler joked.

"You're right, I made a mistake, Isaac. I wasn't cut out for wedded bliss. My marriage to Joseph lasted only a short time, but at least we had a son, John. Now I have three grandchildren."

"I knew that Joseph had died, I'm truly sorry. I was always jealous of him, and I never forgave him for taking my sweetheart away from me, but I bought all his records anyway. I have the complete collection of his concerts. He was a genius."

The jeweler offered Kate a seat on a dark leather sofa, and made himself comfortable at her side. "So you're a widow now?" he added, studying her affection-ately.

"Don't get any ideas, I haven't come looking for sympathy. Or to buy jewelry. Jewels aren't my style," Kate replied.

"I can see that," Isaac Rosenblat noted, casting a

sideways glance at her wrinkled trousers and combat boots, and the travel backpack she set on the floor.

"I want to show you these glass pieces," she said, taking the eggs from her jacket.

The morning light was shining through the window, falling directly on the objects Kate was holding in the palms of her hands. An impossible brilliance blinded Isaac Rosenblat for an instant, making his heart leap. He came from a family of jewelers. Precious stones from the tombs of the Egyptian pharaohs had passed through the hands of his grandfather; his father's hands had fashioned diadems for empresses; his own had dismantled the ruby and emerald jewelry of Russian czars murdered during the Bolshevik Revolution. No one knew more about gems than he did, and very few stones had the power to move him, but what he had before him was something so wondrous that it made his head spin. Without a word, he took the eggs over to his desk and examined them through his loupe beneath a strong light. When he confirmed that his first impression was correct, he heaved a great sigh, took out a white linen handkerchief, and wiped his forehead.

"Where did you steal these, my girl?" he asked, his voice trembling.

"They came from a remote place called the City of the Beasts."

"Are you pulling my leg?" the jeweler asked.

"Well, no. I swear. Are they worth anything, Isaac?"

"They're worth something, yes. Let's say that with these stones you could buy a small country," he murmured.

"Are you kidding?"

"These are the largest and the most perfect diamonds I have ever seen. Where were they? It isn't possible that a treasure like this could have gone unnoticed. I know all the important stones in existence, but I have never heard of these, Kate."

"Ask them to bring us some coffee and a shot of vodka, Isaac. And get comfortable, because I'm going to tell you an interesting story," Kate Cold replied.

And so she informed her good friend about a teenage Brazilian girl who had climbed a mysterious mountain in the Upper Orinoco, led by a dream and by a naked witch man to the place where she found the eggs in an eagle's nest. Kate told him how the girl had entrusted that fortune to Alexander, her grandson, charging him with the mission of using it to help a certain tribe of Indians, the People of the Mist, who were still living in the Stone Age. Isaac Rosenblat listened courteously, not believing a word of the preposterous story. Not even a blithering idiot would swallow a pack of fantasies like that, he thought. He felt sure that his old sweetheart had gotten mixed up in some shady business, or that she had discovered a fabulous mine. He knew that Kate would never tell him the straight story. And, well, that was her right. He sighed again.

"I see you don't believe me, Isaac," the eccentric writer muttered, tossing back another shot of vodka to calm a fit of coughing.

"I suppose you will admit that this is a rather unusual story, Kate?"

"And I still haven't told you about the Beasts, the giant, hairy, stinking . . ."

"That's all right, Kate, I don't think I need further details," the jeweler interrupted, defeated.

"I need to turn these boulders into capital to set up a foundation. I promised my grandson that the money would be used to protect the People of the Mist, which is what those invisible Indians are called, and . . ."

"Invisible?"

"Well, they're not exactly invisible, Isaac, but they seem to be. It's like a magic trick. Nadia Santos says that . . ."

"And who is Nadia Santos?"

"The girl who found the diamonds. I already told you that. Will you help me, Isaac?"

"I'll help you, Kate, as long as it's legal."

And that was how the respectable Isaac Rosenblat became guardian of the three awesome stones; how he was put in charge of turning them into hard cash; how he invested the capital wisely; and how he helped Kate Cold create the Diamond Foundation. He advised her to appoint the anthropologist Ludovic Leblanc president but to keep control of the money in her own hands. Which is how Isaac Rosenblat and Kate Cold renewed a friendship that lay dormant for forty years.

"Did you know that I'm widowed too, Kate?" he confessed that same night as they went out to have dinner together.

"I hope you're not planning to propose, Isaac. I haven't washed a husband's socks for a long time, and I'm not going to start now." Kate laughed.

They toasted the diamonds.

A few months later Kate sat at her computer, wearing nothing over her lean body but a ragged T-shirt that stopped at mid-thigh, revealing her bony knees, her vein- and scar-traced legs, and her strong walker's feet. Above her head the blades of a ceiling fan buzzed like a swarm of flies, doing little to relieve the suffocating heat of New York in the summer. For some time—at least sixteen or seventeen years—the writer had contemplated the possibility of installing air conditioning in her apartment but hadn't yet found the time to do it. Sweat soaked her hair and trickled down her back as her fingers furiously attacked the keyboard. She knew she had only to brush the computer keys, but she was a creature of habit and so she pounded them, as she had once pounded her now-antiquated typewriter.

On one side of her computer stood a pitcher of iced tea spiked with vodka, an explosive mixture she was very proud of having invented. On the other side lay her sailor's pipe, cold. She was resigned to smoking less because her cough was a constant annoyance, but she kept the filled pipe for company: The smell of black tobacco soothed her soul. "At sixty-five there are not many vices an old witch like myself can indulge in," she thought. She was not inclined to give up any of her vices, but if she didn't stop smoking, her lungs were going to explode.

Kate had been working for six months to organize the Diamond Foundation, which she had created with the famous anthropologist Ludovic Leblanc, whom, it should be mentioned in passing, she considered her personal enemy. She detested that kind of work, but if she didn't do it, her grandson, Alexander, would never forgive her. "I'm a professional who likes action, I report on travels and adventure, I'm not a bureaucrat," she sighed between sips of her vodka-spiked tea—or, more accurately, her tea-spiked vodka.

Besides struggling with the matter of the foundation, she had had to fly twice to Caracas to testify in the trial against Mauro Carías and Dr. Omayra Torres, the persons responsible for the deaths of hundreds of Indians infected with smallpox. Mauro Carías was not present at the trial because he was on life support in a private clinic. It would have been better for him had the Indian who clubbed him finished the job.

Things were getting complicated for Kate Cold; *International Geographic* had commissioned her to write an article on the Kingdom of the Golden Dragon. It was not wise for her to keep postponing the trip, because they might give the assignment to another reporter; she knew, however, that she couldn't leave before she cured her cough. That small country was set amid the peaks of the Himalayas, where the climate was very treacherous; the temperature could drop thirty degrees within a few hours. The idea of consulting a physician never entered her mind, of course. She had never gone to a doctor in her life and she wasn't about to start now; she had a terrible opinion of professionals who charge by the hour. (She charged by the word.) It seemed obvious to her that no doctor was in a hurry to have his patient get well, and for that reason she preferred home remedies. She had placed her faith in some tree bark she'd brought back from the Amazon. A hundred-year-old shaman by the name of Walimai had assured her that the bark was good for disorders of the nose and mouth and would leave her lungs like new. Kate had ground this natural remedy in the blender, and then, to disguise the bitter taste, had added it to her iced tea and vodka, drinking the concoction all day with great determination. The medicine had not yet given results, which was what she was explaining that very moment to Professor Ludovic Leblanc by e-mail.

Nothing made Cold and Leblanc as happy as mutually detesting one another—and never losing an opportunity to show it. They had no shortage of excuses, because they were inescapably united by the Diamond Foundation: he being the president and she the money manager. Their common effort for the foundation forced them to communicate almost daily, and they did that by e-mail in order not to hear the other's voice on the telephone. They were determined to see each other as little as possible.

The Diamond Foundation had been created to protect the Amazon tribes in general and the People of the Mist in particular, as Alexander had decreed. Professor Ludovic Leblanc was writing a heavy academic tome on that tribe—and on his own role in that adventure, although the truth was that the Indians had been miraculously saved from genocide by Alexander and his Brazilian friend Nadia Santos, not by Leblanc.

As she looked back on those weeks in the jungle, Kate had to smile. When they had left for their trip to the Amazon, her grandson had been a coddled little boy— or a spoiled brat, as she called him—but by the time they returned, he had become a man. Alexander—or Jaguar as he had got it in his head he wanted to be called—had been very brave; in all fairness she had to admit that. She was proud of him. The foundation existed only because of Alex and Nadia; without them the project would have been nothing but an idea, because the two young people had provided the financing.

In the beginning, the professor tried to have the organization named after him: the Ludovic Leblanc

Foundation. He was convinced that his name would attract the press and possible benefactors who would contribute to the project with grants. Kate, however, did not allow him to finish the sentence. "You will have to walk over my dead body before you put the capital furnished by my grandson in your own name, Leblanc," she interrupted.

The anthropologist had to give in because she had the three fabulous diamonds from the Amazon. Like the jeweler Rosenblat, Ludovic Leblanc did not believe a word of the story about those extraordinary stones. Diamonds in an eagle's nest? Leblanc suspected that the guide, César Santos, Nadia's father, had access to a secret mine deep in the jungle, and that was where the girl had obtained the stones. He cherished the fantasy of returning to the Amazon and convincing the guide to share the riches with him. It was a harebrained dream; he was getting old, his joints hurt, and he no longer had energy to travel to places that didn't have air conditioning. Besides, he was very busy writing his masterwork.

It was impossible to devote himself properly to his important mission on his measly salary as a professor. His office was a hole, dangerous to his health. And it was on the fourth floor of a decrepit building that had no elevator. Disgraceful. If only Kate Cold were a little more generous with the budget. What a disagreeable woman! the anthropologist thought. She was impossible to deal with. The president of the Diamond Foundation should work in style. He needed a secretary and a decent office, but that tightwad Kate would not let loose one penny more than was strictly needed for the tribes. They were arguing by e-mail over the question of an automobile, which to him seemed indispensable. Getting around by the metro was a waste of precious time that would be better utilized in protecting the Indians and the forest, he explained. Leblanc's words were running across Kate's screen: *I'm not asking for anything special, Cold. We're not talking about a chauffeured limousine, only a modest little convertible. . . .*

The telephone rang and Kate ignored it. She didn't want to lose the thread of the heated arguments she was planning to use to nail Leblanc, but the ringing continued until it got under her skin. Furious, she picked up the receiver, growling about the dastardly person who was interrupting her intellectual labors.

"Hi, Grandmother," came the happy voice of her oldest grandchild from California.

"Alexander!" she exclaimed, enchanted to hear his voice. However, she immediately controlled her enthusiasm, as she didn't want her grandson to suspect that she missed him. "Haven't I told you a thousand times not to call me Grandmother?"

"We also agreed that you would call me Jaguar," Alex replied, unfazed.

"Jaguar! You can't even sprout whiskers, you're more like a Chihuahua than a big cat."

"You, on the other hand, *are* my father's mother, so I have the legal right to call you grandmother."

"Did you get my gift?" she asked to divert him.

"It's wonderful, Kate!"

And in fact it was. Alexander had just turned sixteen, and through the mail he had received an enormous box from New York containing his grandmother's present. Kate had given up one of her most precious possessions: the skin of a ten-foot-long python, the same one that had swallowed her camera in Malaysia several years before. Now the trophy was hanging in Alexander's room, the only adornment. Months earlier, he had destroyed everything in his room in a fit of worry about his mother's grave illness. The only things he had left were a gutted mattress to sleep on and a flashlight for reading at night.

"How are your sisters?"

"Andrea won't come into my room because she's freaked out by the snakeskin, but Nicole is my slave if

I let her touch it. She's offered to trade me everything she has in the world for that python, but I will never give it to anyone."

"I hope *not*. And how's your mother doing?"

"Much better. You can tell because she's gone back to her painting. You know what? Walimai, the shaman, told me I have the power to heal, and that I must use it well. I've about decided that I'm not going to be a musician, the way I'd planned; I'm going to be a doctor instead. How does that sound to you?" Alex asked.

"I suppose you think you cured your mother," his grandmother laughed.

"I didn't do it, it was the 'water of health' and the medicinal plants I brought back from the Amazon."

"And the chemotherapy, and the radiation . . ." she interrupted.

"We won't ever know what cured her, Kate. Other patients who received the same treatment in the same hospital have died, but my mother is in full remission. I know cancer is very treacherous, and can come back at any moment, but I think that the plants the shaman Walimai gave me, and also the miraculous water, will keep her well."

"You paid a big price to get them," Kate commented.

"I did come close to getting killed when . . ."

"Oh that was nothing, I was talking about leaving your grandfather's flute behind," she cut in.

"Your concern for me is very moving, Kate," Alexander joked.

"Oh, well! Too late now. I suppose I should ask about your family."

"It's your family, too, and as far as I know, you don't have any other. But if you're interested, I am pleased to inform you that we are gradually getting back to a normal family life. Mother's hair is growing back—curly and gray. Although she looked prettier when she was bald," Kate's grandson said.

"I'm happy that Lisa is getting well. I like her. She's a good painter," Kate Cold admitted.

"And a good mother . . ."

There was a pause of several seconds on the line before Alexander could gather the courage to mention the reason for his call. He explained that he had saved some money; for several months he had given music lessons and worked in a pizzeria. His intention had been to replace the things he'd destroyed in his room, but he'd changed his mind.

"I don't have time to listen to your financial plans. Get to the point. What do you want from me?" his grandmother said gruffly.

"My vacation starts tomorrow . . ."

"And?"

"I was thinking that if I paid my way, maybe you'd take me with you on your next trip. Didn't you tell me you were going to the Himalayas?"

Another glacial silence followed the question. Kate Cold was making an enormous effort to contain the satisfaction that swept over her: everything was going according to plan. If she had invited her grandson, he would have offered a list of objections, as he had when the trip to the Amazon had come up, but this way the idea came from him. She was so sure that Alexander would be going that she had prepared a surprise for him.

"Are you there, Kate?" Alexander asked timidly.

"Of course. Where would I be?"

"Will you think about it, at least?"

"So. I thought that young people today were devoted to smoking grass and looking for dates over the Internet . . ." she grumbled.

"That comes a little later, Kate. I'm sixteen, and my budget won't stretch far enough even for a virtual date." Alexander laughed, and added, "I think I proved to you that I'm a good travel companion. I won't get in your way, and I can be of help. You're getting a little old to go by yourself. . . ."

"Watch what you're saying, pipsqueak!"

"I meant, well . . . I can carry your luggage, for example. And I can take photos."

"You think that *International Geographic* would publish your snapshots? Timothy Bruce and Joel González will be coming, the same photographers who went with us to the Amazon."

"Is González all right?"

"His broken ribs healed, but he's jumpy about everything and anything. Timothy looks after him like a mother."

"And I'll look after you like a mother, Kate. You might get trampled by a herd of yaks in the Himalayas. And the air's very thin, you could have a heart attack," her grandson pleaded.

"I do not intend to give Leblanc the pleasure of seeing me die before he does." Kate gritted her teeth, and added, "But I see that you know a little about the region."

"You can't imagine how much I've been reading about it. Can I go with you? Please!"

"All right, but I'm not going to sit and wait for you. We'll meet at John F. Kennedy Airport next Thursday, where we'll take a night flight to London and fly from there to New Delhi. Do you have that?"

"I'll be there, I promise!"

"Bring warm clothing. The higher we climb, the colder it will get. I'm sure you'll have occasion to do a little mountaineering, so you can also bring your climbing gear."

"Thanks, thank you, Grandmother!" Alex exclaimed, jubilant.

"If you call me Grandmother one more time, I'm not going to take you anywhere!" Kate replied. She hung up the phone and brayed with laughter like a hyena.

CHAPTER FOUR

The Collector

THIRTY BLOCKS AWAY FROM Kate Cold's tiny apartment, on the top floor of a skyscraper in the heart of Manhattan, the second wealthiest man in the world, who had made his fortune by stealing the ideas of his employees and his partners in the field of computers, was talking by telephone with someone in Hong Kong. The two had never seen one another, nor would they ever.

The multibillionaire called himself the Collector, and the person in Hong Kong was simply the Specialist. The former did not know the identity of the latter. Among other security precautions, both had filters on their telephones to disguise their voices, and a device to prevent having their telephone numbers traced. That conversation would not be heard anywhere else. Not even the FBI, with the most sophisticated espionage systems in the world, would be able to learn what the secret transaction between those two parties consisted of.

The Specialist accomplished things—for a price. The Specialist could assassinate the president of Colombia, put a bomb on an airplane, make off with the royal crown of England, kidnap the pope, or replace the *Mona Lisa* in the Louvre with a fake. The Specialist didn't have to advertise, because there was never a lack of work; on the contrary, clients often had to wait months on a list before their turn came. The mode of operation was always the same: the client deposited a certain six-figure fee—nonrefundable—and waited patiently as his personal data were being painstakingly verified by the criminal organization.

After a brief time, the client received a visit from an agent, usually someone with an innocent appearance, perhaps a student seeking information for a thesis, or a priest representing a charitable institution. The agent would interview the client regarding the details of the mission, and would then disappear. On the first visit, the price was never mentioned; it was understood that if the client needed to ask what the service would cost, he would never be able to pay. Later the deal would be sealed with a personal telephone call from the Specialist. The call could originate from any place in the world.

The Collector was forty-two. He was a man of

medium stature and ordinary appearance; he wore thick eyeglasses, his shoulders were bowed, and he was balding prematurely, all of which made him seem much older. He dressed carelessly; his sparse hair always seemed greasy, and he had the bad habit of picking his nose when he was deep in thought, which was most of the time. He had been an only child, plagued with complexes and bad health; he had no friends and was so brilliant that he was bored in school. His school-mates despised him because he got the best grades in class without trying, and his teachers liked him no better because he was pompous and always knew more than they did. He had begun his career when he was fif-teen, building computers in his father's garage. By the time he was twenty-three, he was a millionaire and, owing to his intelligence and his absolute lack of scru-ples, at thirty he had more money in his personal accounts than the entire budget for the United Nations.

As a boy, like almost everyone, he'd collected postage stamps and coins; in his teens he collected racecars, medieval castles, golf courses, banks, and beauty queens; now, in early maturity, he'd started a collection of "rare objects." He kept them hidden in armored vaults spread across five continents, so that in case of some disaster not all of his precious collection would be destroyed. The drawback to that method was that it did not allow him to stroll among his treasures and enjoy them all at the same time; he had to hop onto his jet and travel from place to place to see them, but in truth he didn't have to do that too frequently. It was enough to know they existed, that they were safe, and that they were his. He wasn't motivated by artistic appreciation of his booty, only clear and simple greed.

Among other items of incalculable value, the Collector possessed the oldest manuscript known to man, the authentic funeral mask of Tutankhamen (the museum example being a copy), the brain of Einstein cut into sections and floating in a formaldehyde solution, Averroes' original texts written in his own hand, a human skin completely covered with tattoos from neck to feet, rocks from the moon, a nuclear bomb, the sword of Charlemagne, the secret diary of Napoleon Bonaparte, several of St. Cecilia's bones, and the formula for Coca-Cola.

Now the multibillionaire meant to acquire one of the rarest treasures in the world, a prize that few knew existed and to which only one living person had access. It was a golden dragon encrusted with precious stones, and for eighteen hundred years it had been seen only by the crowned monarchs of a small sovereign kingdom that lay in the mountains and valleys of the Himalayas. The dragon was wrapped in mystery and protected by a curse, as well as by ancient and complex security. It was not mentioned in any book or tourist guide, though many people had heard of it, and there was a description of it in the British Museum. There was also a drawing on an ancient parchment that a Chinese general discovered in a monastery at the time China invaded Tibet. That brutal military occupation forced more than a million Tibetans to flee, among them the Dalai Lama, the supreme spiritual leader of Buddhism.

Before 1950, the hereditary prince of the Kingdom of the Golden Dragon had been given special instruction between the ages of six and twenty in the Tibetan monastery where the parchments describing the dragon and its uses had been guarded for centuries. It was part of the prince's training to study them. According to the legend, the dragon was not merely a valuable statue, it was a miraculous device for telling the future, which only the crowned monarch could use in solving problems of his kingdom. The dragon could make predictions as varied as changes in climate, which anticipated the yield of the harvests, to the militaristic intentions of neighboring countries. Thanks to that valuable information, and to the wisdom of its rulers, the tiny kingdom had been able to enjoy peace and prosperity and maintain its fierce independence.

For the Collector, the fact that the statue was made of gold was irrelevant, for he had all the gold he wanted. What interested him were the dragon's magical properties. He had paid a fortune to the Chinese general for the stolen parchment, and then had it translated; he knew that the statue was worthless without instructions. The multibillionaire's tiny ratlike eyes glittered behind his thick glasses when he contemplated how he would be able to control the world economy once he had that object in his hands. He would know the ups and downs of the stock market before they happened, and could act before his competitors and multiply his billions. It annoyed him greatly to be the *second* richest man in the world.

The Collector had learned that during the Chinese invasion, at the time the monastery was destroyed and several of the monks murdered, the hereditary prince of the Kingdom of the Golden Dragon, Prince Dil Bahadur's father, had escaped through mountain passes disguised as a peasant. He had managed to reach Nepal and from there, always incognito, traveled back to his country.

The Tibetan lamas had not been able to complete the prince's preparation, but his father, the king, had personally continued his education. He had not, however, been able to provide his son the same high mental and spiritual training he himself had received. When the Chinese attacked the monastery, the monks had not as yet opened his mind to the ability to see auras and thus judge an individual's character and intentions. Nor had he been trained in the art of telepathy that allowed him to read thoughts. His father could not teach him those things, but at least when he died his son would be prepared to occupy the throne with dignity. The new king possessed a deep knowledge of the teachings of Buddha, and with time proved to have a commendable combination of the authority needed to govern, the practicality required for meting out justice, and the spirituality that safeguarded him from the corruption of power.

Dil Bahadur's father was just twenty when he ascended to the throne, and many thought he would not be capable of ruling as other monarchs of that kingdom had before him. From the beginning, nevertheless, the new king gave evidence of maturity and wisdom. The Collector knew that this monarch had been on the throne for more than forty years, and that his government had been characterized by peace and well-being.

The sovereign of the Kingdom of the Golden Dragon did not welcome outside influences, especially those from the West, which he considered materialistic and decadent, a culture that posed grave dangers to the values that had always prevailed in his nation. The official state religion was Buddhism, and the king was determined to keep things that way. Every year he commissioned a survey to measure the index of national contentment, its focus not on the numbers of problems, since many problems are inescapable, but on the level of compassion and spirituality among his kingdom's inhabitants. The government discouraged tourism and admitted only a small number of qualified visitors each year. As a result, tourist agencies referred to the country as the Forbidden Kingdom.

Recently installed, television was transmitted a few hours each day, and then only those programs the king considered inoffensive, such as sports, science, and cartoons. National dress was obligatory; Western clothing was forbidden in public places. That restriction had motivated fervent petitions from university students who were dying to wear American jeans and sports shoes, but the king was inflexible on that point, as he was on many others. He counted on the unconditional support of the remainder of the population, which was proud of its traditions and had no interest in foreign styles.

The Collector knew very little about the Kingdom of the Golden Dragon, whose historical and geographical riches meant nothing to him. He never planned to visit. Nor would it be his problem to acquire the magical statue: for that he was paying a fortune to the Specialist. If that icon could predict the future, as he had been assured, he could fulfill his ultimate dream: to become the richest man in the world, to become Number One.

Dil Bahadur was the youngest son of the monarch of the Kingdom of the Golden Dragon, and the chosen heir to the throne. He lived with his master in his "home" in the mountains. The entrance to their grotto was camouflaged by a natural screen of rocks and bushes and located on a kind of terrace or balcony on the side of the mountain. The monk chose it because it was nearly inaccessible on three sides, and because no one could find it unless he was very familiar with the area.

Tensing had lived for several years as a hermit in

that cave, in silence and solitude, until the king and queen of the Forbidden Kingdom delivered their son to his care. Tensing was to tutor the lad, who would be with him until he was twenty. During that time he would shape him into a perfect ruler by following a program so rigorous that few humans would survive it. All the training in the world, however, would not achieve the desired results unless Dil Bahadur proved to have superior intelligence and a spotless heart. Tensing was content; his disciple had exceeded his hopes in regard to those attributes.

The prince had been with the monk twelve years now, sleeping on rock, his only shelter the skin of a yak, eating a strictly vegetarian diet, dedicated totally to religious practice, study, and physical exercise. And he was happy. He would not change his life for any other, and it was with regret that he saw the day approaching when he must rejoin the world. He remembered very well, nonetheless, how terrified and lonely he had felt when at the age of six he had found himself in a hermit's cave in the mountains alongside a gigantic stranger who let him cry for three days; cry until he had no more tears to shed. He never wept again. Beginning with that day, the giant had replaced his mother, his father, and the rest of his family; he became his best friend, his master, his Tao-shu instructor, his spiritual guide. From Tensing he learned nearly everything he knew.

Tensing led the prince step by step along the path of Buddhism, tutored him in history and philosophy, introduced him to nature, animals, and the curative powers of plants, developed the youth's intuition and imagination, and taught him the skills of war while teaching him the value of peace. He initiated Dil Bahadur into the secrets of the lamas and helped him discover the mental and physical equilibrium he would need in order to govern. One of the exercises the prince had to practice was shooting his bow while standing on tiptoe with raw eggs beneath his heels, or crouched with eggs tucked behind his knees.

"Hitting the target with your arrow is not enough, Dil Bahadur; you must also develop strength, stability, and muscle control," the lama repeated patiently.

"Perhaps it would be more productive for us to eat the eggs, honorable master," the prince would sigh when he broke them.

Dil Bahadur's spiritual apprenticeship was even more intense. When he was ten, the boy could enter a state of trance and rise to a higher level of consciousness; at eleven he could communicate telepathically and move objects without touching them; at thirteen, he made astral journeys. On his fourteenth birthday his master opened an orifice in his forehead to enable him to see auras. The operation actually perforated the bone and left a circular scar the size of a pea.

"All organic matter radiates energy, or an aura, a halo of light invisible to the human eye except in the case of certain persons with psychic powers. You may learn many things from the color and shape of an aura," Tensing explained.

During three consecutive summers, the lama traveled with the boy to cities in India, Nepal, and Bhutan, to train him in reading the auras of the people and animals he saw there. He did not, however, take him to the beautiful valleys and cultivated terraces in the mountains of his own country, the Forbidden Kingdom. He would return there only when his education was complete.

Dil Bahadur learned to use the eye in his forehead with such precision that by now, at the age of eighteen, he could identify the medicinal properties of a plant, the ferocity of an animal, or the emotional state of a person, just from viewing the aura.

In only two years the prince would be twenty, and his master's work would be done. Then Dil Bahadur would return for the first time to the affection of his family, and would go to study in Europe, because there was crucial knowledge to be learned in the modern world, information Tensing could not teach him but he would need if he was to govern his nation.

Tensing was devoting all his energies to preparing the prince to be a good king and to be able to decipher the messages of the Golden Dragon. Dil Bahadur's course of studies was intense and complex, so that sometimes he lost patience, but Tensing, unyielding, prodded him to keep working until both were exhausted.

"I do not want to be king, master," Dil Bahadur said one day.

"Possibly my student would rather renounce his throne and not have to study," smiled Tensing.

"I want to live a life of meditation, master. How shall I achieve enlightenment amid the temptations of the world?"

"Not everyone can be a hermit like me. It is your karma to be a ruler. Your illumination must come as you travel a path much more difficult than that of meditation. You will have to achieve that while serving your people."

"I do not want to leave you, master," said the prince, his voice breaking.

The lama pretended not to see the tears in the youth's eyes.

"Wishes and fears are illusions, Dil Bahadur, not realities. You must practice detachment."

"Must I also detach myself from affection?"

"Affection is like the noonday sun; it does not need the presence of another to be manifest. Separation between beings is also an illusion, since all things in the universe are connected. Our spirits will be together always, Dil Bahadur," Tensing explained, noting, with some surprise, that he himself was not immune to emotion, and that he shared the sadness his disciple felt.

He, too, was distressed when he thought of the impending day when he must return the prince to his family, to the world, and to the throne of the Kingdom of the Golden Dragon for which he was destined.

CHAPTER FIVE

Eagle and Jaguar

❋

THE PLANE CARRYING ALEXANDER Cold landed in
New York at five forty-five in the evening. At that
hour, the heat of the June day had not yet faded. The
youth remembered with good humor his first trip alone
to that city, when almost as soon as he left the airport,
an inoffensive-looking girl stole everything he owned.
What was her name? He'd nearly forgotten . . .
Morgana! A name from medieval sorcery. It seemed to
him that years had gone by since that incident, though
it was only a few months. He felt like a different
person: he'd grown up, he was more sure of himself,
and he no longer had fits of anger and despair.

His family's crisis was behind them. It seemed that
his mother had beat her cancer, though there was
always the fear that it would come back. His father was
smiling again, and his sisters, Andrea and Nicole, were
beginning to grow up, too. He almost never fought
with them anymore, just enough to be a true brother.
He had gained a lot of respect among his friends. Even

the beautiful Cecilia Burns, who used to pay about as much attention to him as she would to a flea, now asked him to help her with her math assignments. Well, more than just help. He had to do all the problems and then let her copy his work, but the girl's radiant smile was more than enough reward for him. All Cecilia Burns had to do was shake that shining mane of hair, and Alexander's ears turned red. Ever since he had returned from the Amazon with half his head shaven, with a proudly displayed scar and a string of incredible stories, he'd become very popular at school. Even so, he felt as if he didn't really fit in. His friends were not as much fun as they had been. Adventure had aroused his curiosity; the little town where he'd grown up was a barely visible dot on the map of Northern California. He felt he was suffocating there, he wanted to escape and explore the wide, wide world.

Alexander's geography professor suggested that he give an oral report to the class about his adventures. He arrived at school with his blowgun—though, to avoid accidents, without the curare-poisoned darts—photos of him swimming with a dolphin in the Rio Negro, subduing a crocodile with his bare hands, and wolfing down meat impaled on an arrow. When he explained that the meat was a hunk of anaconda, the world's largest water snake, his classmates' amazement reached the point of disbelief. And he hadn't even told them the most interesting part: his journey into the territory of the People of the Mist, where he had encountered fabulous prehistoric creatures. Nor had he told them about Walimai, the aged shaman who helped him obtain the "water of health" for his mother, because that story would have made them think he'd lost his mind. He had written everything down very carefully in his diary, because he was planning to write a book. He even had the title; he would call it "City of the Beasts."

He never said a word about Nadia Santos, or Eagle, as he called her. His family knew that he had left a friend in the Amazon, but only his mother, Lisa, guessed the depth of their relationship. Eagle was more important to him than all his friends put together, including the beautiful Cecilia Burns. He had no intention of exposing his memory of Nadia to the curiosity of a mob of ignorant teenagers who would never believe that the girl could talk with animals, or that she had found three fabulous diamonds, the largest and most valuable in the world. And certainly he couldn't mention that she had learned the art of making herself invisible. He himself had witnessed the Indians disappear at will, like chameleons taking on the colors and textures of the jungle; it was impossible to see them in broad daylight and from only six feet away. He had attempted their disappearing act but had never learned the skill. Nadia, on the other hand, did it as easily as if becoming invisible were the most natural thing in the world.

Jaguar wrote to Eagle almost every day, sometimes a paragraph or two, sometimes more. He stored up the pages and every Friday mailed them in a large envelope. The letters took over a month to reach Santa María de la Lluvia, which was on the border between Brazil and Venezuela, but the two friends were resigned to the delays. Eagle lived in an isolated and primitive little village where the only telephone belonged to the police, and e-mail had never been heard of.

Nadia answered his letters with laboriously written brief notes, as if writing were a difficult task for her, but all it took was a few words from one of her letters and Alexander could sense her beside him, like a real presence. Each of those letters brought a breath of the jungle to California: sounds of water and concerts of birds and monkeys. Sometimes Jaguar thought that he could actually smell the damp of the trees, and that if he held out his hand he would be able to touch his friend. In her first letter, Eagle had told him that he should "read with his heart," just as before he had learned to "listen with his heart." According to her, that was the way to communicate with animals, or to understand an unknown language. With a little practice, Alexander learned to do that; then he discovered that he didn't need paper and ink to feel that he was in contact with Nadia. If he was alone, and if it was quiet, he simply thought about Eagle and could hear her. But he enjoyed writing her anyway. It was like keeping a diary.

When the door of the plane opened in New York, and the passengers finally could stretch their legs after six hours of immobility, Alexander exited carrying his backpack, hot and cramped but very happy at the idea of seeing his grandmother. His tan had faded, and his hair had grown; it now covered the scar on his head. He remembered that on his previous visit Kate had not met him at the airport, and he recalled how upset he had been. It was, after all, the first time he had traveled alone, but now he laughed to think how afraid he'd been. This time his grandmother had been very clear: they were to meet *at* the airport.

Almost as soon as he came off of the long ramp into

the gate area, he saw Kate Cold. She hadn't changed: the same spiky hair, the same broken eyeglasses mended with tape, the same jacket with a thousand pockets—all filled, the same knee-length, baggy shorts revealing thin, muscled legs scored like tree bark. The only surprise was her expression, which ordinarily conveyed concentrated fury. Alexander had not often seen his grandmother smile, although she frequently burst out laughing at the least opportune times—an explosive laugh like yipping dogs. Now she was smiling with something that resembled tenderness, although it was highly unlikely that she was capable of such a sentiment.

"Hi, Kate!" he greeted her, a little frightened by the possibility that his grandmother might be going a little soft in the head.

"You're a half hour late," she spit out, coughing.

"All my fault," he replied, calmed by her tone. She was the grandmother he'd always known; the smile had been an optical illusion.

Alexander took her arm as unemotionally as possible and planted a loud kiss on her cheek. She pushed him away, wiped off the kiss, and invited him for a soda, because they had two hours to kill before taking off for London on their way to New Delhi. Alex followed her to the clubroom for frequent flyers. The writer, who traveled often, at least allowed herself that luxury. Kate showed her card and they went in. Then, only nine feet away, he saw the surprise his grandmother had prepared for him: Nadia Santos.

Alex gave a shout, dropped his backpack, and opened his arms impulsively, but immediately contained himself, embarrassed. Nadia, too, blushed and hesitated a minute, not knowing how to act before this person who suddenly seemed like a stranger. She didn't remember his being so tall, and in addition his face had changed, his features were sharper. Finally happiness overcame confusion, and she ran and threw herself against her friend's chest. Alexander found that Nadia hadn't grown at all during those months; she was still the same ethereal little girl, honey-colored from head to toe, with a ring of parrot feathers holding back her curly hair.

As she waited for her vodka at the bar, Kate pretended to be giving all her attention to a magazine. The two friends, overjoyed at being reunited after their long separation and at starting off together on a new adventure, kept murmuring each other's totemic name: Jaguar . . . Eagle . . .

• • •

The idea of inviting Nadia to come along on the trip had been in Kate's head for months. She kept in touch with César Santos, the girl's father, because he was supervising the programs of the Diamond Foundation in their effort to preserve the native forests and indigenous cultures of the Amazon. Santos knew the region better than anyone; he was the perfect man for that job. Through him, Kate learned that the People of the Mist, whose leader was a colorful and ancient woman named Iyomi, showed signs of adapting rapidly to the changes they were being forced to make. Iyomi had decided to send four young people—two boys and two girls—to Manaos to study. She wanted them to learn the customs of the *nahab*, as her people called anyone who was not an Indian, so they could serve as a link between the two cultures.

While the rest of the tribe stayed in the jungle, living off what they hunted and fished, the four representatives were dropped right into the middle of the twenty-first century. As soon as they got used to wearing clothes and had mastered a basic vocabulary in Portuguese, they threw themselves valiantly into learning "the magic of the *nahab*," beginning with two formidable inventions: matches and buses. In fewer than six months, they had learned of the existence of computers, and at the rate they were going, according to César Santos, one day in the not too distant future they would be able to engage in cutthroat combat with the feared lawyers of corporations that were exploiting the Amazon. As Iyomi had said: "There are many kinds of warriors."

Kate told César Santos that it was important to let his daughter come visit her. She argued that just as Iyomi had sent the young people to study in Manaos, he ought to send Nadia to New York. The girl was old enough now to leave Santa María de la Lluvia and see something of the world. It was all very well to live with nature and to know the ways of the Beasts and the Indians, but his daughter should also be receiving a formal education. A couple of months in civilization would be very good for her, the writer maintained. Secretly, she was hoping that a temporary separation would ease César Santos's mind, and then maybe in the near future he would decide to send his daughter to the United States to study.

For the first time in her life, Kate was willing to be responsible for someone. She hadn't taken responsibility even with her own son, John, who after her divorce had lived with his father. Her work as a journalist, her trips, her eccentric lifestyle, and her chaotic apartment were not ideal for taking in visitors, but Nadia was a case apart. It seemed to Kate that this girl, at thirteen, was much wiser than she was at sixty-five. She was sure that Nadia had a very old soul.

Of course Kate had not spoken a word of her plans to her grandson, Alexander; it wouldn't do for the lad to think she was getting soft. There was not an ounce of sentiment in her plan, the writer reasoned, her motives were purely practical. She needed someone to organize her papers and files, and besides, she had an extra bed in her apartment. If Nadia came to live with her, Kate planned to work her like a slave—there would be no babying. Of course that would be later, when she came to her house to stay, not now, when the hard-headed César Santos had finally agreed to send his daughter to the States for a few weeks.

Kate had never imagined that Nadia would arrive with nothing but the clothes she was wearing. Her luggage consisted of a sweater, two bananas, and a cardboard box with holes punched in the top. Inside was the tiny black monkey that was always with her, Borobá, as frightened as she. It had been a long trip. César Santos had driven his daughter to the plane, where a flight attendant took responsibility for Nadia until she landed in New York. In case she got lost, Santos had taped strips of adhesive with Kate's telephone number and address to his daughter's arms. Getting the tape off was not an easy job.

Nadia had never flown except in her father's old prop plane, and because of her fear of heights she didn't like flying in general. Her heart had turned over when she saw the size of the commercial airplane in Manaos and realized that she would be on it for many hours. She was terrified as she boarded, and Borobá didn't feel much better. The poor monkey, accustomed to fresh air and freedom, was tortured by the sound of the motors. When his owner lifted the lid of the box in the New York airport, he shot out like an arrow, shrieking and leaping across people's shoulders and sowing panic among the travelers. It took Nadia and Kate half an hour to catch him and calm him down.

For the first few days, the experience of living in an apartment in New York was difficult for Borobá and his mistress, but soon they learned to find their way around the streets and made friends in the neighborhood. Everywhere they went they attracted attention. A monkey that behaved like a human, and a young girl with feathers in her hair created a stir. New Yorkers chatted with them, and tourists took their picture.

"New York is a collection of villages, Nadia. Each neighborhood has its own character. Once you get to know the owners of the grocery store and the laundry, the mail carrier, my friend at the Italian coffee shop, and a few others, you'll feel as much at home as you do in Santa María de la Lluvia," Kate reassured Nadia, and soon the girl found that she was right.

The writer treated Nadia like a princess, all the time saying to herself that there would be time later on to tighten the thumbscrews. She showed her all the sights: tea at the Plaza Hotel, a horse-drawn carriage ride through Central Park, the view from the top of several skyscrapers, the Statue of Liberty. She had to teach her about elevators, escalators, and revolving doors. They also went to the theater and to the movies, experiences Nadia had never had. What impressed her most, however, was the ice on the Rockefeller Center skating rink. Having known only the tropics, she never tired of admiring the coldness and whiteness of the ice.

"You will soon be bored with ice and snow, because I'm thinking of taking you with me to the Himalayas," Kate told her.

"Where is that?"

"On the other side of the world. You'll need stout

shoes there, and heavy clothes and a waterproof parka."

The writer thought that taking Nadia to the Kingdom of the Golden Dragon was a stupendous idea; she wanted the girl to see more of the world. She bought Nadia warm clothing and proper footwear; and for Borobá, a baby-size snowsuit and a special travel tote for pets, a black bag with mesh that allowed air to circulate and the pet to see out. It was lined with soft lambskin and had little ports for water and food. She also bought diapers. It wasn't easy to get the monkey to wear them, even with Nadia's long explanations in the language she shared with the animal. For the first time in his placid lifetime, Borobá bit a human. Kate went around with a bandaged arm for a week, but the monkey learned to wear the diapers, an indispensable step in preparing for a trip as long as the one they were planning.

Kate had not told Nadia that Alexander would be meeting them at the airport. She wanted it to be a surprise for both of them.

Soon Timothy Bruce and Joel González joined them in the airline's clubroom. The photographers hadn't seen the writer or the young people since their trip to the Amazon. They hugged each other warmly as

Borobá jumped from one head to another, excited at seeing his old friends.

Joel proudly lifted his shirt to show them the marks of the Amazon anaconda's ferocious embrace. Several of his ribs had been broken, and his chest would always be slightly sunken. As for Timothy, he looked almost handsome despite his long horse-face, and, when questioned by the relentless Kate, he confessed that he had had his teeth straightened. In place of the big, crooked, yellow teeth of old, and the overbite that had made it difficult for him to close his mouth, he now displayed the resplendent smile of a movie actor.

At eight o'clock that evening their party boarded the plane for India. The flight lasted hours and hours, but for Alexander and Nadia it seemed short: they had a lot to talk about. They kept checking, and were relieved to find that Borobá was quite content, cuddled deep in his lambskin. While the rest of the passengers tried to sleep in their narrow seats, the two young people entertained themselves talking and watching movies.

Timothy Bruce could barely fit his long limbs into the small space of his seat, and every so often he got up to do his yoga exercises in the aisle, to avoid cramping. Joel González was more comfortable, because he was short and slim. Kate had her own system for long flights: she took two sleeping pills with several swallows of vodka. The effect was like being clubbed.

"Even if there's a terrorist on board with a bomb, don't wake me," she instructed them before covering herself to her forehead with a blanket and curling up like a shrimp in her seat.

Three rows behind Nadia and Alexander sat a man with long hair combed into dozens of small braids that were in turn tied back with a leather thong. He had a bead necklace around his neck, and a suede pouch tied with a black cord rested on his chest. He was wearing stained jeans, worn cowboy boots, and a Stetson that sat low on his forehead; they learned later that it was never removed, not even when he slept. Alexander and Nadia thought that he was a little old to be dressed like that.

"He must be a rock star," Alexander noted.

Nadia didn't know what a rock star was, and Alexander decided that it would be very difficult to explain. He promised that the first chance he had he would outline the basics of movies and popular music to his friend, something any self-respecting teenager should know.

Judging by the wrinkles around the strange hippie's eyes and mouth, and the deep furrows in his tanned face, they calculated that he had to be over forty. What they could see of the hair tied back in the ponytail was steely gray. In any case, whatever his age, the man seemed to be in good physical shape. They had first seen him in the New York airport, carrying two pieces of luggage: a canvas tote and, slung over one shoulder, a sleeping bag cinched with a belt. After that they had glimpsed him dozing, cowboy hat tipped over his face, in the London airport as he waited for a flight, and now they were on the same plane bound for India. They waved to him from their seats.

As soon as the pilot turned off the FASTEN SEAT BELTS sign, this odd man took a few steps down the aisle, stretching his muscles. He walked up to Nadia and Alexander and smiled. For the first time they could see that there was no expression in his startlingly blue eyes; it was as if he were hypnotized. His smile rearranged the wrinkles on his face, but went no farther than his lips. His eyes looked dead. The stranger asked Nadia what she was carrying in the case on her lap, and she showed him Borobá. The man's smile turned into a laugh when he saw a monkey wearing diapers.

"They call me Tex Armadillo, because of the boots, you know?" he introduced himself. "They're armadillo hide."

"Nadia Santos, from Brazil," the girl said.

"Alexander Cold, from California."

"I noticed that you guys were carrying a guide book about the Forbidden Kingdom. I saw you reading it in the airport."

"That's where we're going," Alexander informed him.

"Not many tourists visit that country. I understand they let only a hundred or so foreigners in every year," said Tex Armadillo.

"We're with a group from *International Geographic.*"

"That right? You seem pretty young to be working for a magazine," he commented.

"That's right," confirmed Alexander, who had decided not to be too forthcoming.

"That's my plan, too, but I don't know whether I'll get a visa once I get to India. They don't have much sympathy in the Kingdom of the Golden Dragon for hippies like me. They think we come to get drugs."

"Are there a lot?" Alexander asked.

"Marijuana and opium grow wild everywhere, it's just a matter of going out and harvesting it. It would be a snap."

"So drugs must be a serious problem," Alexander commented, surprised that his grandmother hadn't mentioned that.

"There's no problem. The only thing they use 'em for is medicine. They don't know the treasure they're sitting on. Can you imagine the money they could make exporting them?" said Tex Armadillo.

"I can imagine," Alexander answered. He didn't like the direction the conversation was going, and he didn't like the man with the dead eyes.

CHAPTER SIX

Cobras

THEY LANDED IN NEW DELHI in the morning. Kate
and the photographers, used to traveling, felt pretty
good, but Nadia and Alexander, who hadn't closed
their eyes all night, looked like survivors of an earthquake. Neither of the two was prepared for the spectacle of that city. The heat struck them like a slap in the
face. The minute they stepped outside they were surrounded by a sea of men who rushed at them offering
to carry their luggage, act as guides, and sell them
everything from fly-covered bananas to statues of
Hindu gods. Dozens and dozens of children crowded
around them, their small hands reaching for coins. A
leper, his face half-eaten by the illness, his fingers completely missing, pressed against Alexander, begging,
until an airport guard threatened him with a club.

A human mass of dark skin, delicate features, and
enormous black eyes swirled around them. Alexander
was used to a minimum of twenty inches of private
space, the custom in his country. He felt as if he were

95

being attacked. He could barely breathe. Suddenly he realized that Nadia had disappeared, swallowed up by the throng, and he panicked. He began to call to her, frantic, trying to free himself from the hands tugging at his clothing, until after several heart-stopping minutes he saw, some distance away, the colorful feathers she wore in her ponytail. He elbowed his way through the crowd, grabbed her hand, and dragged her in the wake of his grandmother and the photographers, who had been in India several times before and knew the drill.

It took them half an hour to gather their luggage, count the pieces, defend them from would-be helpers, and hail the two taxis that drove them to the hotel—driving on the left, English-style, through nearly impassable streets. All kinds of vehicles were circulating in total chaos, disregarding the occasional traffic lights and police whistles: cars, broken-down buses painted with religious figures, motorcycles with four people astride, carts pulled by buffaloes and rickshaws pulled by humans, bicycles, decrepit vans crammed with students, and even a placid elephant adorned for some ceremony.

They were tied up for forty minutes in a traffic jam caused by a dead cow surrounded by starving dogs and enormous black birds pecking at the decomposing flesh. Kate explained that cows are considered sacred, and no one drives them off, which is why they wander at will through the streets. There was, however, a special branch of the police that collected dead cows and herded live ones to the city's outskirts.

The sweating and patient masses contributed to the chaos. A holy man with long tangled hair to his heels, completely naked and followed by a half-dozen women tossing flower petals at him, crossed the street at a turtle's pace, and no one even turned to look at him. Evidently he was a familiar sight.

Nadia, who had grown up in a village with twenty houses, in the silence and solitude of the forest, hovered between fright and fascination. Compared to this city, New York was a wide spot in the road. She never imagined that there were this many people in the world. In the meantime, Alexander was fending off the hands reaching into the taxi to offer merchandise or ask for money through the windows they were unable to close because they would have smothered.

Finally they reached the hotel. Once inside the gates protected by armed guards, they found themselves in a Garden of Eden where absolute peace reigned. The noise of the street had disappeared as if by magic; all they could hear was the trilling of birds and the song of many fountains. Peacocks strutted across grassy lawns, dragging their bejeweled tails. Several bellboys dressed in brocade and gold-embroidered velvet and wearing tall turbans decorated with pheasant feathers, like illustrations in a book of fairy tales, seized their luggage and led them inside.

The hotel was a palace of white marble so extravagantly carved that it looked like lace. The floors were covered with enormous silk carpets; the furniture was made of the finest woods inlaid with silver, mother-of-pearl, and ivory; the tables held huge porcelain jars overflowing with flowers whose perfumes filled the air. Everywhere they saw lush tropical plants in hammered-copper pots, and scores of intricately fashioned cages filled with brightly colored songbirds. The palace had once been the residence of a maharajah who had lost his power and his fortune when India declared its independence from England, and now it was leased to an American hotel chain. The maharajah and his family still lived in one wing of the building, separate from the hotel guests. In the afternoon, however, they often came down to have tea with the tourists.

The room that Alexander shared with the photographers was luxurious and richly furnished. The bath featured a tiled pool and a fresco on the wall depicting a tiger hunt: The hunters, armed with shotguns, were riding on elephants, surrounded by a train of servants on foot carrying lances and bows and arrows. Their room was on the highest floor, and from the balcony they could appreciate the fabulous gardens insulated from the street by a high wall.

"The people you see camping down there are whole families that live and die in the street. Their only possessions are a few cooking pots and the rags on their backs. They are the 'untouchables,' the poorest of the poor," Timothy Bruce explained, pointing out some ragged tents on the sidewalk outside the wall.

The contrast between the opulence of the hotel and the absolute poverty of those people moved Alexander to fury and horror. When he tried to share his feelings with Nadia, she did not understand what he meant. She owned nothing but what she was wearing, and to her the splendor of the palace was oppressive.

"I think I would be more comfortable outside with the untouchables than I am here with all these things around me, Jaguar. I feel dizzy. There isn't an inch of wall space that isn't decorated; there's no place for your eyes to take a rest. It's *too* luxurious. I'm choking. And why do these princes keep bowing to us?" she asked, pointing to the men dressed in brocade and plumed turbans.

Her friend smiled wryly. "They're not princes, Eagle, they're hotel employees."

"Tell them to go away, we don't need them."

"It's their job. If I tell them to leave us alone, they'll be offended. You'll get used to it."

Alexander went back to the balcony to watch the untouchables in the street. They survived in abject poverty, barely able to clothe themselves. Upset by such a spectacle, Alexander took some dollars from the few he had, exchanged them for rupees, and went outside to give them to the poor. Nadia watched from the balcony. From her vantage she could see the gardens, the hotel walls, and the masses of poor on the other side. She saw her friend go through the wrought-iron gate protected by the guards, venture out alone among the crowd, and begin to hand out coins to the nearest children. Instantly, he was mobbed by dozens of desperate beggars. The news flashed like gunpowder that a foreigner was handing out money, and more and more people rushed toward him, like an uncontainable human avalanche.

When Nadia realized that within minutes Alexander

would be crushed, she rushed downstairs screaming. Hotel guests and employees came running, which only added to the alarm and general commotion. Everyone had a suggestion, but seconds were racing by. There was no time to lose but no one seemed capable of making a move. Suddenly Tex Armadillo stepped forward, and took charge of the situation.

"Quick! Come with me!" he ordered the armed guards posted at the gates of the garden.

He led them straight into the heart of the uproar in the street, where he began throwing punches as the guards attempted to clear a way with their clubs. Armadillo grabbed a weapon from one of them and shot twice into the air. The people nearest him froze in their tracks, but others kept pushing in from behind them.

Tex Armadillo took advantage of the few seconds of confusion to get to Alexander, who had been thrown to the ground, his clothes in tatters. He grabbed him under the armpits and with the help of the guards managed to drag him to safety inside the hotel gates, even rescuing the boy's eyeglasses, which by some miracle still lay unbroken on the ground. The gates of the palace were slammed shut, as the shouting grew louder and louder outside.

"You are dumber than you look, Alexander. You can't change anything with a few dollars. India is India, you have to accept it as it is," was Kate's comment when she saw her battered grandson.

"Following those guidelines we'd all still be living in the age of the cave dwellers!" he replied, wiping his bloody nose.

"We are, child, we are," she said, disguising how proud she was of him.

Sitting beneath a large white umbrella with gold fringe on the hotel terrace, a woman had observed the entire episode. She was fortyish—though a very well-cared-for fortyish—slim, tall, and athletic. She wore sandals and khaki-colored cotton slacks and shirt. Her travel-worn leather handbag lay on the ground between her feet. Her smooth mane of black hair, highlighted by a wide white streak at the forehead, framed a face of classic features: chestnut-colored eyes, thick, arched eyebrows, straight nose, and expressive mouth. Despite the simplicity of her attire, she had an elegant, aristocratic air.

"You are a brave young man," the stranger said to Alexander an hour later, when the *International Geographic* group had assembled on the terrace.

The youth felt his ears burn.

"But you must be cautious, you're not in your own country," she added in English that was perfect but flavored with a slight Central European accent difficult to pinpoint.

At that moment two waiters appeared carrying large silver trays of *chai*, an Indian-style tea prepared with milk, spices, and a lot of sugar or honey. Kate invited the traveler to join them. She had also invited Tex Armadillo, grateful for his prompt action in rescuing her grandson, but he declined, saying that he preferred a beer and his newspaper. Alexander was puzzled that this self-proclaimed hippie, who had only a canvas tote and a sleeping bag for luggage, would be staying in a maharajah's palace, but he concluded that the room rate must be very reasonable. India was cheap for anyone who had American dollars.

Soon Kate and her guest were exchanging observations, and that was how they discovered that all of them were on their way to the Kingdom of the Golden Dragon. The stranger introduced herself as Judit Kinski, a landscape architect, and she told them that she was traveling at the official invitation of the king, whom she had had the honor of meeting recently. She said that when she learned that the monarch was interested in growing tulips in his country, she had written him offering her services. She thought that under certain conditions the bulbs could be adapted to the climate and terrain of the Forbidden Kingdom. The king had immediately requested an interview, and, given the world fame of Dutch tulips, she had chosen to have it in Amsterdam.

"His Majesty knows as much about tulips as any expert. To be honest, he doesn't need me at all; he could have carried out this project on his own, but apparently he liked the designs of the gardens I showed him, and was kind enough to offer me a contract," she explained. "We talked a lot about his plans to create new parks and gardens for his people, preserving native species and introducing others. He is aware that this must be accomplished very carefully in order not to upset the ecological balance. There are plants, birds, and a few small mammals in the Forbidden Kingdom that have disappeared from the rest of the world. The country is a nature sanctuary."

The group from *International Geographic* thought that the monarch must have been as enchanted with Judit Kinski as they were. The woman made a memorable impression: She radiated a combination of strength of character and femininity. Seen at close range, the harmony of her face and the natural elegance of her movements were so extraordinary that it was difficult to tear one's eyes away.

"This king is a white knight for the ecology. What a shame there aren't more rulers like him," Kate replied in turn. "He subscribes to *International Geographic.* That's why he approved our visas and is allowing us to do an article."

"It's an extremely interesting country," Judit said.

"Have you been there before?" Timothy asked.

"No, but I've read a lot about it. I tried to prepare for this trip, not only those things that have to do with my work but anything I could find about the people and their customs and ceremonies . . . I don't want to offend them with my rude Western codes of behavior," she smiled.

"I suppose you've heard about the fabulous Golden Dragon . . ." Timothy prompted.

"I'm told that no one has seen it except their kings. It may be a legend," she replied.

The subject did not come up again, but Alexander noticed the gleam of excitement in his grandmother's eyes, and guessed that she would do anything possible to find a way to that treasure. The challenge of being the first person to prove its existence was irresistible.

Kate and Judit agreed to exchange information and help one another, as befitted two foreign women in an unfamiliar region. At the other end of the terrace, Tex Armadillo was drinking his beer with his newspaper folded on his lap. Mirror-lensed sunglasses covered his eyes, but Nadia could feel his gaze lingering upon their group.

They had only three days to act like tourists. In their favor was the fact that many people here spoke English, since for more than two hundred years India had been a colony of the British Empire. Even so, as Kate told them, they would not be able to scratch the surface of New Delhi in such a short period of time, much less understand the complex society of India. The contrasts were extreme: incredible poverty on the one hand, beauty and opulence on the other. There were millions of illiterates, but the universities were producing large numbers of technicians and scientists. The villages had no potable water, but the nation was building nuclear bombs. India had the largest film industry in the world, but also the greatest number of holy men, who doused themselves in ashes and never cut their hair or finger-nails; just the thousands of Hindu gods, or the caste system alone, could take years of study.

Alexander was used to the American belief that everyone should be able to do what they want in life. He was horrified at the idea that in India, people's lives are determined by the caste into which they're born. Nadia, on the other hand, listened to Kate's explanations without offering a criticism.

"If you had been born here, Eagle, you wouldn't be able to choose your husband. You would have been wed at the age of ten to a fifty-year-old man. Your father would have arranged your marriage, and you would have nothing to say about it," Alexander told her.

Nadia smiled. "I'm sure my father would choose better than I."

"Are you nuts? I would never permit such a thing!" Alex exclaimed.

"If we'd been born into the tribe of the People of the Mist in the Amazon, we would have to hunt for food with poisoned darts. If we'd been born here, it wouldn't seem strange to have fathers arrange marriages," Nadia argued.

"How can you defend this system? Look at the poverty! Would you like to live like that?"

"No, Jaguar, but I don't want more things than I need, either," she replied.

Kate took the two young people to visit palaces and

temples, and also walked them through the markets, where Alexander bought bracelets for his mother and sisters while Nadia's hands were being painted with henna, like a bride's. The design was as intricate as embroidery, and it would stay on her skin for two or three weeks. Borobá, as always, rode on his mistress's shoulder or hip, but he didn't attract attention there as he had in New York; in New Delhi monkeys were more common than dogs.

In one square they came upon two snake charmers sitting on the ground, legs crossed, playing their flutes. Their cobras rose from their baskets and stayed erect, swaying, hypnotized by the movement of the flutes. When Borobá saw them, he jumped from his mistress, shrieking, and scrambled up a palm tree. Nadia walked over to the charmers and began to murmur something in the language of the jungle. Immediately the serpents turned toward her, hissing, as their tongues knifed through the air. Four elliptical eyes stared daggers at the girl.

Before anyone could react, the cobras slithered from their baskets and zigzagged toward Nadia. People began shouting, panicked, and ran. Within an instant there was no one left but Alexander and his grandmother, both of them paralyzed with surprise and terror. The snake charmers tried in vain to control the serpents with their instruments, but they didn't dare go near them. Nadia was composed, with a rather amused expression on her golden face. She did not move an inch as the serpents coiled around her legs and climbed up her slim body as high as her neck and face, hissing constantly.

Kate, bathed in cold sweat, thought she was going to faint for the first time in her life. She slipped to the ground and sat there, pale as death, eyes bulging, unable to utter a sound. After the first instant of stupor, Alexander realized that he mustn't move. He knew his friend's strange powers very well. In the Amazon he had seen her pick up a *surucucú*, one of the most poisonous serpents in the world, in one hand, whirl it over her head, and throw it far away. He assumed that if no one did anything stupid to disturb the cobras, Eagle was safe.

This scene lasted several minutes, until the girl gave an order in her jungle tongue and the serpents snaked down her body and returned to their baskets. The charmers quickly slapped down the lids, picked up the baskets, and ran from the square, convinced that the foreign girl with feathers in her hair was a demon.

Nadia called Borobá and, once he was back on her

shoulder, continued her walk through the square as if nothing had happened. Alexander followed, smiling, without a word, highly amused to see that for once his grandmother had completely lost her composure at a sign of danger.

CHAPTER SEVEN

The Sect of the Scorpion

✹

ON HER LAST DAY IN NEW DELHI, Kate Cold had to spend hours in a travel agency trying to get tickets on the one weekly flight to the Kingdom of the Golden Dragon. It wasn't that there were that many passengers, just that the plane was so small. Since she had to make those arrangements, she gave Nadia and Alexander permission to go by themselves to the Red Fort, an ancient landmark near the hotel, which was a must for tourists.

"Don't get separated for any reason, and come back to the hotel before sunset," the writer ordered.

The fort had been used by English troops during the time that India was a colony. This enormous country had been the most glorious jewel in the British crown until finally it gained its freedom in 1947. Since then the fort had been deserted. Tourists visited only a small part of the enormous compound. Very few people knew the inner workings of the fort, a true labyrinth of corridors, secret rooms, and underground passageways that stretched beneath the city like the tentacles of an octopus.

Nadia and Alexander followed a guide lecturing in English to a group of tourists. The suffocating heat of midday did not penetrate the fort; inside it was cool, and the walls were stained with the green patina of moisture collected over the centuries. There was a disagreeable odor in the air, which the guide said was the urine of the thousands and thousands of rats that lived in the cellars and came out at night. The horrified tourists covered their noses and mouths, and several left the tour.

Suddenly Nadia pointed out Tex Armadillo in the distance, leaning against a column and looking around as if he were expecting someone. Her first impulse had been to wave to him, but Alexander realized what she was about to do and caught his friend's arm.

"Wait, Eagle, let's see what this guy is up to. I don't trust him at all," he said.

"Don't forget that he saved your life when you were being crushed by the crowd."

"Yes, but there's something about him I don't like."

"What?"

"He seems to be something he isn't. I don't think he's really a hippie interested in finding drugs, as he told us on the plane. Have you noticed his muscles? He moves like one of those karate experts you see in the movies. A drug-addicted hippie wouldn't look like that," Alexander said.

They waited, unseen among the mass of tourists, never taking their eyes off Tex. After a while they saw a tall man walking toward him; he was wearing a tunic and a blue-black turban that was nearly the same tone as his skin. He had a broad sash about his waist, also blue-black, and tucked into it a curved knife with a bone handle. His eyes glowed like coals in his dark face, and he had a long beard and prominent eyebrows.

The friends could tell that the newcomer and the American obviously knew one another, and watched as the man with the turban disappeared around the corner of a wall, followed by Tex. They needed no discussion; wordlessly they agreed to investigate. Nadia whispered to Borobá that he shouldn't chatter or jump around. The little monkey clung to his mistress, tight as a backpack.

Slipping along, hugging the walls and hiding behind columns, they stayed within fifteen or twenty feet of Tex Armadillo. Sometimes they lost sight of him because the architecture of the fort was complex and it was evident that the man did not want to call attention to himself. However, thanks to Nadia's infallible instinct, they always found him again. They were a good distance from the other tourists now, and they didn't see or hear anybody. Alex and Nadia cut through rooms, went down narrow stairways with treads worn by use and time, and crept along endless corridors, always with the sensation that they were walking in circles. A growing murmur, like a chorus of crickets, was added to the penetrating odor.

"We shouldn't go any farther, Eagle. That's the sound of rats. They're very dangerous," Alexander said.

"If those men can go into the cellars, why can't we?" she replied.

The friends did not speak as they went deeper and deeper into that underground world; they realized that echoes would repeat and amplify their voices. Alexander was worried that they wouldn't be able to find their way back, but he didn't want to voice his doubts aloud and frighten Nadia. Neither did he say anything about the possibility of snakes, because after the episode with the cobras, his apprehension seemed out of place.

At first, light had sifted in through small openings in the ceilings and walls, but now they were forced to walk long stretches in darkness, feeling along the walls as a guide. From time to time when they passed a weak lightbulb they could see rats scurrying along the walls. Wires dangled dangerously from the ceiling. They noticed that the floor was damp, and in some places they could see little streams of foul-smelling water. Soon their feet were wet, and Alexander tried not to think about what would happen if something triggered a short circuit. However, being electrocuted worried him less than the increasingly aggressive rats all around them.

"Pay no attention to them, Jaguar. They won't dare come near us unless they smell that we're afraid; then they'll attack," Nadia whispered.

Once again they had lost sight of Armadillo. The two friends were now in a small domed room that had been used to store munitions and provisions. Three arches opened onto what appeared to be long dark corridors. Alexander signaled Nadia, asking which they should choose; for the first time she hesitated, confused. She wasn't sure. She took Borobá, set him on the floor, and gave him a slight push, asking him to pick. The monkey climbed right back on her shoulder; he hated getting wet and was terrified of the rats. She repeated the order, and though the little primate wouldn't let go he pointed a trembling paw toward the opening on the right, the narrowest of the three.

The two friends followed Boroba's indication, crouching down and feeling their way because now there wasn't even a weak lightbulb and the darkness was nearly total. Alexander, who was much taller than Nadia, bumped his head and muttered "what the . . . !" For a few minutes they were enveloped in a cloud of bats, stirring panic in the heart of Boroba, who immediately dived under his mistress's shirt.

It was time to call on the black jaguar. Alex concentrated, and in only seconds he could see about him as if he had antennae. He had practiced this skill for months, ever since he had learned in the Amazon that the jaguar, the king of the South American jungle, was his totemic animal. Alexander was slightly nearsighted, and even with glasses he did not see well in darkness, but he had learned to trust the instinct of the jaguar that he sometimes could invoke. Now he followed Nadia confidently, "seeing with his heart," as he did more and more often.

Suddenly Alex stopped short, taking his friend's arm; ahead, the passageway made a sharp turn. Farther on, he could see a faint glow, and they could hear the murmur of voices. Using extreme caution, Alex peered around the corner and could see that ten feet away the corridor opened up into a room like the one they'd just come from.

Tex Armadillo, the man in black, and two other individuals dressed in the same kind of tunics were kneeling around an oil lamp that flickered faintly but produced enough light for the two young people to see. It was impossible to get any closer, as there was nothing to hide behind, and they knew that if they were caught, they would be in trouble. The thought flashed through Jaguar's mind that no one knew where they were. They could die in those cellars and no one would find their bodies for days, maybe weeks.

The men were speaking English, and Armadillo's voice was clear, but the other three had a nearly incomprehensible accent. It was obvious, nevertheless, that they were talking about a business deal. They watched Armadillo hand over a sheaf of bills to the person who had the air of being the leader of the group. Then they heard a long discussion about what seemed to be a plan of action that included weapons, mountains, and maybe a temple or a palace, they couldn't be sure.

The leader unfolded a map on the dirt floor, smoothed it with the palm of his hand, and with the tip of his knife traced out a route for Tex Armadillo. The light of the oil lamp fell full on the man's face. From where they were watching they couldn't see the map very well, but they could easily make out a brand on the man's dark hand and note that the same design was repeated on the bone handle of the knife. It was a scorpion.

Alex calculated that they had seen enough, and should start back before the men ended their meeting. The only way out of the room was the corridor where Alex and Nadia were hiding. Again Nadia consulted Borobá, who from his mistress's shoulder unhesitatingly pointed the way. Relieved, Alexander remembered what his father always advised him when they went mountain climbing together: *Confront obstacles as they appear, don't waste energy fearing what you may meet in the future.* He smiled, thinking that he shouldn't worry so much, since he wasn't always the one in charge. Nadia was a resourceful person, as she had demonstrated on many occasions. He should never forget that.

Fifteen minutes later they were back at street level, and soon heard the voices of tourists. They walked faster and blended into the crowd. They did not see Armadillo again.

• • •

"Do you know anything about scorpions, Kate?" Alexander asked his grandmother when they all met back at the hotel.

"Some of the kinds they have in India are very poisonous. You can die from their bites. I hope that won't happen, because that would delay our trip, and I don't have time for funerals," she replied, feigning indifference.

"I haven't been bitten yet."

"Then why are you interested?"

"I wanted to know if the scorpion means something. Is it a religious symbol, for instance?"

"The serpent is, especially the cobra. According to legend, a gigantic cobra watched over Buddha as he meditated. But I don't know anything about scorpions."

"Can you find out?"

"I would have to get in touch with that dreadful Ludovic Leblanc. Are you sure you want to ask me to make that sacrifice, child?" the writer grumbled.

"I think it could be very important, grandmother . . . Sorry, I mean Kate."

So Kate plugged in her laptop and sent an e-mail to the professor. Given the difference in time, it wasn't feasible to call him. She didn't know when the answer would come, but she hoped it would be soon, because she wasn't sure she could use her computer in the Forbidden Kingdom. Following a hunch, she sent another message to her friend Isaac Rosenblat, asking if he knew anything about the Golden Dragon that supposedly existed in the country they were traveling to. To her surprise, the jeweler replied immediately.

Dear girl! What a pleasure to hear from you! Of course I know about that statue. Every serious jeweler knows its description, it's one of the rarest and most precious objects in the world. No one has seen your famous dragon, and it has never been photographed, but there are drawings of it. It's about two feet long and is thought to be solid gold, but that isn't all: the craftsmanship is very ancient and very beautiful. In addition, it is covered with precious stones. According to legend, its eyes alone—just those two perfect, absolutely symmetrical, star rubies—are worth a fortune. Why do you ask? I don't suppose that you're planning to steal the dragon, the way you did the diamonds in the Amazon?

Kate e-mailed back, assuring the jeweler that robbery was precisely what she was planning, and decided not to remind him that Nadia had found the diamonds. It suited her to have Isaac Rosenblat believe she was capable of having stolen them. That way, she calculated, she would keep her former suitor's interest alive. She burst out laughing, but the laughter quickly turned into a fit of coughing. She dug through one of her many carryalls and pulled out a canteen containing her Amazon remedy.

Professor Ludovic Leblanc's reply was long and confusing, like everything he did. He began with an exhausting explanation of how, among his many attributes, he had been the first anthropologist to discover the meaning of the scorpion in Sumerian, Egyptian, Hindu, and ... blah-blah-blah ... mythology; then followed with twenty-three paragraphs on his accomplishments and knowledge. But sprinkled here and there in those twenty-three paragraphs were several very interesting facts, which Kate Cold was able to extract from the tangle. The aging writer heaved a sigh of boredom, thinking what a burden it was to have to put up with that peevish man. She had to reread the message several times to be able to summarize the important parts.

"According to Leblanc, there is a sect in the north of India that worships the scorpion. Its members have that figure branded on their skin, usually on the back of the right hand. They have a reputation for being bloodthirsty, ignorant, and superstitious," she informed her grandson and Nadia.

She added that during the fight for India's independence the sect had done the dirty work for the British troops, torturing and murdering their compatriots. Though they were widely despised, the men of the scorpion sect were still employed today as mercenaries, because they were ferocious fighters, famous for their skill with knives.

"They're bandits and smugglers, and they also kill for hire," Kate informed them.

Alexander then told Kate what he and Nadia had seen in the Red Fort. If Kate was tempted to scold them for having done something so dangerous, she contained herself. On the trip to the Amazon, she had learned to trust the two young friends.

"I have no doubt that the men you two saw belong to that sect. Leblanc says in his e-mail that the members wear cotton tunics and turbans dyed with the indigo plant. The dye rubs off on their skin and over the years becomes indelible, like a tattoo, which is why they are known as the Blue Warriors. They are nomads, and they spend their lives on horseback. They have no belongings except for weapons, and they are trained to fight from the time they are children," Kate explained.

"Do the women have blue skin too?" Nadia asked.

"It's strange that you should ask, child. There are no women in the sect."

"How do they have children if there are no women?"

"I don't know. Maybe they don't."

"If they're trained for war from the time they're small, children *must* be born into the sect," Nadia insisted.

"Maybe they steal them, or buy them. There's so much poverty in this country, so many abandoned children . . . And many parents just sell their children because they can't feed them," said Kate.

"I'm wondering what business Tex Armadillo can have with the Sect of the Scorpion," Alexander mused.

"Nothing good," said Nadia.

"You think it has anything to do with drugs? Remember what he said on the plane, that marijuana and opium grow wild in the Forbidden Kingdom."

"I hope that man doesn't cross our paths again, but if he does, I don't want you to have anything to do with him. Do you understand?" his grandmother ordered firmly.

The friends nodded, but the writer happened to

catch the look they exchanged, and guessed that no warning of hers would restrain Nadia and Alexander's curiosity.

One hour later the group from *International Geographic* assembled at the airport to take the plane to Tunkhala, the capital of the Kingdom of the Golden Dragon. They ran into Judit Kinski there, who was taking the same flight. The landscape architect wore boots, a white linen dress and a matching coat, and she carried the scuffed purse they had seen before. Her luggage consisted of two suitcases of a heavy, tapestrylike cloth, expensive but badly worn pieces. It was obvious that she had traveled a lot, though the general effect of her clothes and her suitcases was anything but shabby. In contrast, the members of the *International Geographic* expedition, with their stained and wrinkled clothes, their bundles and backpacks, looked like refugees fleeing some cataclysm.

The prop plane was an old model with a capacity of eight passengers and two crew. The other two travelers were a Hindu who had business in the Forbidden Kingdom and a young doctor who had graduated from a university in New Delhi and was returning to his country. The travelers commented that their little plane did not seem a particularly safe way to challenge the mountains of the Himalayas, but the pilot smiled and replied that there was nothing to fear: In the ten years he had been flying that route he had never had a serious accident, even though the winds between the precipices were often very strong.

"What precipices?" asked Joel González, uneasy.

"I hope you can see them, they're magnificent. The best time for flying is between October and April, when the skies are clear. If it's cloudy, you can't see anything," said the pilot.

"It's a little cloudy today. What will keep us from crashing into a mountain?" asked Kate.

"These are low clouds. You'll see it clear soon, ma'am. Besides, I know the route by heart, I can fly it with my eyes closed."

"I hope you keep them wide open, young man," Kate replied curtly.

"I estimate that within a half hour we'll have left the clouds behind," the pilot said, hoping to calm her, and added that they were lucky, because sometimes flights were delayed for several days, depending on the weather.

Jaguar and Eagle were just happy that Tex Armadillo wasn't on board.

CHAPTER EIGHT

In the Forbidden Kingdom

✸

NONE OF THE TRAVELERS TAKING that flight for the first time was prepared for what lay ahead. It was worse than a roller coaster in an amusement park. They covered their ears and felt an emptiness in the pits of their stomachs as the airplane shot up like an arrow, then dropped several hundred feet, making them feel as if their guts were glued to their brains. When it seemed that finally they had stabilized, the pilot would bank sharply to avoid a mountain peak, and they would be hanging almost upside down; then he would perform the same maneuver in the opposite direction.

Through the windows they could see mountains on both sides, and below them, very far below, incredible precipices with seemingly bottomless chasms. A single false move, or a brief hesitation on the part of the pilot, and the small plane would threaten to crash against the rocks or drop like a stone. A capricious blast of wind from the stern would hurl them forward, but once past that mountain, the air currents would change and blow toward them, making them feel as if they weren't moving at all.

The merchant from India and the doctor from the Forbidden Kingdom were glued in their seats, less than relaxed, although they said they had lived through that experience before. As for the members of the *International Geographic* team, they held their stomachs with both hands, trying to control their nausea and fear. No one made the least comment, not even Joel González, who was deadly white, quietly praying and rubbing the silver cross he always wore. All of them were impressed by the calm of Judit Kinski, who was composed enough to be leafing through a book on tulips, showing no trace of vertigo.

The flight lasted for several hours that seemed like several days, at the end of which they made a nosedive landing onto a short field cleared in the midst of thick green. From the air they had seen the wonderful countryside of the Forbidden Kingdom: a majestic chain of snow-capped mountains and a series of narrow valleys and terraced hillsides covered with lush semitropical vegetation. The villages looked like clusters of little dollhouses, scattered here and there in almost inaccessible sites. The capital lay in a long narrow valley enclosed on all sides by mountains. It seemed impossible that a plane could land there, but the pilot knew his job well. When at last they touched down, everyone applauded, celebrating his amazing skill. Steps soon were run up to the plane. When the door was opened, the passengers got to their feet with great difficulty and staggered toward the exit, afraid that at any minute they might vomit or faint—all, that is, except for the cool and composed Judit Kinski.

Kate was the first to reach the door. A breath of fresh air hit her in the face, reviving her. She was surprised to see a beautifully woven carpet that ran from the steps to the door of a small building of polychrome wood with a pagoda roof. On either side of the carpet, children waited with baskets of flowers. Set all along the path were slim poles topped with billowing silk banners. Several musicians dressed in vibrant colors and large hats were playing drums and brass instruments.

Right at the foot of the steps stood four dignitaries attired in full ceremonial garb: silk skirts bound at the waist with tight, dark blue sashes, a sign of ministerial rank; long jackets embroidered with coral and turquoise, and tall, pointed leather hats brightened with gold ornamentation and ribbons. They held delicate white scarves.

"Goodness! I wasn't expecting this kind of reception," the writer exclaimed, smoothing her spiky hair and unfashionable thousand-pocketed jacket.

She descended the steps, followed by her companions, smiling and waving, but no one waved back. Her crew passed by the dignitaries and the children holding the flowers without winning a single glance; it was as if they didn't exist.

Judit followed behind, calm, smiling, perfectly poised. At that moment the musicians struck up a deafening chorus, the children began tossing a rain of rose petals, and the dignitaries bowed deeply. Judit Kinski returned their greetings with a modest bow, then held her arms out as the dignitaries stepped forward and draped scarves called *katas* across them.

The reporters from *International Geographic* watched as a party of richly attired individuals emerged from the small building with the pagoda roof. In the center was a man taller than the others, about sixty years old, though young in bearing, wearing a simple, long, dark red skirt, or sarong, that covered the lower half of his body, and a saffron-colored cloth folded over one shoulder. His head was uncovered and shaved. He was barefoot, and his only adornments were a prayer bracelet made of amber beads and a medallion on his chest. Despite his extreme simplicity, which contrasted with the luxurious garb of the others, no one had any doubt that this man was the king. The foreigners stepped aside to let him pass, and automatically bowed deeply, as others were doing. Such was the authority the monarch communicated.

The king greeted Judit Kinski with a nod, which she returned in silence. Then they exchanged scarves with a series of complicated bows. She performed the steps of the ceremony perfectly. She wasn't joking when she told Kate that she had carefully studied the customs of the country. At the end of the ceremony the monarch and the landscape designer smiled openly and shook hands in Western fashion.

"Welcome to our humble country," the sovereign said in a British-accented English.

The monarch and his guest withdrew, followed by the king's entourage, as Kate and her group scratched their heads, confused by what they had just seen. Judit must have made an extraordinary impression on the ruler, who was treating her as he would an honored ambassador, not a landscaper contracted to plant tulips in his garden.

They were collecting their luggage, which included

the bundles containing the photographers' cameras and tripods, when a man approached them and introduced himself as Wandgi, their guide and interpreter. He was wearing the typical sarong tied at the waist with a striped sash, a short, sleeveless jacket, and soft hide boots. Kate noticed his hat, which was the kind the Italian mobsters wear in the movies.

They loaded their equipment onto a broken-down Jeep, settled in as well as they could, and started off for the capital, which, according to Wandgi, was "just over there," but turned out to be a trip of nearly three hours. What he called "the highway" was in fact a narrow curving road. The guide spoke an old-fashioned English and had an accent that was difficult to understand, as if he had learned it from a textbook without having had many opportunities to practice.

Along the way they drove past monks and nuns of all ages, some no more than five or six years old, all with their bowls for begging food. There were also many farm people on foot carrying bundles, young people on bicycles, and carts pulled by buffaloes. These were a very handsome people of medium stature, with aristocratic features and dignified bearing. They were always smiling, as if they were genuinely content. The only motorized vehicles they saw were a very old motorcycle with a parasol serving as improvised roof, and a small bus painted a thousand colors and overflowing with passengers, animals, and bundles. To pass the bus, the Jeep had to pull off to one side, because there wasn't room for two vehicles on the narrow road. Wandgi informed them that his majesty had several modern automobiles and that Judit Kinski was surely at the hotel by now.

"The king dresses like a monk," Alexander observed.

"His majesty is our spiritual leader. He lived the early years of his life in a monastery in Tibet. He is a very devoted man," the guide explained, joining his hands before his face and bowing as a sign of respect.

"I thought monks were celibate," said Kate.

"Many are, but the king must marry in order to provide sons to the crown. His majesty is a widower. His beloved wife died ten years ago."

"How many children did they have?"

"They were blessed with four sons and five daughters. One of his sons will be king. Here it is not as it is in England, where the oldest offspring inherits the crown. The prince with the purest heart becomes our king upon the death of his father," said Wandgi.

"And how do they know which one has the purest heart?" Nadia asked.

"The king and queen know their children well, and usually they simply know, but their decision must be confirmed by the High Lama, who studies the astral signs and subjects the chosen child to several tests before deciding if he or she is truly the reincarnation of an earlier monarch."

He explained that the tests were foolproof. For example, during one of them, the prince or princess recognizes seven objects used by the first ruler of the Kingdom of the Golden Dragon eighteen hundred years before. The objects are placed on the floor, mixed in with others, and the child must choose. If he passes that first test, he must ride a wild stallion. If he is the reincarnation of a king, the beast will recognize his authority and be as tame as if it had been broken. The child must also swim the roaring, icy waters of the sacred river. The current helps those of pure heart; all others drown. This method of testing heirs to the throne had never failed.

Throughout its history, the Forbidden Kingdom has always had fair and visionary monarchs, Wandgi said, and added that the country had never been invaded or colonized, even though it lacked an army capable of confronting its powerful neighbors, India and China. In the present generation, the youngest son, who was only a baby when his mother died, had been chosen to succeed his father. He had passed all the tests at the age of six. The lamas had given him the name he bore in earlier incarnations: Dil Bahadur, "brave heart." No one had seen him since his selection; he was being given instruction in a secret location.

Kate seized the opportunity to ask the guide about the mysterious Golden Dragon. Wandgi did not seem disposed to talk about it, but the group from *International Geographic* were able to deduce a few facts from his evasive answers. Apparently the statue could predict the future, but only the king could decipher the coded language of the prophecies. The reason it was essential for the king or queen to be pure of heart was that the power of the Golden Dragon could be used only to protect the nation, never for personal ends. There could be no greed in the heart of the monarch.

On their way to the capital, the *International Geographic* crew saw peasant homes and many temples, which they identified immediately by the prayer banners similar to the ones they'd seen fluttering in the wind at the airport. The guide exchanged greetings with each person they saw; apparently everyone knew everyone.

They passed lines of boys dressed in the dark red of the monks' tunics, and the guide explained that most teaching took place in the monasteries, where students lived from the time they were five or six years old. Some never left the monastery, because they chose to follow in the footsteps of their teachers, the lamas. Girls went to different schools. There was a university, but usually professionals were trained in India, and in some cases, when the family could afford it or the student won a government scholarship, in England.

The group saw television antennas on a couple of modest shops. Wandgi told them that people in the neighborhood gathered around during the hours programs were broadcast, but that there were frequent blackouts and the daily schedule varied. He added that most of the country was linked by telephone. To make a call you went to the post office—if there was one nearby—or to a school where there was always a telephone available. No one had a phone in their house, of course; there was no need for one. Timothy Bruce and Joel González exchanged doubtful glances. Was it all right to use their cell phones in the Land of the Golden Dragon?

"The range of mobile telephones is greatly limited by the mountains, so they are virtually unknown here.

I've been told that no one speaks face to face in your country anymore, only by telephone," the guide said.

"And by e-mail," Alexander added.

"I've heard about that, but I haven't seen it," Wandgi commented.

The landscape was like a dream, untouched by modern technology. Land was cultivated behind slow and patient buffaloes. Emerald rice paddies glowed on terraces that had been carved out of the sides of the mountains. Unfamiliar trees and flowers grew on the berm along the road, and in the background rose the snowy peaks of the Himalayas.

Alexander made the observation that the agricultural methods seemed far behind the times, but his grand-mother pointed out that not everything is measured in terms of productivity, and added that this was the only country in the world in which the ecology was far more important than the economy. Wandgi was pleased by Kate's words, but did not comment further in order not to embarrass these visitors who came from a country where, from what he had heard, business was definitely more important.

Two hours later the sun had dropped behind the mountains, and evening shadows were stretching across the green rice paddies. In the scattered homes and temples they could see the quavering flames of small yak butter–burning lamps. Faintly, they could hear the guttural sounds from the huge trumpets of the monks calling for evening prayer.

Shortly after, far in the distance, they saw the first buildings of Tunkhala, the capital, which looked like little more than a village. The main street boasted a few street lamps, so they could appreciate the cleanliness and order that were the rule everywhere, as well as the contradictions: yaks plodded through the street beside Italian Vespas, grandmothers carried their grandchildren strapped to their backs, and police dressed like ancient princes directed traffic. The doors of many houses stood wide open, and Wandgi explained that there was virtually no crime, after all, they all knew each other; anyone who came into your house was probably a friend or a relative. The police had very little to do except guard the borders, maintain order during festivals, and control rebellious students.

There was still a lot of activity. Wandgi stopped the Jeep before a shop little larger than a closet, where they sold toothpaste, sweets, Kodak film, sun-faded postcards, and a few newspapers and magazines from Nepal, India, and China. They noticed that empty tin cans, bottles, and bundles of used paper were also being sold. Everything, even the most insignificant object, had value, because everything was in limited supply. Nothing was wasted; everything was used or recycled. A plastic bag or a glass bottle was a treasure.

"This is my humble shop and beside it is my small home, where it will be my great honor to welcome you," Wandgi announced, blushing; he did not want the foreigners to think he was boasting.

A young girl of fifteen came out to greet them.

"And this is my daughter Pema. Her name means 'lotus flower,'" the guide added.

"The lotus flower is a symbol of purity and beauty," said Alexander, blushing like Wandgi, because the moment he said it he felt ridiculous.

Kate cast a sidelong glance at him, surprised. He winked and said that he'd read that in a book in the library before they left.

"What else did you find out?" she muttered out of the corner of her mouth.

"Ask and ye shall know, Kate. I know almost as much as Judit Kinski," Alexander replied in the same tone.

Pema smiled with irresistible charm, joined her hands before her face, and bowed in the traditional greeting. She was as slim and straight as a bamboo cane; in the yellow light of the lamps her skin looked like ivory and her large eyes shone playfully. Her black hair fell like a fine mantle across her shoulders and back. She was dressed like everyone they had seen. There was little difference between male and female clothing; everyone wore a skirt or a sarong, and a jacket or blouse.

Nadia and Pema looked at each other with mutual astonishment. On the one hand there was this girl from the heart of South America, with feathers in her hair and a black monkey clinging to her neck; on the other, a girl with the grace of a ballerina who had been born among the highest peaks of Asia. The two girls felt connected by an instantaneous current of friendship.

"If you want, perhaps tomorrow Pema can teach the girl and the Little Grandmother how to wear a sarong," suggested the guide, with obvious concern.

Alexander cringed when he heard the words "little grandmother," but Kate did not react. The writer had just realized that the shorts she and Nadia were wearing were offensive in this country.

"We would be very grateful," Kate replied, bowing in turn, with her hands joined before her face.

• • •

Finally the exhausted travelers reached the hotel, the only one in the capital, or anywhere in the Forbidden Kingdom. The few tourists who ventured out into the countryside slept in the homes of peasants, where they were always welcomed. No one was refused hospitality. The *International Geographic* group dragged their luggage to the two rooms they were to share—Kate and Nadia in one and the men in the other. Compared to the incredible luxury of the maharajah's palace in India, the rooms in this hotel seemed like monks' cells. They fell into beds without washing or undressing, bone weary, but they soon awoke, stiff with cold. The temperature had dropped sharply. They pulled out their flashlights and found some heavy wool throws stacked neatly in a corner; they wrapped up in those and slept till dawn when they were awakened by the mournful sound of the long, heavy trumpets that called the monks to their prayers.

Wandgi and Pema were waiting with the good news that the king was willing to receive them the next day. As they savored a delicious breakfast of tea, vegetables, and rice balls, which they ate using the three fingers of the right hand, as good manners demanded, the guide gave them a brief course on the protocol for visiting the palace.

To begin with, they would need to buy proper clothing for Nadia and Kate. And the men should wear jackets. The king was a very tolerant person and surely would understand that they were outfitted for their work; nonetheless, it would be more polite to show the proper respect. Wandgi explained how to exchange the *katas*, and told them that they should kneel in the places assigned to them until it was indicated that they might take seats, and that they should not speak to the king before he spoke to them. If they were offered food or tea, they should refuse three times, then eat silently and slowly to demonstrate that they appreciated the food. And it was considered bad form to speak while eating. Borobá would stay with Pema. Wandgi did not know the protocol in regard to monkeys.

Kate succeeded in connecting her laptop to one of the two telephone lines in the hotel and sent messages to the *International Geographic* and to Professor Leblanc. The man might be a neurotic, but she could not deny that he was an inexhaustible source of information. The writer asked him to send her what he knew about how the kings were trained, and about the legend of the Golden Dragon. She promptly received his communication on those subjects.

Pema took Kate and Nadia to a house where sarongs

were sold, and each of them bought three; it rained several times a day and they had to allow time for the skirts to dry. It wasn't easy for either of them to learn how to wrap the cloth around their bodies and secure it with the sash. First they got them so tight that they couldn't take a step; then they wound them so loosely that they fell off with the first movement. Nadia mastered the technique after a few tries, but Kate still looked like a mummy. She couldn't sit down, and she walked like a prisoner in shackles. Alexander and the two photographers burst out in fits of uncontrollable laughter when they saw Kate hobbling along, grumbling and coughing.

The royal palace was the largest building in Tunkhala, with more than a thousand rooms distributed on three visible floors and two below ground level. It was strategically located on a steep hill, and was approached by a curving road lined with prayer flags mounted on flexible bamboo poles. The king's residence was the same elegant style as every other home, including the most modest, but it had several roof levels, tiled and crowned with ancient ceramic figures of mythological creatures. The balconies, doors, and windows were painted in designs of extraordinary colors.

Soldiers dressed in yellow and red, with leather jackets and plumed helmets, were standing guard. They were armed with swords and bows and arrows. Wandgi explained that their function was purely decorative; the actual police carried modern weapons. He added that the bow was the traditional weapon of the Forbidden Kingdom and also the favorite sport. Even the king participated in the yearly competitions.

The party was received by two officials attired in elaborate court dress, and led through several halls in which the only furniture was low tables, large polychrome wooden trunks, and piles of round cushions to sit on. There were occasional religious statues with traditional offerings of candles, rice, and flower petals before them. The walls were decorated with frescoes, some of them so ancient that the motifs had nearly disappeared. A few monks outfitted with paintbrushes, tins of paints, and thin gold leaf, were restoring the frescoes with infinite patience. Everywhere they looked, they saw rich tapestries embroidered with silk and satin threads.

They walked down long corridors with offices on both sides, where dozens of clerks and scribes were at work. Computers had not as yet been adopted; all the data of public administration were still entered by hand. There was also a room for the oracles. That was where people came to ask advice of certain lamas and monks who had the gift of prophecy and could be of help in moments of indecision. For the Buddhists of the Forbidden Kingdom, the road to salvation was always individual, and was rooted in compassion for all things animate and inanimate. They believed that theory served no purpose without practice. A person could correct his course and hasten good results by using a good guide, mentor, or oracle.

Finally they came to a large, unadorned chamber: in its center sat an enormous, gilded Buddha whose head touched the ceiling. They heard music that sounded like mandolins, and then realized that they were hearing several monks, chanting. The melody grew louder and louder. Then suddenly it would fall, adopting a new rhythm. Before the monumental image were a prayer rug, lighted candles, sticks of incense, and baskets of offerings. Imitating the dignitaries, the visitors bowed before the statue three times, touching their foreheads to the floor.

The architecture of the hall where the king received them was as simple and delicate as the rest of the palace, but in this room the walls were decorated with ceremonial masks and tapestries with religious scenes.

Five chairs had been provided in deference to the foreigners.

Behind the king hung a tapestry featuring a creature that surprised Nadia and Alex because it so closely resembled the beautiful winged dragons they'd seen in the distant Amazon, in the *tepui* near the City of the Beasts. They were the last of a species that had been nearly extinct for thousands of years. The royal tapestry proved that in some long-ago epoch those dragons had also lived in Asia.

The monarch was wearing the same tunic he wore the day before, but today he had added a strange headdress that looked like a cloth helmet. On his chest shone the medallion of his authority, an ancient gold disc encrusted with coral. They found him sitting in the lotus position on a dais about a foot and a half high.

Beside the sovereign was a beautiful leopard, stretched out like a cat; it pricked its ears when it saw the visitors and bared its teeth at Alexander. Its master's hand on its back calmed the leopard, but its elongated eyes never left the American youth.

Several dignitaries accompanied the king, splendidly attired in striped cloth, embroidered jackets, and hats adorned with large gold leaves—although some wore Western shoes and carried executive briefcases. A few monks were there in their red tunics. Three girls and two boys, tall and distinguished-looking, stood beside the king. The visitors assumed that these were his children.

As Wandgi had instructed them, they did not accept the offer of the chairs, because it was not polite to sit at the same level as the king; instead they chose the small wool carpets arranged before the royal dais.

After the obligatory greetings and exchange of the *katas*, the foreigners waited for the king's signal to take their places on the floor, the men with crossed legs and the women with their legs folded to one side. It was all Kate, tangled in her sarong, could do to keep from rolling across the floor. And it was all the king and his court could do to keep a straight face.

Before they began their conversation, tea was served, along with nuts and strange fruit sprinkled with salt, which the visitors ate only after refusing three times. The moment had come for the gifts. The writer signaled to Timothy and Joel, who crawled forward on their knees to present the king with a box containing copies of the first twelve issues of *International Geographic*, published in 1888, and a manuscript page of Charles Darwin's writings that the director of the magazine had miraculously obtained from an antiques dealer in London. The king thanked them, and in turn offered them a book wrapped in a cloth. Wandgi had told them that they must not open the package; that would be a sign of impatience acceptable only in a child.

At that moment, an official announced the arrival of Judit Kinski. The members of the expedition of *International Geographic* realized why they hadn't seen her in the hotel that morning: the woman was a guest at the royal palace. She greeted everyone with a slight nod and took her place on the floor with the other foreigners. She was wearing a simple dress and carrying her usual leather purse—which apparently she was never without; her only adornment was a wide African bracelet of carved bone.

As Judit sat down, Tschewang, the royal leopard, which had been quiet but alert, sprang from the dais and took a stance before Alexander, its upper lip pulled back in a threatening grimace that revealed a row of very sharp teeth. Everyone froze, and the two guards stiffened, ready to intervene, but the king stopped them with a gesture and called the beast. The leopard turned toward its master, but did not obey.

Without thinking, Alexander whipped off his glasses, rose on all fours, and assumed the same expression as the big cat; he had made claws of his hands and was growling and showing his teeth.

At that point, Nadia, sitting calmly where she was, began to murmur strange sounds like the purring of a cat. With that, the leopard padded over to her and put its face next to hers, sniffing her and switching its tail. Then, to everyone's astonishment, it lay down before her, turned over, and exposed its belly, which she scratched with no sign of fear, still making the purring sound.

"You can speak with animals?" the king asked in a matter-of-fact tone.

The dumbfounded foreigners deduced that apparently in this kingdom speaking with animals was nothing out of the ordinary.

"Sometimes, your Majesty," the girl replied.

"What is happening with my faithful Tschewang? Usually he is very polite and obedient." The monarch smiled and waved a hand toward the feline.

"Your Majesty, I think he was frightened of a jaguar," Nadia replied.

No one except Alexander understood what she meant. Kate smacked the palm of her hand against her forehead. They were definitely creating a scene; they must seem like a pack of escaped lunatics. The king, however, did not bat an eye at the answer of the little honey-colored foreigner. He merely studied the

American boy who by now had returned to normal and was again sitting before the dais with his legs crossed. Only the sweat on his forehead betrayed the scare he'd experienced.

Nadia Santos laid a silk scarf before the leopard. The big cat picked it up delicately in its jaws and carried it to the feet of the monarch. Then it took its usual place on the royal dais.

"Tell me, child, can you also speak with birds?" the king asked.

"Sometimes, Majesty," she replied.

"We often see interesting birds here," he said.

In truth the Kingdom of the Golden Dragon was an ecological sanctuary where many species could be found that were extinct in other places in the world, but he did not want to seem boastful about that; it would be unpardonable bad manners. Not even the king, who was the ultimate authority in questions of flora and fauna, flaunted his country's treasures.

Later, when the group from *International Geographic* opened the royal gift, they found it was a book of bird photographs. Wandgi told them that the king himself had taken the photos. His name, nonetheless, did not appear anywhere; that would have been another demonstration of vanity.

• • •

The remainder of the interview consisted of talk about the Kingdom of the Golden Dragon. The foreigners noticed that no one ever made a direct statement. The most frequently used words were "possibly," "maybe," and "perhaps," a convenient way to prevent clashes of opinions and confrontations. The avoidance of absolutes provided an honorable way out in case the parties involved were not in agreement.

Judit Kinski seemed to know a lot about the wonders of the region's natural world. This captivated the ruler, along with the rest of the court, because her knowledge was so unusual in a foreigner.

"It is an honor to welcome the representatives of the *International Geographic* magazine to our country," the sovereign said.

"The honor is entirely ours, Majesty. We know that your nation's respect for nature is unique in all the world," replied Kate.

"If we harm the natural world, we must pay the consequences. Only a madman would commit such folly. Your guide, Wandgi, will take you wherever you wish to go. Perhaps you will want to visit the temples or the *dzongs*, the fortified monasteries, where possibly the monks can welcome you as guests and give you the information you need," the king proposed.

Everyone was aware that he was not including Judit, and guessed that the ruler was planning to show her the beauties of his kingdom himself.

The interview had come to an end, and all that was left was to offer their thanks and say good-bye. That was when Kate committed her first blunder. Unable to control her impulse, she asked the king point-blank about the legend of the Golden Dragon. A glacial silence settled over the hall. The dignitaries were paralyzed, and the king's amiable smile disappeared. The pause that followed was thick with tension, until Judit dared speak out.

"Please forgive our disrespect, Majesty. We are not familiar with your customs. I hope that Mrs. Cold's question has not been offensive to you. In truth, she spoke for all of us. I am as curious about that legend as the journalists from *International Geographic*," she said, fixing her chestnut eyes on his.

The king returned her gaze with a very serious expression, as if he was weighing her motives, and at last he smiled. The ice shattered, and everyone began to breathe again, relieved.

"The sacred dragon does exist; it is not merely a legend. However, I regret that you may not see it," said the king, speaking with a firmness he had avoided until then.

"Somewhere I read that the statue is kept in a fortified monastery in Tibet," Judit persisted. "I've always wondered what happened to it after the Chinese invasion."

Kate had thought that no one would dare push the subject any further. This woman had a great deal of confidence in herself and in the attraction the king felt for her.

"The sacred dragon represents the spirit of our nation. It has never left our kingdom," he clarified.

"My apologies, Majesty, I was misinformed. It is only logical that it be kept in this palace, close to you," said Judit.

"That may be," he said, standing to indicate that the interview was over.

The group from *International Geographic* bid their farewells with deep bows, and backed from the room—all except Kate, who was so entangled in her sarong that she had no choice but to pull it up above her knees and stumble out, turning her back to his majesty.

Tschewang, the royal leopard, followed Nadia to the door of the palace, pushing its muzzle against her hand, but also never taking its eyes from Alexander.

"Don't look at him, Jaguar. He's jealous of you," the girl laughed.

CHAPTER NINE

Kidnapped

THE COLLECTOR WAS STARTLED awake by the ringing of the private telephone on his night table. It was two in the morning. Only three people knew that number: his doctor, the chief of his bodyguards, and his mother. It had been months since that telephone rang. The Collector hadn't needed his doctor or his security chief, and as for his mother, at that moment she was somewhere in the Antarctic, photographing penguins. The lady had spent recent years on a series of cruise ships, sailing from port to port on an endless journey. As soon as she arrived at one destination, an employee met her with a ticket in hand for her to board a different ship. Her son had discovered that travel kept his mother happy, and kept him from having to see her.

"How did you get this number?" the second richest man in the world asked indignantly; he recognized the speaker in spite of the filter that distorted the voice.

"Finding out secrets is part of my job," the Specialist replied.

"What news do you have for me?"

"The article we agreed upon will soon be in your possession."

"So why are you bothering me?"

"To tell you that the Golden Dragon will not serve your purposes unless you know how to use it," the Specialist explained.

"I have the translated parchment for that, the one I bought from the Chinese general," the Collector responded.

"Do you think that something as important as that secret would be laid out on a single sheet of parchment? The translation is in code."

"Then get the code! That's what I hired you to do."

"No. You contracted me to get the object, nothing more. That was our deal," the distorted voice informed him coldly.

"I'm not interested in the dragon without the instructions, you understand me? Get them, or you will never see your millions," the client screamed.

"I never amend the terms of a negotiation. You and I made an agreement. I will deliver the statue to you within two weeks, and I will collect the sum we settled on or you will pay the consequences."

The threat was all too clear; the client realized that

he was gambling his life. For once, the second richest man on the planet was frightened.

"You're right. A deal is a deal. I will pay you an additional fee for the code for deciphering the parchment. Do you think you will have it fairly soon? As you know, this is a very urgent matter. I am prepared to pay whatever is necessary, money is no object," the Collector said in a conciliatory tone.

"In this case, price isn't the point."

"Everyone has a price."

"You're wrong," the Specialist replied.

"Didn't you tell me that there is nothing you can't get your hands on?" asked the anguished client.

"One of my agents will be in touch with you soon," the voice replied, and the line went dead.

The multibillionaire could not go back to sleep. He spent the rest of the night in his office, which occupied most of his house and contained his fifty computers, going over and over the figures of a fortune too large to count to the penny. Day and night his employees monitored the most important stock markets in the world. However, no matter how many times the Collector went over the figures, and no matter how often he screamed at his staff, he could not alter the fact that there was a man who had more money than he did. *That* his nerves could not bear.

After a tour of the enchanting city of Tunkhala, with its pagoda-roofed houses, its *stupas*, or religious shrines, its temples, and its dozens of monasteries perched on the slopes of the hills in the midst of exuberant trees and flowers, Wandgi offered to show them the university. The campus was a natural park with waterfalls and thousands of birds. The pagoda roofs, the images of Buddha painted on the walls, and the prayer flags gave the university the look of a complex of monasteries. They saw groups of students standing and talking along the paths in the park, and were struck by their formality, so different from the relaxed air of Western youth.

They were welcomed by the rector, who asked Kate if she would speak to the students and tell them about *International Geographic*, which many of them read regularly in the library.

"We have very few occasions to welcome illustrious visitors to our humble university," he said, bowing repeatedly.

And that was how the writer, the photographers,

Alexander, and Nadia found themselves in a hall before a hundred and ninety university students and their professors. Nearly all of them spoke some English, because that was the favorite subject, but many times Wandgi had to translate. The first half-hour went by very smoothly.

The members of the audience asked naïve questions, very respectfully, bowing before addressing the foreigners. Alexander quickly became bored, and he raised his hand to say, "May we ask a few questions ourselves? We've come a long way to learn about this country."

There was a moment of silence, during which the confused students just looked at each other; this was the first time a speaker had proposed such a thing. After some hesitation and whispering among the professors, the rector gave his consent. During the next hour and a half, the visitors learned very interesting facts about the Forbidden Kingdom, and the students, freed from the strict formality they were accustomed to, grew brave enough to ask questions about American movies, music, clothing, cars, and a thousand other things.

Toward the end, Timothy pulled out a rock 'n' roll CD, and Kate put it in her player. Usually shy, her grandson was struck by an irresistible impulse and jumped to the front of the stage to give a dance demonstration that left the students with their jaws hanging open. Borobá, infected by Alexander's frenetic dance, imitated him to perfection, drawing raucous laughter from the audience. At the end of the "lecture," as their professors watched in amazement, the students accompanied the *International Geographic* group to the edge of the campus, singing and dancing as enthusiastically as Borobá.

"How were they able to learn that American music after hearing it only one time?" Kate asked, impressed.

"The students have been listening to it for years, Little Grandmother. At home they wear jeans, just like you Americans do," Wandgi replied, laughing. "They're smuggled in from India."

By then, Kate was resigned to allowing the guide to call her "little grandmother." It was a sign of good manners, the respectful way to address an older person. Nadia and Alex, for their part, were supposed to call Wandgi "uncle" and Pema "cousin."

"Perhaps, if they are not too tired, my honorable visitors might like to try a typical meal of Tunkhala," Wandgi suggested timidly.

The "honorable visitors" were tired, but they could not miss this opportunity. They ended their very busy day in the home of their guide. Like many in the capital city, the two-story home was constructed of white brick, its walls painted with intricate designs of flowers and birds, like those they'd seen in the palace. It was impossible to know which of the people coming and going belonged to Wandgi's immediate family because everyone was introduced as an uncle, brother, or cousin. No surnames were used. When a child was born, its parents gave it two or three names, to distinguish it from its siblings, but anyone could change their name at will; several times, in fact, during his or her life. The only ones to use family names were royalty.

Pema and her mother, along with several aunts and female cousins, served the meal. Everyone sat on the floor at a round table that held a veritable mountain of red rice and other grains, and a variety of vegetables seasoned with spices and hot pepper. Soon came a stream of delicacies specially prepared in honor of the foreign guests: yak liver, sheep's lungs, pig's feet, goat's eyes, and blood sausage seasoned with so much pepper and paprika that the mere smell of the dishes brought tears to Kate's eyes and sent her into a fit of coughing. They each ate with one hand, forming little balls of food, and courtesy demanded that the host family first offer the little balls to their visitors.

When they tasted the first mouthful, Alexander and Nadia nearly shrieked: neither of them had ever tasted anything so hot. Their mouths were burning, as if they had bitten down on live coals. Kate warned them, between coughs, that they must not offend their hosts, but the natives of the Forbidden Kingdom knew that the foreigners would not be able to swallow their food. As tears streamed down Nadia's and Alexander's cheeks, their hosts roared with laughter and pounded the floor with hands and feet.

Pema, who was also laughing a lot, brought her friends tea to rinse out their mouths, and a new plate of the same vegetables prepared without the hot seasonings. Alexander and Nadia exchanged a glance. In the Amazon they had eaten everything from roast snake to a soup made from the ashes of a dead Indian. Without a word, they simultaneously decided this was not the time to back away. They expressed their thanks, bowing with hands joined before their faces, and then each of them rolled a fiery little ball and bravely ate it.

The next day was the day of a religious festival that coincided with the full moon and the birthday of the king. The entire country had been preparing for the event for weeks. All of Tunkhala poured out into the streets, and peasants came down from the mountains and distant villages, traveling for days on foot or horseback. After being blessed by the lamas, musicians went outside with their instruments, and cooks set large tables with food, sweets, and jugs of rice liquor. At this celebration, everything was free.

The trumpets, drums, and gongs of the monasteries rang out from early morning. The faithful, and the pilgrims arriving from distant places, crowded into the temples to make their offerings, whirl the prayer wheels, and light candles of yak butter. The rancid odor of the grease and smoke from the incense floated through the city.

Before their trip, Alexander had gone to his school library to learn all he could about the Forbidden Kingdom, its customs and its religion, so he was able to give Nadia, who had never heard of Buddha, a brief summary of Buddhism.

"Five hundred and sixty-six years before Christ, in what today is South Nepal, a prince named Siddhartha Gautama was born. At his birth, a seer predicted that the boy would rule all the earth, but that he must be isolated from suffering and death lest he be moved to become a great spiritual leader. His father, who favored the former route for his son, surrounded the palace with high walls so that Siddhartha would live a marvelous life devoted to pleasure and beauty, without ever encountering misery. Even the leaves that fell from the trees were quickly swept up so that he would not see them wither. He married and he had a son, without ever having left that paradise. He was twenty-nine when he ventured outside the garden and saw illness, poverty, pain, and cruelty for the first time. He cut his hair, removed his jewels and clothing of rich silks, and set out in search of Truth. For six years he studied with yogis in India and subjected his body to the most rigorous asceticism."

"What's that?" Nadia asked.

"He lived a life of hardship. He slept on thorns and ate nothing but a few grains of rice."

"Bad idea," Nadia commented.

"That's what Siddhartha himself concluded. After passing from absolute pleasure in his palace to the most unsparing self-sacrifice, he realized that the Middle Path is the most reasonable," Alexander said.

"Why do they call him the Enlightened One?" Nadia wanted to know.

"Because when he was thirty-five, he sat beneath a tree and meditated for six days and six nights without moving. One moonlit night, like the night on which this festival is celebrated, his mind and his spirit opened, and he understood all the principles and processes of life. That is, he became Buddha."

"In Sanskrit, Buddha means 'awakened' or 'enlightened,'" Kate clarified. She had been paying close attention to her grandson's explanations. "Buddha isn't a name, it's a title, and anyone can become Buddha if he lives a noble and spiritual life," she added.

"The basic principle of Buddhism is to have compassion for everything that lives or exists. Buddha said that we must seek truth or illumination within ourselves, not in others or in external things," Alex continued. "That's why Buddhist monks don't go out in the world to preach, the way our missionaries do, but spend their lives in quiet meditation, seeking their own truth. All they own are their tunics, their sandals, and their bowls for begging food. They are not interested in material goods."

To Nadia, who owned nothing but a small bag that held essential clothing and three parrot feathers for her hair, that part of Buddhism seemed perfect.

In the morning there were three archery tournaments, the most popular activity of the Tunkhala festival. The best archers came decked out in colorful clothing and wearing garlands of flowers that girls had draped around their necks. Their bows were nearly six feet long, and very heavy.

Someone offered Alexander a bow, but he had a hard time even lifting it, to say nothing of using it. He pulled back the string with all his might, but the arrow slipped through his fingers and shot off in the direction of an elegant dignitary standing about ten feet from a target. Horrified, Alexander watched the man fall backward and was terrified that he'd killed him, but his victim quickly got to his feet, smiling widely. The arrow had pierced his hat. No one was offended. Waves of laughter celebrated the foreigner's awkwardness, and the dignitary spent the rest of the day wearing the arrow in his hat as a trophy. The king's older son won the archery tournament.

The citizens of the Forbidden Kingdom presented themselves in their finest holiday garb, and most wore masks or had their faces painted yellow, white, and red. Hats, necks, ears, and arms gleamed with silver, gold, ancient coral, and turquoise.

This day the king arrived wearing a spectacular headdress: the crown of the Forbidden Kingdom, which was made of silk embellished with heavy gold embroidery and precious stones. In the center, above his forehead, shone a huge ruby. On his chest he wore the royal medallion. With his eternal expression of calm and optimism, the king walked unescorted among his subjects, who obviously adored him. As a retinue he had only his ever-present Tschewang, the leopard, and his guest of honor, Judit Kinski, who wore the typical dress of the country though she still toted her usual shoulder bag.

In the evening there were theatrical performances with masked actors, acrobats, strolling minstrels, and jugglers. Groups of girls performed traditional dances while the best athletes competed in mock sword fights and a kind of martial art that the foreigners had never seen. They tumbled and moved with such amazing quickness that they seemed to fly above the heads of their opponents. No one could best one slim, handsome youth who had the agility and ferocity of a panther. Wandgi informed the guests that he was one of the king's sons, though not the one chosen to occupy the throne some day. He had a warrior's inclinations, they said; he always wanted to win, he liked applause, he was impatient and willful. It was clear, the guide added, this son did not have the qualities to become a wise ruler.

As the sun set, crickets began to sing, adding to the

sounds of the festival. Thousands of torches were lighted, and lamps with paper shades glowed in the dark.

There were large numbers of masked celebrants in the jubilant crowd. The masks were true works of art, each different, painted gold and brilliant colors. Nadia was surprised to note black beards flowing from beneath a few masks, because the men of the Forbidden Kingdom were close-shaven. Facial hair was simply never seen; it was considered unhygienic. For a while she studied the crowd, and soon she realized that the bearded individuals were not participating in the festivities. She was just about to communicate her observations to Alexander when he came over to her with a worried expression.

"Look at that man over there, Eagle," he said.

"Where?"

"Behind the juggler tossing the lighted torches in the air. The one wearing a Tibetan fur cap."

"What about him?" Nadia asked.

"Let's just quietly get a closer look," said Alexander.

As they drifted nearer, they could see two pale expressionless eyes through the mask: the unmistakable eyes of Tex Armadillo.

"How did he get here? He didn't come on the plane

with us, and the next flight was not until five days from now," Alexander commented after they had moved away a little.

"I don't think he's alone, Jaguar. Those masked men with the beards must be from the Sect of the Scorpion. I've been watching them, and it seems to me they're plotting something."

"If we see anything suspicious, we'll tell Kate. For the moment, let's not lose sight of them," said Alexander.

A family of experts in fireworks had come from China to add to the festivities. Soon the sky was alight and the crowds in the streets celebrated each burst of the marvelous Chinese display with cries of amazement.

There were so many people that it was difficult to move about in the confusion. Accustomed to the tropical warmth of her village, Santa María de la Lluvia, Nadia was shivering with the early evening cold. Pema offered to go back to the hotel with her to get warm clothing, so both set off with Borobá, who was frantic from the noise of the fireworks, while Alexander kept a close watch on Tex Armadillo.

Nadia was thankful that Kate had thought to buy her clothes for high altitudes. Her teeth were chattering as hard as Boroba's. She first put the monkey's snowsuit on him, and then her own pants, heavy socks, boots, and jacket, while Pema watched with amusement. She was very comfortable in her light silk sarong.

"Let's go! We're missing the best part of the festival!" Pema exclaimed.

They ran outside. The moon and cascades of Chinese multicolored stars lit up the night.

"Where are Pema and Nadia?" Alexander asked, judging that it had been more than an hour since they left.

"I haven't seen them," Kate replied.

"They went to the hotel because Nadia wanted to get a jacket, but they should have been back by now. Maybe I'd better go look for them," Alex decided.

"They'll be coming along, there's nowhere for them to get lost here," his grandmother said.

Alexander did not find the girls at the hotel. Two hours later, everyone was worried because no one had seen them in the swirling crowds for a long time. Their guide, Wandgi, borrowed a bicycle and went back to his house, thinking that Pema might have taken Nadia there, but he soon returned, in a panic.

"They've disappeared!" he shouted.

"Nothing could have happened to them. You told us that this is the safest country in the world!" Kate exclaimed.

By then very few people were in the streets. Only a few stragglers and the women who were clearing trash and remnants of food from the tables lingered. The scent of flowers and gunpowder floated on the air.

"They might have gone somewhere with students from the university," Timothy Bruce suggested.

That was not possible, Wandgi assured them. Pema would never do that. No respectable girl went out alone at night and without her parents' permission, he said. They decided to go to the police station, where they were courteously received by two exhausted officers who had been working since dawn and did not seem disposed to go out looking for two girls who surely were with friends or relatives. Kate planted herself before them, flourishing her passport and journalist's credentials, and loudly scolded them in her best voice of command, but nothing could shake them.

"These people received a special invitation from our beloved king," said Wandgi, and that got the police officers' attention.

The rest of the night was spent looking for Pema

and Nadia. By dawn the entire police force—nineteen officers—was on a state of alert, because four other young girls had been reported missing in Tunkhala.

Alexander told his grandmother about his suspicions that Blue Warriors had mixed in among the crowd, and added that he had seen Tex Armadillo disguised as a Tibetan shepherd. He had tried to follow him, but Armadillo must have realized he had been recognized and had slipped away. Kate informed the police, who advised them that it was counterproductive to sow panic when they had no proof.

During the first hours of the day, the chilling news spread that several girls had been kidnapped. Nearly all the shops remained closed and the doors of houses open, as citizens of a peaceful capital poured out into the streets to discuss the disappearance of the girls. Crews of volunteers went out to scour the countryside, but it was a disheartening job because the rough terrain covered with impenetrable vegetation greatly complicated the search. Soon a rumor began to circulate. It grew until it was an uncontainable river of panic sweeping across the city: The Scorpions! The Scorpions!

Two peasants who had not attended the festival

reported having seen several horsemen gallop toward the mountains. The hooves of their horses struck sparks from the stone and their black capes flapped in the wind. In the ghostly light of the fireworks they looked like devils, the terrified peasants said. A little later, a family returning home to their village found a worn canteen filled with liquor on the path, and took it to the police. A scorpion was burned into its leather case.

Wandgi was beside himself. He was kneeling on the floor of his house, moaning, with his face in his hands, while his wife sat silent and tearless, completely stupe-fied.

"Are they referring to the Sect of the Scorpion—the one in India?" Alexander asked.

"The Blue Warriors! I will never see my Pema again," the guide wept.

Little by little, the group from *International Geographic* gathered details. This group of bloodthirsty nomads roamed the north of India, where they often attacked defenseless villages to kidnap girls and convert them into slaves. To them, a woman was less valu-able than a knife; they treated the frightened girls worse than they did their animals, and kept them hidden in caves.

The members of this sect immediately killed any girl child born to them, but they kept the infant boys, whom they took from their mothers at the age of three and trained to fight. To harden them against venom, they exposed the boys to scorpion bites so that by the time they were adolescents they could survive snake and insect poisons that would be fatal to anyone else.

Within a very short time, the young slave girls died of illness or mistreatment, or were simply murdered, and the few who lived to the age of twenty were considered useless and were abandoned, to be replaced by the next group of kidnapped girls. And so the cycle was repeated. Along the rural roads of India one would see the sorrowful figures, these mad women, in rags and begging for food. No one came near them for fear of the Sect of the Scorpion.

"And the police do nothing?" Alexander asked, horrified.

"It all happens in very isolated regions, in miserable little villages with no defenses. No one dares confront the bandits. They live in fear of them; they think they have diabolical powers and that they can send a plague of scorpions to wipe out an entire village. There is no worse fate for a girl than to fall into the hands of the Blue Warriors. For a few years she will live the life of an animal, see her newborn daughters put to death, have her sons taken from her, and, if she doesn't die, end up as a beggar," the guide explained to them. He added that the Sect of the Scorpion were thieves and murderers who knew all the mountain passes in the Himalayas, crossed borders at will, and always attacked by night. They were as silent as shadows.

"Have they been seen in the Forbidden Kingdom before?" asked Alexander, with a terrible suspicion growing in his mind.

"Not until now. They have been active only in India and Nepal," the guide replied.

"Why did they come all this way? It's very strange that they would dare come to a city like Tunkhala. And strangest of all is that they decided to come in the middle of a festival, when the entire town was out celebrating and the police were on guard," Alexander noted.

"We must go immediately and speak with the king. He must mobilize every possible resource," Kate said decisively.

Her grandson was thinking about Tex Armadillo and the alarming men he'd seen in the cellars of the Red Fort. What role was that man playing in all this? What was the significance of the map he and the men had been studying?

Alexander didn't know where to begin to search for Eagle but he was prepared to travel the Himalayas from end to end to find her. He had no doubts about the danger his friend might be in at this very moment. Every minute was precious: he must find her before it was too late. More than ever he needed a jaguar's hunting instinct, but he was so upset that he couldn't concentrate hard enough to invoke it. Sweat was running down his brow and his back, soaking his shirt.

Nadia and Pema never saw their attackers. Two dark cloaks fell over them, enveloping them; then they were tied with cord, like packages, and lifted off the ground. Nadia screamed and kicked and tried to defend herself, but one sharp blow to her head stunned her. Pema, in contrast, gave herself to her fate, sensing that it was useless to fight at that moment, and that she should conserve her energy for later. Two of the kidnappers slung the tied-up girls over the horses they were riding and mounted behind them, holding them with iron grips. Folded blankets were the men's only saddles, and they guided their horses with the pressure of their knees. They were formidable horsemen.

Within a few moments Nadia had recovered consciousness, and as soon as her mind began to clear she

took inventory of her situation. She recognized immediately that she was on a galloping horse, even though
she had never ridden one. With each stride her stomach and chest pounded hard against the animal; she
could barely breathe beneath the blanket, and on her
back she felt the pressure of a large, powerful hand
clamping down on her like a claw.

The penetrating odor of the sweating horse and the
man's clothing was precisely what cleared her mind and
allowed her to think. Accustomed to living in contact
with nature and animals, she had a sharp sensitivity to
odors. Her kidnapper did not smell anything like the
people she had met in the Forbidden Kingdom, in
which everything was scrupulously clean. There the
natural aromas of silk, cotton, and wool blended with
those of the spices its citizens used for cooking and the
almond oil that everyone used to add luster to their
hair. Nadia could recognize a person from the
Forbidden Kingdom with her eyes closed. The man
who had her in his grasp smelled as if his clothes had
never been washed, and his skin exuded a bitter scent
of garlic, charcoal, and dust. She had no doubt that he
was a stranger to this land.

Nadia listened carefully and calculated that besides
the two horses Pema and she were being carried on,

there were at least four more, maybe five. And she could tell that they were riding uphill. When the pace of the horses changed, she realized that they were no longer on a path, but cutting across open country. She could hear the sound of hooves against stone and feel the horse straining to climb. Sometimes it slipped, whinnying, and the voice of the horseman would urge it forward in an unknown tongue.

Nadia's bones felt as if they were being ground to powder by the thumping, but she couldn't get more comfortable because she was immobilized by the rope. The pressure on her chest was so strong that she was afraid her ribs would break. How could she leave some sign, so they could find her? She was sure that Jaguar would try, but these mountains were a labyrinth of peaks and precipices. If she could only drop a shoe, she thought, but that was impossible since she was wearing laced boots.

Shortly afterward, when both girls were badly bruised and half-unconscious, the horses stopped. Nadia tried very hard to listen and concentrate. The horsemen dismounted, and again she felt herself being lifted, then tugged like a sack to the ground. She fell onto stones. She heard Pema moan, and then hands untied the rope and removed the blanket. She gulped fresh air and opened her eyes.

The first thing she saw was the moon and the dark dome of the sky; then two black, bearded faces bending over her. A stinking gust of garlic, liquor, and something like tobacco struck her like a knife. The men's dark eyes shone from sunken sockets and they laughed mockingly; many had missing teeth, and the few they had were nearly black. Nadia had seen people in India with teeth like that, and Kate had explained that the color came from chewing betel nut. Even though it was dark, she recognized the faces of the men she'd seen in the Red Fort, the fearsome warriors of the scorpion sect.

With one jerk, her captors pulled her to her feet, but her knees buckled, and they had to hold her up. Nadia saw Pema a few steps away, doubled over with pain. Pointing and pushing, the kidnappers indicated the way the girls should go. One of the men stayed with the horses and the others climbed the hill, leading the prisoners. Nadia had calculated well: there were five horsemen, plus the two that had carried Pema and her.

After walking for about fifteen minutes, Nadia saw a cluster of men, all wearing the same type of clothing, all dark, bearded, and armed with knives. Nadia tried to conquer her fear and listen with her heart, trying to understand what they were saying, but she was too battered. As the men talked, she closed her eyes and imagined that she was an eagle, the queen of the heights, the imperial bird, her totemic animal. For a few seconds she had the sensation that she was soaring up like that splendid bird, and could see beneath her the chain of the Himalayan mountains and, very far in the distance, the valley of the city of Tunkhala. A shove brought her back to earth.

The Blue Warriors lighted torches made of burlap scraps tied to a stick and soaked in yak butter. In this wavering light, they led the girls down a natural, narrow ravine through the rock. They clung close to the side of the mountain, stepping with great care, because a deep precipice yawned at their feet. An icy wind sliced their skin. There were patches of snow and ice among the rocks, even though it was summer.

Nadia thought that if it was this cold in summer, winter in this region must be frightful. Pema was wearing only her silk sarong and sandals. Nadia tried to hand her jacket to her friend, but the minute she started to take it off one of the men slapped her and forced her to keep walking. Pema was at the end of the file and Nadia couldn't see her from her place in line, but she imagined that her friend was in worse condition than she was. Fortunately they did not have to climb much farther but stopped before some thorny bushes the men parted and held aside. Their torches illuminated the entrance to a natural cave, well hidden in the rough terrain. Nadia felt her hope fade; any possibility that Jaguar would find her was dwindling.

The large cave was composed of several smaller grottos or rooms. The girls saw bundles, weapons, tack for horses, blankets, sacks of rice, lentils, dried vegetables, nuts, and long strings of garlic. To judge by the look of the camp and the quantity of food, it was obvious that their captors intended to stay for a while.

A spine-chilling altar had been set up in a central location. A statue of the fearsome goddess Kali sat atop a pile of bones, surrounded by human skulls, dried rats, snakes, and other reptiles, vessels containing a dark bloodlike liquid, and jars holding live black scorpions. As the warriors walked in, they knelt before the altar, stuck their fingers in the vessels, and then placed them in their mouths. Nadia noticed that each of the men wore an assortment of daggers of different shapes and sizes tucked into the sashes circling their waists.

The two girls were pushed toward the back of the

cavern, where they were given to the care of an old woman. Over her rags she wore a mantle made from the hides of dogs, which gave her the look of a hyena. Her skin was stained the same blue tone as the warriors'; a horrible scar furrowed her right cheek from eye to chin, as if she had been slashed by a knife, and the figure of a scorpion branded her forehead. She carried a short whip.

Huddled beside a fire were four captive girls, trembling with cold and terror. The jailer grunted and gestured to Pema and Nadia that they should join them. The only one of them who was wearing winter clothing was Nadia; all the others were dressed in the silk sarongs they had put on to celebrate the king's birthday. Nadia realized that these girls had been kidnapped under the same circumstances she and Pema had, and that gave her a ray of hope, because by now the police would be moving heaven and earth looking for them.

A chorus of moans greeted Nadia and Pema, but as the woman came toward them with whip raised high, the prisoners fell silent, burying their heads in their arms. The two friends tried to stay close together.

When the guard wasn't looking, Nadia wrapped her jacket around Pema and whispered not to give up hope, they would find a way to get out of this mess. Pema was shivering, but she had succeeded in regaining control. Her beautiful black eyes, which had always been smiling, now reflected courage and determination. Nadia pressed her hand, and each felt strengthened by the other's presence.

One of the members of the scorpion sect could not keep his eyes off Pema, impressed by her grace and dignity. He came toward the terrified girls and stood before her with one hand on the handle of his dagger. He wore the same filthy dark tunic, greasy turban, and had the same tangled beard, strange blue-black skin, and betel-stained teeth as the others, but his attitude radiated authority, and the others respected him. He seemed to be the leader.

Pema stood and bore the cruel gaze of the warrior. He reached out and touched the girl's long hair, which slipped like silk through his filthy fingers. A light fragrance of jasmine was loosed in the air. The man seemed confused, almost moved, as if he had never touched anything so precious. Pema shook her head, pulling her hair from his hand. If she was afraid, she didn't show it. On the contrary, her expression was so defiant that the girls, the old woman with the scar, and even the other bandits froze, sure that the warrior would strike his insolent prisoner, but, to everyone's surprise, he barked a brief laugh and stepped back. He spat on the floor at Pema's feet, then returned to his cronies, who were kneeling around a fire. They were sipping from their canteens and chewing red betel nuts, spitting and talking as they studied a map unfolded on the ground.

Nadia assumed that this map was the same, or similar, to the one she and Alex had glimpsed in the Red Fort. She understood nothing of what was being said, because the brutal events of recent hours had affected her so deeply that she wasn't capable of listening with her heart. Pema quietly told her that they were speaking a dialect of the north of India and that she could understand a few words: dragon, routes, monastery, American, and king.

They had to stop talking, because the woman with the scar, who had heard them, came toward them brandishing her whip.

"Quiet!" she roared.

The girls began to whimper with fear, except for Pema and Nadia, whose manner did not change, although they lowered their eyes in order not to provoke the woman. When the jailer again lost interest in them, Pema whispered to Nadia that women abandoned by the Blue Warriors always had a scorpion branded on their foreheads, and that many were mute because their tongues had been cut out. Shuddering with horror, they did not speak again, but communicated with their eyes.

The four girls who had been brought to the cave a little before them were in such a state of panic that Nadia believed they must know something she didn't, but she didn't dare ask. She realized that Pema, too, knew what was awaiting them, but she was brave and was prepared to fight for her life. Gradually, the other girls felt the comfort of Pema's courage, and, without consulting one another, they inched closer to her, seeking her protection. Nadia was filled with a mixture of admiration for her friend and frustration because she couldn't communicate with the other girls, who didn't speak a word of English. She regretted that she was so different from them.

One of the Blue Warriors gave an order, and for a moment the woman with the scar forgot the captives and left them in order to obey the command. She spooned something into bowls from a black kettle hung over the fire, and served the men. At an order from the leader, she grumblingly served the prisoners as well.

Nadia was handed a bowl of steaming gray gruel. A

blast of garlic struck her nostrils and she had to fight to keep from retching. She must eat, she decided, because she would need all her strength to escape. She signaled Pema, who lifted the bowl to her lips. Neither of the two girls had any intention of resigning themselves to their fate.

CHAPTER TEN

Borobá

THE MOON SANK BEHIND THE snow-topped peaks, and the fire in the cave faded to a pile of coals and ash. The guard was snoring, sitting up, whip still in her hand: Her mouth was agape, and a thread of saliva was trickling down her chin. The Blue Warriors had stretched out on the ground and they, too, were sleeping, but one of them stood guard at the entrance to the cave, holding an ancient rifle. A single torch shed a pale light, projecting sinister shadows onto the rock walls.

The men had tied the captives' ankles with leather thongs, and given them four blankets of rough wool. Barely covered, pressed against one another, the unfortunate girls tried to keep one another warm. Exhausted from crying, they were all asleep, except for Pema and Nadia, who were using the moment to whisper back and forth.

Pema told her friend all she knew about the feared Sect of the Scorpion, how they stole girls and mistreated them. Besides cutting out the tongues of those who spoke too much, they burned the soles of their feet if they tried to escape.

"I don't plan to remain in the hands of these horrible men. I would rather kill myself," Pema concluded.

"Don't talk that way, Pema. Whatever happens, it's better to die trying to escape than to die without a fight."

"You think you can escape from here?" Pema replied, pointing to the sleeping warriors and the guard at the entrance.

"We will find the moment to do it," Nadia assured her as she rubbed her ankles, swollen from the bonds.

After a while even the two friends were overcome with weariness and began to nod off. Several hours had gone by, and Nadia, who had never had a watch but was accustomed to calculating time, thought it must be about two in the morning. Suddenly her instinct warned her something was happening. She felt with her skin that the energy in the air had changed, and she sat up, alert.

A fleet shadow was almost flying across the floor of the cave. Nadia's eyes could not see what it was, but she sensed that it was her loyal Borobá. With a flood of relief, she realized that her tiny friend had followed the kidnappers. The horses had soon left him behind, but the little monkey had been able to follow his mistress's trail and somehow find the cave. Nadia hoped with all her heart that Borobá would not shriek with joy when he saw her, and tried to transmit a mental message to calm him.

Borobá had come to Nadia's arms as soon as he was born, when she herself was nine. He was so small that she had to feed him with an eyedropper. From that time they had never been apart. The monkey grew up at her side, and they complemented one another so well that each could sense what the other was feeling. They shared a code of gestures and intentions, in addition to Borobá's language, which Nadia had learned. The monkey must have picked up his mistress's warning, because he did not come to her. He sat huddled in a dark corner, motionless, for a long time, looking around, calculating the risks, waiting.

When Nadia was sure that no one had noticed Borobá's presence, and the snores of her jailer hadn't changed, she whistled softly. The monkey started working his way toward her, staying close to the wall where he was protected by the shadows, until he reached her and with one leap threw himself around her neck. He had torn off his baby snowsuit, leaving only shreds. His little hands clung to Nadia's curly hair, and he rubbed his wrinkled face against her neck, emotional but silent.

Nadia waited for him to calm down, and thanked him for being so faithful. Then she gave him a command. Borobá immediately obeyed. Slipping back the same way he had come, he approached one of the sleeping men and with his clever and delicate hands, with awesome precision pulled a dagger from his sash, and carried it to Nadia. He sat down in front of her, watching intently, as she cut the thongs from her ankles. The knife was so sharp that it was not difficult.

The moment she was free, Nadia waked Pema.

"This is our chance to escape," she whispered to her.

"How do you plan to get past the guard?"

"I don't know yet, we'll see. One step at a time."

But Pema would not allow her to cut her bonds, and with tears in her eyes whispered that she couldn't go.

"I won't get very far, Nadia. You see how I'm dressed; I can't run like you in these sandals. If I go with you, they will catch us both. You have the best chance if you go alone."

"Are you crazy? I can't go without you!" Nadia murmured.

"You have to try. Get help. I can't leave the other girls; I will stay with them until you get back with reinforcements. Go now, before it's too late," said Pema, taking off the jacket and handing it back to Nadia.

She spoke with such determination that Nadia gave up any idea of trying to change her mind. Her friend would not abandon the other girls. And it was not possible to take them, because there was no way they could all leave without being seen; only she could do that. The two friends hugged briefly and, with her heart in her mouth, Nadia stood up.

The woman with the scar moved in her sleep, stammered a few words, and for an instant it seemed that all might be lost, but then she started snoring with the same rhythm she had before. Nadia waited five minutes, until she was convinced that all the others were asleep as well. She immediately started along the path Borobá had taken, pressing herself against the wall. She took a deep breath and called on her powers of invisibility.

Nadia and Alexander had spent an unforgettable time in the Amazon with the tribe of the People of the Mist, the most remote and mysterious humans on the planet. Those Indians, who were living just as men and women had in the Stone Age, were in some aspects very evolved. They scorned material progress and lived in concert with the forces of nature, in perfect harmony with the world around them. They were part of the complex ecology of the jungle, like the trees, the insects, the humus. For centuries they had survived in the forest with no contact with the outside world, protected by their beliefs, their traditions, their sense of community, and the art of making themselves invisible. When they sensed danger, they simply disappeared. This skill was so absolute that no one actually believed that the People of the Mist existed. When people talked about them, they spoke as if they were telling a legend—and that had protected them from the curiosity and greed of outsiders.

Nadia realized that this skill was not a trick or an illusion but a very ancient art that required continual practice. "It's like learning to play the flute," she had once told Alexander. "You have to study a long time." He had never really believed he could learn, and hadn't made an effort to practice. Nadia, on the other hand, had decided that if the Indians could do it, she could, too. She knew that more was involved than mimicry, agility, delicacy, silence, and knowledge of one's surroundings; mental attitude was most important of all. She learned how to reduce herself to nothingness and visualize her body becoming so transparent it was converted into pure spirit. It was necessary to maintain concentration and interior calm in order to create a formidable psychic field about her person. One distraction could cause failure. Only in that superior state in which spirit and mind were working in unison could invisibility be achieved.

In the months that had passed between the adventure in the City of the Beasts in the heart of the Amazon and the moment when she found herself in that cave in the Himalayas, Nadia had practiced tirelessly. She had made such progress that sometimes her father shouted for her when she was right by his side. When she suddenly materialized, César Santos would jump with surprise. "I've told you not to appear like that. You're going to give me a heart attack!" he would complain.

Nadia knew that in this moment the only thing that could save her was that art she had learned from the People of the Mist. She murmured instructions to Boroba to wait a few minutes before he followed her— she could not become invisible carrying the little monkey—and then turned inward, toward that mysterious space we all have when we close our eyes and expel all thoughts from our minds. Within seconds she entered a state similar to a trance. She felt that she had stepped free of her body, and that she could see herself from above, as if her consciousness had risen ten feet above her own head. From that position, she saw her legs take a step, then another and another, moving away from Pema and the other girls, advancing in slow motion, moving through the darkness of the bandits' lair.

She passed within inches of the horrible woman with the whip, slipped like an unseen shadow among the bodies of the sleeping warriors, continued, almost floating, toward the mouth of the cave where the weary guard was making an effort to stay awake, his eyes lost in the night, but clutching his rifle. She did not lose her concentration for a second, or allow fear or hesitation to send her soul back to the prison of her body. Neither stopping nor changing the rhythm of her steps, she came so close to the man that she was almost touching his back, so close that she could clearly smell his scent of dirt and garlic.

The guard shivered slightly and clutched his weapon, as if at some instinctive level he had sensed her presence near him, but his mind immediately blocked out that suspicion. His hands relaxed and his eyes half-closed, as he struggled against sleep and fatigue.

Nadia glided out of the entrance to the cave like a ghost, and kept walking blindly into the darkness, without turning to look back and without hurrying. The night swallowed her slender silhouette.

Almost as soon as Nadia had returned to her body and taken a look around her, she realized that she would never be able to find her way back to Tunkhala in broad daylight, much less in the shadows of night. She was surrounded by mountains, and since she had been brought to this place with her head covered, she didn't have a single point of reference that would allow her to get her bearings. The one thing she was sure of was that they had been climbing all the way, which meant that she must descend on the return, but if she did that, she would surely run into the other Blue Warriors. She knew that the guard in charge of the horses had stayed behind some distance from the cave, and she didn't know how many more might be scattered among the hills. Considering the confidence with which the bandits moved about, with no apparent fear of being surprised, there must be a lot of them. It would be better to look for a different escape route.

"What do we do now?" she asked Borobá when they were again reunited, but the monkey knew only the route he had followed to come there, the same way the bandits had come.

Borobá, as unaccustomed to the cold as his mistress, was shivering so hard that his teeth were chattering. Nadia held him against her chest beneath her parka, comforted by the presence of her faithful friend. She pulled up her hood and tied it firmly around her face, regretting that she didn't have the gloves Kate had bought her. Her hands were so cold that she couldn't feel her fingers. She held them to her lips and blew on them to warm them, and then stuck them in her pockets, but she wouldn't be able to climb or to keep her balance in that rough terrain without using both hands. She figured that as soon as the sun came up and her captors realized that she'd fled, they would come out en masse to look for her; they couldn't permit one of their prisoners to reach the valley or raise the alarm. It was clear that they were used to moving about in the mountains; she, in contrast, had no idea where she was.

The Blue Warriors would assume that she was fleeing down the mountainside, toward the villages and valleys of the Forbidden Kingdom. To trick them, she decided to climb higher, even though she was aware that by doing so she was moving farther from her goal. She knew there was no time to waste, and that Pema's fate, and that of the other girls, depended on her finding help soon. She hoped to reach the top of the mountain by dawn, and from there plan another way to get to the valley.

Ascending the steep hill turned out to take much longer and be more difficult than she had imagined; the darkness, barely relieved by the moonlight, added to the difficulties of the terrain. She slipped and fell a thousand times. She ached all over from being carried across the galloping horse the day before, and from the blow to her head and her bruises, but she didn't allow herself to think about that. She could barely breathe and her ears were buzzing. She remembered Kate's explanation about there being less oxygen at this altitude.

There were small shrubs growing among the rocks, which disappeared completely during the winter but at this season flourished beneath the summer sun. Nadia grabbed them to make her climb. When her strength ebbed, she remembered that she had climbed toward the peak of the *tepui* in the City of the Beasts until she found the eagle's nest containing the three fabulous diamonds. "I did that, so I can do this; this is much easier," Nadia told Borobá, but the tiny monkey, still numb with cold beneath her jacket, did not even stick his nose out.

By dawn, she was still more than six hundred feet

from the top of the mountain. First came a pale glow, which in only minutes took on an orange cast. When the first rays of the sun shone over the formidable mass of the Himalayas, the sky sang with color: the clouds were tinted with purple and the patches of snow turned rosy pink.

Nadia did not pause to contemplate the beauty of the landscape; making an extraordinary effort, she continued to climb, and soon she stood at the highest point of that mountain, panting and bathed in sweat. She felt as if her heart would burst in her chest. She had thought that from the top of the mountain she would have a view of the valley of Tunkhala, but all she saw before her were the impenetrable Himalayas, one mountain after another, stretching toward infinity. She was lost. When she looked down, she thought she saw figures moving in several directions: the Blue Warriors. She sat down on a boulder, exhausted, fighting despair and fatigue. She had to rest and catch her breath, but she couldn't stay there. If she didn't find somewhere to hide, her pursuers would soon discover her.

Borobá stirred beneath her parka. Nadia unzipped it, and her little friend looked out, his intelligent eyes fixed on hers.

"I don't know which way to go, Borobá. All the

mountains look alike, and I don't see any kind of trail," Nadia said.

The little monkey pointed in the direction they'd come from.

"I can't go that way, because the Blue Warriors will capture me. But they won't notice you, Borobá, there are monkeys everywhere. You can find the way back to Tunkhala. Go look for Jaguar," Nadia commanded.

The monkey shook his head, covered his eyes with his hands and shrieked, but she explained that if they didn't separate they had no chance to save the other girls or save themselves. Pema's fate, and that of the other girls, as well as her own, depended on him. He must find help or they would all perish.

"I will hide somewhere near here until I'm sure they aren't looking for me, then I'll find a way to get down to the valley. In the meantime you must hurry, Borobá. The sun's already up, so it won't be as cold. You can get to the city before the sun sets again," Nadia Santos insisted.

Finally Borobá let go and shot off down the mountainside like an arrow.

Kate sent Timothy and Joel into the countryside to photograph flora and fauna for *International*

Geographic. They would have to work on their own, while she stayed in the capital. She couldn't remember having been so worried and upset in all her life, except for the time Alexander and Nadia were lost in the Amazon jungle. She had assured César that this trip to the Forbidden Kingdom presented no danger. How could she tell a father that his daughter had been kidnapped? And even worse, that she was in the hands of professional murderers who stole girls to make them their slaves?

Kate and Alexander had gone to speak with the king, who met with them in the reception room of his palace along with his commander in chief, his prime minister, and the two lamas who had highest authority after him. Judit Kinski was also there.

"The lamas have consulted the stars and have given instructions to the monasteries to pray and make offerings for the missing girls. General Myar Kunglung is in charge of the military operation. Possibly the police have already been mobilized?" asked the king, whose serene face did not reflect his extreme concern.

"Possibly, Your Majesty . . . Also, soldiers and palace guards alert. Borders being watched." The general spoke using his poor English so the foreigners could understand.

And he added, "Perhaps people, too, will look for girls. I never heard nothing like this ever in our country. Possibly news will be here soon."

"Possibly? That doesn't sound good enough to me!" sputtered Kate, and then immediately bit her lips; she knew that she had been terribly rude.

"Perhaps Mrs. Cold is the least bit upset," offered Judit, who apparently had already learned to speak in the vague terms that were considered polite in the Kingdom of the Golden Dragon.

"Perhaps so," said Kate, bowing, with her hands before her face.

"Perhaps it would be improper to ask how the honorable general plans to organize the search?" Judit inquired.

The next fifteen minutes went by with questions from the foreigners, who received increasingly vague answers until it became obvious that there was no way they could press the king or the general any further. Kate and Alexander were so frustrated that they had broken out in a sweat. Finally the monarch stood, and there was nothing to do but say good-bye and back out of the room.

"It's a beautiful morning, perhaps there will be a lot of birds in the garden," Judit suggested to the king.

"Perhaps," he agreed, leading her outside.

. . .

The king and Judit strolled along the narrow path that twisted through the vegetation of the park where everything seemed to be growing in a wild state; a trained eye, however, could appreciate the calculated harmony of the whole. It was there, amid that glorious abundance of flowers and trees, among the concerts of hundreds of birds, that Judit had proposed to begin the experiment with the tulips.

The king believed that he did not deserve to be the spiritual leader of his nation. He felt very far from having reached the degree of preparation that was needed. All his life he had practiced detachment from earthly matters and material possessions. He knew that nothing in the world is permanent; everything changes, decomposes, dies, and is renewed in a different form; it is, therefore, futile to cling to things of this world, which can only cause suffering. The path of Buddhism lies in accepting that premise. Sometimes the monarch had the illusion that he had succeeded, but the visit of this foreign woman had caused his doubts to return. He felt attracted to her, and that made him vulnerable. It was a feeling he had not experienced before, because the love he had shared with his wife had flowed like water in a tranquil stream. How could he protect his kingdom if he could not protect himself from the temptations of love? There was nothing bad about wanting love and intimacy with another person, the king argued to himself, but in his position he could not permit himself that freedom; the remaining years of his life must be wholly dedicated to his people. Judit interrupted his musings.

"What an extraordinary pendant that is, Majesty!" she commented, pointing to the jewel he wore on his chest.

"The kings of this country have worn it for eighteen hundred years," he explained, removing the medallion and handing it to her so that she could examine it more closely.

"It's very beautiful," she said.

"Very old coral, like this, is greatly appreciated among us, because it is rare. It is also found in Tibet. The fact that it is found here indicates that perhaps millions of years ago the waters of the seas reached the peaks of the Himalayas," the king explained.

"What does the inscription say?" she asked.

"They are the words of Buddha: *Change must be voluntary, not imposed.*"

"And what does that mean?"

"All of us may change, but no one can force us to do

it. Change may occur when we confront an unquestionable truth, something that forces us to revise our beliefs," he said.

"That's a strange phrase to have been chosen for the medallion."

"This has always been a very traditional country. The duty of the ruler is to defend his people from changes that are not based on a truth," the king replied.

"The world today is changing rapidly. I understand that the students in your country want changes," she commented.

"Some young people are fascinated with the lifestyle and products of other lands, but not all modern things are good. The majority of my people do not want to adopt Western ways."

They had come to a pond, where they stopped to contemplate the dance of the carp in the crystal-clear water.

"I suppose that on a personal level the inscription on the medallion means that every human can change. Do you believe that an already formed personality can be modified, Majesty? For example, that a villain can become a hero, or a criminal a saint?" asked Judit, returning the jewel.

The monarch smiled. "If the person does not change

in this lifetime, perhaps he will have to return to do it in another incarnation."

"Each of us has his karma. Perhaps the karma of a bad person can't be changed," she suggested.

"Perhaps the karma of that person will be to encounter a truth that forces him, or her, to change," the king replied, noting, intrigued, that the chestnut eyes of his guest were moist.

They walked through an isolated section of the garden that was bare of exuberant blooms, a simple patio of sand and rock where an elderly monk was tracing a design with a rake. The king explained to Judit that he had copied the idea from gardens in the Zen monasteries he had seen when he visited Japan. A little farther on, they crossed a carved wooden bridge that spanned a stream rippling over stones. Just ahead was the small pagoda where they were to have a tea ceremony. The awaiting monk greeted them with a bow. As Judit was removing her shoes, she and the king continued their conversation.

"I don't want to seem impertinent, Majesty, but I have the impression that the disappearance of those girls is a very harsh blow for your nation," said Judit.

"Perhaps . . ." the sovereign replied, and, for the first

time, she noticed that his expression changed and a deep furrow marked his brow.

"Isn't there anything that can be done? Something more than military action, I mean . . ."

"What do you have in mind, Miss Kinski?"

"Please, Majesty, please call me Judit."

"Judit is a beautiful name. Unfortunately, no one calls me by my name. I fear that it is a demand of protocol."

"On an occasion as serious as this, possibly the Golden Dragon could be of great help—if the legend of its magic powers is true," she suggested.

"The Golden Dragon is consulted only for matters that concern the well-being and security of this kingdom, Judit."

"Forgive my boldness, Majesty, but perhaps this is one of those times. If citizens have disappeared, that means that their well-being and security are not being assured," she insisted.

"Possibly you are right," the king admitted, lowering his head.

They went inside the pagoda and sat on the floor facing the monk. The circular wooden room was dimly lighted by the coals where water was boiling in an ancient iron vessel. They sat meditating in silence while the monk led them step by step through the long, slow ceremony that consisted of nothing more than serving them bitter green tea in two small clay cups.

CHAPTER ELEVEN

The White Eagle

THE SPECIALIST COMMUNICATED with the Collector through an agent, as was the usual procedure. This time the messenger was Japanese, and he requested a meeting with the second richest man in the world to discuss a strategy for negotiations in the Asian gold markets.

That day a spy had sold the Collector the key to the ultrasecret Pentagon archives. The American military archives could be very valuable in his dealings in armaments. For investors like himself, world conflict was essential: peace was not good business. He had calculated precisely the percentage of humanity that must be at war in order to stimulate the arms market. If the number was low, he would lose money, and if it was high, the stock market became very volatile and the risk was too great. Fortunately for him, it was easy to foment wars, although not so easy to end them.

When an assistant informed the Collector that a person unknown to him was requesting an urgent interview, he guessed that it must be the Specialist's envoy. Two words gave him the clue: gold and Asia. He had been waiting impatiently for several days, and he received the visitor immediately. The agent spoke in flawless English. The elegance of his suit and his impeccable manners went right over the Collector's head; he was not known for his refinement.

"The Specialist has identified the only two people who have full knowledge of how to manipulate the statue that interests you: the king and the prince who is heir to the throne, a young man whom no one has seen since he was five or six years old," he reported.

"Why is that?"

"He is being educated in a secret place. All the monarchs of the Forbidden Kingdom go through special training in their childhood and youth. The parents turn the child over to a lama, who prepares him to govern. Among many other things, the prince must learn the code of the Golden Dragon."

"Then that lama, or whatever you call him, must also know the code."

"No. He is only a mentor, a guide. No one, other than the monarch and his heir, knows the complete code. The code is divided into four parts, and each one is kept in a different monastery. The mentor takes the prince to all of them during his training, a process that takes twelve years, during which he learns the complete code," the agent explained.

"How old is this prince?"

"About eighteen. His education is nearly complete, but we are not sure that he knows how to decipher the code as yet."

"Where is he now?" the Collector asked impatiently.

"We believe that he is in a secret hermitage in the peaks of the Himalayas."

"Well, what are you waiting for? Bring him to me."

"That will not be easy. I have just told you that his location is uncertain, and we are not absolutely sure that he has all the information you need."

"Then find out! That's what I'm paying for, man. And if you don't find him, then bribe the king."

"How shall we do that?"

"These little kings of second-rate countries are all corrupt. Offer him whatever he wants: money, women, automobiles, whatever," said the multibillionaire.

"You have nothing that can tempt this king. He is not interested in material things," replied the Japanese agent, without veiling the scorn he felt for the client.

"And power? Nuclear bombs, for example?"

"Definitely not."

"Then kidnap him. Torture him. Do whatever you have to do to drag the secret out of him."

"In his case torture will not work. He will die without telling us anything. The Chinese tried those methods with the lamas in Tibet, and they rarely have any effect. Those people are trained to separate body from mind," said the Specialist's envoy.

"How do they do that?"

"Let's say that they ascend to a higher mental plane. The spirit detaches itself from its physical connection. Do you understand?"

"Spirit? You believe in that?" the Collector scoffed.

"It doesn't matter whether I believe or not. The fact is they do it."

"You mean they're like those circus fakirs who don't eat for months and lie on beds of nails?"

"I am speaking of something much more mystical than that. Certain lamas can remain outside their bodies for as long as they wish."

"And?"

"That means they feel no pain. They can even die at will. They simply stop breathing. It is futile to torture a person who is like that," the agent explained.

"And truth serum?"

"Drugs are ineffective because the mind is on a

different plane, not connected with the brain."

"Are you trying to tell me that the king of some dinky country can do that?" the Collector roared.

"We do not know with certainty, but if the training he received in his youth was complete, and if he has practiced throughout his lifetime, that is exactly what I'm trying to tell you."

"The man has to have some weakness!" the Collector exclaimed, pacing around the room like a caged animal.

"He has very few, but we are looking for them," said the agent and placed a card on the table on which he had written in purple ink the amount, in millions of American dollars, the operation would cost.

It was incredibly high, but the Collector concluded that he was not dealing with a normal kidnapping, and that in any case he could pay it. When he had the Golden Dragon in his hands and controlled the world's stock markets, he would recover his investment a thousand times over.

"All right, but I don't want problems of any kind; you must be discreet and not provoke an international incident. It is crucial that no one connect me with this matter; if they did, my reputation would be ruined. Your job is to make the king talk, even if you have to blow that country to bits. You got it? I don't care how you do it."

"You will have news soon," said the visitor, standing and silently disappearing.

It seemed to the Collector that the agent had evaporated. He shuddered: he regretted that he had to have dealings with such people. However, he couldn't complain; the Specialist was a first-class professional whose services he required to become the richest man in the world—number one, the richest person in the history of humanity, richer than the ancient Egyptian pharaohs or Roman emperors.

The morning sun was blazing over the Himalayas. Master Tensing had finished his meditation and prayers. He had washed, with the deliberation and precision that characterized all his movements, in a slender thread of water trickling down from the mountains, and now he was preparing their one meal of the day. His disciple, prince Dil Bahadur, had boiled water with tea, salt, and yak butter. One part was left in a gourd to be drunk during the day and the other was mixed with toasted barley flour, for their *tsampa*. Master and disciple carried their staples in a small sack tucked among the folds of their tunics.

Dil Bahadur had also boiled a few vegetables that they had coaxed with great effort from the arid land of a natural terrace a long way from the humble, ancient hermitage where they lived. The prince had had to walk several hours to obtain a handful of greens for their meal.

"I see you are limping, Dil Bahadur," the master observed.

"No, no . . ."

The master locked eyes with his student, who noted a spark of amusement in the lama's pupils.

"I fell," he confessed, showing the scratches and bruises on one leg.

"How?"

"I was not concentrating. I am sorry, master," said the youth, bowing deeply.

"The elephant trainer needs five virtues, Dil Bahadur: good health, confidence, patience, sincerity, and wisdom," the lama said, smiling.

"I forgot the five virtues. At this moment I do not have perfect health because I lost confidence as I walked. I lost confidence because I was hurrying; I was not patient. And when I told you I was not limping, I was not sincere. In sum, I have far to go before I am wise, master."

Both laughed happily. The lama went to a wooden box, took out a ceramic bottle containing a greenish ointment, and gently rubbed it on the prince's leg.

"Master, I believe that you have achieved enlightenment but have been left here on this earth only in order to teach me," Dil Bahadur sighed, and as answer, the lama gave him an affectionate tap on the head with the bottle.

They prepared for the brief ceremony of thanks they always performed before eating, then sat in the lotus position high atop their mountain with their bowls of *tsampa* and tea in front of them. Between mouthfuls, which they chewed deliberately, they admired the landscape in silence, because they never spoke as they ate. Their eyes were lost in the magnificent chain of snowy peaks stretching before them. The sky was turning a deep cobalt blue.

"It will be very cold tonight," the prince said when they had finished their meal.

"*This* is a very beautiful morning," the master responded.

"Oh, of course. The here and now. We must rejoice in the beauty of this moment instead of thinking of the storm to come," the student recited in a slightly ironic tone.

"Very good, Dil Bahadur."

"Perhaps there is not all that much that I must yet learn," the youth smiled.

"Almost nothing, only a little modesty," the lama replied.

As they talked a bird appeared in the sky. It flew in great circles, spreading its enormous wings, and then disappeared.

"What was that bird?" the lama asked, getting to his feet.

"It looked like a white eagle," said the youth.

"I have never seen one here."

"You have been observing nature for many years. Possibly you know all the birds and beasts of this region."

"It would be an unpardonable arrogance on my part to pretend that I know everything that lives in these mountains, but in truth I have never seen a white eagle," the lama replied.

"I must go to my lessons, master," said the prince, picking up the bowls and going inside.

High up on the mountain, in a cleared circle, Tensing and Dil Bahadur were exercising, practicing Tao-shu, a combination of several martial arts invented by the monks at the remote fortified monastery of Chenthan Dzong. The survivors of the earthquake that destroyed the monastery had scattered throughout Asia to teach their art. Each trained only one person, male or female, selected for physical capacity and moral integrity. That was how their knowledge was transmitted. The total number of warriors expert in Tao-shu never exceeded twelve in each generation. Tensing was one of them, and the student he had chosen to replace him was Dil Bahadur.

The rocky ground was treacherous this time of year; there was frost at dawn, and the rocks were slippery. Dil Bahadur enjoyed the exercise more in the fall and winter because soft snow cushioned the falls. Besides, he liked the feel of the winter air. Enduring the cold was part of the harsh apprenticeship his master was submitting him to, such as walking barefoot most of the time, eating very little, and sitting motionless for hours and hours to meditate. By noon that day the sun was shining and there was no refreshing breeze; his bruised leg hurt, and with every badly executed tumbling pass he landed on rocks, but he did not ask for a break. His master had never heard him complain.

In size, the prince, who was slim and of medium height, contrasted greatly with Tensing, who came from the eastern region of Tibet where people are unusually tall. The lama was nearly seven feet, and throughout his lifetime he had been devoted to both spiritual practice and physical exercise. He was a giant with the muscles of a weight lifter.

"Forgive me if I have been too rough, Dil Bahadur. Possibly in a former life I was a cruel warrior," Tensing apologized after he overthrew his student the fifth time.

"Possibly in a former life I was a fragile maiden," Dil Bahadur replied, lying flat on the ground and panting.

"Perhaps it would help if you did not try to control your body with your mind. You must be like the tigers that range through the Himalayas: pure instinct and determination," the lama suggested.

"Perhaps I shall never be as strong as my honorable master," said the youth, struggling to his feet.

"The storm tears the mighty oak from the soil, but not the reed, because it bends. Do not judge my strength, only my weaknesses."

"Possibly my master has no weaknesses." Dil Bahadur smiled as he assumed the defense posture.

"My strength is also my weakness, Dil Bahadur. You must use it against me."

Seconds later, close to three hundred pounds of

muscle and bone came flying through the air in the prince's direction. This time, however, with the grace of a dancer, Dil Bahadur stepped toward the hurtling mass almost upon him. At the instant when the two bodies made contact, he twisted slightly to the left, deflecting Tensing's charge. The master dropped to the ground, rolling easily on his shoulder and hip. He immediately sprang to his feet and with a formidable leap renewed the attack. Dil Bahadur was waiting for him. Despite his weight, the lama sprang like a cat, tracing an arc in the air, but his ferocious kick failed to reach the youth, because Dil Bahadur was not there to receive it. In a fraction of a second the student was behind his opponent and striking a quick blow to the nape of his master's neck. That was one of the passes of Tao-shu that could immediately paralyze and even kill, but the prince's force was calculated to drop his instructor without injuring him.

"Possibly Dil Bahadur was a maiden *warrior* in a former life," said Tensing, standing up, very satisfied, and bowing deeply to his student.

"Perhaps my honorable master forgot the virtues of the reed." The youth smiled and bowed in return.

At that moment both looked up as a shadow fell onto the ground: overhead was the same white bird they had seen hours earlier, circling above them.

"Do you notice anything strange about that eagle?" asked the lama.

"Perhaps my sight is failing, master, but I cannot see its aura."

"Nor can I."

"What does that mean?" the youth inquired.

"You tell me what it means, Dil Bahadur."

"If we cannot see its aura, master, it may be because it has none."

"That is a very wise conclusion," the lama joked.

"How can it not have an aura?"

"Possibly it is a mental projection," Tensing suggested.

"Let us try to communicate with it," said Dil Bahadur.

Both men closed their eyes and opened their minds and hearts to receive the energy of the powerful bird circling overhead. They stood for several minutes in deep concentration. So strong was the bird's presence that they could feel the vibration from its wings on their skin.

"Is it saying anything to you, master?"

"I sense nothing but its anguish and confusion. I cannot decipher a message. And you?"

"No, I cannot."

"I do not know what this means, Dil Bahadur, but the eagle has a reason for seeking us," Tensing concluded. He had never had a similar experience, and he was disturbed by it.

CHAPTER TWELVE

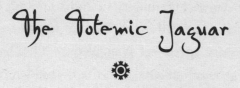

The Totemic Jaguar

✵

THERE WAS GREAT CONFUSION IN the city of Tunkhala. The police were interrogating half the population, as detachments of soldiers set off for the interior of the country, some in Jeeps and others on horseback, since no wheeled vehicle could travel the steep mountain trails. Monks with offerings of flowers, rice, and incense congregated around religious statues. Prayer flags were fluttering all around the city, and trumpets sounded in the temples. For the first time since it was inaugurated, the television station broadcast all day long, repeating the same news over and over and showing photographs of the missing girls. Not even a pin could have been squeezed into the homes of the victims: friends, relatives, and neighbors arrived constantly to offer their condolences, bringing food and prayers written on paper they burned before their religious images.

Kate Cold was able to communicate by telephone

222 · *Isabel Allende*

with the American embassy in India and ask for their help, but she had little faith that aid would arrive with the necessary speed—if it arrived at all. The official who took the call told her that the Forbidden Kingdom was not under his jurisdiction, and that Nadia Santos wasn't an American citizen in any case—she was Brazilian. In view of that conversation, Kate had decided to cling to General Myar Kunglung like his shadow. He was the person in charge of the only military resources in the country, and she did not intend to allow him to be distracted for an instant. She ripped off the sarong she'd been wearing the last few days, put on her usual explorer's outfit, and climbed into the general's Jeep—and no one could dissuade her.

"You and I are going to organize a campaign," she announced to the surprised general, who did not understand everything the writer said though he understood her intentions perfectly.

"You stay here in Tunkhala, Alexander, because if Nadia can, she will communicate with you. Call the embassy in India again," she directed her grandson.

To sit there with his arms crossed was torture to Alex, but he realized that his grandmother was right. He went to the hotel, where there was a telephone, and was able to talk with the ambassador, who was a little more amiable than the first official had been, though he could promise nothing concrete. Alex also spoke with *International Geographic* in Washington. As he waited, he made a list of every detail he could think of, even the most insignificant, with the hope that it might lead to a trail.

As he thought about Eagle, his hands trembled. Why had the Sect of the Scorpion specifically chosen her? Why had they risked kidnapping a foreigner, something that would undoubtedly provoke an international incident? What was the significance of Tex Armadillo's having shown up in the middle of the festival? Why was he in disguise? Were the masked men Blue Warriors, as Eagle believed? These and a thousand other questions were racing around in his mind, increasing his frustration.

It occurred to him that if he found Tex Armadillo, he might pick up the end of a thread that would lead him to Nadia, but he didn't know where to begin. In search of any clue, he carefully reviewed every word he had exchanged with the man or had overheard when he followed him down into the cellars of the Red Fort in India. He jotted down his conclusions:

- Tex Armadillo and the Sect of the Scorpion were connected.
- Tex Armadillo had nothing to gain from kidnapping the girls. That was probably not his mission.
- Events might have something to do with drug trafficking.
- Capturing the girls did not fit in with a drug operation, because it attracted too much attention.
- Until that moment, the Blue Warriors had never kidnapped girls within the Forbidden Kingdom. They must have a powerful reason for doing so now.
- That reason just might be that they wanted to attract attention and distract the police and the armed forces.
- If that was the case, they had a different objective. What? Where would they attack?

Alexander concluded that his list clarified very little: he was going in circles.

At about two in the afternoon, Alex received a telephone call from his grandmother Kate, who was in a village two hours from the capital. General Myar

Kunglung's soldiers had searched every community, every temple, monastery and home in search of the criminals. There was no new information, but there was no longer any doubt that the feared Blue Warriors were in the country. Several peasants had seen the black-clad horsemen from a distance.

"Why are they looking there? The kidnappers aren't going to hide the girls in a place that is easy to find!" Alexander exclaimed.

"We're looking for any clues we can find, Alex. Soldiers are scouring the hills, too," Kate explained.

Alex remembered having heard that the Sect of the Scorpion knew all the mountain passes in the Himalayas. It was only logical that the men would be hiding out in some inaccessible spot.

Alex decided that he couldn't wait in the hotel any longer. "I'm not named Alexander, defender of men, for nothing," he murmured, sure that the definition of his name must also include defending women. He put on his parka and climbing boots—the ones he wore when he went rock climbing with his father in California— counted his money, and went out to look for a horse.

As he left the hotel, he found Borobá lying on the ground near the door. He swallowed a moan as he bent down to pick up the little monkey, thinking he was dead. Happily, the minute Alex touched him, Borobá opened his eyes. As he stroked him and murmured his name, Alex carried Nadia's close companion to the kitchen, where he found fruit to feed him. The poor creature had foam around his mouth, his eyes were red, his body was covered with scratches, and he had bleeding cuts on all four little paws. However, as soon as he ate a banana and drank some water, he perked up a little.

"Do you know where Nadia is?" Alex asked as he wiped the monkey's wounds, but he could not decipher the screeches and gestures Borobá made in response.

Alex was truly sorry that he had never learned to communicate with Borobá. He had had plenty of opportunity to learn the language of monkeys during the three weeks he was in the Amazon, and several times Nadia had offered to teach him. She said the language was composed of very few sounds and, according to her, it was something anyone could learn. It hadn't seemed necessary to him, however; he couldn't think of much he and Borobá would have to talk about, and Nadia was always there to translate. Now it turned out that the monkey had information that was the most important thing in the world to him.

Alexander changed the battery of his flashlight and

put it in his backpack along with the rest of his climbing equipment. The gear was heavy, but one look at the chain of mountains surrounding the city was enough to convince him it would be necessary. He packed a lunch of fruit, bread, and cheese, then rented a horse right at the hotel; several were available, since horses were the most common means of transport in the country. He had ridden during the summers he went to his grandparents' ranch with his family, but the land was flat there. He assumed that the horse would have the experience he lacked in climbing steep trails. He made Borobá comfortable inside his jacket, and set off at a gallop in the direction the monkey indicated.

As the light began to fade and the temperature fell, Nadia realized that her situation was desperate. After sending Borobá for help, she had stayed for a while to see what was happening on the steep slopes below. The rampant vegetation that grew in the valleys and hills of the Forbidden Kingdom became sparse the higher you climbed, and disappeared completely on the peaks of the mountains. That allowed her to see, though not clearly, the movements of the Blue Warriors, who had come out to search for her as soon as they were aware she had fled. One of them went downhill to where they had left the horses, undoubtedly to warn the rest of the gang. Judging by the quantity of supplies and equipment for horses she had seen, Nadia had no doubt that there were other men, though it was impossible to know the precise number.

Some of the warriors had searched the area around the cave where the woman with the scar was guarding the kidnapped girls. It wasn't long before it occurred to them to check out the peak. Nadia knew that she couldn't stay where she was; her pursuers would pick up her trail very quickly. She couldn't hold back a sob as she looked around her. There were many places she could hide, but it would also be easy to get lost. Finally she chose a deep ravine, like a slice cut into the mountain, to the west of where she stood. It seemed perfect; she could hide in one of the deep clefts in the terrain, though she wasn't sure whether she could get out later.

If the Blue Warriors didn't find her, then neither would Jaguar. She prayed that he wouldn't try to come alone, because one person could never take on the Scorpion warriors. Knowing her friend's independent character, and how impatient he was with the indecisive ways of the inhabitants of the Forbidden Kingdom, she feared he wouldn't ask for help.

When she saw several men climbing toward her, she

had to make a decision. The cleft she had chosen as her hiding place seemed much less deep than it actually was, as she was able to confirm as soon as she began the downward climb. She had no experience in this land, and she was afraid of heights, but she remembered the time she'd had to climb the abrupt walls of a waterfall in the Amazon, following the Indians' lead, and that gave her courage. True, on that occasion she had been with Alexander and now she was alone.

She had gone only two or three yards, clinging like a fly to the vertical rock wall, when the root that was holding her weight pulled loose as she was feeling for a foothold. She lost her balance and tried to grab something to steady herself, but her hand found only patches of ice. She began to tumble toward the bottom of the ravine. For a second she panicked, sure that she was going to die, but almost immediately she landed in some brush that miraculously cushioned her fall. Bruised and scraped and scratched, she tried to change position, but the movement tore a sharp cry from her lips. With horror she saw that her left arm was hanging at an abnormal angle. She had dislocated her shoulder.

In those first minutes she felt nothing, her body had lost all sensation, but gradually the pain became so intense that she thought she was going to faint. And when she moved, the pain was much worse. She made an effort to stay alert and evaluate her situation; she could not allow herself the luxury of losing her head.

As soon as Nadia could think a little, she looked upward and saw that she was surrounded with slanting rock; overhead was the infinite peace of a clear blue sky that looked as if it had been painted on. She summoned her totemic animal to her aid, and with an enormous psychic effort transformed herself into a powerful eagle that flew out of the canyon in which she was trapped, high above the mountains. She glided silently above the heights, observing from above the landscape of snowy peaks and, much lower, the intense green of that beautiful country.

In the following hours, Nadia evoked the eagle every time she felt overwhelmed by hopelessness. And every time the great bird brought relief to her spirit.

Gradually she was able to move, holding the helpless arm with her other hand, until she was hidden beneath some brush. And that was good, because the Blue Warriors had reached the summit she had fallen from and were exploring the area. One of them tried to climb down into the ravine but it was too steep, and he assumed that if he couldn't do it, then neither could the fleeing girl.

From her hiding place Nadia heard the bandits call to one another in a language she made no effort to understand. When finally they left, silence returned to the mountain peaks, and she felt the measure of their immense solitude.

Despite her parka, Nadia was freezing. The cold was easing the pain of her injured shoulder and she was irresistibly sinking into sleep. She hadn't eaten since the previous night but she felt no hunger, only a terrible thirst. She scratched at the pools of dirty ice that had formed among the rocks, and sucked a handful eagerly, but when it dissolved it left the taste of mud in her mouth. She realized that night was near and that the temperature would fall below zero. She closed her eyes. For a while she fought against fatigue, but then decided that if she slept the time would pass more quickly.

"Maybe I will never see another dawn," she murmured.

Tensing and Dil Bahadur had returned to their modest hermitage on the mountain. It was a time usually set aside for study, but neither of them made any move to take the parchments from the trunk where they were stored; they had other things on their minds.

They lit a small brazier and warmed their tea. Before meditating, they chanted *Om mani padme hum* for fifteen minutes and then they prayed, asking for the mental clarity to understand the strange sign they had seen in the sky. They went into a trance, and their spirits abandoned their bodies to journey on a different plane.

It was about three hours before sunset when the master and his disciple opened their eyes. For a few moments they sat motionless, allowing time for their souls, which had been far away, to settle again into the reality of the surroundings in which they lived. In their trances, both had had similar visions, so no discussion was necessary.

"I suppose, master, that we will go to help the person who sent the white eagle," said the prince, sure that this was also Tensing's decision, since that was the path signaled by Buddha: the path of compassion.

"Perhaps," the lama replied, simply out of habit, for his determination was as strong as his disciple's.

"How will we find this person?"

"Possibly the eagle will guide us."

They dressed in their wool tunics, threw yak skins across their shoulders, put on the leather boots they wore only on long walks and during the harsh winter, and picked up an oil lantern and their tall staffs. At their waists they bound packets of yak butter and flour for their *tsampa*. Tensing added a flask with rice liquor and a small wooden case that held his acupuncture needles, along with a selection of his medicines. Dil Bahadur slung one of his shortest bows and a sheath filled with arrows over his shoulder. Without further words, they set out in the direction the great white bird had taken.

Nadia Santos surrendered to death. She was no longer tormented by pain, cold, hunger, or thirst. She was floating in a waking sleep, dreaming of the eagle. For moments at a time she would wake up, and then she would have flashes of consciousness in which she knew where she was and the condition she was in. She knew that her chances of survival were very slim, but by the time night enveloped her, her spirit had already liberated itself from fear.

Earlier, however, she had suffered. Once the Blue Warriors had left and she didn't hear them anymore, she made one try to drag herself up the steep cliff, but immediately realized that with her useless arm it would be impossible to climb without assistance. She didn't try to take off her parka and examine her arm, because every movement was torture, but she could see that her hand was very swollen. From time to time she blacked out from the pain, but if she concentrated on it, it was much worse. She tried to keep her mind busy thinking other thoughts.

Several times during the day she knew despair. She wept, thinking of her father, whom she would not see again; she called to Jaguar with her thoughts. Where was her friend? Had Borobá found him? Why didn't he come? Once or twice she screamed and screamed until she lost her voice. She didn't care if the men of the scorpion sect heard her, she would rather deal with them than stay there by herself, but no one came. A little later she heard footsteps, and her heart lurched with joy until she saw it was a pair of wild goats. She called to them in their language, but could not get them to come near.

Nadia had lived her life in the warm, humid climate of the Amazon. She had never known cold. In Tunkhala, where people wore only cotton and silk, she had not taken off her sweater. She had never seen snow, and hadn't known what ice was until she saw it on an artificial skating rink in New York. Now she was shivering. In the small recess in which she was a prisoner, she was protected from the wind, and thickets of brush made it slightly less cold, but with all that she found the temperature unbearable. She curled up in a ball for hours, until her stiff body lost all feeling. Finally, when the sky began to grow dark, she felt the strong presence of death. She recognized it because she had seen it before. In the Amazon she had seen people and animals be born and die; she knew that every living creature completes the same cycle. In nature, everything is renewed. She opened her eyes, looking for stars, but as yet she could see nothing; she was sunk in absolute darkness, for the faint glow of the moon lighting the peaks of the Himalayas did not reach the ravine. Again she closed her eyes, and imagined that her father was with her, holding her. The image of the witch doctor Walimai's wife flashed through her mind, the transparent spirit who was always with him, and she wondered if it was only the souls of Indians that could come and go between heaven and earth as they pleased. She guessed that she would be able to do it, too, and decided that if that were true she would come back in spirit and console her father and Jaguar. Every thought, however, was costing her enormous effort; she wanted only to die.

Nadia let go of the bonds that held her to the world and gently drifted upward, effortlessly, without pain, as gracefully as she had risen when she turned into an eagle and her powerful wings held her above the clouds, carrying her higher and higher toward the moon.

Borobá led Alexander to the place where he had left Nadia. The little monkey was so drained from having made the trip three times without resting that he lost his way several times, but was always able to pick up the trail again. About six in the evening they came to the narrow path that led to the Blue Warriors' cave. By then the men had tired of looking for Nadia, and had gone back to their normal routine. The frightening-looking fellow who seemed to be in charge had decided that they couldn't waste any more time on the girl who had escaped their grasp; instead, they should follow their plan and rejoin the rest of the band in accord with the instructions they'd received from the American who had hired them.

Alex observed that the ground was badly trampled and saw horse droppings everywhere; it was obvious that the bandits had been there, although he didn't see any sign of them now. He realized that he couldn't go any farther on horseback; the sounds of the hooves echoed like a giant bell; it would be impossible not to hear him, if someone were standing guard. He dismounted and let the horse go, in order not to signal his approach. On the other hand, he was sure that he couldn't catch it again even if he went back the same way.

He began to make his way up the mountain, taking cover among stones and boulders, following the course pointed out by Borobá's trembling little paw. Dragging himself on his belly, he passed within sixty yards of the entrance to the cave, where he saw three men on guard, armed with rifles. He deduced that the others must be inside, or that they had moved on to another spot, because he didn't see anyone on the slopes of the mountains. He supposed that Nadia was in the cave with Pema and the other missing girls, but alone, and without weapons, he could not take on the warriors of the scorpion sect. He hesitated, not sure what he should do, until Borobá's insistent gestures made him doubt that Nadia was inside the cave.

The monkey kept tugging at his sleeve and pointing toward the top of the mountain. One look was enough to tell him that it would take several hours to reach the summit. He could make better time if he weren't carrying his backpack but he hated to leave his climbing gear behind.

He was torn between returning to Tunkhala to get help, which would take a lot of time, and continuing his search for Nadia. The former course might save the captive girls, but it could be fatal for Nadia if she was in trouble, which Borobá seemed to indicate. The latter choice might help his friend, but it could be dangerous for the other girls. He reasoned, however, that it would not be in the Blue Warriors' best interest to harm their captives. If they had gone to the trouble of kidnapping those girls, it was because they needed them for something.

Alexander continued his climb, and when he reached the top it was already deep night, though an enormous moon was shining like a great silver eye. Borobá looked around, confused. He jumped out of the protection of the parka and scurried around in a frenzy, screeching with anguish. Alexander realized that the monkey had expected to find his mistress there. Crazed with hope, he began to call Nadia's name in a low voice; he was afraid that echoes would carry his voice down the mountain and, in that absolute silence, reach the bandits' ears. Soon he realized the futility of continuing to search in this rugged terrain with only the light of the moon, and concluded that it would be best to wait until morning.

He settled in between two rocks, using his backpack as a pillow and sharing his food with Borobá. Then he lay quiet, with the hope that if he listened with his heart, Nadia could tell him where she was, but no voice came to him.

I have to sleep a little if I want to get my strength back, he thought, exhausted, but sleep didn't come.

Near midnight, Tensing and Dil Bahadur found Nadia. They had followed the white eagle for hours. The powerful bird flew silently above their heads and at such a low altitude that even at night they could sense it. Neither of the two was sure what they were actually seeing, but its presence was so strong that they didn't have to consult one another to know what they had to do. If they strayed, or stopped, the bird would circle, showing them the correct route. And that was how it had led them directly to the place where they were to find Nadia. Once they were there, the white eagle disappeared.

A hair-raising growl stopped the lama and his disciple short. They were a few yards from the precipice Nadia had tumbled into but they could go no farther because an animal they had never seen before, a large cat, black as night itself, blocked their path. The beast was ready to spring, hair standing up along its spine, claws unsheathed. Its gaping jaws revealed enormous, sharp teeth, and its blazing yellow pupils shone fiercely in the flickering light of the oil lamp.

Tensing's and Dil Bahadur's first impulse was self-defense, and both had to exert control not to call on the art of Tao-shu, which they trusted more than Dil Bahadur's arrows. With a great effort of will, they stood still as stone. Breathing calmly, to keep from panicking and to prevent the beast from picking up the unmistakable scent of fear, they concentrated on sending positive energy, just as they had done with the snow leopard and the ferocious Yetis. They knew that the worst enemy, as well as the greatest ally, may well be one's own thoughts.

For an instant, which nonetheless seemed eternal, men and beast stood facing one another, until Tensing's serene voice could be heard whispering a basic mantra. The oil lamp flickered as if it was going to go out, and before their eyes, in place of the cat, appeared a strange-looking youth. They had never seen anyone with such pale skin, or anyone wearing clothes like his.

As for Alexander, he had seen a faint light that at first seemed like an illusion, but gradually became more real. Behind that glow he could see two human silhouettes moving toward him. He thought the two were from the Sect of the Scorpion, and he leaped up, alert, ready to die fighting. He felt the spirit of the black jaguar rush to his aid; he opened his mouth, and a savage roar shook the quiet night. It was only when the two strangers were but a few yards away, and he could see their faces better, that Alex realized they were not the sinister bearded bandits.

The three stared at each other with equal curiosity: on one side, two Buddhist monks wrapped in yak hides; on the other, an American youth in blue jeans and boots, with a monkey holding onto his neck. When they had collected themselves, all three joined their hands before their faces and bowed in unison in the traditional greeting of the Forbidden Kingdom.

"*Tampo kachi*," said Tensing. May happiness be yours.

"Hi," Alexander replied.

Borobá shrieked and put his paws over his eyes, as he did when he was frightened or confused.

The situation was so bizarre that all three laughed. Alexander desperately searched for some word in the language of the country but couldn't remember a one. He had the impression, however, that his mind was an open book to these men. Although he didn't hear them speak a word, the images forming in his brain revealed their intentions, and he realized that they were there for the same reason he was.

Tensing and Dil Bahadur learned telepathically that the stranger was looking for a missing girl he called Eagle. They naturally deduced that it was the same person who had sent them the white bird. It was not surprising to them that the girl had the ability to transform herself into a bird, just as it was no surprise to them that the youth had appeared before their eyes in the guise of a great cat. They believed that nothing is impossible. In their trances and astral journeys, they themselves had taken on the form of different animals or beings of other universes. They also read in Alexander's mind his suspicions about the bandits of the Sect of the Scorpion, which Tensing had heard about in his travels through the north of India and Nepal.

At that instant, a cry from the skies interrupted the current of ideas flowing among the three men. They looked up, and there, once again, was the great bird. They watched it trace a tight circle and then descend in the direction of a dark precipice a little farther ahead.

"Eagle! Nadia!" yelled Alexander, first with wild joy and then with terrible apprehension.

The situation was critical, because climbing to the

bottom of that ravine at night was next to impossible. Even so, they had to try, because the fact that Nadia had not answered Alexander's repeated calls, or Borobá's shrieks, meant that something very serious had happened to her. She had to be alive, the mental projection of the eagle proved that, but she could be badly injured. There was no time to lose.

"I'm going down," Alexander said in English.

Tensing and Dil Bahadur did not need a translation to understand his decision, and they prepared to help him.

Alex congratulated himself for having brought his mountain-climbing gear and flashlight, and he was also thankful for the experience he'd acquired climbing and rappelling with his father. He put on his harness, drove a metal spike into the rocks, tested its firmness, secured his rope and, before the astonished eyes of Tensing and Dil Bahadur, he scrambled down the precipice like a spider.

CHAPTER THIRTEEN

Medicine for the Mind

✺

THE FIRST THING NADIA NOTICED when she regained consciousness was the rancid smell of the heavy yak hide wrapped around her. She half-opened her eyes but she couldn't see anything. She tried to move, but she was immobilized; she tried to speak, but no sound came out. She felt an unbearable stab of pain in her shoulder, which within seconds spread through the rest of her body. Again she sank into darkness, with the sensation that she was falling into an infinite void that enveloped her totally. While in that state, she floated calmly, but the moment she had a spark of consciousness she felt pain shooting through her. Even in a faint, she moaned.

Finally she began to come to, but she felt as if her brain were enveloped in a whitish, cottony matter she couldn't shake free of. When she did open her eyes, she saw Jaguar bending over her and assumed that she had died, but then she heard his voice calling her. At last she was able to focus, and with the burning stab in her shoulder, she knew she was still alive.

"Eagle, it's me . . ." said Alexander, so frightened and worried about his friend that he was near tears.

"Where are we?" she murmured.

A bronze-colored face with almond-shaped eyes and a serene expression came into view.

"*Tampo kachi*, brave little girl," Tensing greeted her. He was holding a wooden bowl and indicating that she should drink the liquid it held.

With difficulty, Nadia swallowed the warm, bitter liquid that fell like mud into her empty stomach. She felt nauseated, but the lama pressed his hand firmly against her chest, and the discomfort immediately disappeared. She drank a little more, and soon Jaguar and Tensing faded away and she fell into a deep, tranquil sleep.

Using his rope and flashlight, Alexander had descended into the ravine in a matter of seconds; he had found Nadia curled up amid some brush, icy and motionless, like someone dead. When he confirmed that she was still breathing, he yelled with relief. As he tried to move her, he saw the dangling arm and assumed she had broken some bone, but didn't pause to find out. The first priority was to get her out, though she wouldn't be easy to lift, in her unconscious state.

He removed his harness and fitted it around Nadia, then used his belt to strap her arm tightly to her chest. Dil Bahadur and Tensing raised the girl very cautiously, careful to keep her from swinging against the rocks, and then threw the rope back down to Alexander so he could climb up.

Tensing examined Nadia and decided that before anything else they would have to get her warm; they would tend to the arm later. He tried to give her a little of the rice liquor, but she was unconscious and wouldn't swallow. Among the three of them, they rubbed her from head to toe for a long time, restoring her circulation, and as soon as some color came back, they wrapped her in one of the hides like a package, covering even her face.

With their long staffs, Alexander's rope, and the second yak hide they improvised a litter and transported the girl to a small refuge nearby, one of the many natural caves in the mountains. To carry Nadia back to Tensing and Dil Bahadur's hermitage would be too difficult and take too long. The lama decided that they would be safe from the bandits where they were, and should rest the remainder of the night.

• • •

Dil Bahadur found some dry roots and used them to build a small fire that provided some warmth and light. With extreme care, he removed Nadia's parka, and Alexander yelped with fear when he saw his friend's shoulder out of its socket, and her dangling arm swollen to twice its normal size. In contrast, Tensing showed no sign of emotion.

The lama opened his small wooden case and began to place his needles at certain points on Nadia's head to suppress the pain. Then he took herbs from his pouch and ground them between two stones while Dil Bahadur melted some yak butter in his bowl. The lama stirred the powders into the fat to form a dark, pleasant-smelling salve. His expert hands reset Nadia's shoulder, and then spread the salve over the area of the injury. The girl did not make the slightest movement, completely tranquilized by the needles. With telepathy and gestures Tensing explained to Alexander that pain produces tension and resistance, which blocks the mind and slows the natural ability to heal. Besides killing pain, the acupuncture activated the body's immune system. Nadia was *not*, he assured Alexander, suffering.

Dil Bahadur tore off the lower edge of his tunic to make bandages. He boiled water with a few coals from the fire and soaked the cloth strips in that liquid; the lama then used them to wrap the injured shoulder. Finally Tensing immobilized Nadia's arm with a scarf, removed the acupuncture needles, and demonstrated to Alexander how to cool Nadia's forehead and lower her fever with snow collected from among the rocks.

In the hours that followed, Tensing and Dil Bahadur concentrated on healing Nadia with their mental powers. It was the first time the prince had practiced this skill on a human being. His master had been training him for years in this method of healing, but up till now he had tried it only on wounded animals.

Alexander realized that his new friends were focusing the energy of the universe and channeling it to give strength to Nadia. Dil Bahadur passed Alex a message telepathically, telling him that his master was a physician and, in addition, a powerful *tulku*, who could call on the enormous wisdom of previous incarnations. Although he wasn't sure that he had fully grasped the telepathic message, Alexander had the good judgment not to interrupt or ask questions. He stayed close by Nadia's side, cooling her with snow and giving her water to drink when she awoke. He kept the fire going until the roots they were using as fuel were exhausted. Soon the first light of dawn slit the mantle of night, while the monks, sitting in the lotus position with their eyes closed and their right hands on his friend's body, murmured mantras.

Later, when Alexander was able to analyze what he had experienced during that strange night, the one word that occurred to him to define what that pair of mysterious men had done was "magic." Nothing else could explain how they had healed Nadia. He assumed that the powder they had used to make the salve was some powerful remedy unknown to the rest of the world, but he was sure that it was Tensing's and Dil Bahadur's mental powers that had produced the true miracle.

During the hours that the lama and the prince were applying their psychic powers to heal Nadia, Alexander thought about his mother, far away in California. He imagined the cancer as a merciless terrorist lurking in her body, ready to attack at any moment. Lisa Cold's family had celebrated her recovery, but all of them knew that the danger was not past. Chemotherapy and the "water of health" Alex had brought from the City of the Beasts, in combination with the witch man Walimai's herbs, had won the first round, but the battle was not over. Throughout the night that he watched Nadia improve with such amazing speed as the monks silently prayed, he formed a plan to bring his mother to the Kingdom of the Golden Dragon—or else study that awesome method of healing for himself.

At dawn, Nadia awakened without fever, with good color in her face, and with a voracious appetite. Borobá, huddled by her side, was the first to greet her. Tensing prepared *tsampa*, and she devoured it as if it were a delicacy, although it was nothing but a grayish gruel with the flavor of toasted barley. She also eagerly drank the medicinal potion the lama gave her.

In English, Nadia reported her adventure with the Blue Warriors, the kidnapping of Pema and the other girls, and the location of the cave. She was aware that the two men who had saved her were capturing the images forming in her mind. From time to time Tensing interrupted her to clarify some details, and since she listened with her heart, she understood him. The person who had the most difficulty in communicating was Alexander, even though the monks could divine his thoughts. He was exhausted; he couldn't keep his eyes open, and he couldn't imagine how the lama and his disciple were so alert after having spent part of the night rescuing Nadia and the rest of it praying.

"We must save those poor girls before they suffer irreparable harm," said Dil Bahadur after listening to Nadia's story.

But Tensing was not in as great a hurry as the prince. He questioned Nadia to learn exactly what she had heard in the cave, and she repeated the few words Pema had recognized. Tensing asked if she was sure that they had mentioned the Golden Dragon and the king.

"My father may be in danger!" the prince exclaimed.

"Your father?" Alexander asked, surprised.

"The king is my father," Dil Bahadur explained.

"I've been thinking about all this, and I am sure that those criminals didn't come to the Forbidden Kingdom just to steal some girls. They could have done that more easily in India," Alexander offered.

"So you think they came here for some other reason?" Nadia asked.

"I think they kidnapped the girls as a diversion, and that their real goal has something to do with the king and the Golden Dragon."

"Stealing the statue, maybe?" Nadia theorized.

"I understand that it's very valuable. I have no idea why the kidnappers mentioned the king, but it can't be for anything good," Alex concluded.

The usually unemotional Tensing and Dil Bahadur could not hold back a grunt. They discussed the matter in their language for a few minutes and then the lama announced that they must all rest for three or four hours, before moving into action.

When the friends awakened, the location of the sun told them it was about nine A.M. Alexander looked around him and could see nothing but mountains and more mountains; it was as if they were at the end of the world. He knew, however, that they were not far from civilization, it was merely well out of sight. The hiding place the lama and his disciple had chosen was protected by large rocks and was difficult to reach unless one knew it was there. It was obvious that the monks had used it before, because there were candle stubs in one corner. Tensing explained that to go down to the valley they would have to make a long detour; it wasn't that far, but they were cut off by a high cliff, and the Blue Warriors blocked the one trail that led to the capital.

Nadia's temperature was back to normal, she felt no pain, and the swelling in her arm had gone down. She was hungry again, and ate everything she was offered, including a serving of a vile-smelling cheese from Tensing's pouch. The lama again applied the salve to the girl's shoulder and wrapped it in the same strips of cloth, since they had no others, and then he helped her take a few steps.

"Look Jaguar, I'm completely well! I can lead you to the cave where Pema and the other girls are," Nadia exclaimed, giving a few hops to prove what she was saying.

But Tensing ordered her to lie down again on her improvised bed; she was not completely well and she needed more rest, he told her. Her body was the temple of her spirit, and she must treat it with respect and care. Her task was to visualize her bones in the correct places, her shoulder without swelling, and her skin clear of the bruises and scratches she had suffered in the last day or two.

"We are what we think. Our being emerges from our thoughts. Our thoughts construct the world," the monk told her telepathically.

Nadia captured the broad stroke of his idea: She could heal herself with her mind. That was what Tensing and Dil Bahadur had done for her during the night.

"Pema and the other girls are in serious danger. They may still be in the cave I escaped from, but it's also possible that they've already been taken somewhere else," Nadia explained to Alexander.

"You said that they had a camp there with weapons, provisions, and equipment for their horses. I don't think it would be easy to move all that in a few hours' time," he reasoned.

"In any case, you have to hurry, Jaguar."

Tensing indicated that she was to stay and rest while he and the two young men rescued the captive girls. It wasn't far, and Borobá could lead them there. Nadia tried to explain that they would have the ferocious Sect of the Scorpion to deal with, but it seemed as if the lama did not understand, because his only response was a calm smile.

Tensing and Dil Bahadur had no weapons other than the prince's bow and arrows, and the two tall wooden staffs they always carried; everything else was back in their hermitage. Their one amulet was the magic piece of petrified dragon dropping from the Valley of the Yetis that the prince was wearing around his neck. When they competed in earnest, as they did sometimes in the monasteries where the prince was educated, they used a variety of weapons. The competitions were friendly, and rarely was anyone injured, since the warrior monks were experienced and careful not to do harm. The gentle Tensing would wear a hard armor of padded leather that covered his chest and back, in addition to metal guards on his legs and forearms. His size, enormous in itself, was thus doubled, turning him into a true giant. Atop that massive body, his head looked too small, and the sweetness of his expression seemed entirely out of place. His favorite weapons were metal discs with knife-sharp spurs, which he threw with incredible precision and speed, and his heavy sword, which no other man could lift with both hands and which he brandished effortlessly with one. He was able to disarm another man with a single move, split an armor in two with his sword, and brush the cheeks of his opponents with his discs without wounding them.

Dil Bahadur did not have the strength or skill of his master, but he was quick as a cat. He did not wear armor or other protection, because it slowed his movement; speed was his best defense. In a tournament he could dodge knives, arrows, and lances, flexing his body like a weasel. To see him in action was a wondrous sight, he seemed to be dancing. His favorite weapon was the bow, because he had infallible aim: wherever the target was, there sped his arrow. His master had taught him that the bow was part of his body and the arrow an extension of his arm; he must shoot by instinct, sighting with his third eye. Tensing had insisted on making him a perfect archer because, he claimed, it cleansed the heart. According to the lama, only a pure heart can master that weapon. The prince, who never missed a shot, contradicted him, joking that his arm knew nothing at all about the impurities of his heart.

Like all experts in Tao-shu, master and disciple used their physical power as a form of exercise to temper character and soul, never to harm another living being. Respect for every form of life, the basis of Buddhism, was their creed. They believed that any living creature could, in a previous life, have been their mother, and therefore must be treated with love and kindness. Anyway, as the lama always said, it doesn't matter what you believe or don't believe, only what you do. They could not hunt a bird to eat it, far less kill a man, even in self-defense. They must see the enemy as a teacher who gives them opportunity to control their passions and learn something about themselves. The prospect of attacking a fellow being had never presented itself until now.

"How can I shoot my arrow against other humans and have a pure heart, master?"

"That is permitted only if there is no alternative, and if one has the certainty that the cause is just, Dil Bahadur."

"It seems to me, master, that in this case that certainty exists."

"May all living beings have good fortune; let none experience suffering," master and student recited together, wishing with all their hearts not to find themselves forced to use any of their deadly martial knowledge.

Alexander, for his part, had the temperament of a peacemaker. In all his sixteen years of living he had never found it necessary to fight, and in fact he didn't know how. Besides, he had nothing he could use to defend himself. His only tool was the jackknife his grandmother had given him to replace the Swiss Army knife he'd given the witch man Walimai in the Amazon. It was a good tool, but as a weapon it was ridiculous.

Nadia sighed. She didn't understand weapons, but she had met the men of the Sect of the Scorpion, who were famous for their brutality and their skill with knives. Those men lived for crime and war, and were trained to kill. What could a pair of peaceful Buddhist monks and a young American tourist do against a band of renegades? She told them good-bye and with great anxiety watched them leave. Her friend Jaguar went in the lead, with Borobá riding his neck and clutching his ears; the prince followed, and the huge lama brought up the rear.

"I hope I will see you alive again," Nadia murmured as they disappeared among the tall rocks that protected the small grotto.

Once the three men began the descent toward the cave of the Blue Warriors, they could move faster. They were almost running. Despite the brilliant sun, it was cold. The air was so clear that they could see the distant valleys, and from so high among the mountains, the view was dazzling. They were surrounded by snowy peaks, but below lay hill after hill covered with glorious vegetation, and terraces of green rice paddies cut from the hillsides. Scattered in the distance they could see the white *stupas* of the monasteries, small villages with their houses of clay, wood, stone, and straw, pagodalike roofs and twisting streets, all blending into nature like an extension of the terrain. There time was measured by seasons, and the rhythm of life was slow and unchanging.

Had they carried binoculars, they would have seen prayer flags fluttering everywhere, large images of Buddha painted on the rocks, lines of monks hurrying toward the temples, buffaloes pulling plows, women on the way to market in their necklaces of turquoise and silver, children playing with balls made from rags. It was nearly impossible to imagine that this small nation, so peaceful and so beautiful, preserved intact for centuries, was now menaced by a band of assassins.

Alexander and Dil Bahadur hurried a little faster, thinking of the girls they must rescue before their foreheads were branded with a red-hot iron, or something worse happened to them. They didn't know what dangers awaited in the course of the rescue, but they were sure they would be considerable. Tensing, in contrast, was not overly concerned. The captive girls were just the first part of his mission; the second part preoccupied him much more: saving the king.

In the meantime, despite General Myar Kunglung's efforts to keep the news secret, word had spread in Tunkhala that the king had vanished. They had been waiting for him at the television station because he was going to address the country, but he had not appeared. Now no one knew where to find him. It was the first time in the history of the nation that such a thing had happened. The king's older son, the one who had won the archery tournaments during the festival, was taking his father's place for the time being. If the king did not show up within a few days, the general and the high lamas would have to seek out Dil Bahadur so that he could fulfill the destiny for which he'd been preparing for more than twelve years. Naturally, everyone hoped that would not be necessary.

Rumors were circulating that the king was in a monastery in the mountains, where he had retired to meditate; that he had traveled to Europe with the foreign woman named Judit Kinski; that he was in Nepal with the Dalai Lama; and a thousand other speculations. None of them, however, aligned with the sovereign's serene and pragmatic nature. Neither was it possible that he could travel incognito, and in any case, the weekly airplane wasn't scheduled until Friday. The monarch would never abandon his responsibilities, especially when the country was in crisis over the kidnapped girls. The conclusion of the general and the rest of the inhabitants of the Forbidden Kingdom was that something of grave consequence must have happened to him.

Myar Kunglung abandoned the search for the girls and returned to the capital. Kate refused to be left behind, and so learned some of the confidential details. At the gate to the palace she found the guide Wandgi sitting beside a column awaiting news of his daughter, Pema. The man threw his arms around the journalist, weeping. He seemed like a different person, as if he had aged twenty years in the last two days. Kate quickly freed herself, because she did not like emotional demonstrations, and as consolation offered him a swig of vodka-spiked tea from her ever-present canteen. Wandgi took the drink out of courtesy but when he had a taste of the foul liquid, he quickly spewed it out. Kate grabbed him by one arm and forced him to follow the general with her, so he could translate. Myar Kunglung's English was about at the level of Hollywood's Tarzan.

They learned that the king had spent the afternoon and part of the night in the hall of the Great Buddha in the heart of the palace, accompanied by Tschewang, his leopard. Only once did he interrupt his meditation: when he took a brief stroll through the garden and drank a cup of jasmine tea brought to him by a monk. The monk informed the general that his majesty always prayed several hours before consulting the Golden Dragon. At midnight, he said, he had brought him another cup of tea. By then most of the candles had burned out, and in the shadowy room he could see that the king was no longer there.

"You didn't find out where he was?" Kate asked through Wandgi.

"I supposed he had gone to consult the Golden

Dragon," the monk replied.

"And the leopard?"

"He was chained in one corner. His majesty cannot take him to the Chamber of the Golden Dragon. Sometimes he leaves him in the Buddha Hall, and other times he leaves him in the care of the guards at the Magnificent Door."

"Where is that?" Kate wanted to know, but instead of an answer she received a scandalized look from the monk and a glare from the general. It was clear that this information was not provided to outsiders, but Kate was not easily put off.

The general explained that very few people knew the location of the Magnificent Door. The men who guarded it were blindfolded and led there by one of the ancient monks who served in the palace and were trusted with the secret. That door was the threshold to a sacred part of the palace that no one except the monarch could enter. On the other side began the obstacles and deadly traps that protected the Sacred Passageway. Unless a person knew where to step, he would meet a horrible death.

"Would it be possible to speak with Judit Kinski, the European woman who is a guest at the palace?" the writer persisted.

When a servant went to look for her, he discovered that she had disappeared as well. Her bed had been slept in, and her clothes and personal effects were still in the room—with the exception of the leather purse she always had slung over one shoulder. The thought that the king and the expert in tulips had run off to some amorous rendezvous flashed through Kate's mind but was immediately discarded as absurd. Such behavior did not fit the character of either of the two, and besides, there was no need to run off to be together.

"We must look for the king," said Kate.

"Possibly that idea had already occurred to us, Grandmother," General Kunglung muttered, clenching his teeth.

The general sent for a nun who could guide them to the lower floors of the palace. He was forced to tolerate Kate and Wandgi's tagging along because the writer was clinging to his arm like a leech and wouldn't let go. This was the rudest woman he had ever seen, the general thought.

They followed the nun down two stories, passing through a hundred interconnecting rooms, and finally came to the hall that contained the Magnificent Door. They didn't have a chance to admire it, because, to their horror, they found two guards outfitted in the uniform of the royal house lying facedown in pools of their own blood. One was dead, but the other was still alive. With his last breath he told them that the Blue Warriors, led by a white foreigner, had rushed into the Sacred Passageway. Not only had they managed to get in alive and make their way back out again, but worse, they had kidnapped the king and stolen the Golden Dragon.

Myar Kunglung had spent forty years in the armed forces but he had never confronted a situation as perilous as this. His soldiers occupied themselves with war games and marching in parades, but until that moment, violence had been unknown in his country. He had never found himself in the position of needing to use his weapons, and none of his soldiers knew true danger. The notion that their ruler had been kidnapped in his own palace was inconceivable to him. The general's strongest emotion at that moment, greater even than fear or anger, was shame. He had failed in his duty; he had been incapable of protecting his beloved king.

Kate no longer had anything to do in the palace. She took her leave of the wretched general, and set off at a gallop in the direction of the hotel, dragging Wandgi in her wake. She needed to make plans with her grandson.

"Possibly the American boy has rented a horse, and

perhaps he has left. I believe he is not back yet," the owner of the hotel informed her with big smiles and bows.

"When was that? Did he go alone?" she asked, worried.

"Possibly he left yesterday, and it may be that he had a monkey with him," said the man, striving to be at his most amiable with the foreign grandmother.

"Borobá!" exclaimed Kate, guessing immediately that Alexander had gone to look for Nadia.

"I should never have brought those children to this country!" she added in the middle of a coughing fit, dropping onto a chair in a daze.

Without a word, the hotel owner poured a glass of vodka and placed it in her hands.

CHAPTER FOURTEEN

The Golden Dragon

✸

THAT NIGHT THE KING HAD MEDITATED for hours before the Great Buddha, as he always did before going to the Sacred Passageway. His ability to understand the enlightenment he would receive from the statue depended upon the state of his spirit. He had to have a pure heart, free of desire, fear, expectation, memories, or negative intent, and as open as the lotus flower. He prayed fervently, because he knew that his mind and his heart were vulnerable. He felt that his hold on the reins of his kingdom, and on those of his own psyche, was dangerously weak.

The king had been very young when he ascended to the throne after the early death of his father, at a time when he had not completed his training with the lamas. There were things he had never learned, and he had not developed his paranormal abilities as he should have. He could not see peoples' auras or read their thoughts; he had not experienced astral journeys, and he did not know how to heal with the power of his mind, although he could do such things as stop his breathing and will himself to die. He had compensated for deficiencies in his preparation and for his psychic limitations with common sense and continual spiritual practice. He was a generous man with no personal ambition, dedicated wholly to the well-being of his kingdom. He surrounded himself with loyal followers who helped him make fair decisions, and he maintained an efficient information network in order to keep up with what was going on in his country and in the world. He ruled with humility, because he felt unfit to play the role of king. He hoped to retire to a monastery when his son Dil Bahadur ascended to the throne, but after he met Judit Kinski he had doubted even his religious calling. For the first time since the death of his wife, he was attracted to a woman. He was very confused, and in his prayers he asked simply that he be able to carry out his destiny, whatever it might be, without harm to others.

As a youth, the monarch had learned the code for deciphering the messages of the Golden Dragon; what he lacked was the intuition of the third eye, which was also required. He could interpret only part of what the statue communicated. Every time he consulted it, he lamented his own limitations. His consolation was that his son Dil Bahadur would be much better prepared to govern the nation than he had been.

"This is my karma in this incarnation: to be king, though I am not deserving of it," he used to murmur sadly.

That night, after several hours of intense meditation, he felt that his mind was clear and his heart open. He bowed deeply before the Great Buddha, touching his forehead to the floor; he asked for inspiration, and rose. His knees and back hurt after such a long period of immobility. He chained his faithful Tschewang to a ring that was set in the wall, drank the last sip of his now cold jasmine tea, picked up a candle, and left the hall. His bare feet slipped noiselessly across the polished stone floor. Along the way he came across several servants silently cleaning the palace.

By order of General Myar Kunglung, most of the guards had been called out to reinforce the kingdom's sparse military and police forces while they looked for the missing girls. The king barely noticed their absence, the palace was a very secure place. The guards fulfilled a decorative function during the day, but as they were generally not needed, only a handful remained at night. The security of the royal family had never been threatened.

The thousand rooms of the palace were interconnected by a multitude of doors. Some rooms had four exits, others, that were hexagonal in shape, had six. It was so easy to get lost that on the three upper floors of the ancient edifice the architects had carved signs on the doors as guides; on the lower floors, however, to which only a few monks and nuns, selected guards, and the royal family had access, there were no signs. And as the floors were below ground level and, additionally, without windows, there were no points of reference.

These underground rooms, ventilated through an ingenious system of pipes, had absorbed a strange odor over the centuries: a combination of dampness, grease from the lamps, and several kinds of incense, which the monks lighted to frighten away rats and evil spirits. Some rooms were used to store public administration parchments, statues, and furniture; others were depositories of medicines, provisions, or the antiquated weapons no one used anymore, but most were empty. Walls were covered with paintings of religious scenes, dragons, devils, long texts in Sanskrit, descriptions of the horrible punishments evil souls suffer in the Beyond. The ceilings were painted as well, but soot from the lamps had turned them black.

As the king progressed deeper into the palace, he

lighted lamps from the flame of his candle, thinking that the time had come to install electricity throughout the building; at present, it was available in only one wing of an upper floor, the one the royal family occupied. He opened doors and walked through rooms without hesitation; he knew the way by heart.

Soon he came to a rectangular room, larger and with higher ceilings than the others; it was lighted with a double row of gold lamps, and at the far end was a spectacular door of bronze and silver, incrusted with jade. Two young guards, attired in the age-old uniform of royal heralds, with plumed blue silk headgear and lances adorned with colorful ribbons, were standing watch on either side of the door. They looked tired; they had been on duty several hours in the solitude and sepulchral silence of this chamber. When they saw the king, they fell to their knees, touched their heads to the floor, and stayed in that position until he gave them his blessing and told them to get to their feet. Then they turned their faces to the wall, as demanded by protocol, so they couldn't watch as the sovereign opened the door.

The king twirled several of the many jade medallions that embellished the door, and pushed. The door swung heavily on its hinges. He stepped inside the room and the massive door closed behind him. From that moment, the security system that had protected the Golden Dragon for almost eighteen hundred years was automatically activated.

Hidden among the gigantic ferns in the park around the palace, Tex Armadillo followed every step the king took through the subterranean rooms of the palace, as clearly as if he were dogging his heels. Thanks to modern technology, he could see the king perfectly on the small screen of his laptop. The monarch had no suspicion that he was wearing a tiny, high-precision camera on his chest, which allowed the American to observe as the king avoided the series of obstacles and disarmed the security mechanisms that protected the Golden Dragon. At the same time, he was plotting the coordinates of the route the king was following, outlining with the help of a Global Positioning System an exact map that he could follow later. Tex couldn't help smiling as he thought of the genius of the Specialist, who left nothing to chance. The apparatus he was using, much more sensitive, precise, and with broader capabilities than any currently in use, had been developed in the United States for military purposes, and was not available to the general public. The Specialist, however, could obtain anything; that was what contacts and money were for.

Crouching among the plants and sculptures of the garden were the twelve fiercest Blue Warriors of the sect, all under Armadillo's command. The remaining members were carrying out the other half of the plan in the mountains, where they were preparing the escape with the statue and where they held the kidnapped girls. That distraction, too, was the product of the Machiavellian mind of the Specialist. Because the police and soldiers were busy looking for the girls, the intruders were able to get into the palace without meeting resistance.

Even though they felt very confident, the murderous men were proceeding with caution. The Specialist's instructions had been exact: They must not attract attention. They would need several hours' head start to hide the statue in a safe place and extract the code from the lips of the king. They knew the exact number of guards still on duty and where they were located. They had already taken care of the four that patrolled the gardens, and did not expect their bodies to be discovered until the following morning. They themselves were armed with an arsenal of knives, which they had more faith in than firearms. The American was carrying a Magnum pistol with a silencer, but if everything worked out as planned, he would not have to use it.

Tex Armadillo did not take any particular pleasure in violence, though it was inevitable in his line of work. He believed that violence was for hit men, and he thought of himself as an intellectual, a man of ideas. Secretly he harbored the ambition of replacing the Specialist or of forming his own organization. He did not enjoy the company of the Blue Warriors, they were brutal and treacherous mercenaries with whom he could barely communicate, and he wasn't sure, should the need arise, whether he could control them. He had tried to convince the Specialist that he needed no more than a couple of the best men to perform the mission, but the response he received was to stick to the plan. Armadillo knew that the least insubordination or divergence from instructions could cost him his life. The one person he feared in this world was the Specialist.

His orders were clear: He was to watch the king's every movement through the hidden camera, wait until he arrived in the Chamber of the Golden Dragon and was consulting the statue—to be sure it was functioning—and then rush into the palace and, using the Global Positioning System, go as far as the Magnificent

Door. He was to take six men inside: two to carry the treasure, two to kidnap the king, and two for protection. He would have to skirt all the traps on his way to the Sacred Chamber and, to do that, he was counting on the video he had recorded.

The idea of kidnapping the leader of a nation and stealing his most precious object would have been absurd in any country other than the Forbidden Kingdom, where crime was nearly unknown and where, therefore, there were almost no defenses. For Armadillo it was child's play to stage an attack in a country whose citizens still used candles to light their houses and who believed that the telephone was some kind of magic. His sneer disappeared, however, as he witnessed on his laptop the ingenious ways the Golden Dragon was defended. The mission might not be as easy as he had imagined. The minds that had invented those traps eighteen centuries before were not in the least bit primitive. He owed his advantage to the Specialist's superior mind.

When Armadillo saw that the king had reached the final room, he motioned to six Blue Warriors to guard the rear, as planned, and he headed toward the palace with the others. They went in through a service entrance on the ground floor and immediately found themselves in a room with four doors. Referring to the GPS map, the American and his followers moved with little hesitation from one room to the next, until they reached the heart of the palace. In the hall of the Magnificent Door they encountered the first obstacle: the two soldiers standing guard. When the king's guards saw the intruders, they raised their lances, but before they could take a step forward, two lethal knives, perfectly thrown from several yards' distance, struck each in the chest. They collapsed to the floor.

Replaying the video on his screen, Armadillo followed it step by step. He twisted the same jades the king had turned before him. The door opened heavily, and the bandits walked through into a round room with nine narrow doors, all identical. The lamps the monarch had lighted were burning, casting wavering illumination on the precious stones that decorated the doors.

At that point, the king had stepped onto an eye painted on the floor, opened his arms wide, and then had turned at a forty-five-degree angle, so that his right arm was pointing to the door he needed to open. Tex Armadillo imitated him, followed by the superstitious men of the scorpion sect, who by now each had a knife between his teeth and one in each hand. The

American suspected that the camera had not recorded all the risks they would meet; some would undoubtedly be purely psychological, or tricks of illusion. He had watched the king pass unhesitatingly through certain rooms that seemed to be empty, but that didn't mean that they were. They would have to move forward with great caution.

"Don't touch anything," he warned his men.

"We hear demons and witches and monsters live in this place here," one of the men murmured in his mangled English.

"There are no such things," Armadillo replied.

"They say, too, that the man who touch the Dragon . . . that something horrible happen him."

"Nonsense! Those are just superstitions, pure ignorance."

The man was insulted when the American's comment was translated, and the entire group shuffled and muttered, ready to turn on Armadillo.

"I thought you were warriors, but I see that you're really little babies! Cowards!" Armadillo spit out with infinite scorn.

The first bandit, outraged, raised his knife, but Armadillo already had his pistol in his hand, and there was a murderous gleam in his pale eyes. By now the Blue

Warriors were very sorry they had accepted this job. Their band had always survived by committing simple crimes; this was unknown territory. They had made a deal to steal a statue, and in exchange they were to receive quantities of modern firearms and a pile of money to buy horses and anything else that occurred to them. No one had warned them, however, that the palace was bewitched. And it was too late to turn back, they had no choice but to follow the American to the end.

After overcoming the obstacles, one by one, that protected the treasure, Tex Armadillo and four of his men found themselves in the Chamber of the Golden Dragon. Even though they had the advantage of modern technology, which allowed them to see how the king had avoided falling into the traps, they had already lost two men to horrible deaths: one fell into a deep well and the other's flesh was eaten in a matter of minutes by a rampaging acid.

Just as the American had thought, they had not been subjected merely to physical ambushes but to psychological tricks as well. To Armadillo, it was like descending into a psychedelic hell, but he maintained his self-control by telling himself over and over that most of the horrifying images that assaulted them were only in his mind. He was a professional who exercised complete control over his body and mind. For the primitive men of the Sect of the Scorpion, on the other hand, the journey toward the dragon had been much more harrowing, for they were unable to distinguish between what was real and what was imaginary. They were used to meeting danger head on but they were terrified by things that could not be explained. The mysterious palace rubbed their nerves raw.

The invaders had no idea what they would find when they went into the Chamber of the Golden Dragon; the images on the laptop screen had not been very clear. They were blinded by the brilliance of the gold-sheathed walls, which reflected light from count-less oil lamps and thick beeswax candles. The scents from the lamps and from the burning incense and myrrh filled the air. They paused at the threshold, deaf-ened by a hoarse, guttural sound impossible to describe, something that at first impression suggested the moan of a whale inside a vast metal tube. After a moment, however, they could detect a certain coher-ence in the song, and soon it was evident that they were hearing some sort of language. Seated in the lotus posi-tion before the statue, the king had his back to them, so immersed in the sounds and absorbed in his task that he didn't hear them come in.

The monarch's voice was rising and falling, chanting strange wordlike sounds, and then from the mouth of the statue would come the response, rumbling throughout the room. The intense vibration could be felt on the skin, and in the brain, and on the nerves; it was like standing inside a reverberating bell.

And there, before the eyes of Armadillo and the Blue Warriors, stood the Golden Dragon, in all its splendor: leonine body, paws with great claws, curled-up reptilian tail, plumed wings, a ferocious head with four horns, protruding eyes, and gaping maw filled with two rows of sharp teeth and a forked serpent's tongue. The gold work was delicate and perfect: each scale on the body and tail was set with a precious stone, the feathers of the wings were tipped with diamonds, the tail displayed an intricate design of pearls and emeralds, the teeth were ivory, and the eyes were perfect star-rubies, each the size of a dove's egg. The fabled animal was mounted on black stone, in the center of which was a strip of yellow quartz.

The bandits were stupefied, trying to digest the assault of the lights, the rarefied air, and the thundering sound. None of them had expected the statue to be so extraordinary; even the most ignorant man in the band realized that he was standing before an object of unimaginable value. Their eyes glinted with greed, and each of the men thought about how just one of those precious stones could change his life.

Armadillo had also succumbed to the magical fascination of the statue, though he had never thought of himself as a particularly ambitious man—he did this work because he liked adventure. He prided himself on living a simple life, completely free of sentimentality or any other kind of bond. He treasured the idea of retiring when he was older, when he grew weary of seeing the world, and of spending his last years on his ranch in the western United States, where he planned to breed race horses. In some of his missions he had held a fortune in his hands, and had not felt any temptation to appropriate it. He was satisfied with his commission, which was always very generous. However, when he saw the statue, it crossed his mind to betray the Specialist. With the statue in his power, nothing could stop him. He would be enormously rich; he could fulfill all his dreams, including that of having his own organization, one more powerful even than the Specialist's. For a brief moment, he abandoned himself to the pleasure of that idea, but quickly returned to reality. "That must be the statue's curse: overpowering greed," he thought. He had to exert great self-discipline to concentrate on the next steps of the plan. Silently, he signaled his men, and they moved toward the king with knives in hand.

CHAPTER FIFTEEN

The Cave of the Bandits

❋

IT WAS NOT DIFFICULT FOR ALEXANDER and his new friends to find the general area of the Blue Warriors' cave; Nadia had given them the approximate location, and Borobá took care of the rest. The little monkey was still riding Alexander's shoulders, with his tail wrapped around the youth's neck and his hands buried in Alexander's hair. He did not like climbing mountains, and he liked going down them even less. Every so often, Alex would slap at the monkey to let go, because Borobá's tail was choking him and his nervous little hands were pulling out tufts of hair.

Once the party was sure of the whereabouts of the cave, they approached with great caution, taking advantage of the cover of shrubs and the irregular terrain. They did not note any activity, or hear anything but the wind among the hills and, from time to time, the cry of a bird. In that silence, their footsteps, even their breathing, sounded deafening. Tensing picked up a few stones and tucked them into the folds his tunic formed at the waist, then telepathically ordered Borobá to go scout what lay ahead. Alexander breathed a sigh of relief when finally the monkey jumped down.

Borobá went loping off in the direction of the cave, and within ten minutes he was back. He could not voice what he had seen, but in the monkey's mind Tensing saw confused images of several persons, and in that way verified that the cave was not empty, as they had feared. Apparently the captive girls were still there, guarded by a few Blue Warriors, though most of the men had left. That made their immediate task easier, but Tensing did not consider it good news: it meant that the others must be in Tunkhala. He had no doubt that, as the young American had suggested, the criminals had not come to the Forbidden Kingdom to kidnap a half-dozen girls but to steal the Golden Dragon.

The three men and the monkey crawled close to the cave, where a man sat on his haunches, supporting himself with his rifle. The light shone directly on him, and at that distance he made an easy target for Dil Bahadur who, however, would have to stand to use his bow. Tensing gestured to him to stay flat on the ground, and pulled out one of the stones he had gathered. Mentally, he asked forgiveness for the act he was

284 · *Isabel Allende*

about to commit, and then, without hesitation, he
threw the stone with all his strength. To Alexander it
seemed as if the lama hadn't aimed at all, so he was
dumbfounded when the guard fell forward with barely
a sound, knocked unconscious by the stone that had
struck him squarely between the eyes. Tensing
motioned to the others to follow him.

Alexander picked up the guard's weapon, though he
had never fired a rifle and didn't even know if it was
loaded. The weight of the gun in his hands gave him
confidence, and awakened an unfamiliar sense of com-
bativeness. He felt a strong flow of energy; in an
instant his doubts disappeared and he was ready to
fight like a wild beast.

All three ran into the cave at the same time. Tensing
and Dil Bahadur were yelling bloodthirsty yells, and
without thinking about what he was doing, Alexander
imitated them. Normally he was a rather shy person,
and he had never made such an uproar. All his rage,
fear, and strength were concentrated in those cries;
thanks to them, and the charge of adrenaline surging
through his veins, he felt invincible, like the jaguar.

Inside the cave they found four bandits, the woman
with the scar, and the prisoners, who were in the back

of the cavern with their ankles tied. Surprised by that trio bellowing like madmen, the Blue Warriors hesitated only an instant and then reached for their knives, but that instant was enough to allow Dil Bahadur's first arrow to hit its mark, piercing the right arm of one of the men.

The arrow did not stop him. With a howl of pain, he threw his dagger with his left hand, and immediately drew another from the sash at his waist. The dagger hissed as it flew straight toward the prince's heart. Dil Bahadur stepped to one side. The dagger brushed his armpit without wounding him, as he raised his arm to shoot a second arrow; he was calm as he stepped forward, sure that he was protected by the magic shield of the dragon dropping.

At the same time, Tensing, with incredible skill, was dodging the knives flying about him. A lifetime of training in the art of Tao-shu allowed him to predict the course and speed of each dagger. He didn't need to think, his body reacted instinctively. He eliminated one of the men with a quick leap and a sharp kick to the jaw. With a swipe of one arm he dislodged the gun from another who was aiming to fire, but the Blue Warrior immediately pulled out his knives.

Alexander didn't have time to aim at anything. He

pulled the trigger and a shot echoed through the air, exploding against the rock walls. He felt a push from Dil Bahadur, stumbled, and escaped by a hair from being the target of one of the knives. When he saw that the bandits still standing were going for their rifles, he grabbed his by the barrel, which was hot, and charged them, yelling at the top of his lungs. Without conscious thought, he slammed the rifle butt down on the shoulder of the nearest man; the blow did not put him out of commission but stunned him enough that it gave Tensing time to get his hands on the man and press a key point on his neck. His paralyzed victim felt an electric charge travel from his neck to his heels; his knees buckled and he dropped like a rag doll, eyes bulging and a scream stuck in his throat, unable to move a finger.

In only a few minutes the four Blue Warriors were on the ground. The guard had recovered slightly from being struck with the stone, but he had no opportunity to use his knives. Alexander placed the barrel of his rifle to his temple and ordered him to join the others. He spoke in English, but the tone was so clear that the man did not hesitate to obey. While Alexander stood guard with the weapon he didn't know how to use, trying to look as bold and cruel as possible, Tensing bound the Blue Warriors with rope he found in the cave.

As Dil Bahadur, bow at the ready, started toward the girls at the back of the cave, he was stopped short by a loud scream. About midpoint in the ten yards that separated him from them was a pit of glowing charcoal. The woman with the scar had deserted her cooking pots; she held a whip in one hand and, in the other, an open basket that she was shaking over the heads of the five captives.

"One more step and I'll drop the scorpions over them," the jailer shrieked.

The prince did not dare shoot his arrow. From that distance he could fell the woman with no difficulty, but he couldn't prevent her from spilling the lethal insects on the girls. The Blue Warriors, and surely the woman as well, were immune to the venom, but anyone else was at risk of dying from their stings.

Everyone froze. Alexander kept his eyes and his weapon trained on the prisoners, two of whom had not yet been tied up by Tensing and were waiting for an unguarded moment to jump him. The lama did not dare act, either. From where he stood, the only weapons he could use against the woman were his extraordinary parapsychological powers. He tried to project a mental image that would freeze her with fear; there was too much confusion and distance between them to try to hypnotize her. He could see enough of her aura to recognize what a primitive and cruel creature she was, and one who was frightened besides; he knew they would have to use force to subdue her.

The standoff lasted a few seconds, but that was enough to shift the balance of power. One more instant and Alexander would have had to shoot the two men who were primed to leap on Tensing. Then something totally unexpected occurred. One of the girls threw herself against the woman with the scar, and the two of them rolled across the cave floor as the basket arced through the air and hit solid ground. A hundred black scorpions scrabbled toward the back of the cave.

The girl who had jumped in was Pema. Despite her slim, almost ethereal build, and the fact that she was tied at the ankles, she took on her jailer with suicidal determination, ignoring the whip the woman was wielding blindly, and the imminent threat of the scorpions. Pema pounded the woman with her fists, bit her, and pulled her hair, fighting for her life; the girl was at a clear disadvantage, because the woman was stronger, and by now she had dropped the whip and pulled out the kitchen knife she wore at her waist. Pema's actions gave Dil Bahadur the opportunity to drop his bow, seize a tin of the kerosene the bandits used in their lamps, pour the combustible fluid on the ground, and light it with a twig from the fire. A curtain of flames and thick smoke swirled up, singeing his eyelashes.

Indifferent to the fire, the prince ran to Pema, who was on her back on the ground with the evil woman on top of her, straining with both hands to hold back the knife inching closer and closer to her face. The tip of the knife was scratching Pema's cheek, as the prince grabbed the woman around the neck, pulled her back, and with one chop to the temple knocked her unconscious.

Pema sat up and desperately slapped at the flames licking her long skirt, but the silk was blazing like dry tinder. With one tug the prince yanked off the skirt and then turned to the other girls who were huddled against the wall and crying with terror. Using the woman's knife, Pema cut through her bonds and then helped Dil Bahadur free her companions. She led them through the curtain of fire—where charred scorpions were twisting and crackling—toward the entrance to the cave, now filling with smoke.

Tensing, the prince, and Alexander dragged their prisoners outside and left them tightly tied two by two, back to back. Borobá took advantage of the bandits' defenselessness to make fun of them, tossing clods of dirt at them and sticking out his tongue, until Alexander called him. The monkey leapt to his shoulders, curled his tail around his neck, and clamped onto his ears. Alex sighed with resignation.

Dil Bahadur took the clothes from one of the bandits and handed his monk's habit to Pema, who was half-naked. It was so big on her that she had to fold it over twice around her waist. With great revulsion, the prince put on the black, stinking clothes of a Blue Warrior. Although he would have preferred a thousand times over to wear only his loin cloth, he knew that as soon as the sun set and the temperature fell, he would need some protection. He was so impressed with Pema's courage and self-possession that giving her his tunic seemed the least he could do. He couldn't take his eyes off her. The girl acknowledged his gesture with a shy smile, and wrapped herself in the rough, dark red habit typical of the monks of her country, never suspecting that she was wearing the clothing of the heir to the throne.

Tensing interrupted the emotion-charged glances between Dil Bahadur and Pema to ask the girl what she had heard in the cave. She confirmed what he already suspected: The other members of the band were planning to steal the Golden Dragon and kidnap the king.

"I understand the first part of the plan, the statue is very valuable, but not the second. What do they want of the king?" the prince asked.

"I do not know," she replied.

Tensing quickly studied the aura of the prisoners in order to select the most vulnerable, and planted himself before him, piercing him with a penetrating gaze. The always-sweet expression of his eyes had changed completely: the pupils had narrowed to slits and the man had the sensation that he was facing a snake. Tonelessly, the lama recited some words in Sanskrit that only Dil Bahadur recognized, and in less than a minute the frightened bandit was in Tensing's power, sunk in a hypnotic trance.

The lama's questions clarified certain aspects of the Sect of the Scorpion's plan, and confirmed that it was already too late to stop the band from getting into the palace. The man did not believe that they had harmed the king; the American's instructions had been to take him alive, they needed him. That was all the Blue Warrior knew. The most important information they gained was that the sovereign and the statue would both be taken to the abandoned monastery of Chenthan Dzong.

"How do they think they can escape from there?" the prince asked, surprised. "It's in the middle of nowhere."

"By air," the bandit said.

"They must have a helicopter," Alexander put in. Even though he did not know the language, from the images forming in his mind he was able to grasp the broad outlines of what was being discussed. These pictures conveyed most of the communication between the lama and the prince, until Pema was able to fill in details.

"Are they referring to Tex Armadillo?" asked Alexander.

He could not get a clear answer, because the bandits knew him only as "the American," and Pema had never seen him.

Tensing brought the man out of his hypnotic trance and announced that they were going to leave the bandits there, after making sure they could not work free from their bonds. It wouldn't hurt them to spend one or two nights outdoors, until they were found by the royal guard or, if they were lucky, their own men. Joining his hands before his face, and bowing slightly, the lama apologized to his prisoners for the discourteous way he had treated them. Dil Bahadur did the same.

"I will pray that you are rescued before black bears, snow leopards, or tigers find you," Tensing said with all seriousness.

Alexander was intrigued by this show of courtesy. If the situation had been reversed and they had been the victims, those men would have murdered them without a hint of a bow.

"Perhaps we should go to the monastery," Dil Bahadur proposed.

"What shall we do with the girls?" Alexander asked, indicating Pema and her friends.

"Possibly," Pema offered, "I can lead them back to the valley and advise the king's troops to join you at the monastery."

"I don't think it would be wise to use the bandits' trail; they must have men posted through these mountains. You will have to take a shortcut," Tensing replied.

"My master has forgotten the cliff," the prince murmured.

The lama smiled. "Perhaps the cliff is not an entirely bad idea, Dil Bahadur."

"Possibly my master is joking?"

The lama's answer was a broad smile that lit up his face, and he motioned for the young people to follow him. They went back the way they had come, in order to rejoin Nadia. Tensing went first, helping the girls, who had great difficulty making their way, dressed as they were in sandals and sarongs. They had no experience at all in moving across such steep terrain, but no one complained. They were too grateful to have been rescued from the Blue Warriors, and the gigantic monk inspired absolute confidence.

Alexander, who brought up the rear after the prince and Pema, took one last look at the pathetic group of bandits they were leaving behind. It seemed incredible to him that he had been part of a skirmish with professional killers: It was like a scene from an action film. He had just survived something nearly as violent as his experience in the Amazon, when Indians and soldiers clashed and left several people dead, or when he had seen a couple of bodies that had been destroyed by the claws of the Beasts. He could not smother his smile; definitely, traveling with his grandmother Kate was not for softies.

Nadia watched her friends walking single file along the steep path that led to her hiding place, and ran out to meet them, greatly relieved that they were back. She stopped when she saw one of the Blue Warriors in the group. A second look told her it was Dil Bahadur. They had taken less time than they'd expected, but those few hours had seemed endless to her. During that time she had summoned her totemic animal with the hope that she could watch them from the air, but the white eagle had not appeared, and she'd had to resign herself to waiting with a knot in her throat. She learned that she could not transform herself into the great bird on a whim; that happened only in moments of great danger or of extraordinary mental clarity. The eagle represented her spirit, the essence of her character. When she'd had her first experience with her totemic animal in the Amazon, she'd been very surprised that it was a bird, since she suffered from vertigo and heights paralyzed her with fear. She had never dreamed of flying, like other young people she knew. If anyone had asked her what her totemic spirit might be, she would have answered, a dolphin, of course; that intelligent and playful animal was something she could identify with. The eagle, which flew with such grace above the highest peaks, had helped her a lot in overcoming her phobia, although sometimes she was still afraid of heights. At that very moment, the sight of the steep cliffs yawning at her feet made her tremble.

"Jaguar!" she called, and ran toward her friend.

Alexander's first impulse was to throw his arms around her, but he stopped in time; he didn't want the others to think that Nadia was his girlfriend or anything like that.

"What happened?" she asked.

"Not much," he replied with a gesture of feigned indifference.

"How did you free the girls?"

"Easy. We disarmed the bandits, beat them up, burned the scorpions, smoked out the cave, tortured one of the men to get information, and left the rest tied up without water or food to die a slow death."

Nadia stood open-mouthed until Pema gave her a hug. The two girls quickly exchanged details about everything they'd gone through since they were separated.

"Do you know anything about that monk?" Pema whispered into Nadia's ear, pointing to Dil Bahadur.

"Not much."

"What's his name?"

"Dil Bahadur."

"That means 'brave heart,' an appropriate name. Perhaps I will marry him," Pema said.

"But you just met him! And he already asked you to marry him?" Nadia whispered, laughing.

"No. Usually monks don't marry. But possibly I will ask him if I get a chance," Pema replied casually.

CHAPTER SIXTEEN

The Cliff

TENSING DECIDED THAT THEY should eat something and rest before planning how to get the girls down to the floor of the valley. Dil Bahadur commented that there wasn't enough flour and yak butter for everyone, but he offered his meager provisions to Pema and the girls, who hadn't eaten in many hours. Tensing asked him to build a fire to boil water for tea and to melt yak butter. As soon as that was ready, the monk dug into the folds of his tunic, where he usually carried his beggar's pouch, and, like a magician, began to extract handfuls of cereal, garlic, dried vegetables, and other foods for their meal.

"This is like the loaves and fishes you read about in the New Testament," Alexander commented, amazed.

"My master is a very holy man. This isn't the first time I've seen him work miracles," said the prince, bowing with profound respect before the lama.

"Perhaps your master is not so holy as he is quick with his hands, Dil Bahadur. There were great stores of provisions in the bandits' cave, and I didn't want to waste them," the lama replied, bowing in turn.

"My master stole?" exclaimed the disciple, unbelieving.

"Let us say that your master borrowed," said Tensing.

The young people exchanged a puzzled glance and then burst out laughing. This explosion of happiness worked like opening a valve through which the terrible anxiety and fear they had lived with for days could escape. Soon all of them were on the ground, rocking with uncontainable laughter while the lama amiably stirred the *tsampa* pot and served tea without any change in his serene face.

Finally the young people calmed down, but the minute the master served their austere meal, they doubled over again, unable to stop laughing.

"Possibly when you come to your senses, you will listen to my plan," Tensing said, patient as ever.

The plan put an end to any idea of humor. What the lama proposed was nothing less than to lower the girls down the cliff face. They took one look over the edge and backed away, breathless: before them was approximately two hundred and forty feet of vertical fall.

"Master, no one has ever gone down there," said Dil Bahadur.

"Perhaps the moment has come for someone to be the first," Tensing replied.

All the girls started crying except Pema, who from the beginning had been an example of strength to the others, and Nadia, who right there and then decided she would rather die in the hands of the bandits or freeze in a glacier up at the peak than go down the face of that precipice. Tensing explained that if the girls used the shortcut, they could reach a village in the valley and ask for help before nightfall the next day. Otherwise, they would be stuck where they were and also run the risk that a band from the scorpion sect would find them. It was important to return the girls to their homes and to warn General Myar Kunglung so he could rescue the king from the fortified monastery before the bandits killed him. As for the master and Dil Bahadur, they would go on ahead in order to reach Chenthan Dzong as quickly as they could.

Alexander did not take part in the discussion, but began to study the matter. What would his father do in such a situation? Surely John Cold would find a way not only to get down the cliff but back up as well. His father had climbed steeper mountains than this, and had done it in midwinter, sometimes for pure sport and other times to help climbers who had met with an accident or become trapped. John was a cautious and methodical man, but no danger would stop him when it was a matter of saving a life.

"I think I can go down if I use my rappelling equipment," he said.

"How many feet is it?" Nadia asked, taking care not to look down.

"A lot. My rope won't reach that far, but there are several outcroppings, like ledges; we can stairstep the descent," Alex explained.

"It may be possible," Tensing replied, who had formulated his audacious plan after watching Alexander rescue Nadia from the ravine she'd fallen into.

"It's risky, but with luck I can do it; how, though, will we get these girls down? They have no experience in mountain climbing," said Alexander.

"Possibly we will think of a way to do it," the lama replied, and immediately asked for silence; it had been many hours since he had prayed.

While Tensing meditated, sitting on a rock facing the infinite heavens, Alexander measured his rope, counted his pitons, tested his harness, calculated his possibilities, and discussed the best way of carrying out this risky maneuver with the prince.

"If only we had a kite!" Dil Bahadur sighed.

He told his foreign friends that in the Kingdom of the Golden Dragon they practiced the ancient art of making silk kites in the form of birds with two sets of wings. Some were large and strong enough to carry a man standing between the wings. Tensing was an expert in that sport, and he had taught his disciple. The prince remembered his first flight a couple of years before, when during a visit to a monastery he had crossed between two mountains utilizing air currents that allowed him to steer his fragile craft while six monks held onto the end of the kite's long cord.

"You could die doing that," said Nadia.

"It isn't as difficult as it seems," the prince assured her.

"It must be like piloting a glider," Alexander commented.

"An airplane with wings of silk. I don't think I'd like to try that," Nadia said, thankful that there weren't any kites available.

Tensing prayed that the wind would be calm, for that would affect their attempt at a descent. He also prayed that the American boy had sufficient experience and determination, and that the others' courage would not falter.

"It's difficult to estimate the height from here, Master Tensing, but if my ropes will reach that narrow terrace you see down there, I can do it," Alexander assured him.

"And the girls?"

"I will lower them one by one."

"Except me," Nadia interrupted firmly.

"Nadia and I want to go with you and Dil Bahadur to the monastery," said Alexander.

"Who will take the girls on to the valley?" asked the lama.

"Perhaps the honorable master will allow me to do that," said Pema.

"Five girls? Alone?" interrupted Dil Bahadur.

"Why not?"

"That is your decision, Pema, no one else's," said Tensing, confident after observing the girl's golden aura.

"Possibly any of you can do it better than I can, but if the master authorizes me and will support me with his prayers, perhaps I can carry out my part with honor," the girl offered.

Dil Bahadur was pale. He had decided, with the unshakable certainty of first love, that Pema was the only woman in the world for him. The fact that he had never known others, and that his experience was zero, did not enter into his thoughts. He was afraid that Pema would fall to her death from the cliff, or, should she reach the bottom safe and sound, that she would get lost or encounter other dangers. There were tigers in that region, and he could not get the Sect of the Scorpion out of his mind.

"It's very dangerous," he said.

"Perhaps my disciple has decided to go with the girls?" asked Tensing.

"No, master, I must help you rescue the king," the prince murmured, lowering his eyes with embarrassment.

The lama led him aside, where the others couldn't hear.

"You must have faith in her. Her heart is as valiant as yours, Dil Bahadur. If it is your karma to be together, it will happen no matter what. If that is not to be, nothing you do can change the course of your life."

"I didn't say I wanted to spend my life with her, master!"

Tensing smiled. "Perhaps it is not necessary for you to say so."

Alexander decided to use the remaining daylight

hours in preparing for the next day. First of all, he had to be sure that with his two fifty-yard ropes he could make the descent. He spent half an hour explaining to the others the basic principles of rappelling, from how to wear the harness, which they would sit in as they went down, to techniques for releasing and stopping the rope. The second rope would be used as a safety line. He didn't need it, but it would be indispensable for the girls.

"Now I'm going down as far as that ledge, and once I'm there I'll measure the distance to the bottom of the cliff," he announced after he had secured his rope and put on the harness.

Everyone watched what he was doing with intense interest, except Nadia, who didn't dare look over the edge. To Tensing, who had spent his life climbing through the Himalayas like a mountain goat, Alexander's technology was engrossing. Amazed, he examined the strong, light rope, the metal carabiners, the belaying devices, the ingenious harness. He watched Alexander give a wave of his hand and drop into the void, sitting in his harness. Alex used his feet to kick away from the vertical rock face and his hands to let out the rope so that he slipped down ten to fifteen feet at a time, with no apparent effort. In fewer than five minutes he reached the lip of the ledge. From above he looked very small. For half an hour, he measured the distance to the bottom with the second rope, which he carried coiled at his waist. Then he climbed back up, not as easily as he'd gone down, but with no major difficulty. Back on top, he was greeted with applause and happy cheers.

"We can do it, Master Tensing, the ledge is wide and firm enough to hold all five girls and me. The rope reaches the bottom, and I think I can teach them to use the harness. But there is one problem," Alexander said.

"What is that?"

"I will need both ropes once I'm on the terrace, because they can't go down without a safety rope. One will be attached to the harness and the second to a piton I've driven into rock and left down there; that will help me ease the girls down. We really have to have that safety in case they lose control of the first rope, or if the system fails for some reason. Since they aren't experienced, they can't do it without that second rope."

"I understand that, but we *have* two ropes; what is the problem?"

"We'll use those getting down to the terrace. Then you will drop them so I can secure them there and lower the girls to the bottom. I can't climb back up if both ropes are on the terrace. And I can't scale that vertical wall without gear. An expert climber could do it, over a matter of hours, but I don't think I can. It means that we will have to have a third rope of some kind," Alexander explained.

"Or at least a cord that we can use to pull up one of the ropes from the terrace," added Dil Bahadur.

"Exactly."

They didn't have a hundred and fifty feet of cord. Their first thought, of course, was to cut narrow strips from the clothes they were wearing, but that would leave them too exposed to the cold and in danger of frostbite or death. The girls were wearing nothing but thin silk sarongs and short jackets. Tensing thought about the rolls of yak hair rope he kept in his hermitage, but that was far away and there wasn't time to get it.

By then the sun had gone down and the sky was beginning to turn an indigo blue.

"It's very late. Perhaps the hour has come for us to prepare to spend the night as comfortably as we can. Tomorrow we shall see what solution occurs to us," the lama said.

"This cord we need doesn't have to be terribly strong, does it?" asked Pema.

"No, but it must be long. All we need it for is to pull up one of the ropes," Alexander replied.

"Perhaps we can make one," she suggested.

"How? With what?"

"We all have very long hair. We can cut it and braid it."

An expression of absolute amazement lit every face. The other girls immediately began to stroke the long locks that hung to their waists. Scissors never touched the hair of women from the Forbidden Kingdom; it was considered their greatest attribute of beauty and femininity. Unmarried women wore their hair loose and perfumed it with musk and jasmine; married women bathed theirs in almond oil and braided it in elaborate hairdos they decorated with silver pins, turquoise, amber, and coral. Only female monks sacrificed their crowning glory and lived their lives with shaved heads.

"Possibly each of us can provide twenty strands. Multiplied by five, that's a hundred. Let's say that each length of hair is about twenty-four inches long; we will have over a hundred and fifty feet of hair. And possibly I can get twenty-four strands from my head, so even after it's braided we will have more than enough," Pema explained.

"I have hair too," Nadia offered.

"It's pretty short, I don't think it will work," Pema observed.

One of the girls burst into inconsolable tears. Cutting her hair was too great a sacrifice, she said. They couldn't ask her to do that. Pema sat down beside her and began gently persuading her that hair was less important than their lives and the safety of the king. After all, the hair would grow back.

"And while it's growing, how will I show my face in public?" the girl sobbed.

"With enormous pride, because you will have contributed to saving our country from the Sect of the Scorpion," Pema replied.

While the prince and Alexander looked for roots and dry animal droppings to build a small fire to keep them warm during the night, Tensing examined Nadia and adjusted her bandages. He was very satisfied; her shoulder was still bruised, but healed, and she felt no pain.

Pema used Alexander's knife to cut her hair. Dil Bahadur was so agitated that he couldn't watch. Pema's cutting of her hair seemed too intimate, almost painful. As the silky hair fell and the girl's long and fragile neck appeared, her beauty was transformed; she looked like a handsome youth.

"Now I can go out and beg like a monk," Pema joked, pointing to the prince's tunic she was wearing, and her head, where only a few clumps stood up among the stubble.

The other girls took the knife and began to cut each other's hair. Then they sat in a circle and braided a fine, gleaming black cord that smelled of musk and jasmine.

The group rested as well as they could in their small refuge among the rocks. In the Kingdom of the Golden Dragon there was never physical contact among people of different sexes, except among children and married couples, but that night it was necessary; it was cold, and they had no shelter other than the clothes on their backs and two yak hides. Tensing and Dil Bahadur had lived in the high mountains, and they tolerated the cold better than the others. They were also accustomed to privation, so they gave the yak hides and the larger portions of food to the girls. Although his stomach was growling with hunger, Alexander followed their lead; he did not want to be less gallant than the other men. He also shared a chocolate bar he found broken at the bottom of his backpack.

Since they had only a limited amount of fuel, they had to keep the fire very low, but even those weak flames offered a certain security. At least it would deter the tigers and snow leopards that lived in those hills. They heated water in a bowl and prepared tea with yak butter and salt, which helped them endure the rigors of the night.

They slept huddled together like cubs to give each other warmth, protected from the wind in their cleft in the mountainside. Dil Bahadur did not dare choose a place as close to Pema as he would have liked; he dreaded his master's teasing gaze. He realized that he hadn't told Pema that his father was the king and that he was not an ordinary monk. It seemed to him it wasn't the right moment for that; on the other hand, he felt that not to tell her was as bad as deceiving her. Alexander, Nadia, and Borobá formed a tight little knot and slept soundly until light began to appear on the horizon.

Tensing led the first prayer of the morning, and in chorus they all recited *Om mani padme hum* several times. They were not worshiping a deity, for Buddha was simply a human who had achieved illumination, that is, supreme comprehension. They were sending their prayers like beams of positive energy into infinite space, and to the spirit that reigns in all things. Alexander, who had grown up in a family of agnostics, marveled that in the Forbidden Kingdom even the most trivial things were suffused with a sense of the divine. Religion in that country was a way of life; every person cared for the Buddha carried within him or her. He was surprised to find himself reciting the sacred mantra with true enthusiasm.

The lama blessed the food and divided it as Nadia passed two bowls with hot tea.

"Possibly this will be a beautiful day, sunny and without wind," Tensing announced, studying the sky.

"Perhaps if the honorable master wishes, we could get started as soon as possible," Pema suggested. "The road to the valley will be a long one."

"I believe that, with a little luck, all of you will be down in less than an hour," said Alexander, checking his gear.

Shortly after, they began the descent. Alexander snapped on his equipment and in only a few minutes, light as a fly, he had lowered himself to the ledge halfway down the vertical wall of the rock face. Pema made it clear that she wanted to be the first to follow. Dil Bahadur took the rope, fit the harness around her, and once again explained the mechanism of the cara-biners.

"You must drop down in short spurts. If there's a problem, don't be afraid; I will hold you safe with the second rope until you get your rhythm, understand?" he asked.

"Perhaps it will be wise not to look down. We will support you with our thoughts," Tensing added, stepping back to concentrate on sending mental energy to Pema.

Dil Bahadur drove a piton into the rock and knotted on a rope he tied around his waist; he signaled Pema that he was ready. She walked to the edge of the precipice and smiled to veil the panic she was feeling.

"I hope we will see each other again," Dil Bahadur whispered, not daring to say anything more for fear of revealing the secret love that had been choking him from the first moment he saw her.

"I hope so, too. I will send my prayers to the heavens and make offerings for the king to be saved. Please be careful," she replied, moved.

Pema closed her eyes, commended her soul to heaven, and dropped into the void. She fell like a stone for several yards, until she could control the carabiner that tightened the rope. Once she got the feel of the mechanism and mastered the rhythm, she continued with more confidence. She used her legs to kick away from the rock and maintain her momentum. Dil Bahadur's tunic—which she was wearing—floated in the air, and from above she looked like a bat. Sooner than she expected, she heard Alexander's voice saying that she was almost there.

"Perfect!" he yelled, as he caught her.

"Is that it? It was over just when I was beginning to enjoy it," she replied.

The terrace was so narrow and exposed that a small wind could have affected her balance, but just as Tensing had predicted, the weather was cooperating. High on the cliff, they pulled up the harness and put it on another of the girls. She was terrified, and did not have Pema's character, but the lama fixed his hypnotic eyes on her and was able to calm her. One by one, they lowered the four girls without major problems, because every time one slipped or let go, Dil Bahadur held them with the safety rope. Once everyone was on the narrow lip of the ledge, it was difficult to move, and there was a substantial threat that one of them would fall off. Alexander had foreseen that difficulty, and the previous day had driven in pitons they could hold onto. They were ready to begin the second phase of the descent.

Dil Bahadur dropped down the ropes, and Alexander used them to repeat the operation from the ledge to the foot of the precipice. This time Pema had no one to catch her at the bottom, but she had gained confidence and started down with no hesitation. Her companions followed shortly after.

Alexander waved good-bye to them, wishing with all his heart that those four girls who looked so fragile dressed in their tattered festival saris and golden sandals, and led by another girl dressed in a monk's tunic, would quickly find the road to the nearest village. He watched them start down the mountainside toward the valley and grow smaller until they were tiny dots, then disappear. The Kingdom of the Golden Dragon had few roads, and many could not be traveled during the rainy season or winter snows, but at this time of year they would fare better. If the girls found a road, someone would give them a ride.

Alexander gave a sign, and Dil Bahadur picked up the long length of black braid, which had a stone tied on the end. After making sure where it would land, the prince dropped the braided hair onto the terrace and Alexander picked it up. He rolled one rope and secured it at his waist, then tied the second to the braid and

signaled them to pull it up. Dil Bahadur pulled carefully until he held the end of the rope in his hand. He
knotted that onto a piton, and Alexander began his
climb to the top.

CHAPTER SEVENTEEN

The Yeti Warriors

✸

ONCE THEY WERE ASSURED THAT Pema and the other
girls had started off in the direction of the valley, the
lama, the prince, Alexander, Nadia, and Borobá began
their trek up the mountain. The higher they climbed
the colder it got. Once or twice they had to use the
monks' long staffs to cross narrow crevasses. Those
improvised bridges were more secure than they seemed
at first glance. Alexander, who had practice in keeping
his balance because of his climbing with his father, was
not hesitant to step on the pole and jump to the other
side, where the steadying hand of Tensing was waiting.
But for Nadia the bridges were impossible, especially
after suffering the dislocated shoulder. Dil Bahadur
and Alexander stretched a rope tight between them,
one on each side of the fissure, while Tensing made the
jump with Nadia tucked under his arm like a precious
package. The idea was that the rope would give
Tensing a bit of security should he waver, but he was so
experienced that neither felt a tremor as he went

across: the monk's hand barely brushed the rope. Tensing's foot touched the staffs for only an instant, as if he were floating, and before Nadia could panic they were on the other side.

"Possibly I am in error, honorable master, but it seems to me that Chenthan Dzong does not lie in this direction," the prince hesitantly suggested a few hours later, when they stopped briefly to rest and brew some tea.

"If we took the usual route, it might, perhaps, take several days, and that would give the bandits the advantage," Tensing replied. "It perhaps is not a bad idea to take a shortcut."

"The Yetis' tunnel!" Dil Bahadur cried.

"I believe we will have need of a little help if we are to face the Sect of the Scorpion."

"My honorable master intends to ask the Yetis?

"Perhaps."

"With all respect, master, I believe that the Yetis have about as much of a brain as this monkey," the prince replied.

"In that case," Nadia interrupted, offended, "we'll be fine, because Borobá has as much of a brain as you do."

Alexander tried to follow the conversation and capture the images that were forming telepathically in his mind, but he could not be certain what they were talking about.

"Did I understand? You're talking about a Yeti? The Abominable Snowman?" he asked.

Tensing nodded.

"Professor Ludovic Leblanc searched for him for years in the Himalayas and concluded that he doesn't exist, that he's only a legend," said Alexander.

"Who is this professor?" Dil Bahadur wanted to know.

"My grandmother Kate's enemy."

"Perhaps he did not search where he should have," Tensing interjected.

The prospect of seeing a Yeti was as exciting to Nadia and Alexander as the extraordinary encounter with the Beasts in their marvelous golden city in the Amazon. Those prehistoric animals had also been compared to the Abominable Snowman because of the enormous tracks they left, as well as for their elusiveness. It had also been said of the Beasts that they were only of legend, but their existence has been proven.

"My grandmother will have a heart attack if she learns we saw a Yeti and didn't take photographs," Alexander sighed, remembering that he had put everything in his backpack but a camera.

No one spoke as they continued; each word cost them breath. Unaccustomed as they were to that altitude, Nadia and Alexander were suffering the lack of oxygen most. Their heads ached, they were light-headed, and by dusk both were at the limits of their strength. Soon Nadia had a nose bleed, and she bent over and vomited. Tensing decided they would stop where they were, and he began to look around for a protected spot. While Dil Bahadur prepared *tsampa* and boiled water for a medicinal tea, the lama eased Nadia's and Alexander's discomfort with his acupuncture needles.

"I believe that Pema and the other girls are safe by now. That means that soon General Myar Kunglung will know that the king is in the monastery," said Tensing.

"How do you know that, honorable master?" asked Alexander.

"Pema's mind is transmitting less anxiety. Her energy is different."

"I've heard of telepathy, master, but I never imagined it could function like a cell phone."

The lama smiled amiably. He didn't know what a cell phone was.

The young people tried to make themselves comfortable among the boulders while Tensing rested his body and mind; however, since these peaks were the land of the great white snow leopards, he kept watch with a sixth sense. That night seemed very long and very cold.

The next day the party reached the entrance of the long natural tunnel that led to the secret Valley of the Yetis. By then Nadia and Alexander were totally fatigued; their skin was burned by the sun reflecting off the snow, and their lips were dry and cracked. The tunnel was so narrow and the smell of sulfur so strong that Nadia thought they would suffocate, but for Alexander, who had wormed through the depths of the earth in the City of the Beasts, this was a walk in the park. Tensing, who was almost seven feet tall, could barely squeeze through some parts of the tunnel, but since he had come this way once before, he kept moving forward with assurance.

Nadia and Alexander were amazed when finally they emerged into the Valley of the Yetis. They had not been prepared to find a place bathed in warm mists buried deep within the frozen peaks of the Himalayas, a land where they saw vegetation unknown anywhere else in the world. Within a few minutes their bodies recovered the warmth they hadn't felt in days, and they were able to take off their parkas. Borobá, who had made the journey beneath Nadia's jacket, clinging tight to her and numb with cold, poked out his head; when he felt the warm air he recovered his habitual good humor: at last he was in his element.

If Nadia and Alexander had not been prepared for tall columns of steam, warm mists and pools of sulfurous waters, fleshy purple flowers and herds of *chegnos* grazing the dry valley's pastures, they were even less prepared for the Yetis when they appeared.

At a turn in the path, a horde of males armed with clubs blocked their way, yelling as if possessed by devils. Dil Bahadur took his bow in hand; he realized that since he was dressed in one of the bandit's clothing, the Yetis had no way of recognizing him. Instinctively, Nadia and Alexander, who had never imagined the Yetis would be so horrible-looking, stepped behind Tensing. He, in contrast, walked forward confidently and, placing his hands together before his face, bowed and greeted them with mental energy and with the few words he knew in their language.

Two or three eternal minutes passed before the Yetis' primitive brains recalled the lama's visit several months before. They were not actually friendly when they remembered, but at least they stopped waving their clubs a few inches from the visitors' heads.

"Where is Grr-ympr?" Tensing inquired.

Still growling, and never taking their eyes off them, the Yetis led the party to the village. Pleased, the lama noticed that things had changed; the warriors were filled with energy, and in the village he saw females and children who appeared to be healthy. He noticed that none had a purple tongue, and that the whitish hair that covered them from neck to foot was no longer matted with filth. Some females not only were more or less clean, but seemed in addition to have smoothed their coat, which intrigued him immeasurably, since he knew nothing of feminine wiles.

The village itself hadn't changed; it was still a warren of dens and underground caves beneath the crust of petrified lava that was the prevailing feature of the topography. A thin layer of soil lay on top of that crust, which, thanks to the warmth and moisture in the valley, was reasonably fertile and produced some food for the Yetis and their only domesticated animals, the *chegnos*. Once there, the Yetis led them straight to Grr-ympr.

The sorceress had aged visibly. When they had met her, she was already ancient, but now she seemed a thousand years old. If the other Yetis looked healthier and cleaner than before, she, in contrast, had become a bundle of rickety bones covered with a greasy hide; foul secretions trickled from her nose, eyes, and ears. The smell of filth and decay she emitted was so repugnant that not even Tensing, with his extensive medical training, could ignore it. The two communicated telepathically, occasionally throwing in the few words they shared.

"I see that your people are healthy, honorable Grrympr."

"Lavender-colored water: forbidden. He who drinks: beatings," she replied summarily.

"The remedy seems worse than the illness," Tensing said with a smile.

"Illness: no more," the aged woman confirmed, missing the monk's irony.

"I am happy. Have children been born?"

She indicated two on her fingers, and added in her language that they were healthy. Tensing had no difficulty understanding the images that formed in his mind.

"With you: who are they?" she grunted.

"You know this one; he is Dil Bahadur, the monk who discovered the poison in the lavender water of the spring. The others are also friends, and they come from very far, from another world."

"For what?"

"With all respect, honorable Grr-ympr, we came to ask your help. We need your warriors to rescue our king, who has been kidnapped by bandits. We are only three men and a girl, but with your warriors perhaps we can overcome them."

The ancient woman understood less than half of that speech, but she knew that the monk had come to collect the favor she owed him. He wanted her warriors. There would be a battle. She did not like the idea, primarily because for decades she had been trying to keep the tremendous aggressiveness of the Yetis under control.

"Warriors fight; warriors die. Village without warriors; village die, too," she summarized.

"You are right. What I ask is a very great favor, honorable Grr-ympr. Possibly there will be a dangerous battle. I cannot guarantee the safety of your warriors."

"Grr-ympr, dying," the woman muttered, striking her chest.

"I know that, Grr-ympr," said Tensing.

"Grr-ympr dead: many problems. You cure Grr-ympr: you take warriors," she offered.

"I cannot cure old age, honorable Grr-ympr. Your time in this world has come to an end; your body is tired and your spirit wants to go. There is nothing bad in that," the monk explained.

"Then no warriors," she decided.

"Why are you afraid to die, honorable elder?"

"Grr-ympr: needed. Grr-ympr commands: Yetis obey. Grr-ympr dead: Yetis fight. Yetis kill, Yetis die: end," she concluded.

"I understand. You cannot leave this world because you fear that your people will suffer. Is there no one to take your place?"

Sadly, she shook her head. Tensing realized that the sorceress was afraid that at her death the Yetis, who now were healthy and energetic, would go back to killing one another as they had before, until they disappeared forever from the face of the earth. Those semi-human creatures had depended on the strength and wisdom of their leader for several generations; she was a severe, just, and wise mother. They obeyed her blindly, because they believed she was gifted with supernatural powers; without her, the tribe would be set adrift. The lama closed his eyes and for several minutes both of them sat with their minds blank. When Tensing opened his eyes again, he announced his plan aloud, so that Nadia and Alexander would understand it.

"If you lend me some of your warriors, I promise that I will come back to the Valley of the Yetis and stay here for six years. Very humbly, I offer to take your place, honorable Grr-ympr, so that you may go to the world of the spirits in peace. I will look after your people; I will teach them to live as well as possible, not to kill one another, and to use the resources of the valley. I will train the most capable one among them so that at the end of six years you will have a chieftain or chieftainess of the tribe. This is what I offer you."

When he heard those words, Dil Bahadur jumped to his feet and stood before his master, pale with horror, but the lama stopped him with a gesture; he could not lose mental communication with the ancient woman. It was several minutes before Grr-ympr absorbed what the monk was saying.

"Yes," she accepted with a deep sigh of relief; at last she was free to die.

As soon as they had a moment of privacy, Dil Bahadur, his eyes filled with tears, asked his beloved master for an explanation. How could he have offered such a thing to the sorceress? he wailed. The Kingdom of the Golden Dragon needed him much more than the Yetis did; his own education was not complete, and the master should not abandon him in that manner.

"Possibly you will be king before it was planned, Dil Bahadur. Six years go by quickly. In that amount of time perhaps I will be able to help the Yetis."

"And me?" cried the youth, unable to imagine his life without his mentor.

"Possibly you are stronger and better prepared than you believe. After six years I plan to leave the Valley of the Yetis to begin the education of your child, the future ruler of the Kingdom of the Golden Dragon."

"What child, master? I have no child."

"The child you will have with Pema," Tensing replied calmly, as the prince blushed to the tips of his ears.

Nadia and Alexander followed the discussion with some difficulty but they captured the sense of it, and neither of them showed any surprise regarding Tensing's prophecy about Pema and Dil Bahadur, or about his plan to become the Yetis' mentor. Alexander was amused to think how a year ago he would have qualified everything that was happening as madness, but now he knew how mysterious the world is.

Through telepathy, the few words he had learned of the tongue of the Forbidden Kingdom, the words Dil

Bahadur had acquired in English, and Nadia's incredible gift for languages, Alexander managed to communicate to his friends that his grandmother had once written an article for *International Geographic* on a kind of puma in Florida that was destined for extinction. It was confined to a small, inaccessible area, and because when it bred it had always reproduced within the same family group, it had grown weak and unsocial. The best guarantee for any species is diversity. He explained that if, for example, there was only one strain of corn, soon pests and changes in climate would destroy it, but when there are hundreds of varieties, if one dies, others live. Diversity guarantees survival.

"What happened to the puma?" Nadia asked.

"They brought experts to Florida who introduced similar cats into their habitat. They interbred and in less than ten years the species was renewed."

"Do you think that's what's happening with the Yetis?" Dil Bahadur asked.

"Yes. They've lived for so long in isolation; there are very few of them, they breed among themselves, and that's why they're still weak."

Tensing sat thinking about what the foreign youth had said. Whatever happened, even though the Yetis left the valley, they would not find anyone to interbreed with; there were no others of their species in the world, and no human would be willing to mate with them. Sooner or later, however, they would have to be exposed to the outside world, it was inevitable, and it would have to be done with great care, otherwise the encounter with humans could be fatal to both. Only in the protected surroundings of the Forbidden Kingdom might that be accomplished.

During the next few hours the party ate and rested briefly to nourish their depleted bodies. When they heard that there would be a battle, all the Yetis wanted to go, but Grr-ympr would not allow that, she did not want to leave the village unprotected. Tensing warned them that they might die, because they were going to meet some evil humans called Blue Warriors, who were very strong and who had daggers and firearms. The Yetis did not know what those things were, and Tensing explained using the most extreme terms he could, describing the kind of wound the weapons produced, the streams of blood, and other gruesome details to excite the Yetis. That doubled the frustration of those who were going to stay in the valley; none of them wanted to miss the opportunity to have fun fighting against humans. One by one they passed before the lama, leaping and uttering harrowing yells and showing off their teeth and muscles to impress him. From them, Tensing chose the ten who had the worst characters and reddest auras.

The lama personally checked the Yetis' leather shields, which might deflect the thrust of a dagger but would be ineffective against a bullet. Those ten creatures, only slightly more intelligent than a chimpanzee, would not be able to outfight the men of the scorpion sect, no matter how fierce they were, but the lama was counting on the element of surprise. The Blue Warriors were superstitious, and although they had heard of the Abominable Snowman, they had never seen one.

That afternoon, by Grr-ympr's orders, a pair of *cheg-nos* had been slaughtered in honor of the visitors. With great repugnance, because they could not conceive of sacrificing any living creature, Dil Bahadur and Tensing collected the animals' blood and smeared the hairy coats of the chosen warriors with it. Using the horns, the longest bones, and strips of the hide, they constructed terrifying, blood-covered helmets, which the Yetis donned with shrieks of pleasure while females and children leaped about with admiration. The master and his disciple concluded with satisfaction that the Yetis looked frightening enough to intimidate the bravest opponent.

Alexander did not want to expose Nadia to the dangers that awaited them; the other men agreed, so they planned to have Nadia stay in the Yetis' village. It was pointless to try to convince her of that, however, and finally they had to agree to let her come with them.

"We may none of us come out alive, Eagle," he argued.

"In that case, I would have to spend the rest of my life in this valley, with no companions but the Yetis. No, thanks. I'll go with the rest of you, Jaguar," she replied.

"At least here you would be relatively safe. I don't know what we're going to find in that abandoned monastery, but I'm sure it won't be pleasant."

"Don't treat me like a child. I know how to take care of myself, I've done it for thirteen years. Besides, I think I can help."

"All right," Alex conceded, "but I want you to do exactly what I say."

"Not a chance. I'll help any way I can," Nadia replied. "You aren't an expert; you know as little about fighting as I do." Alex had to admit that she wasn't far off the mark.

"Perhaps it will be best to leave by night; that way we will reach the other end of the tunnel at dawn, and can use the morning hours to get to Chenthan Dzong," Dil Bahadur proposed, and Tensing agreed with his plan.

After filling their bellies with a generous meal, the Yetis all lay down and started to snore—without removing the new helmets they had adopted as a symbol of bravery. Nadia and Alexander were so hungry that they wolfed down their ration of roasted *chegno* despite the bitter taste and bits of singed hair. Tensing and Dil Bahadur prepared their *tsampa* and tea, then sat to meditate facing the enormity of the firmament, whose stars they could not see, because by night, when the temperature fell in the mountains, the mists from the fumaroles turned into a thick fog that covered the valley like a cottony mantle. The Yetis had never seen stars, and for them the moon was an inexplicable halo of blue light that sometimes shone through the mists.

The Fortified Monastery

✦

TEX ARMADILLO PREFERRED THE original plan for getting out of Tunkhala with the king and the Golden Dragon: a helicopter outfitted with a machine gun, which would land in the palace gardens at a specified moment. No one would have been able to stop them. The air force of that country consisted of four antiquated planes acquired from Germany more than twenty years before and flown only on New Year's Day to drop paper birds over the capital, to the delight of the children. It would have taken several hours to get them ready to give chase, and by then the helicopter would have had more than enough time to reach safe haven. The Specialist, however, had changed the plan at the last moment, without explanation. The message had said that it was not in their best interests to attract attention, and even less to machine-gun the peaceful inhabitants of the Forbidden Kingdom; that would provoke an international scandal. Their client, the Collector, demanded discretion.

Armadillo had no choice but to accept the second plan, which was, in his opinion, much riskier than the first. As soon as he captured the king in the Sacred Chamber, Armadillo had taped his mouth and given him an injection that anaesthetized him within five seconds. The instructions were not to harm him; the monarch had to be alive and uninjured when he reached the monastery so they could extract the information they needed if they were to decipher the statue's messages.

"Be cautious. The king is trained in martial arts, he can defend himself. I warn you, though, that if you hurt him you will pay for it dearly," the Specialist had said.

Tex Armadillo was beginning to lose patience with his boss but he didn't have time to state his misgivings.

The four bandits were frightened and impatient, though that didn't stop them from stealing some of the gold candelabra and incense burners. They were starting to pry the precious metal from the walls with their daggers when the American barked his orders.

Two of them took the inert king by the shoulders and ankles, while the others lifted the heavy gold statue from the pedestal of black stone where it had stood for eighteen centuries. The reverberation of the dragon's chants and bizarre noises still echoed in the room. Tex

Armadillo did not pause to examine the statue, but he assumed that it functioned as some kind of musical instrument. He didn't believe it could predict the future; that was a myth concocted for the ignorant, but it didn't really matter: the intrinsic value of the object could not be measured. How much would the Specialist make from this mission? Many millions, he was sure. And what would his share be? Barely a tip by comparison.

Two of the Blue Warriors strapped some cinches from their horses under the statue. As they struggled to lift it, Armadillo realized why the Specialist had told him to bring six men. Now he badly needed the two he had lost in traps in the palace.

Even knowing the way and how to skirt the obstacles did not make their return easier; the king and the statue slowed them down greatly. They soon realized, however, that, taken in reverse order, the traps were not being activated. That afforded them some relief, but they didn't linger or lower their guard; they feared that this palace held further disagreeable surprises. They reached the Magnificent Door without incident. There they saw the bodies of the two guards they had attacked, just as they had left them. No one noticed that one of the young soldiers was still breathing.

Using the GPS, the robbers made their way through the labyrinth of rooms and doors and finally emerged into the dark garden of the palace. The rest of the band was waiting, along with Judit Kinski, whom they held prisoner. They had followed orders and did not drug or mistreat her. The bandits, who had never seen the woman before, did not understand the purpose of taking her with them, and Armadillo did not offer any explanation.

The men had commandeered a truck from the palace, which was parked outside, beside the Blue Warriors' horses. Tex Armadillo avoided looking Judit in the eye. She was quite calm, given the circumstances; he motioned to his men to put her in the truck bed along with the king and the statue, and cover them all with a tarp. He got behind the wheel—no one else here knew how to drive—and the leader of the Blue Warriors and one of his men joined him in the cab. As the truck headed toward the narrow mountain road, the remaining men scattered. They would meet later at a spot in the Forest of the Tigers, again following the orders of the Specialist, and from there they would begin the trek toward Chenthan Dzong.

As they expected, the truck was stopped as they left Tunkhala, where General Myar Kunglung had posted sentries to control the road. It was child's play for Tex Armadillo and the bandits to overpower the three men who were standing guard, and to take their uniforms. The trunk was painted with the emblems of the royal house, and in the sentries' garb they passed the remaining road blocks without being stopped, heading toward the Forest of the Tigers.

The enormous woods had originally been the royal hunting estate, but it had been several centuries since anyone had devoted himself to that cruel sport. The huge park had been turned into a nature preserve where the rarest species of plants and animals in the Forbidden Kingdom flourished, and tigresses went there in the spring to drop their cubs. The unique climate of that country, which, according to season, ranged from the temperate humidity of the tropics to the winter cold of high mountain regions, encouraged the growth of extraordinary flora and fauna, a true ecological paradise. The beauty of the surroundings, with its thousand-year-old trees, crystal-clear streams, orchids, rhododendrons, and brightly colored birds, had absolutely no effect on Tex Armadillo or on the bandits. The one thing that mattered to them was not to run into any tigers and to get out of there as quickly as possible.

The American untied Judit Kinski.

"What are you doing?" yelled the head bandit threateningly.

Without a word, the woman rubbed her wrists and ankles where the rope had rubbed raw red marks. Her eyes were studying the place, following every movement of her kidnappers, and always returning to Armadillo, who studiously avoided meeting her eyes, as if he couldn't take the force of her gaze. Without asking permission, Judit walked to where the king lay and delicately, taking care not to strip the skin from his lips, removed the adhesive gag. She bent over him and listened to his chest.

"The effect of the injection will wear off soon," Armadillo commented.

"Don't give him any more, his heart could stop," she said in a tone that seemed more like a command than a plea, fixing her chestnut-colored eyes on Armadillo.

"It won't be necessary. We just have to get him on a horse," he replied, turning his back to her.

As the first rays of the sun filtered through the trees, the light turned as golden as honey, waking the monkeys and birds that erupted in a noisy chorus. The night dew evaporated from the ground, wrapping the landscape in a yellow fog that blurred the outlines of the gigantic trees. A pair of pandas rocked lazily in the branches above their heads. The sun was completely up by the time all the band of the scorpion sect had gathered. With the full light, Armadillo shot a number of Polaroid photos of the statue, then gave the order to wrap it in the tarp they had used in the truck and tie it up with rope.

Now they would have to abandon the vehicle and continue up the mountain on horseback, following overgrown trails that no one had used since the earthquake had changed the local topography, and Chenthan Dzong, as well as other monasteries in that region, had been abandoned. The Blue Warriors, who spent their lives on horseback and were comfortable in every kind of terrain, would have the least difficulty getting there. They knew mountains well, and they also knew that once they collected their reward in money and weapons they could reach the northern border with India in three or four days. As for Armadillo, he had the helicopter, which was to pick him up at the monastery with his prize.

The king had regained consciousness, but was still under the effect of the drug; he was confused and dizzy, with no idea of what had happened. Judit helped him sit up, and explained that they had been kidnapped and that the bandits had stolen the Golden Dragon. She took a small flask from her purse, which, miraculously, she hadn't lost in the confusion, and gave him a sip of whisky. The liquor brought him to his senses, and he was able to get to his feet.

"What does this mean?" the king exclaimed in a tone of authority that no one had heard before.

When he saw that they were loading the statue onto a metal, wheeled platform to be pulled by horses, he realized the magnitude of the disaster.

"This is a sacrilege. The Golden Dragon is the symbol of our country. There is a very ancient curse that will fall upon the person who profanes the statue," the king warned them.

The leader of the bandits raised a fist to quiet the king, but the American pushed him away.

"Shut up and obey, if you don't want more problems," Armadillo ordered.

"Release Miss Kinski," the king replied firmly. "She's a foreigner, she doesn't play any part in this matter."

"You heard me, shut up or she'll pay the consequences, do you understand?" Armadillo warned him.

Judit took the king's arm and whispered please to be calm, there was nothing they could do for the moment and it would be better to wait for their chance to act.

"Come on, let's not waste any more time," the spokesman for the bandits said.

"The king isn't up to riding yet," Judit said when she saw him stagger like a drunk.

"He will ride with one of my men until he can look after himself," the American decided.

Armadillo drove the truck into a hollow, where it was half-hidden, then covered it with branches. As soon as that was done, they began their trek, single file, up the mountain. The day was clear, but the peaks of the Himalayas were lost in patches of clouds. They would have to climb continually, passing through a region lush with bananas, rhododendrons, magnolias, hibiscuses, and many other semitropical species. Higher up, the landscape changed abruptly; the forest disappeared and they would encounter dangerous precipices and often be blocked by huge boulders that had rolled from the peaks, or waterfalls that turned the ground into a slippery mud pit. The ascent was risky, but the American had confidence in the skill of the Blue Warriors and the great strength of their mounts. Once they were in the mountains, no one could catch up with them, because no one would have any idea where to look for them and, in any case, they would be too far ahead of everyone else.

· · ·

Armadillo did not suspect that while he was stealing the statue in the palace, the bandits' cave had been dismantled, and its occupants, hungry and thirsty, bound two by two, lay terrified that a tiger would catch their scent and finish them off for dinner. The prisoners were lucky, because before the big cats—so plentiful in this region—found them, a dispatch of royal soldiers had arrived, sent by the general after Pema had told him the location of the camp.

Pema and her exhausted companions had come upon a rural road where finally they met a farmer who was taking his produce to market in a horse-drawn cart. First, because of their close-cropped heads, he had thought the girls were nuns, but then he noticed that all of them except one were dressed for a festival. The man had no access to newspapers or television, but, like everyone in the country, he had heard over the radio that six young people had been kidnapped. He hadn't seen their photographs, and had no way of recognizing them, but one look was enough for him to realize that these girls were in trouble. Pema had planted herself with outstretched arms in the middle of the road, forcing him to stop, and in a few words had summed up their situation.

"The king is in danger; I must get help immediately," she concluded.

The farmer turned around and, urging his horse to a fast trot, took them to the small village he'd just left. There they found a telephone, and while Pema tried to communicate with the authorities, the women of the village began tending to her companions. The girls, who had shown great courage during those terrible days, broke down and cried when they knew they were safe, begging to be taken to their families as soon as possible. Pema was not thinking about her family, however; her concern was for Dil Bahadur and the king.

General Myar Kunglung took the call as soon as he was notified of what had happened, and spoke directly with Pema. She repeated what she knew but refrained from mentioning the Golden Dragon: first, because she wasn't sure the bandits had actually stolen it, and second, because she knew instinctively that if that were the case it would be better if no one knew. The statue represented the soul of the nation. She did not want to spread what might be a false alarm, she decided.

Myar Kunglung sent instructions to the nearest guard post to pick up the girls from the village and bring them to the capital. With Wandgi and Kate Cold by his side, he himself met them halfway. When Pema saw her father, she leaped from the Jeep and ran to hug him. The poor man was sobbing like a baby.

"What did they do to you?" cried Wandgi, looking Pema over from head to toe.

"Nothing, Papa, nothing happened, I promise. But that isn't important now, we must rescue the king, who is in danger of his life."

"That is something for the army, not you. You will come home with me!"

"I can't, Papa. It is my duty to go to Chenthan Dzong!"

"And why is that?"

"Because I promised Dil Bahadur," she replied, blushing.

Myar Kunglung studied the girl with his eagle-sharp eyes and he must have seen something in the color of her cheeks and the tremor of her lips, because he bowed deeply before the guide, hands before his face.

"Perhaps honorable Wandgi will allow his courageous daughter to accompany this humble general?" he asked. "She will have good guard by my soldiers."

The guide realized that despite the bow and humble

346 · *Isabel Allende*

tone, the general would not accept no for an answer. He would have to allow Pema to go with him, and pray to heaven that she would return safe and sound.

The good news that the girls had escaped the grasp of their kidnappers flew through the country. In the Forbidden Kingdom, word spread from mouth to mouth so quickly that when four of the girls, their bare heads covered with silk scarves, appeared on television to tell of their experience, everyone already knew about it. People ran outside to celebrate. They took branches of magnolias to the girls' families and gathered in temples to make offerings of thanks. Prayer wheels and banners carried their elation to the skies.

The one person who had nothing to celebrate was Kate Cold, who was on the verge of a nervous collapse because Nadia and Alexander had not as yet been accounted for. She was still trailing Myar Kunglung. On horseback, Pema and she were on their way toward Chenthan Dzong at the head of a detachment of soldiers, following a road that snaked up toward the heights. When Pema told them what she had heard about the Golden Dragon from the mouths of the bandits, the general had confirmed her suspicions.

"One man guard at Forbidden Door lived past his wounds; he saw bandits take away honorable, beloved king and dragon. Must be secret, Pema. You were good, did well, not to say on telephone. Statue is valued at fortune. All know that, but who can tell me why the king was took?" he said.

"Master Tensing, his disciple, and two young foreigners were going straight to the monastery," Pema informed the general. "They started many hours ahead of us. Possibly they will get there before we do."

"That may not have been the wisest thing to do, Pema. Oh, my. If something happens with our prince Dil Bahadur, who will move up to throne?" the general sighed.

"Prince? What prince?" Pema interrupted.

"Dil Bahadur is heir to the throne, that you did not know, girl?"

"No one told me that. At any rate, nothing will happen to the prince," she stated, but she knew immediately that she had been discourteous, and corrected herself. "That is, possibly the karma of the honorable prince will be to rescue our beloved sovereign and emerge unharmed."

"Perhaps." The general nodded, preoccupied.

"Can't you send planes to the monastery?" Kate queried, impatient with this war being waged on horseback, as if they'd regressed several centuries in time.

"Is nowhere to land. Perhaps a helicopter could do it, only expert pilot could do such flying. Where he lands is funnel of air currents," the general explained.

"Possibly the honorable general agrees with me that at least it must be tried," begged Pema, with the glint of tears in her eyes.

"We know only one pilot who is good enough, can do job. He lives in Nepal. He is a *big* hero, he flew a helicopter up Everest mountain to rescue lost climbers."

"I remember that. The man is famous, we interviewed him for *International Geographic*," Kate commented.

"Is possible we can reach him. Maybe in next few hours. Ask him to come here," said the general.

Myar Kunglung had no way of knowing that that pilot had been hired much earlier by the Specialist, and that this very day he was flying from Nepal to the mountains of the Forbidden Kingdom.

Tensing, Dil Bahadur, Alexander, Nadia with Borobá on her shoulder, and the ten Yeti warriors were approaching the steep cliff topped by the ancient stone ruins of Chenthan Dzong. Excited, growling, the Yetis were pushing and shoving each other and exchanging friendly nips, joyously readying themselves for the thrill of battle. For many years they had waited for an opportunity to really let themselves go, and now the time had come. Tensing had to pause from time to time to calm them.

"Master," Dil Bahadur whispered to Tensing. "I think that finally I remember where I had heard the Yeti language before: in the four monasteries where I was taught the code for the Golden Dragon."

"Perhaps my disciple also recalls that in our visit to the Valley of the Yetis I told him that there was an important reason for our being there," the lama replied in the same tone.

"Something to do with the Yeti language?"

"Possibly . . ."

The view was breathtaking. They were surrounded by incomparable beauty: snowy peaks, enormous rocks, waterfalls, ravines sliced into the mountainside, corridors of ice. Seeing that landscape, Alexander Cold understood why the citizens of the Forbidden Kingdom believed that the highest peak in their land, some twenty-one thousand feet high, was the world of the gods. The young American felt as if he were filled with light and pure air, that something had opened in his mind, that minute by minute he was changing, maturing, growing. He would be very sad to leave this country and return to so-called civilization.

Tensing interrupted Alex's musings to explain that the *dzongs*, or fortified monasteries, which existed only in Bhutan and the Kingdom of the Golden Dragon, were a blend of convent for monks and bunker for soldiers. They stood at the confluence of rivers, and in valleys, to protect nearby towns. They were constructed without plans or nails, always following the same design. The royal palace in Tunkhala was originally a *dzong*, until the needs of government forced it to be enlarged and modernized and turned into a labyrinth of a thousand rooms.

Chenthan was an exception. It rose from a natural terrace so sheer that it was difficult to imagine how the materials were brought there to build it, or how it had withstood winter storms and avalanches for centuries, until it was destroyed by the earthquake. Narrow steps had been cut into the rock, but the monks had so little contact with the rest of the world that it had seldom been used. That path, practically carved from the mountain, was interrupted from time to time by fragile rope and wooden bridges strung across crevasses. The route had not been used since the earthquake, and the bridges were in very poor repair, with the wood rotted and half the rope eaten through, but Tensing and his group could not stop to consider the danger; there were no alternatives. The Yetis crossed them with complete confidence; they had come this way before in their brief excursions outside their valley to look for food. When the party saw a body lying in the depths of a ravine, they knew that Tex Armadillo and his crew had been here before them.

"The bridge isn't safe, that man fell," Alexander said, pointing.

"His horse isn't down there. Maybe he didn't fall from the bridge, maybe he was pushed," Dil Bahadur suggested.

"Why would they be killing each other? That doesn't make sense," Alexander replied.

"Possibly there was an argument, and maybe that man disobeyed the leader," Dil Bahadur ventured.

"We don't have time to find out. We have to get across," Nadia interrupted.

"If the bandits made it on horseback, and maybe even dragging that heavy Golden Dragon, then we can do it, too," Dil Bahadur pointed out.

"That may have weakened the bridge even more. Perhaps it would not be unwise to test it before we start," Tensing determined.

The chasm was not very wide, but neither was it narrow enough to use Tensing's and the prince's wood staffs. Nadia suggested that they could tie a rope to Borobá and send him to test the bridge, but the monkey was very light, so there was no guarantee that if he crossed others could do it, too. Dil Bahadur scanned the terrain and saw that by luck there was a stout root on the other side. Alexander tied one end of his rope to an arrow and the prince shot it with his usual precision, driving it firmly into the root. Alexander tied the other rope to his waist and, steadied by Tensing, slowly ventured onto the bridge, carefully testing every bit of wood before he put his weight on it.

If the bridge gave way, the first rope would hold him briefly. They didn't know whether the arrow would hold, but if not, the second rope would keep Alexander from dropping into the void; however, he could still splatter like an insect against the sidewall of the chasm. He hoped that his experience as a climber would help.

Very gingerly, Alexander started across. He had made it halfway when two planks split and he slipped. A scream from Nadia echoed among the peaks. For a minute or two, no one moved, until the swaying of the bridge stopped and Alex regained his balance. Very slowly he pulled out the leg that was hanging through the broken boards, then lay back and, using the first rope, got back on his feet. He was debating whether to go forward or return when he was startled by a strange noise, as if the mountain were snoring. They first suspected one of the tremors so common in that region, but then they saw the stones and snow rumbling down from the peak. Nadia's scream had triggered a land-slide.

Helpless, the friends and the Yetis watched the deadly river of rock hurtle toward Alexander and the delicate bridge. There was nothing he could do, it was impossible to go forward or back.

Automatically, Tensing and Dil Bahadur concentrated on sending their energy to Alex. In different circumstances, Tensing would have attempted the ultimate test of a *tulku*—a reincarnation of a great lama—he would have altered the will of nature. In moments of true necessity, certain *tulkus* could halt the wind, change the course of storms, stop floods in times of rain, and prevent ice storms, but Tensing had never needed to do that. It was not something that could be practiced, like astral journeys. At that moment, it was too late to try to change the path of the avalanche and save the American boy. Tensing used his mental powers to transmit the enormous strength of his own body to Alexander.

Alexander heard the roar of the stones and saw the cloud of snow it raised before it blinded him. He knew he was going to die, and the rush of adrenaline was like a huge charge of electricity, erasing all thought from his mind and leaving him at the mercy of instinct alone. He was filled with supernatural energy, and, in a thousandth of a second, he was transformed into the black jaguar of the Amazon. With a terrible roar and a formidable leap, he sprang to the far side of the precipice, landing on four cat paws as stone rattled behind him.

His friends did not know he had been miraculously saved; snow and dust from the cliffs masked their view. No one saw him, except Nadia, until the landslide settled. In the instant death threatened, when she believed that Alexander was lost, she had a similar reaction, the same charge of powerful energy, the same fantastic transformation. Borobá was left behind on the ground as she rose into the skies, converted into the white eagle. And from the height of her elegant flight she could see the black jaguar, its claws digging into terra firma.

As soon as the immediate danger had passed,

Alexander returned to his usual form. The one sign of his magical experience were his bleeding fingers and the expression on his face: lips drawn back and teeth exposed in a ferocious grimace. He also sensed the strong jaguar scent on his skin, the smell of a carnivorous beast.

The landslide had carried off a section of the narrow path and destroyed most of the wood of the bridge, but both the old ropes and Alexander's were intact. That was what allowed them to continue—after Alex had tied his rope tightly on one side, and Tensing secured the second on the other. The Yetis were agile as monkeys, and accustomed to the terrain, so they had no difficulty in swinging across. Dil Bahadur reasoned that if he'd learned to use a staff as a bridge, he could manage a tightrope, as his master did with such grace. Tensing didn't need to carry Nadia, only Borobá, since the eagle was still circling above their heads. Alexander wondered why Nadia hadn't been transformed into her totemic animal when she dislocated her shoulder and instead had to send a mental projection in search of help. The lama explained that pain and exhaustion had held her in her physical form.

It was the great white eagle that informed them that Chenthan Dzong lay just a few meters ahead, around a turn. The mounts tethered outside betrayed the presence of the bandits, but Nadia didn't see anyone standing guard; it was obvious that they weren't expecting visitors. She counted nineteen horses, and they were again amazed at the animals' ability to move about in the mountains. They now had an idea of the number of horsemen, since they assumed that none of the bandits had come on foot.

Tensing received the eagle's telepathic message, and gathered his party to plot the best course of action. The Yetis had no concept of strategy; their way of fighting was simply to charge, swinging their clubs and yelling like demons, a tactic that could be very effective if they weren't welcomed with a salvo of bullets. First they would have to find out exactly how many men were in the monastery and where they were located, how many weapons they had, and where they were holding the king and the Golden Dragon.

Suddenly Nadia was back among them, so naturally that it was as if she had never flown as a great eagle high above them. No one commented.

"If my honorable master will permit it, I will go ahead," Dil Bahadur requested.

"That, perhaps, is not the best plan. You are the future king. If anything happens to your father, the nation has only you to count on," the lama replied.

"If the honorable master will permit it, I will go," said Alexander.

"If the honorable master will permit it," Nadia interrupted, "I think I am the best person to go, because I have the power of invisibility."

"No way!" Alexander cried.

"Why? Don't you trust me, Jaguar?"

"It's too dangerous."

"It's no more dangerous for me than it is for you. There's no difference."

"Possibly our girl-eagle is right. We offer the talents we have," Tensing replied. "In this case it will be an enormous advantage to be invisible. You, Alexander, great jaguar heart, you must fight alongside Dil Bahadur. The Yetis will come with me. I fear that I am the only one here who can communicate with them and control them. Once they learn that we are near the enemies, they will go wild."

"Now is when we need modern technology. A walkie-talkie would really come in handy. How will Eagle tell us when we can attack?" Alexander asked.

"Possibly in the same way we are communicating now," Tensing suggested, and Alex burst out laughing; he realized that for quite some time they had been exchanging ideas without speaking.

"Try not to be frightened, Nadia," the prince advised, "because that will jumble thoughts. Do not doubt the method, because that, too, will interfere with reception. Concentrate on one image at a time."

"Don't worry, telepathy is like talking with your heart," she soothed him.

"Our one advantage, possibly, is surprise," the lama reassured them.

"If the honorable master will permit a suggestion, I think that possibly it would be more effective to be more direct when you're speaking to the Yetis," Alexander said sarcastically, imitating the educated manner of speaking in the Forbidden Kingdom.

"Perhaps the young foreigner should have a little more faith in my master," Dil Bahadur interjected as he tested the tension of his bow and counted his arrows.

"Good luck," said Nadia, quickly kissing Alexander's cheek.

She set Borobá down, and he ran and jumped up on Alexander, holding tight to his ears as he had in his mistress's absence.

At that moment, a noise that sounded like the avalanche froze everyone in place. Only the Yetis understood immediately that this was something different, something terrifying that they had never heard before. They threw themselves flat on the ground and hid their heads in their arms, trembling, their clubs forgotten and all their ferocity replaced with the whimpering of frightened pups.

"It sounds like a helicopter," said Alexander, signaling that they should take cover among the shadows and rock crevices so they wouldn't be seen from the air.

"What is a helicopter?" the prince asked.

"Something like an airplane. And an airplane is like a huge kite with a motor," Alex added, amazed that in the twenty-first century there were people still living as if in the Middle Ages.

"I know what an airplane is, I've seen them go by every week on the route to Tunkhala," said Dil Bahadur, not offended by his new friend's tone.

A metal craft appeared in the sky beyond the ruins of the monastery. Tensing tried to calm the Yetis but there was no room in the minds of those creatures to absorb the idea of a flying machine.

"It is a bird that obeys orders. We do not have to be afraid of it, we are fiercer than it is," the lama told them finally, thinking that was something they could understand.

"This means there is a place where the 'copter can

land. Now I know why they took the trouble to come here, and how they intend to get out of the country with the statue," Alexander concluded.

"Let's attack before they get away—that is, if my honorable master thinks it wise," the prince proposed.

Tensing made a sign that they should wait. Almost an hour passed before the helicopter landed. They couldn't see the maneuvers from where they were, but they imagined it must be very complicated, because the pilot made a number of attempts, only to gain altitude, turn, and descend again. Finally the noise of the motor was stilled. In the pristine silence of those peaks they heard human voices close by, and assumed it was the bandits. When the voices faded, Tensing decided the time had come to move closer.

Nadia concentrated on becoming as transparent as air, and started toward the monastery. Alexander was trembling with worry for her; his heart was beating so loudly that he was afraid that three hundred feet ahead their enemies could hear it.

CHAPTER NINETEEN

IN THE MONASTERY OF CHENTHAN Dzong the last part of the Specialist's plan was being set into motion. When the helicopter finally landed in the small, snow-covered area leveled by an avalanche, it was welcomed with cheers; it was a truly remarkable feat. Tex Armadillo, as instructed by his boss, had marked the site with an X traced with strawberry Kool-Aid powder. From the air the cross looked the size of a quarter, as the pilot flew closer it was clearly visible. In addition to the small size of the landing field, which demanded all the pilot's skill to keep the giant blades from clipping the side of the mountain, that master airman also had to contend with air currents. The peaks formed a kind of funnel in which the wind circled like a tornado.

The pilot was a hero of Nepal's air force, a man of proven courage and integrity who had been offered a small fortune to pick up "a package" and two people at this site. He did not know what the cargo was, or feel any great curiosity to know; it was enough for him that it had nothing to do with drugs or weapons. The agent who had contacted him introduced himself as a member of an international team of scientists who were studying rock formations in that area. The two passengers and the "package" were to be transported from Chenthan Dzong to an unknown destination in northern India, where the pilot would receive the other half of his payment.

However, the pilot didn't like the look of the men who helped him down from the helicopter: They were not the foreign scientists he expected but nomads with blue skin and frightening expressions, with a half-dozen knives of different shapes and sizes tucked into their sashes. An American with sky-blue eyes cold as a glacier welcomed the pilot and invited him to have a cup of coffee inside the monastery while the others loaded "the package" into the helicopter, a heavy, strangely shaped bundle wrapped in canvas and tied with rope. Since it took several men to lift it, the pilot assumed it was the rock samples.

The American led him through several rooms in complete ruins. The ceilings were about to cave in and the floor had buckled from the effects of earthquakes and the roots that had pushed up during years of abandonment. Hard, dry weeds had sprung up in the cracks. There were animal droppings everywhere, possibly from snow leopards and mountain goats. The American explained to the pilot that in their hurry to escape the disaster, the warrior monks who had lived in the monastery had left behind weapons, tools, and a few pieces of art. Wind and subsequent tremors had toppled the religious statues that lay shattered on the ground. It was difficult to pick their way through the ruins, and once, when the pilot started in a different direction, the American took him by one arm and pleasantly but firmly led him to a small, improvised kitchen where he was offered instant coffee, condensed milk, and crackers.

The Nepalese hero saw a number of the men with blue-black skin, but he did not see a slender, honey-colored girl who passed very near him, slipping like a ghost among the ruins of the ancient monastery. He wondered who the thuggish-looking men with their turbans and tunics really were, and what connection they might have with the supposed scientists who had hired him. He didn't like the turn this assignment had taken; he suspected that the matter was not as legal and clean as it had been presented to him.

"We have to get going soon," the pilot warned.

"After four the wind picks up."

"We won't be long. Please stay right here. The build-ing is about to fall down, it's very dangerous," Tex Armadillo replied, and left the pilot with a cup in his hand, watched by the men with the knives.

The king and Judit Kinski were at the other end of the monastery, many debris-filled rooms away. They were alone, not tied or gagged, because, as Tex Armadillo had said, escape was impossible; both the monastery's isolation and the watchful eyes of the Sect of the Scorpion assured that. As she moved through the monastery, Nadia counted the bandits. She saw that the external stone walls were as damaged as the internal ones. Snow had drifted high in the corners, and there were recent tracks of the wild animals that had their lairs there but had been frightened away by the human presence. Communicating with her heart, Nadia transmitted her observations to Tensing. After she looked into the room where the king and Judit were waiting, she notified the lama that they were alive. Tensing decided that the moment had come to act.

Armadillo had given the king another drug to lower his defenses and weaken his will, but thanks to the monarch's control of body and mind, he had maintained a deliberate, stubborn silence throughout his interrogation. Armadillo was furious. He could not complete his mission without learning the code for the Golden Dragon. He knew that the statue "sang," but those sounds would be useless to the Collector without the key to interpreting them. In view of his failure to achieve results with drugs, threats, and blows, the American had informed his prisoner that he was going to torture Judit until the king revealed the secret, even kill her if he had to, in which case her death would weigh on the conscience and karma of the king. He was preparing to carry out his threat when the helicopter arrived.

"I deeply regret that you find yourself in this situation because of me, Judit," the king murmured, weakened by the drugs.

"It isn't your fault." Her words were meant to be soothing, but it seemed to the king that she was truly frightened.

"I cannot allow them to harm you, but neither can I trust these men, they're merciless. I believe that they plan to kill us whether I give them the code or not."

"In truth, Majesty, it isn't death I fear, but torture."

"My name is Dorji. No one has called me by that

name since my wife died, many years ago," he murmured.

"Dorji? What does your name mean?"

"It means beam, or ray, of true light. The beam symbolizes the enlightened mind, but I am very far from having reached that state."

"I believe that you deserve that name, Dorji. I have never known a person like you. You have absolutely no vanity, even though you are the most powerful man in this kingdom," she said.

"Perhaps this will be my only opportunity to tell you, Judit, that before these monstrous events took place, I had considered the possibility that you might join me in the mission of looking after my people . . ."

"I don't quite know what you mean."

"I was thinking of asking you to be queen of this modest land."

"In other words . . . marry you?"

"I realize that it is absurd to speak about that now, when we are about to die, but it was my intention. I have meditated about this long and hard. I feel that you and I are destined to do something together. I do not know what, but I feel that it is our karma. We will not be able to do it in this life, but possibly it will be in our next incarnation," said the king, not daring to touch her.

"Another lifetime? When?"

"A hundred years, a thousand, it doesn't matter," the king responded. "After all, the spirit has but one life. The life of the body, on the other hand, races by like a fleeting dream. Pure illusion."

Judit turned away from him and stared at the wall, so the king could not see her face. He assumed that she was troubled, as he was himself.

"You don't know me, you don't know who I really am," Judit murmured finally.

"I cannot read your aura or your mind, as I would wish, Judit, but I can appreciate your intelligence, your great culture, your respect for nature . . ."

"But you can't see inside me!"

"Within you there must be beauty and loyalty," the monarch assured her.

"The inscription on your medallion suggests that people can change. Do you truly believe that, Dorji? Can we be totally transformed?" Judit asked, turning to meet his eyes.

"The one certainty is that everything in this world changes constantly, Judit. Change is inevitable, since all things are transitory. Nevertheless, it is very difficult for us humans to modify our essence and evolve into a superior state of consciousness. We Buddhists believe that we can change through effort of will if we are convinced of a truth, but that no one can force us. That is what happened to Siddhartha Gautama: he was a spoiled prince, but when he saw the misery of the world he was transformed into Buddha," the king replied.

"I believe that it is very difficult, to change. Why do you have faith in me?"

"I have so much faith in you, Judit, that I am prepared to give you the code of the Golden Dragon. I cannot endure the thought of you suffering; least of all because of me. I do not want to be the one who decides how much you can bear; that is your decision. And that is why the secret of the kings of my nation must be in your hands. You can give it to these criminals in exchange for your life," the king offered. "But please, do that only after I am dead."

"They wouldn't dare kill you!" she cried.

"That will not happen, Judit. I will end my life myself, I do not want my death to weigh on anyone's conscience. My time here is ended. Do not worry, it will not be violent, I shall simply cease to breathe," the king explained.

"Listen carefully, Judit. I will give you the code and you must memorize it," he continued. "When they question you, explain that the Golden Dragon emits seven sounds. Each combination of four sounds represents one of the eight hundred and forty ideograms of a lost language, the language of the Yetis."

"You mean the Abominable Snowmen? They really exist?" she asked, incredulous.

"There are only a few remaining, and they have degenerated. Now they are like animals and communicate using only a few words; three thousand years ago, however, they had a language and a civilization of sorts."

"Is that language written anywhere?"

"It is preserved in the memories of four lamas in four different monasteries. Except for my son, Dil Bahadur, and me, no one knows the complete code. It was once written on a parchment, but that was stolen by the Chinese when they invaded Tibet."

"So the person who has the parchment can decipher the dragon's prophecies," she said.

"The code is written in Sanskrit, but when the parchment is moistened with yak milk, a dictionary appears in a different color, with each ideogram translated into the four sounds that represent it. Is that clear, Judit?"

"Perfectly!" cried Armadillo, who had a pistol in his

hand and an expression of triumph on his face. "Everyone has his Achilles heel, Majesty. You see, we got the code after all. I admit that I was a little worried. I thought you would carry the secret to the tomb, but my boss was too clever for you," he added.

"What does this mean?" murmured the bewildered monarch.

"You never suspected her? Good God, man! You never wondered how or why Judit Kinski walked into your life at just this moment? I can't imagine that you didn't check the credentials of the landscape designer who specialized in tulips before you brought her to your palace. How naïve can you be! Look at her. The woman you were willing to die for is my boss, the Specialist. She's the brains behind this whole operation," the American trumpeted.

"Is it true what this man says, Judit?"

"How do you think we managed to steal your Golden Dragon? We knew how to get into the Sacred Chamber because she attached a camera to your medallion. And in order to do that she had to gain your confidence," said Armadillo.

"You took advantage of my feelings for you," the monarch murmured, pale as ash. His eyes never left Judit, who could not look him in the face.

"Don't tell me you even fell in love with her! What a joke!" exclaimed the American, snorting with laughter.

"That's enough, Armadillo," Judit snapped.

"She was sure we couldn't drag the secret from you by force, and that's when she thought of the threat to torture her. She's such a professional that she was ready to go through with it, just to frighten you and force you to tell us," Armadillo explained.

"All right, Armadillo, we've done it. We won't have to hurt the king further, we can go now," Judit ordered.

"Not so fast, boss. Now it's my turn. You don't think I'm going to hand over the statue to you, do you? Why would I do that? It's worth much more than its weight in gold, and I mean to negotiate directly with the client."

"Are you crazy, Armadillo?" the woman barked, but before she could say anything more, he cut her off by shoving his pistol into her face.

"Give me the tape or I'll blow your brains out, woman," Armadillo threatened.

For a second, Judit's always-alert eyes shifted to her purse, which lay on the ground. It was barely a flicker, but that tipped Armadillo off. He bent down and picked up the purse, never shifting the pistol, and emptied the contents onto the ground. Out fell cosmetics, a pistol, photographs, and a number of electronic gadgets the king had never seen before. Several small tapes also fell out. The American kicked them aside, they weren't what he was looking for. He was interested only in the one that had been in the recorder.

"Where's the recorder?" he yelled, furious.

With one hand he pressed the gun into Judit's chest, and with the other he patted her down. Then he ordered her to take off her belt and boots, but found nothing. Suddenly he focused on the wide bracelet of carved bone at her wrist.

"Take that off!" he commanded.

Clenching her teeth, she removed the bracelet and handed it to him. Armadillo stepped back several paces to examine it in the light, then grunted with satisfaction. It held a tiny recorder that would have thrilled the most sophisticated spy. In matters of technology, the Specialist was in the vanguard.

"You will regret this, Armadillo, I promise you. No one sells me out," Judit sputtered, her face distorted with rage.

"But you and this pathetic old man are not going to be here to get your revenge. I'm tired of obeying orders. You're history, boss. I have the statue, the code, and the helicopter. That's all I need. The Collector will be very pleased."

In the split second before Tex Armadillo pressed the trigger, the king stepped in front of Judit, protecting her with his body. The bullet intended for her hit him squarely in the chest. The second bullet struck sparks from the stone wall, because Nadia Santos had raced like a meteor and thrown herself as hard as she could upon the American, who tumbled to the ground.

Armadillo, however, jumped back on his feet with an agility born of many years of training in martial arts. He punched Nadia in the face and sprang like a cat toward the pistol, which had spun some feet away. Judit was also racing toward it, but Armadillo was quicker, and it was he who picked it up.

Tensing and the Yetis exploded into the far end of the monastery where most of the Blue Warriors had gathered, while Alexander and Dil Bahadur went in a different direction to search for the king, following the images Nadia had sent telepathically. Although Dil Bahadur had been there before, he didn't really remember the plan of the building, and the piles of rubble and obstacles scattered everywhere made it even more difficult to recognize anything. Dil Bahadur ran with an arrow drawn and ready to shoot, with Alexander close behind, inadequately armed with the wood staff the prince had lent him.

They had hoped to evade the bandits, but soon happened upon two of them, who were for a brief instant stopped in their tracks by surprise. That hesitation gave the prince enough time to send an arrow into the leg of one of the Blue Warriors. In accord with his principles, he did not shoot to kill, only to immobilize. That man fell to the ground with a scream from his gut, but his companion already had a knife in each hand, which he fired at Dil Bahadur. Things were happening so fast that Alexander couldn't keep up with them. He would never have been able to dodge the daggers, but the prince moved only slightly, as if performing an elegant dance step, and the sharp steel passed by, barely brushing him. His enemy had no time to pull out another knife, because an arrow struck his chest with unbelievable precision—below the clavicle, a few centimeters from his heart, without touching any vital organ.

Alexander used that diversion to club the first bandit, who, though lying on the ground and bleeding, was struggling to pull out another of his many knives. Alex acted without thinking, moved by desperation and the urgency of the moment, but as the heavy staff made contact with the man's skull, he heard a sound like a nut being cracked. A wave of nausea swept over him as reason was restored, and he recognized the brutality of his action. He broke out in a cold sweat, and his mouth filled with saliva; he thought he was going to vomit, but Dil Bahadur was already running forward, and Alex had to suppress his squeamishness and follow.

The prince had no fear of the bandits' weapons, because he believed he was protected by the magic amulet he wore around his neck, the petrified dragon dropping Tensing had given him. Much later, when Alexander described events to Kate, she commented that it was his training in Tao-shu that allowed Dil Bahadur to dodge the daggers, not the amulet. "I don't care what it was, it worked," her grandson had replied. Dil Bahadur and Alexander rushed into the room where the king lay wounded just as Tex Armadillo's hand closed over the pistol, a fraction of a second before Judit Kinski reached it. In the time it took the American to place his finger on the trigger, the prince shot his third arrow, piercing Armadillo's forearm. The American uttered a terrible scream but he didn't drop the weapon. He still clasped the pistol, although it seemed probable that he lacked the strength to aim or fire it.

"Don't move!" Alexander shouted, nearly hysterical, with no idea how to back up his command with only a staff against the American's bullets.

Armadillo seized Nadia with his good arm and lifted her like a doll, protecting himself with her body. Borobá, who had followed Dil Bahadur and Alexander, ran to cling to his mistress's leg, screeching desperately; one kick from Armadillo sent the little monkey flying. Although still stunned from being punched in the face, Nadia tried weakly to break loose, but Armadillo's iron grip did not allow the least movement.

The prince reviewed his possibilities. He had blind faith in his aim, but the risk that the man would shoot Nadia was too great. Helpless, he watched Armadillo back out of the room, dragging the inert girl in the direction of the small field where the helicopter sat waiting on a thin layer of snow.

Judit took advantage of the confusion to run off in the opposite direction, disappearing among the rubble of the monastery.

While all this was happening at one end of the building, a violent scene was unfolding at the other.

Most of the Blue Warriors had congregated around the improvised kitchen, where they were drinking liquor from their canteens, chewing betel, and discussing in low tones their chances of betraying Armadillo. They were unaware, of course, that it was Judit who was actually giving the orders; they thought that she was a hostage, like the king. The American had paid them the agreed-upon sum in cash, and they knew that in India the weapons and horses that completed the deal were waiting, but after they'd seen the gold statue studded with precious stones, they believed they were owed considerably more. They didn't like the fact that the treasure was stowed in the helicopter beyond their reach, although they realized that that was the only way to get it out of the country.

"We have to kidnap the pilot," their leader grunted, glancing toward the Nepalese hero who was over in a corner, drinking his cup of coffee with condensed milk.

"Who will go with him?" one of the bandits asked.

"I will," the leader said.

"And how do we know that you won't go off with the statue?" put in another of his men.

Insulted, the leader reached for one of his knives, but he didn't complete his move because at that moment Tensing, followed by the Yetis, stormed into the south wing of Chenthan Dzong. The small war party was truly terrifying. In the lead came the monk, armed with two chain-linked sticks that he had found among the ruins of what had once been the armory of the famous warrior monks who had lived in the fortified monastery. By the way he moved and held the heavy sticks, anyone could see he was expert in the martial arts. After him came the ten Yetis, who were awesome to see even under normal conditions, and who in this instance were monsters out of anyone's worst nightmare. They seemed to have multiplied to twice their number, creating the tumult of a horde. Armed with clubs and rocks, in their leather breast-plates and tribal helmets with blood-smeared horns, they shouted and leaped about like crazed orangutans, thrilled with this opportunity to swing their clubs and—why not—take a few blows, too, since that was part of the fun. Tensing ordered them to attack, resigned to his inability to control them. Before they burst into the monastery, he had sent a brief prayer to the heavens, asking that there be no deaths in the melee because he would carry them on his conscience. The Yetis were not responsible for their acts; once their aggression was awakened, they lost what little reason they had.

The superstitious Blue Warriors thought they were victims of the curse of the Golden Dragon, and that an army of demons had been loosed to avenge the sacrilege they had committed. They could stand up to the most savage enemies, but the idea of facing the forces of hell terrified them. They started running, closely followed by the Yetis, to the stunned amazement of the pilot. He had flattened himself against the wall to let them pass, cup still in hand, with no idea of what was happening around him. He thought he had come to meet some scientists, and instead he found himself in the midst of an uproar of blue-skinned barbarians, extraterrestrial apes, and a gigantic monk armed as if he were in a kung fu movie.

Once the stampede of bandits and Yetis had gone by, the lama and the pilot found themselves alone.

"*Namasté*," the pilot said in greeting, once he had recovered his voice. It was all he could think of to say.

"*Tampo kachi*," Tensing returned in his language, bowing briefly, as if he were at a social gathering.

"What the hell is going on here?" the pilot asked.

"It may possibly be a little difficult to explain. The ones wearing helmets with horns are my friends, the Yetis. The others stole the Golden Dragon and kidnapped the king," Tensing informed him.

"Are you talking about the legendary Golden Dragon? Then that's what they put in my helicopter!" cried the hero of Nepal, and shot off toward the landing field.

Tensing followed. The situation seemed slightly comic to him, because he still didn't know that the king was wounded. Through a hole in the wall he watched as the terrorized members of the Sect of the Scorpion scuttled down the mountain, pursued by the Yetis. In vain, he tried to summon the latter mentally, but Grrympr's warriors were having far too good a time to pay attention to him. Their hair-raising battle cries had turned to shrieks of anticipated pleasure, like children at a party. Tensing prayed once again that they would not catch up with any of the bandits: he did not want to add indelible marks to his karma with further acts of violence.

Tensing's good humor changed the minute he left the monastery and saw what was developing before his eyes. A stranger, who according to what Nadia had reported had to be the American in charge of the Blue Warriors, was standing beside the helicopter. An arrow had completely run through one of his arms, but that hadn't prevented him from waving a pistol. With the other arm he held Nadia, feet barely touching the ground, tight against his body, so that she served as his shield.

About ninety feet away stood Dil Bahadur, the string of his bow pulled back to shoot, accompanied by Alexander, who was too stunned to do anything.

"Drop the bow! Move back or I kill the girl!" Armadillo threatened, and no one doubted that he would do it.

The prince dropped his weapon, and the two young men retreated toward the ruins of the monastery, as Armadillo fought to climb into the helicopter, dragging Nadia, whom he pushed inside with brutal force.

"Wait! You can't leave here without me!" the pilot yelled, running forward, but the American had already started the engine and the blades were beginning to turn.

This was the moment for Tensing to use his supernatural psychic powers and alter the course of nature by calling on his resources as a *tulku*. He had only to concentrate and call on the wind to prevent the American from fleeing with the sacred treasure of his nation. However, if a wind sheer caught the helicopter in midflight, Nadia, too, would perish. The lama rapidly weighed the possibilities and decided that he couldn't risk it: a human life was more important that all the gold in the world.

Dil Bahadur was pulling back the string of his bow again, but his arrows were useless against the metal craft. Alexander had finally absorbed the fact that the vicious American was taking Nadia with him, and he began screaming his friend's name. She couldn't hear him, but the roar of the engine and the draft from the blades cleared her mind. She had fallen like a sack of rice across the seat where her captor had pushed her. As the helicopter began to lift off the ground, Nadia took advantage of Armadillo's struggle with the controls, which he was operating with only one hand since the wounded arm was hanging useless. She slid toward the door. She opened it, and without a second thought, never looking down, she dropped into empty space.

Alexander ran to her, oblivious of the helicopter that was racketing above his head. Nadia had fallen several feet, but snow cushioned the fall that otherwise might have killed her.

"Eagle! Are you all right?" yelled Alexander, terrified.

She saw him running toward her, and waved, more amazed at her accomplishment than frightened. The roar of the helicopter drowned out their voices.

Tensing went to her, too. As soon as Dil Bahadur saw that she was alive he turned and ran toward the room where he had left his father wounded by Tex Armadillo's bullet. When Tensing bent over Nadia, she shouted that the king was badly hurt and gestured for him to go. The monk rushed after the prince, while Alexander folded his jacket and tried to make his friend comfortable amid the wind and blowing snow the helicopter had stirred up. Nadia was bruised from her fall, but the shoulder she had earlier dislocated had not been reinjured.

"It seems I'm not meant to die young," Nadia commented, gathering herself to get up. Her mouth and nose were bleeding from the punch she'd taken from Armadillo.

"Don't you move till Tensing comes back," ordered Alexander, who was in no mood for jokes.

From where she lay on her back, Nadia watched the helicopter ascend like a great insect, silver against the deep blue of the sky. It flew along the sheer side of the mountain and rose unsteadily through the funnel formed by the peaks of the Himalayas. Minute after minute it seemed to grow smaller in the sky, receding into the distance. Nadia pushed away Alexander, who wanted her to lie still in the snow, and with a great effort got to her feet. She put a fistful of snow into her mouth and immediately spit it out rosy with blood. Her face had begun to swell.

"Look!" shouted the pilot, who had not taken his eyes from his craft.

The helicopter was shuddering like a fly stopped by a windowpane. The Nepalese hero knew exactly what was happening: it had been caught in a burst of whirling air and the blades were vibrating dangerously. He began to wave his arms in the air, shouting instructions that, of course, Armadillo couldn't hear. The one possibility of escaping the whirlwind was to fly with it in an ascending spiral. Alexander thought it must be something like surfing: if one didn't take the wave at the exact moment and use its impetus, the ocean would roll the surfer under.

Armadillo had logged in many hours of flying, as this skill was indispensable in his line of work, and he had flown all kinds of aircraft—small planes, gliders, helicopters, even a dirigible. This was often how he sneaked unseen across borders with his illegal weapons, drugs, and stolen goods. He thought of himself as an expert, but nothing had prepared him for this.

Just as the helicopter was emerging from the funnel and he was whooping with triumph, he felt a powerful vibration shake the craft. It began to whirl faster and faster, as if it were in a blender, and he realized he couldn't control it. Added to the deafening sound of the engine and blades was the roar of the wind. He tried to be rational, calling on his steel nerves and store of experience, but nothing he tried worked. The helicopter continued to spin crazily, and a violent *crack!* warned Armadillo that the rotor had snapped. He stayed airborne several more minutes, held by the force of the wind, until suddenly it veered. For an instant there was silence, and Tex Armadillo had the fleeting hope that he still could steer, but immediately the 'copter began to drop.

Later Alexander wondered whether the man had been aware of what was happening, or whether death took him in a flash, without warning. From where he stood, Alex couldn't see where the helicopter fell, but they all heard the violent explosion, followed by a heavy black cloud of smoke billowing toward the sky.

Tensing found the king lying on the ground with his head in the lap of his son Dil Bahadur, who was stroking his hair. The prince hadn't seen his father since he was a boy of six, the age when he was taken from his bed one night to be deposited in Tensing's arms, but he recognized him because he had held his father's image in his memory all those years.

"Father, father . . ." he murmured, helpless at the sight of the man whose life was draining away before his eyes.

"Majesty, it is I, Tensing," said the lama, in turn leaning over the sovereign.

The king opened his eyes, glazed with death agony. As he focused, he saw a handsome young man who closely resembled his dead wife. He motioned him to bend closer.

"Hear me, my son, I must tell you something," he murmured.

Tensing moved away, to give them a moment of privacy.

"Go immediately to the Chamber of the Golden Dragon in the palace." The monarch spoke with difficulty.

"But, father, the statue has been stolen," the prince replied.

"Nevertheless . . . go!"

"How can I do that if you do not come with me?"

From the most ancient times, the king had always accompanied the heir on his first visit, to instruct him on how to avoid the lethal traps that protected the

Sacred Passageway. That first experience of father and son before the Golden Dragon was a rite of initiation and marked the end of one reign and the beginning of another.

"You must do it alone," ordered the king and closed his eyes.

Tensing approached his disciple and put one hand on his shoulder.

"Perhaps you should obey your father, Dil Bahadur," said the lama.

At that moment Alexander came into the room, supporting Nadia, who was still weak-kneed, by one arm; also with them was the Nepalese pilot who had not yet recovered from the loss of his helicopter and the string of surprises he'd encountered on this mission. Nadia and the pilot stayed at a prudent distance, not wanting to interfere in the drama that was being played out between the king and his son. Alexander, mean-while, stooped down to examine the contents of Judit's handbag, which still lay scattered on the ground.

"You must go to the Chamber of the Golden Dragon, son," the king repeated.

"May my honorable master Tensing come with me? My training is only theoretical. I do not know the palace or the traps. Death awaits me beyond the

Magnificent Door," the prince declared.

"It will not be of help for me to go, Dil Bahadur," the lama replied sadly. "I do not know the way either. Now my place is here, with the king."

"Can you save my father, honorable master?" Dil Bahadur pleaded.

"I will do everything I can."

Alexander went to Dil Bahadur and handed him a small object that the prince did not recognize or know the use of. "This will help you know what to do in the Sacred Passageway," he said. "It's a GPS."

"A what?" asked the prince, confused.

"Let's say it's an electronic map that will help you orient yourself inside the palace. You can find the Chamber of the Golden Dragon the way Armadillo and his men did when they stole the statue," his friend explained.

"How was that?" asked Dil Bahadur.

"I imagine that someone recorded the secrets," Alex explained.

"That's impossible. No one except my father has access to that part of the palace. No other person can open the Magnificent Door or avoid the traps."

"Armadillo did both, and he must have used this system. Judit Kinski and he were partners. Maybe your father showed her the way," Alexander insisted.

"The medallion!" cried Nadia, who had witnessed the scene between the Specialist and Tex Armadillo before her friends came into the room. "Armadillo said something about a camera hidden in the king's medallion!"

Nadia apologized for what she was going to do, then, with the greatest care, she felt along the prostrate body of the monarch until she found the royal medallion, which had lodged between the king's neck and his jacket. She asked the prince to help her remove it, but he was reluctant: the medallion represented royal power and it would be disrespectful for him to take it from his father. The urgency in Nadia's voice, however, forced him to act.

Alexander carried the jewel to the light and quickly examined it. He immediately discovered the miniature camera hidden among the coral insets. He showed it to Dil Bahadur and the others.

"Judit Kinski undoubtedly put it there. This camera, no bigger than a pea, filmed the king's movements through the Sacred Passageway. That's how Armadillo and the Blue Warriors were able to follow him. Every step he took was recorded on the GPS."

"Why did she do that?" asked the horrified prince;

in his mind there was no concept of betrayal or greed.

"I suppose she wanted the statue, which is extremely valuable," ventured Alexander.

"Did you hear the explosion? The helicopter crashed and the statue was destroyed," said the pilot.

"Perhaps it is better so," sighed the king, without opening his eyes.

"With the greatest humility, please permit me to suggest that the two young foreigners accompany the prince to the palace," said Tensing. "Alexander-Jaguar and Nadia-Eagle are pure of heart, like prince Dil Bahadur, and possibly they can help him in his mission, Majesty. Young Alexander knows how to use this modern apparatus and the girl Nadia knows how to see and listen with her heart."

"Only the king and his heir may enter there," murmured the monarch.

"With the deepest respect, Majesty, I dare to contradict you. Perhaps there are moments when tradition must be broken," the lama insisted.

A long silence followed Tensing's words. It seemed that the wounded man's strength had reached its limits, but soon he spoke again.

"So be it. The three shall go," the sovereign finally agreed.

"Perhaps it would not be entirely futile, Majesty, for me to take a look at your wound," Tensing suggested.

"And why, Tensing? We have another king, my time is over."

"Possibly we will not have another king until the prince proves that he is worthy," replied the lama, lifting up the wounded monarch in his powerful arms.

The Nepalese hero found a sleeping bag that Armadillo had left behind, and they arranged a sort of bed where Tensing laid the monarch. The lama opened the king's blood-soaked jacket and washed his chest to examine it. The bullet had gone completely through, leaving an ugly hole where it had exited his back. From the look and location of the wound, and the color of the blood, Tensing realized that the lungs were involved. There was nothing he could do. All his skills of healing and his tremendous mental powers were of little use in a case like this. The dying man knew that as well, but he wanted a little more time to carry out his last responsibilities. The lama stanched the hemorrhage, bound the king's chest tightly, and ordered the pilot to bring boiling water from the improvised kitchen so he could prepare a medicinal tea. An hour later the monarch was fully conscious, and was lucid, though very weak.

"Son, you must be a better king than I was," he told Dil Bahadur, indicating that he should put the royal medallion around his neck.

"Father, that is impossible . . ."

"Hear me, because I have very little time. These are my instructions. First: Soon you must marry a woman as strong as you. She will have to be the mother of our people, and you the father. Second: Preserve the natural world and the traditions of our kingdom; trust nothing that comes from outside. Third: Do not punish Judit Kinski, the European woman. I do not want her to spend her life in prison. She has made serious errors, but it is not our place to cleanse her karma. She will have to return in another incarnation to learn what she has not learned in this."

Only then did they remember the woman responsible for their tragedy. They felt sure that she could not have gotten very far. She didn't know the region, she had no weapon, provisions, or warm clothing, and apparently she was barefoot, since Armadillo had made her take off her boots. But it was Alexander's opinion that if she had been clever enough to steal the dragon in such spectacular fashion, she was clever enough to escape hell itself.

"I don't feel prepared to govern, father," moaned the prince, head bowed.

"You have no choice, son. You have been trained, and you are brave and pure of heart. You can seek counsel from the Golden Dragon."

"It has been destroyed!"

"Lean closer, I must tell you a secret."

The others stepped back to leave them alone as Dil Bahadur put his ear to the king's lips. The prince listened intently to the most vital secret of the kingdom, the secret that for eighteen centuries only the crowned monarchs had known.

"Perhaps it is the hour for you to say good-bye, Dil Bahadur," Tensing suggested.

"May I stay with my father to the end?"

"No, my son, you must leave now," the sovereign whispered.

Dil Bahadur kissed his father on the forehead, and got to his feet. Tensing clasped his disciple in a strong embrace. They were saying good-bye for a long time, possibly forever. Before the prince lay the test of his initiation, and it might be that he would not survive it. For his part, the lama had to fulfill the promise made to Grr-ympr to take her place for six years in the Valley of the Yetis. For the first time in his life, Tensing felt overwhelmed by emotion. He loved that young man like a son, more than himself; the pain of being separated from him burned like fire. The lama tried to distance himself and calm his anxiety. He observed the process of his own mind and breathed deeply, taking note of his unleashed emotions and of the fact that he still had a long road to travel before he achieved absolute detachment from earthly matters, including affection. He knew that separation does not exist on the spiritual plane. He remembered that he himself had taught the prince that every being is a part of a single whole, that all things are connected. Dil Bahadur and he would weave through this and other incarnations eternally. Why then was he feeling such anguish?

"Will I be able to reach the Sacred Chamber, honorable master?" asked the prince, interrupting his thoughts.

"Remember that you must be like the tiger: Listen to the voice of intuition and instinct. Trust in the virtues of your heart," the monk replied.

The prince, Nadia, and Alexander began their return journey to the capital. Since they now knew the route, they were prepared for the obstacles. They used the shortcut through the Valley of the Yetis, so they didn't happen upon any of the detachments of General Myar Kunglung, who at that moment was climbing the steep mountain trail accompanied by Kate and Pema.

The Blue Warriors, on the other hand, ran straight into Kunglung's party. They had scrambled down the mountainside as fast as the rough terrain allowed, fleeing from the horrific demons chasing them. The Yetis did not catch up with them, because they dared go no lower than their habitual range. These creatures had one fundamental rule engraved in genetic memory: not to go near beings of a different kind. Only rarely did they abandon their secret valley, and when they did, it was only to look for food in the most inaccessible peaks, far from any humans. That was the salvation of the Sect of the Scorpion: the Yetis' self-preservation instinct was stronger than their desire to catch their enemies, and the moment came when they simply stopped. They did not do so willingly, because giving up a juicy battle, perhaps the only one that would come along in years, was an enormous sacrifice. For a long time they stood howling with frustration, but then they gave one another a few wallops in consolation, and, heads hanging, began the trek back to their own haunts.

The Blue Warriors didn't know why the devils in the

bloody helmets had quit pursuing them, but they gave thanks to the goddess Kali that they had. The men were so frightened that the thought of going back to claim the statue, as they had planned, never crossed their minds. They continued down the one usable trail, where, inevitably, they met Kunglung's soldiers.

"There they are! It's the Blue Warriors!" Pema shouted as soon as she sighted them from a distance.

General Myar Kunglung had no difficulty capturing the men; they had no way of escaping. They gave up without a fight. One officer was assigned to take them back to the capital, guarded by most of the soldiers, and Pema, Kate, the general, and a few of his best men continued toward Chenthan Dzong.

"What will they do to those bandits?" Kate asked the general.

"Is possible their case will be studied by lamas. Then judges will consider. In end, the king will decide punishment. At least always it has been done before. Though is fact that we have so little practice to punish criminals."

"In the United States they would spend the rest of their lives in prison."

"And they would achieve wisdom there?" the general asked.

Kate laughed so hard that she almost fell off her horse.

"I doubt it, General," she replied, drying her tears, when finally she regained control.

Myar Kunglung had no idea what had seemed so hilarious to the writer. He concluded that foreigners are such strange people, with such incomprehensible ways, that it wasn't worth the energy to try to analyze them. One just had to accept them.

By then night was approaching, and they had to stop and set up a small camp on one of the terraces cut into the mountain. They were eager to get to the monastery, but they knew that to go on with only their flashlights would be foolish.

Kate was exhausted. In addition to the demands of the trail, there was the altitude, to which she was not acclimated, and her cough, which left her no peace. Only her iron will and the hope that she would find Alexander and Nadia kept her going.

"Perhaps you should not worry, Little Grandmother," Pema said soothingly. "Your grandson and Nadia are safe. Nothing can happen to them when they are with the prince and Tensing."

"Something very bad must have happened up there to make those thugs run away like that," Kate replied.

"They mentioned something about the curse of the Golden Dragon and being chased by devils. Do you believe there are demons in these mountains, Little Grandmother?" the girl asked.

"I don't believe any of that nonsense, child," Kate replied, resigned now to being called "grandmother" by everyone in this country.

The night was very long, and no one got much sleep. The soldiers prepared a simple breakfast of salted tea with butter, rice, and some dried vegetables that looked and tasted like shoe leather, then they continued their march. Kate kept up, despite her sixty-five years and lungs wracked by tobacco. General Myar Kunglung said nothing; he did not even glance toward her, for fear of meeting her penetrating blue eyes. Even so, admiration was beginning to grow in his warrior's heart. At first he had detested her and had counted the hours until he would be rid of her, but as the days passed, he ceased to think of her as an impossible old woman and began to respect her.

The rest of the trip passed without incident. When at last they could see the fortified monastery in the distance, they thought there was no one there. Absolute silence lay over the ancient ruins. Alert, with weapons at the ready, the general and his soldiers advanced, followed closely by the two women. They went through room after room until they came to the last, where they were intercepted by a gigantic monk armed with two sticks joined with a chain. He raised his weapon, moved his feet in a series of complicated steps, and, before the group could react, looped the chain around the general's neck. The soldiers stopped where they were, unsure of what to do as their chief kicked his feet in the air, suspended between the monk's monumental arms.

"Honorable Master Tensing!" Pema exclaimed, thrilled to see him.

"Pema?" he asked.

"Yes, it's me, Honorable Master!" she said, and added, pointing to the humiliated general, "perhaps it would be wise to release the honorable General Myar Kunglung."

Tensing set the man down delicately, removed the chain from his neck, and bowed respectfully with hands joined at the level of his forehead.

"*Tampo kachi*, Honorable General," he greeted him.

"*Tampo kachi*. And where is king?" the general replied, trying to mask his indignation as he straightened the jacket of his uniform.

Tensing stepped aside, and the group went inside the large chamber. Half of the roof had caved in years before, and the rest was dangerously close to collapsing entirely; there was a large hole in one of the outside walls where the pale light of day was filtering in. A cloud trapped at the peak of the mountain had created a misty ambience in which everything seemed faded, like images in a dream. A threadbare tapestry hung on one ruined wall, and an elegant statue of a reclining Buddha, miraculously intact, lay on the ground as if just roused from a nap.

The body of the king lay upon an improvised table, surrounded with a half dozen lighted yak-butter candles. A draft of air cold as crystal made the candles dance in the golden snow. The heroic Nepalese pilot, keeping watch near the corpse, did not move as the military contingent burst in.

It seemed to Kate that she was witnessing an unbelievable drama. The scene was unreal: the ruined chamber wrapped in thick white fog; the scattered remains of centuries-old statues and broken columns; the patches of snow and frost in the rough spots of the floor. The people were as theatrical as the setting: the enormous monk with a Mongol warrior's body and face of a saint, with the tiny Borobá teetering on his shoulder; the stern General Myar Kunglung, several soldiers, and the pilot, all in uniform, as if they had dropped in by accident; and finally the king, whose serene and dignified presence was imposing even in death.

"But where are Alexander and Nadia?" the grandmother asked.

CHAPTER TWENTY

❋

ALEXANDER WAS IN THE LEAD, following the indications on the video and the GPS, because the prince did not understand how they worked and this was not the moment to give him a lesson. Alexander was by no means an expert, and these mechanisms were also the last word in technology, used only by the United States Army, but he was familiar with electronic devices and it had not been difficult for him to figure out how to operate them.

Dil Bahadur had spent twelve years of his life preparing for the moment he would walk through the labyrinth of doors on the lowest floor of the palace, open the Magnificent Door, and one by one overcome the obstacles on the way to the Sacred Chamber. He had memorized the instructions, confident that if his recollections failed him, his father would be at his side until he was able to do it alone. Now he had to face the test with only the presence of his new friends, Nadia and Alexander. At first he stared, unconvinced, at the small screen Alexander carried in his hand, until he realized that it was guiding them directly to the proper door. Not once did they have to turn back, and they never opened the wrong door, so soon they found themselves in the room with the golden lamps. Now no one was guarding the Magnificent Door. All traces of blood had been cleaned from the floor. The guard who had been killed by the Blue Warriors, as well as the body of his wounded colleague, had been taken away and no one had replaced them.

"Wow!" Nadia and Alexander cried in unison when they saw the door.

"We must turn the correct jades; if we are mistaken, the system will lock and we will not be able to go in," the prince warned.

"All we have to do is pay close attention to what the king did. It's all here on the video," Alexander explained.

They watched the video twice, until they were absolutely sure, and then Dil Bahadur turned four jade pieces carved in the shape of a lotus flower. Nothing happened. The three young people waited breathlessly, counting the seconds. Slowly the two panels of the door began to move.

They found themselves in the circular room with nine identical doors and, as Tex Armadillo had done days before, Alexander stepped upon the eye painted on the floor, opened his arms, and turned at a forty-five-degree angle. His right hand pointed to the door they should choose.

As it swung open, they heard a hair-raising chorus of laments, and were struck by the foul odor of the tomb. They saw nothing, only unrelieved blackness.

"I will go first, because my totemic animal, the jaguar, is supposed to be able to see in the dark," Alexander offered, stepping inside, followed by his friends.

"Do you see anything?" Nadia asked.

"Nothing," Alexander confessed.

"This is the time it would be helpful to have a totemic animal a little humbler than a jaguar. A cockroach, for example," Nadia said, and laughed nervously.

"Possibly it would not be a bad idea to use your flashlight," the prince suggested.

Alexander felt like a fool: He had completely forgotten that he was carrying his flashlight and his jackknife in the pockets of his parka. As he snapped on the light, they saw they were in a corridor, along which they moved with hesitation until they came to the door at the end. They opened it with extreme caution. The stench was much worse, but there was enough light to allow them to see. They were surrounded with human skeletons hanging from the ceiling and swinging in the air with a macabre clicking of bones; at their feet seethed a revolting living carpet of snakes. Alexander yelled and tried to back out, but Dil Bahadur seized his arm.

"The bones are ancient; they were put here centuries ago to discourage intruders," he said.

"And the snakes?"

"The men of the scorpion sect went past them, Jaguar; that means that we can do it, too," Nadia said encouragingly.

"Pema said that those men are immune to insect and snake poisons," Alexander reminded her.

"Perhaps these snakes are not poisonous. According to what my honorable master Tensing taught me, the shape of the head of dangerous serpents is more triangular. We go ahead," the prince ordered.

"Those snakes don't show up in the video," Nadia noted.

"The camera was on the king's medallion, so it filmed only what was ahead of him, not what was at his feet," Alexander explained.

"Which means that we must be very cautious regarding what's lower and higher than the king's chest," she concluded.

The prince and his friends pushed aside the skeletons and, treading on the snakes, stumbled to the next door, which opened into an empty, shadowy room.

"Wait!" Alexander called. "Here your father did something before he stepped in."

"I remember! There is a pineapple carved in the wood," said Dil Bahadur, feeling along the doorframe.

He found the button he was looking for, and pushed. The pineapple yielded, and immediately they heard a terrible rattle, and watched as a forest of lances fell from the ceiling, stirring a cloud of dust. They waited until the last lance buried itself in the floor.

"This is when we need Borobá. He could scout the way. Well, I will go first, because I am the lightest and thinnest," Nadia decided.

"It occurs to me that possibly this trap is not as simple as it seems," Dil Bahadur warned them.

Slithering like an eel, Nadia slipped past the first metal rods. She had gone six or seven feet when her elbow brushed one of them, and suddenly the floor opened before her feet. Instinctively she grabbed the nearest lance, where she clung, kicking above empty space. Her hands slipped down the metal as her feet searched for some kind of support. By then Alexander had reached her, unmindful of where he was stepping in his haste to help her. He hooked his arm around her waist and pulled her up, holding her tight against his body. The whole room seemed to shudder, as if there was an earthquake, and several more lances fell from the ceiling, but none close to them. For several minutes the two friends didn't move, arms about one another, waiting. Then, very slowly, they moved apart.

"Don't touch anything," Nadia whispered, afraid that even the breath they exhaled would provoke a new danger.

They reached the other side of the room and signaled Dil Bahadur to follow, though he had already started, because he had no fear of the lances: He was protected by his amulet.

"We could have died like a butterfly on a pin," Alexander commented, cleaning his glasses, which were fogged over with sweat.

"But that didn't happen, did it?" Nadia reminded him, though she was as frightened as he was.

"If you take three deep breaths, let the air flow down to your stomach and then let it out slowly, possibly you will feel better," the prince advised.

"We don't have time to do yoga. Let's keep going," Alexander interrupted.

The GPS indicated which door they should open, and, as soon as they did, the lances rose and the room again seemed empty. Ahead of them were two rooms, each with a variety of doors but free of traps. They relaxed a little and began to breathe normally, but were as cautious as ever.

Ahead of them everything was dark.

"You can't see anything on the video, the screen is black," said Alexander.

"What can it be?" Nadia inquired.

The prince took the flashlight and shone it on the floor, where they saw a leafy tree filled with fruit and birds, painted with such mastery that it seemed to rise tall in the center of the room, firmly rooted in the earth. It was so beautiful and so innocent-looking that it invited them to come closer and touch it.

"Do not take a single step!" Dil Bahadur cried, for once forgetting his good manners. "This is the Tree of Life. I have heard stories about the dangers of stepping on it."

The prince pulled out the small bowl he used to prepare his meals, which he always carried with him, and threw it on the floor. The Tree of Life was painted on a length of delicate silk stretched across a deep pit. One step forward would have launched them into the void. They didn't know that one of Armadillo's men had perished in that very place. The bandit lay at the bottom of a deep well where rats were picking his bones.

"How do we get by?" Nadia asked.

"Perhaps it would be better for you to wait here," the prince indicated.

With great caution, Dil Bahadur felt with one foot until he found a narrow lip along the edge of the wall. It was invisible, because it was painted black and blended into the color of the floor. With his back pressed against the wall, he inched forward. He moved his right leg a short distance, tested his balance, and then moved the left. In that way he reached the other side.

Alexander realized that for Nadia that would be one of the most difficult tests, because of her fear of heights.

"Now you must call on the spirit of the eagle. Give me your hand, close your eyes, and focus on your feet," he told her.

"Why don't I just wait here?" she asked.

"No. We're going together," her friend insisted.

They had no idea how deep the hole was and did not mean to find out. The man who had fallen into the well had slipped before anyone could catch him. For an instant he had seemed to float in the air, held in the branches of the Tree of Life, spread-eagled, flapping in his black clothing like a giant bat. The illusion lasted only the blink of an eye. With a scream of absolute terror, the man disappeared into the black mouth of the well. His companions heard the thud of the body when it touched bottom, then a chill silence. Fortunately Nadia knew nothing of that. She clung to Alexander's hand and, step by step, followed him to the other side.

Upon opening another door, the three friends found themselves surrounded with mirrors. Mirrors not only lined the walls, they were also on the ceiling and the floor, multiplying images to infinity. To add to the illusion, the room was tilted, like a cube sitting on one corner. They couldn't walk, they had to crawl, clinging to each other, completely disoriented. They couldn't see the doors because they, too, were mirror-covered. Within a few seconds they felt nauseated; they felt that their heads were bursting and that they were losing their reason.

"Don't look to the side, concentrate on what's ahead.

Follow me; stay in line and don't let go," Alexander ordered. "The direction is mapped on my screen."

"I don't know how we're going to get out of here," said Nadia.

"If we open the wrong door, we could activate a lock that would trap us here forever," the prince warned with his habitual calm.

"We have the most modern technology to help us," Alexander said comfortingly, although he could scarcely control his own nerves.

The doors were all alike, but thanks to the GPS he knew in which direction to go. The king had paused in several places before he opened the correct door. Alexander rewound the video to check the details, and noticed a distorted image of the king reflected in a mirror.

"One of the mirrors is concave. That's our door," he concluded.

When Dil Bahadur saw himself fat and stumpy, he pushed; the door yielded and they were safely out. Now they were in a long, narrow corridor that spiraled back on itself. It was different from other areas of the palace in that there were no visible doors, but they had no doubt they would find one at the end, for that is what the video showed. Here there was no place to get lost, it was simply a matter of going forward. The air was thin and filled with a fine dust, which glittered like gold in the light of the small lamps hanging from the ceiling. On the video they could see that the king had moved along quickly, without hesitation, but that didn't mean they were safe, since there could be dangers the video didn't record.

They walked into the corridor, looking all around, not knowing where the next threat would come from but aware that they could not drop their guard for a second. They had gone a few steps before they became aware that they were sinking into something soft and springy. It was like walking on a long strip of canvas that gave under the weight of their bodies.

Dil Bahadur covered his mouth and nose with his tunic and desperately signaled his friends to do the same. He had realized that they were moving across a series of bellows. With every step they were pumping out the dust they had noticed on entering. Within a few seconds the air was so saturated that they couldn't see a foot ahead. The urge to cough was unbearable, but they controlled it as best they could, because when they breathed their lungs filled with the dust. The only solution was to try to reach the exit as quickly as possible. They began to run, trying not to inhale, which was impossible considering the length of the passage. They feared a lethal poison, but they thought that since the king had passed through it more than once in his life, it couldn't be deadly.

Nadia was a good swimmer, because she had grown up in the Amazon, where life is lived on the water, and she could stay under for more than a minute. That allowed her to hold her breath longer than her friends, but even she had to gasp for air a couple of times. She figured that Alexander and Dil Bahadur had inhaled considerably more of that strange powder than she had. With four long strides she reached the end of the passage, opened the only door, and pulled the others toward it.

Without a thought for the dangers the next room might hold, the three friends burst out of the corridor, falling over each other, choking, gulping air, and trying to brush the powder off their clothes. They saw nothing menacing on the video; the king had moved through this room as confidently as he had through the corridor. Nadia, who was in better shape than her companions, signaled them not to move while she checked out the room. It was well lit, and the air seemed normal. There were several doors, but the screen clearly indicated which one to open. As she moved forward a couple of steps, she became aware that it was difficult to focus: Thousands of brilliantly colored dots and lines and geometric figures were dancing before her eyes. She held out her arms, trying to keep her balance. She turned back and saw that Alexander and Dil Bahadur were staggering, too.

"I feel sick," Alexander muttered, suddenly sinking to the floor.

"Jaguar! Open your eyes!" Nadia shook him. "The effect of that dust is like the potion the Indians gave us in the Amazon. You remember? We saw visions."

"A hallucinogen? You think we've been drugged?"

"A hallucinogen?" asked the prince, who was still on his feet thanks only to his unusual control of his body.

"Yes, I think so. Each of you is seeing something different. It isn't real," Nadia explained, taking her friends' arms to help them forward, never imagining that within a few seconds she would plunge into the hell of the drug.

Despite Nadia's warning, none of the three suspected the terrible power of the golden dust. The first symptom took the form of a psychedelic labyrinth of colors and iridescent figures whirling at dizzying speed. Making a supreme effort, the three kept their eyes open and lurched forward, wondering how the king had averted the drug's spell. They felt they were losing contact with the world and with reality, as if they were dying, and they couldn't contain their moans of anguish. By then they had come to the next room, which was much larger than the previous ones. When they saw what was ahead, they panicked, even though a part of their brains kept telling them that the images were the fruit of their imaginations.

They were in hell, surrounded with monsters and demons circling like a pack of snarling beasts. On every side they saw mangled bodies, torture, blood, and death. A horrifying chorus of cries deafened them, hollow voices called out their names, like ghosts hungry to claim them.

Alexander had a clear vision of his mother in the claws of a powerful, black, menacing bird of prey. He reached out to try to rescue her just at the moment the bird of death bit off her head. He screamed at the top of his lungs.

Nadia was standing on a narrow beam on the top floor of one of the skyscrapers she had visited with Kate in New York, fighting to keep her balance. Thousands of feet below, everything was covered with red-hot lava. The vertigo of death invaded her mind, erasing her ability to reason, as the beam tipped more and more. She heard the fatal temptation of the call of the abyss.

As for Dil Bahadur, he felt his spirit separate from his body, race through the skies like a lightning bolt; it reached the ruins of the fortified monastery at the exact moment his father was dying in Tensing's arms. Then he watched as an army of bloodthirsty creatures attacked the defenseless Kingdom of the Golden Dragon. And the only thing standing between them was himself, naked and vulnerable.

The visions were different for each of them, but all were atrocious; they represented what each most feared, their worst memories, nightmares, and weaknesses, their personal journeys to the forbidden chambers of their own consciousnesses. However, it was a much less arduous journey for them than it had been for Tex Armadillo and the Blue Warriors; because the three young people had good souls, they weren't carrying the weight of the others' unspeakable crimes.

The first to come around was the prince, who had had many years of practice in controlling mind and body. With sheer will he broke away from the evil figures attacking him and took a few steps into the room.

"Everything we're seeing is illusion," he shouted,

and, taking his friends by the hands, he pulled them toward the exit.

Alexander was not able to focus on the screen to follow the instructions, but he was sane enough to realize that he hadn't seen anything on the video but an empty room, proof that Dil Bahadur was right and that these diabolical scenes were nothing but his imagination. Leaning close together, they sat down on the floor to calm down enough to confront the horrendous hallucinogenic visions, even though they did not disappear. After a while, lending strength to one another, the three young friends were able to stand. The king had gone straight to the correct door, apparently without falling prey to any of the torments that had affected them; surely he had learned not to inhale the dust, or else he carried an antidote to the drug. In any case, on the video the king seemed to have escaped the psychological torture they suffered.

In the last room protecting the Golden Dragon, the largest of all, the demons and scenes of horror instantly disappeared and were replaced by a wondrous landscape. The ill effects of the drug gave way to an inexplicable euphoria. All three of them felt light as air, strong, invincible. In the warm glow of hundreds of small oil lamps they saw a garden enveloped in a soft, rosy fog rising from the ground toward the treetops. Angelic voices filled their ears and they smelled the penetrating fragrance of wild flowers and tropical fruits. The ceiling had disappeared, and in its place was a sky at the hour of sunset, crisscrossed by birds with vivid plumage. They rubbed their eyes, incredulous.

"This isn't real either. I'm sure we're still drugged," Nadia murmured.

"Are we all seeing the same thing? I see a park," Alexander added.

"So do I," said Nadia.

"And I. If the three of us see the same thing, it isn't a vision. This is a trap, perhaps the most dangerous of all," Dil Bahadur warned. "It will be best if we do not touch anything, and walk through quickly."

"So we're not dreaming? This looks like the Garden of Eden," commented Alexander, still slightly groggy from the golden dust of the previous room.

"What garden is that?" asked Dil Bahadur.

"The Garden of Eden appears in the Bible. It was where the Creator placed the first man and woman. I think nearly all religions have such a garden. Paradise is a place of eternal beauty and happiness," his friend explained.

Alexander first thought that what he was witnessing might be virtual images or film projections, but then he realized it couldn't be modern technology. The palace had been constructed many centuries before.

Through the fog filled with delicate butterflies came three human figures: two girls and a youth, all radiantly beautiful, with silken hair ruffled by the breeze; they were dressed in airy, embroidered silks and had large wings of golden feathers. They moved with extraordinary grace, calling to them with open arms. The temptation to go to those translucent creatures and surrender to the pleasure of being carried off by their powerful wings was nearly irresistible. Alexander took one step forward, hypnotized by one of the maidens, and Nadia smiled at the youthful stranger, but Dil Bahadur had enough presence of mind to catch his two friends by the arms.

"Don't touch them," he begged. "That would be fatal. This is the garden of temptations."

But Nadia and Alexander, beyond reason, tried to break free from the hands of the prince.

"They aren't real, they're painted on the wall, or they're statues. Ignore them," he repeated.

"They move and they're calling to us," Alexander murmured, enchanted.

"It's a trick, an optical illusion. Look over there!" Dil Bahadur cried, forcing them to look toward one corner of the garden.

Lying face-down on the ground across a pot of painted flowers lay the lifeless body of one of the Blue Warriors. Dil Bahadur led his friends there. The prince bent down and turned the body over; they all saw the horrible way he had died.

The warriors of the scorpion sect had come into this fantastic garden as if in a dream, drugged by the golden powder, which made them believe everything they saw. They were brutes who had spent their lives on horse-back; they slept on the hard ground and were accustomed to cruelty, suffering, and poverty. They had never seen anything beautiful or delicate; they knew nothing of music, flowers, fragrances, or butterflies like those in this garden. They worshipped serpents, scorpions, and bloodthirsty gods. They feared demons and Hell, but they had never heard of Paradise or angels like the ones they were seeing in this final trap of the Sacred Passageway. The closest thing to intimacy or love they knew was the rough camaraderie they shared. Tex Armadillo had had to threaten them with his pistol to keep them from wandering through the bewitched garden, but he had not been able to prevent one of them from yielding to temptation.

The man had reached out and touched the hand of one of the beautiful, winged damsels. He felt the cold of marble, except the texture wasn't smooth like marble, it was rough as sandpaper or ground glass. He pulled back his hand in surprise, and saw the scratches in his palm. That instant his skin began to crack and pull open, and his flesh dissolved as if it were burned to the bone. The others ran to him when he screamed, but there was nothing they could do: the lethal poison had already entered his bloodstream and moved up his arm like corrosive acid. In less than a minute, the poor wretch was dead.

Now Alexander, Nadia, and Dil Bahadur were standing before his corpse, which in the intervening days had dried like a mummy from the effect of the poison. The body had shrunk; it was a skeleton with black hide stuck to bones that emitted a lingering odor of mushrooms and moss.

"As I said, best not to touch anything," the prince repeated but his warning was no longer necessary. After seeing the corpse, Nadia and Alexander had wakened from their trance.

At last the three young people were in the Chamber of the Golden Dragon. Although he had never seen it,

Dil Bahadur immediately recognized it from the descriptions the monks had given him in the four monasteries where he had learned the code. Here were the gold-sheathed walls covered with bas-relief gold engravings of the life of Siddhartha Gautama, the pure gold candelabra holding beeswax candles, the delicate oil lamps with shades of filigreed gold, the gold incense burners with myrrh and other exotic scents. Gold, gold everywhere. The gold that had spurred the greed of Tex Armadillo and the Blue Warriors left Dil Bahadur, Alexander, and Nadia completely indifferent; they thought that the yellow metal was actually rather ugly.

"Perhaps it would not be too much to ask what we're doing here," Alexander said to the prince, unable to avoid the sarcasm in his tone.

"Perhaps I am not sure myself," Dil Bahadur replied.

"Why did your father tell you to come here?" Nadia wanted to know.

"Possibly to consult the Golden Dragon."

"But the dragon was stolen! There's nothing here but that black stone with the quartz inset; that must be the base where the statue stood," said Alexander.

"That *is* the golden dragon," the prince informed them.

"What is?"

"The stone base. The thieves spoke of taking a very valuable statue, but in fact the oracle's predictions issue from the stone. That is the kings' secret, which even the monks in the monasteries do not know. That is the secret my father told me and that you must never repeat."

"So how does it work?"

"First I have to chant the question in the language of the Yetis, then the quartz in the stone begins to vibrate and emits a sound that I must interpret."

"Are you pulling my leg?" asked Alexander.

Dil Bahadur didn't know what that meant. He didn't have the least intention of pulling anyone's leg.

"We'll see how it works. What do you want to ask it?" inquired Nadia, always the practical one.

"Perhaps most important would be to know my karma, so I can fulfill my destiny without straying from the path," Dil Bahadur decided.

"We risked our lives only to learn what your karma is?" Alexander joked.

"I can tell you that: You are a good prince and you will be a great king," was Nadia's comment.

Dil Bahadur asked his friends to sit quietly at the back of the room, and then he approached the platform where the paws of the magnificent statue had rested.

He lighted incense burners and candles, then sat with his legs crossed for a time that seemed very long to Nadia and Alexander. He meditated in silence until his anxieties were calmed and his mind cleansed of all thoughts, desires, and fears—and curiosity. He opened inwardly like the lotus flower, as his master had taught him, to receive the energy of the universe.

The first notes were barely a murmur, but the prince's chant quickly changed to a powerful roar that burst from the earth itself, a guttural sound his two friends had never heard. It was difficult to imagine the sound was human; it seemed to issue from a huge drum in the heart of an enormous cavern. The harsh notes rolled, ascended, fell, acquired rhythm, volume, speed, then faded . . . only to rise again, like the waves of the sea. Each note shattered against the gold walls and was returned multiplied. Fascinated, Nadia and Alexander felt the vibration deep inside them, as if it were born of them. Soon they realized that a second voice had been added to the chant of the prince, a very different voice: the answer, originating in the small section of yellow quartz set in the black stone. Dil Bahadur fell silent in order to listen to the stone's message, which lingered in the air like the echo of great brass bells tolling in unison. The prince's concentration was absolute; not a muscle of his body quivered, as his mind grouped the notes by fours and simultaneously transposed them into the ideograms of the lost language of the Yetis, which he had been memorizing for twelve years.

Dil Bahadur's song lasted more than an hour, which to Nadia and Alexander seemed only a few minutes; the extraordinary music had transported them to a higher level of consciousness. They knew that for eighteen centuries this chamber had been visited only by the kings of the Forbidden Kingdom, and that no one before them had ever witnessed the ceremony of the oracle. Mute, eyes round with amazement, the two young people followed the rising and falling tones of the stone, not understanding exactly what Dil Bahadur was doing, but sure that it was something miraculous, with deep spiritual meaning.

Finally, silence fell over the Sacred Chamber. The section of quartz, which had seemed to glow with light from within during the chanting, turned opaque, as it had been in the beginning. The prince, drained, sat motionless for some time, while his friends waited, not wanting to interrupt him.

"My father is dead," Dil Bahadur said finally, standing.

"Is that what the stone said?" Alexander asked.

"Yes. My father waited until I was here, and then was free to abandon himself to death."

"How did he know you were here?"

"My master, Tensing, told him," said the young prince sadly.

"What else did the stone tell you?" Nadia asked.

"It is my karma to be the next-to-the-last monarch of the Kingdom of the Golden Dragon. I shall have a son, who will be the last king. After him, the world and this kingdom will change, and nothing will ever again be the same. To govern with justice and wisdom, I shall have the help of my father, who will guide me in my dreams. I shall also have Pema, whom I am going to marry, and Tensing, and the Golden Dragon."

"You mean the stone, because there's nothing left of the statue but ash," Alexander noted.

"Perhaps I did not understand clearly, but I believe it will be recovered," commented the prince, signaling that it was time to start back.

Timothy Bruce and Joel González, the *International Geographic* photographers, had carried out Kate's orders to the letter. They had spent that time traveling to the most inaccessible parts of the kingdom, guided by a short, stocky sherpa who carried the heavy equipment

and tents without ever losing his calm smile or unvary-
ing pace. The foreigners, in contrast, were faint from
the effort of following him, and from the altitude, in
which they could scarcely breathe. The photographers,
who knew nothing about their companions' exploits,
arrived with great excitement to tell of their adventures
with rare orchids and panda bears, but Kate didn't
show the slightest interest in their tales. She floored
them with the news that Nadia and her grandson had
contributed to eliminating a criminal organization, rescued five kidnapped girls, captured a band of dangerous bandits, and placed Prince Dil Bahadur on the
throne—all this with the help of a tribe of Yetis and a
mysterious monk with mental powers. Timothy and
Joel did not open their mouths again until it was time
to board the airplane to return to their country.

"One thing is for sure, I'm not traveling with
Alexander and Nadia again," declared the writer, who
still hadn't recovered from recent alarms. "They attract
danger like honey draws flies. I'm far too old to be so
scared."

At that, Alexander and Nadia exchanged knowing
glances, because they had decided that they were going
with her on her next reporting assignment, no matter
what. They would not miss the chance to experience

another adventure with Kate Cold.

The young people had not shared the secrets of the Sacred Chamber with Kate, or of the miraculous piece of quartz, because they had sworn never to tell. They limited themselves to saying that Dil Bahadur, like all the monarchs of the Forbidden Kingdom before him, could go there to hear predictions about the future.

"In ancient Greece there was a temple in Delphi where people went to hear the prophecies of an oracle," Kate told them. "The words she spoke in her trance were always puzzling, but the people who came to the oracle found meaning in them. Today it's known that a gas, probably ether, escaped from the ground at that spot. The priestess was dizzied by the gas and spoke in code; the rest was imagined by her naïve clients."

"This isn't the same thing. What we saw can't be explained by gas," her grandson replied.

The writer laughed dryly.

Alexander smiled. "Our roles have been reversed, Kate. Once I was the skeptic who didn't believe anything unless I saw the proof, you were the one who kept telling me that the world is a mysterious place and that not everything can be explained rationally."

His grandmother couldn't answer because she was laughing so hard that she started coughing and was nearly choking. Her grandson clapped her on the back a few times, a little harder than necessary. Nadia went to get a glass of water.

"It's too bad that Tensing has left for the Valley of the Yetis, otherwise he could have cured your cough with his magic needles and prayers. I'm afraid you're just going to have to give up smoking, Grandmother," said Alexander.

"Don't . . . call . . . me . . . grandmother!"

The afternoon before leaving for the United States, after attending the king's funeral service, the members of the *International Geographic* expedition met in the palace of the thousand rooms with the royal family and General Kunglung. The monarch had been cremated, according to tradition, and his ashes had been divided into four antique alabaster vessels the country's premiere soldiers had carried on horseback to the four cardinal points of the kingdom, where they were scattered on the wind. Neither his people nor his family, who loved him so, wept over the king's death; they believed that weeping obliges the spirit to stay in the world to console the living. The correct thing to do was to show happiness so the spirit can be content to go live out another turn of the wheel of reincarnation, evolving in each life until finally it reaches illumination and heaven—or Nirvana.

"Perhaps my father will honor us by reincarnating in our first son," said Prince Dil Bahadur.

Pema's teacup rattled in her hand, betraying her emotion. She was wearing silk brocade, soft leather shoes, and gold jewelry at her wrists and ears, but her head was bare because she was proud of having contributed her beautiful hair to a cause that was just. Her example helped the other four girls with shaved heads escape a complex over being bald. The long, hundred and fifty-foot strand they had woven from their hair had been placed as an offering before the Great Buddha in the palace, where people made pilgrimages to see it. There had been so much talk about the girls, and they had been seen so often on television, that a kind of mass hysteria had resulted, and hundreds of girls had shaved their own heads in imitation. Dil Bahadur had to appear in person on the screen to assure his people that the kingdom did not need such extreme expressions of patriotism. Alexander commented that in the United States shaved heads were fashionable, along with tattoos and noses, ears, and belly buttons pierced to display rings, but no one believed him.

They were all sitting in a circle on cushions on the

floor, drinking *chai*, the sweet, aromatic tea of India. They tried to swallow bites of an inedible chocolate cake the nuns who were the palace cooks had invented to honor the foreign visitors. Tschewang, the royal leopard, had stretched out beside Nadia, completely relaxed. Following the death of the king, its master, the handsome feline had been depressed. For several days it hadn't wanted to eat, until Nadia convinced the great cat that it was the leopard's responsibility to guard Dil Bahadur.

"As my honorable master Tensing left to go fulfill his mission in the Valley of the Yetis, he gave me something for you," Dil Bahadur said to Alexander.

"For me?"

"Not exactly for you, but for your honorable mother," the new king replied, handing Alexander a small wooden box.

"What is it?"

"A dragon dropping."

"A what?" Alexander, Nadia, and Kate asked in unison.

"It has the reputation of being a very potent medicine. Possibly if you dissolve it in a bit of rice liquor and give it to her, your honorable mother might be cured of her illness," said Dil Bahadur.

"How can I ask my mother to swallow such a

thing?" cried Alex, offended.

"Possibly it would be better not to tell her what it is. It is petrified. Which is not, I believe, the same as fresh excrement . . . In any case, Alexander, it has magical powers. A small piece saved me from the daggers of the Blue Warriors," Dil Bahadur explained, pointing to the tiny rock hanging from a leather cord around his neck.

Kate could not help rolling her eyes, and a mocking smile danced briefly on her lips, but Alexander, moved, thanked his friend for the gift and put it in his shirt pocket.

"When the helicopter went up in fire, exploded, Golden Dragon melted. Very serious. Our people believe golden statue keeps borders safe for us. Many years it defends our borders and keeps our nation prosperous," said General Kunglung.

"Perhaps it isn't the statue but the wisdom and prudence of your rulers that has kept the nation safe," Kate replied. She surreptitiously offered her chocolate cake to the leopard, who sniffed it, wrinkled its muzzle with distaste, and went back to lie beside Nadia.

"How can we make people understand that young King Dil Bahadur is good man—is honorable man, strong even without the sacred dragon?" asked the general.

"With all respect, honorable General, possibly your people will have another statue before long," said the writer, who finally had learned to speak as the courtesy of the country required.

"Does the honorable Little Grandmother wish to explain what she is saying?" Dil Bahadur interrupted.

"Possibly a friend of mine can resolve the problem," said Kate, and went on to explain her plan.

After a few hours' battle with the primitive telephone company of the Forbidden Kingdom, the writer had succeeded in speaking directly to Isaac Rosenblat in New York City, and had asked him if it would be possible for him to craft a dragon similar to the one that was destroyed, based on four Polaroid photographs, some rather fuzzy video film, and a detailed description given by the bandits of the scorpion sect, who were hoping to please the nation's authorities.

"Are you asking me to make a statue out of gold?" Isaac Rosenblat shouted from the other side of the planet.

"Yes, Isaac. More or less the size of a dog. Plus, set it with several hundred precious stones, including diamonds, sapphires, emeralds—and, of course, a pair of identical star rubies for the eyes."

"And who, for God's sake, is going to pay for all this?"

"A certain collector who has an office very near yours, Isaac," replied Kate, howling with laughter.

The writer was very proud of her plan. She had had a special recorder sent from the United States, one that was not sold commercially but that she had obtained thanks to her contacts with a CIA agent with whom she had become friends while reporting in Bosnia. With that gadget she had been able to listen to the miniaturized tapes Judit Kinski had hidden in her handbag. They contained the information needed to identify the client called the Collector. Kate intended to use that evidence to trap him. She would leave him alone only if he replaced the lost statue; it was the least he could do to repair the harm that had been done. The Collector had taken precautions to prevent his telephone calls from being intercepted, but he didn't suspect that each of the agents the Specialist had sent to close their deal had taped the negotiations. For Judit, those tapes were life insurance she could use if things became ugly. That was why she carried them with her at all times—until she had lost her handbag in the struggle with Tex Armadillo. Kate Cold knew that the second wealthiest man in the world would not allow his connection with a criminal organization, which included kidnapping the monarch of a peaceful nation, to appear in the press, and that he would have to give in to her demands.

Kate's plan caught the court of the Forbidden Kingdom off guard.

"Perhaps it would be wise for the honorable Little Grandmother to discuss the matter with the lamas. Her plan is well intentioned, but possibly the course she means to follow is slightly illegal," Dil Bahadur suggested amiably.

"Perhaps it is not, shall we say, legal, but the Collector deserves no better. Leave the matter to me, Majesty. In this case I am fully prepared to darken my karma with a little blackmail. And by the way, if it is not inappropriate, may I ask Your Majesty what will happen to Judit Kinski?" Kate asked.

The woman had been found, unconscious and stiff with cold, by one of the parties of soldiers General Kunglung had sent to search for her. She had wandered through the mountains for days, lost and hungry, until her feet were frostbitten and she could go no farther. The cold made her sleepy, and she had rapidly lost her desire to live. Judit had abandoned herself to her fate with a kind of secret relief. After so much danger and greed in her life, the temptation of death seemed sweet. In her brief moments of lucidity it was not her past triumphs that came to mind but the serene face of Dorji, the king. What was the reason for his stubborn presence in her memory? She had never loved him. She had pretended to because she needed him to give her the code to the golden dragon, nothing more. She did, she admitted to herself, admire him. That gentle man had made a profound impression on her. She thought that under different circumstances, or if she had been a different woman, she would have inevitably fallen in love with him. But that hadn't happened, she was sure. Which was why she was surprised that the king's spirit stayed with her in that icy place where she awaited death. The sovereign's placid, caring eyes were the last thing she saw before she slipped into darkness.

The patrol found her just in time to save her life. As they spoke, Judit was in the hospital, where they were keeping her sedated after amputating several fingers and toes that had been badly frostbitten.

"Before he died, my father told me not to sentence Judit Kinski to prison. I want to offer the woman the chance to improve her karma, and evolve spiritually. I will send her to spend the rest of her life in a Buddhist monastery on the border with Tibet. The climate is harsh, and the place is isolated, but the nuns are, as you say, saintly. I've been told that they get up before sunrise, spend the day meditating, and eat nothing but a few grains of rice."

"And you think that Judit will gain wisdom there?" asked Kate, smiling sarcastically and exchanging glances with General Myar Kunglung.

"That depends on her alone, honorable Grand-mother," the prince replied.

"May I ask Your Majesty please to call me Kate? That's my name."

"It will be a privilege to call you by name. Perhaps our honorable grandmother Kate, her valiant photog-raphers, and my friends Nadia and Alexander will want to return to this humble kingdom where Pema and I will always welcome you," said the young king.

"You bet!" exclaimed Alexander, but an elbow from Nadia reminded him of his manners, and he added; "Although possibly we do not deserve the generosity of Your Majesty and his worthy bride, perhaps we will be sufficiently bold to accept such an honorable invita-tion."

Everyone burst out laughing, unable to help them-selves, even the nuns who were ceremoniously serving tea, and little Borobá, who started excitedly leaping around, tossing pieces of chocolate cake into the air.

P.S.

Ideas,
interviews
& features...

About the author

About the book

Read on

Interview with Isabel Allende

by Eithne Farry

JANUARY 8TH IS always an auspicious day for Isabel Allende. She confides: 'I get up very early and I meditate a little bit, and then I do a little ceremony that's becoming more and more complicated. I burn sage, light a candle.' There is a delicate pause and then the highly acclaimed author, whose work has been translated into at least twenty-seven languages, lets out a bark of laughter. 'You know, that kind of New Age bull!'

And that's the way the interview goes. Moments of seriousness and introspection are undone with a brash statement, a flash of self-deprecating humour, a quick-fire bit of emotional honesty to help the conversation along. Isabel talks about her love of words, her family, her 'outsiderness', and her fondness for make-up and 'very high heels' – 'they make me feel four inches taller, which is good when you are only five feet tall'. And she talks very seriously and very intensely about her work, about the need 'to be alone, for sometimes ten or fourteen hours a day, to allow me to see how things relate to each other. I need to be aware of memory, to sit in the quiet and recall all the details, and see how they connect.'

For Isabel, writing is an almost magical process, and January 8th is always the day she chooses to sit down to work on a new book. 'I'm always a little scared that maybe it won't work, that this time it won't happen. But I've been writing for twenty-two years now and I've learned that if you have patience the words will come.' This tradition started with *The House of the Spirits* – the debut that catapulted Isabel into the literary limelight and which began life as a letter to her dying Chilean grandfather. 'I started writing a spiritual letter to him on the 8th January, to tell him that people only die when you forget them, and that I would never forget him. But I soon realized that he would never read it, and that somehow it was turning itself into a book.'

It was a particularly poignant time for Isabel. She was living in exile in Venezuela following the 1973 coup in Chile and was unable to return home. 'You know, because of all that it is very hard for me to write a story about normal people, who have normal lives sheltered by the establishment. My characters are marginal – people who have either come to a new place and don't know the rules, or they are different and therefore they are not accepted. So that's the kind of people I am interested in – the people on the fringes of society – and those are the stories I write.' She adds: 'I always write from the perspective of the outsider, because that is what I feel I am. Even when I write about Chile I am an outsider, because I have not lived there for many years. I am different now, I have changed, the country has changed and I don't fit in. But I don't really fit in anywhere so it's fine, I'm used to it.'

She has lived in America for twenty years and has fallen in love with Marin County, ▶

6 My characters are marginal – people who have either come to a new place and don't know the rules, or they are different and therefore they are not accepted. 9

BORN

Isabel was born in 1942 in
Lima, Peru, and lived in
Chile until 1974. She
worked in Venezuela from
1975 to 1984 and then
moved to America. She
now lives in California
with her husband Willy
Gordon.

CAREER

Isabel Allende has
worked as a TV presenter,
journalist, playwright
and children's author. Her
first book for adults – the
acclaimed *House of the
Spirits* – was published
in Spanish in 1982 and
won her international
attention and praise when
it was translated into
twenty-seven languages.
She has gone on to write
the novels *Portrait in
Sepia*, *Daughter of
Fortune*, *The Infinite Plan*,
Eva Luna, *Of Love and
Shadows* and *Zorro* plus a
short-story collection, *The
Stories of Eva Luna*. She
has also published the

Interview *(continued)*

◄ California, though she still holds on tightly
to her Chilean roots. 'I look Chilean. I cook,
dream, write and make love in Spanish. My
books have an unmistakable Latin American
flavour.' She continues: 'When I speak
English I am a different person. In Spanish
I am very funny. I'm smarter too.' She regrets
leaving her homeland, relatives and friends,
but believes that being an exile made her
the writer she is today. 'It forced me to do
things that I would never have done. I had
to develop strengths that I didn't know I was
capable of. It was traumatic, deeply
traumatic, but it made me strong.'

This strength was severely tested in 1992
when Isabel's daughter became critically
ill with the rare blood disorder porphyria
and fell into a coma. Isabel stayed by her
bedside and wrote her a letter, in an
attempt to express her love and grief and
bewilderment, but her daughter never
regained consciousness. The letter became
Isabel's soul-baring memoir *Paula*, a literary
tour de force which Isabel describes as 'the
most important book that I will ever write.
It is the event that marked me the most,
that changed me the most. It is something
that I remember every single day.' She
continues: 'After Paula's death I thought I
was never going to write again. I had to pull
myself out of a very dark depression.'

She didn't write again for three years.
'I would sit in front of my computer and
nothing would come out. And then I
remembered that I was a journalist – sure
I was a lousy journalist – but I could research
a subject. So I gave myself a theme that would

be as far removed from death as possible.
I decided to write about food and sex.' The
result was *Aphrodite*, a celebration of the
senses. She recalls the research gleefully:
'I just started asking people what turns
them on, wonderful stuff came up, fantastic
stories.'

And, insists Isabel, it is the stories that
count. 'If I can hear a story, if I can tell a story,
that is the most important thing.' This love
affair with words goes back to her childhood
in Chile. 'I was greedy for stories. I would
read anything. I was always enchanted by
the poetry of Pablo Neruda because he could
say things in a way that would amaze me.
He would describe olive oil as liquid gold,
and suddenly I could see it that way. It was
a revelation.' Even now, after seven novels, a
collection of short stories, three memoirs
and a trilogy for children, the process of
writing still excites her. 'I jump out of bed
very early, put on my make-up and high
heels and run to my little casita at the back
of the house and work all day. I am totally
immersed in the story. I go through the
threshold and I enter a space that is dark.
Inside is the story and my job is to show up
in front of the computer every day and
illuminate that space word by word until I
get the story.' ∎

memoir *Paula*, which
she wrote following the
death of her daughter, a
celebration of the senses
entitled *Aphrodite*, and
My Invented Country, in
which she recalls her life
in Chile until Pinochet's
military coup forced her
into exile. She has also
published an adventure
trilogy for children –
City of the Beasts,
*Kingdom of the Golden
Dragon* and *Forest of the
Pygmies* – which takes the
environment and ecology
as its themes.

Favourite
Reads

Poetry
Pablo Neruda

One Hundred Years of Solitude
Gabriel García Márquez

The Female Eunuch
Germaine Greer

His Dark Materials Trilogy
Philip Pullman

The Aleph
Jorge Luis Borges

The Tin Drum
Günter Grass

La Lumière des justes
Henri Troyat

War and Peace
Leo Tolstoy

A Thousand and One Nights

Aunt Julia and the Scriptwriter
Mario Vargas Llosa

Sandokan
Emilio Salgari

Q & A

What are the differences between writing for adults and children?

I think that writing for young adults requires more action, velocity, dialogue and humour than for adults. A strong plot and memorable characters are important. Less description is probably better.

Did you enjoy the challenge?

I enjoyed the challenge very much! And I learned a new genre. My hardest critics are my grandchildren. They always teach me a lot.

Where did the idea to write three books for children come from?

I had promised my three grandchildren that I would write a novel for them. They liked the first one so much that I ended up writing two more.

What did you feel like when you were writing them? Did you remember what it was like to be a child again? Or is that something that you can access all the time anyway?

I remembered the books I loved as a teenager that helped me. I have been writing novels for twenty-two years, so it was not hard to change the style to write juvenile books.

What is your most vivid memory of childhood?

Stories. I was a great reader and I invented stories for my brothers. ▶

Q & A *(continued)*

◀ **Is it important to you to write books for children that have a theme like the environment, ecology, and the Buddhist belief that 'we must seek truth and illumination within ourselves, not in others or in external things'? Should there be a message as well as an exciting story?**

I don't want to be didactic in my books. Who am I to teach kids anything? But unavoidably my ideas and beliefs appear in everything I write.

You've dedicated the book 'to my friend Tabra Tunoa, tireless traveller, who took me to the Himalayas, and told me about the Golden Dragon'.

My friend Tabra Tunoa took me to India and Nepal. We trekked in the Himalayas (not too high, though). She told me about Tibet and Bhutan. I was impressed by the landscape of tall mountains and beautiful valleys. The people are unforgettable. Their culture and religion are based on tolerance and compassion.

Did you eat the monks' diet of tsampa, as well as local delicacies? What did each taste like?

I ate the local food. Tsampa and tea with yak butter had a slightly stale and smoky taste, but you soon get used to it. We mainly ate vegetarian food, because they eat very little meat.

Is the Hidden Kingdom a real place, like Mustang, or imagined?

The model for the kingdom of my book is really Bhutan.

Do you think writing about it could be harmful in that more people will want to visit and therefore begin to destroy the harmonious balance?

Only a few tourists a year are allowed in Bhutan. The government and the people protect their environment fiercely.

Did you do a massive amount of research?

Yes, I had to do much research for each one of the books.

What would you suggest people read to find out more?

I read dozens of books for the research. The best ways to start are a good travel book and the Internet.

Do you have a totemic animal?

I had a very important dream in which I discovered that my totemic animal is the eagle. I do not particularly like eagles. I have seldom seen one, and I do not know why this bird is my spirit animal. When I meditate, often I feel that I can see from above and can fly great distances. The eagle is solitary and fierce. ▶

Q & A *(continued)*

◄ **Why that particular one? What does it say about you as a person?**

The fact that the eagle is always in the air, far above everything else, gives it distance to see what others do not see. Maybe that is why I am a storyteller. I observe quietly from a distance and thus I get the stories.

Is Buddhism important to you?

Buddhism is very attractive to me but I am not a religious person. I have a private spiritual practice but I do not belong to any church.

Is there a special skill from any of the three books that you wish you had, for example, being invisible, reading auras, fighting in the Tao-shu style, talking with and understanding animals?

I would like to have all the skills that I mention in the trilogy! I would love to be able to fly or to transform myself into an eagle – wouldn't you?

Do you believe in yetis?

I believe that the world is a very mysterious place. Anything is possible, including yetis.

Are the Blue Warriors based on a real gang?

The Blue Warriors are based on a tribe of nomads in Northern India who worship the scorpion.

What is your most treasured memory of that trip?

My best memory is trying to communicate in broken English and sign language with the sherpas, the monks and the people in the remote villages. They are beautiful people. Their faces are soft, they are polite and calm, and they always smile.

Did you bring back any souvenirs?

I brought back some old beads, and thousands of photographs.

Now that the trilogy is complete, do you have plans to write more books for children?

For the time being I have no plans to write for children. I just finished a book on Zorro. It was written for adults but I suppose that kids that are good readers will enjoy it. ∎

Have You Read?

Other titles by Isabel Allende

City of the Beasts
Isabel Allende's first novel for children, this is an eco-thriller that introduces the reader to Alex Cold, his redoubtable grandmother Kate, and sensitive Nadia. Here the trio head down the Amazon River on the track of a legendary 9-foot beast. They also encounter anthropologists, anacondas, and the mysterious People of the Mist, whose harmonious life style is being threatened by the encroachment of 'civilization'. It's up to Alex and Nadia to find a way to help them out of their predicament.

'Allende's writing is so vivid we hear the sounds, see the bright birds, smell and even taste the soft fruit'   *The Times*

The House of the Spirits
Allende's debut was an immediate success on its publication in 1982, garnering critical acclaim and a huge international fan base for the Chilean author. It's a grand sweep of a novel, following the fortunes of the charismatic Trueba family as they negotiate the emotional and political upheavals that beset their lives. Written in lush, lyrical prose, Allende introduces clairvoyants, fortune tellers, playboys, mystics, gentlemen landowners and reformers to 'the big house on the corner' and the reader to the enchantment of 'magical realism'.

'Nothing short of astonishing ... In *The House of the Spirits* Isabel Allende has indeed shown us the relationships between past and

present, family and nation, city and country,
spiritual and political values. She has done so
with enormous imagination, sensitivity, and
compassion'   *San Francisco Chronicle*

....

Paula
Justly regarded as Allende's tour de force, this
hugely moving memoir began as a letter to
her daughter Paula, who became gravely ill in
December 1991. Allende wrote the story of
her family for her comatose daughter,
including anecdotes, descriptions of
relatives, and accounts of Chile in the
turbulent years leading up to Pinochet's
military coup. Paula never regained
consciousness and Allende published the
book as a memorial to her daughter and a
meditation on grief, faith and loss.

'Beautiful and heart-rending . . . Memoir,
autobiography, epicedium, perhaps even
some fiction: they are all here, and they are
all quite wonderful'
                    Los Angeles Times Book Review

....

Daughter of Fortune
Orphan Eliza Sommers goes on a search for
love, but ends up on a journey of self-
discovery. Brought up in the British colony of
Valparaíso in Chile by the well-intentioned
spinster Miss Rose (and her more stuffy
brother Jeremy), Eliza falls unsuitably in
love with the humble but handsome clerk
Joaquín. When he heads to California to take
part in the 1849 gold rush, Eliza follows ▶

Have You Read? *(continued)*

◄ him. But in the rough-and-tumble life of San Francisco our unconventional heroine finds that personal freedom might be a more rewarding choice than the traditional gold band on the wedding finger.

'Memory and imagination and myth weave their spells ... Allende creates world upon world in dazzling descriptive prose'
Independent on Sunday

My Invented Country
Exploring the events of her life and the country in which she lived until Pinochet's military coup, Isabel Allende takes us on an up-close and personal tour of her Chile. Two life-altering world events mark out her reappraisal of the concept of home – the military coup in Chile in the 1970s, which sent her into exile, and the events of 9/11 in her adopted country. Family and friends are recalled in all their exasperating, entertaining glory, and the effects of the political upheavals are vividly described. But she also explores the roles of myth and memory in shaping her books, concluding that nostalgia is a huge inspiration.

'Allende is incapable of telling a bad story. She writes of her own experiences with a kind of wild candour' *Independent*

If You Loved This,
You'll Like ...

Forest of the Pygmies
The final instalment of Isabel Allende's
trilogy follows Alex and Nadia's adventures
in Kenya. Here you can read the first few
pages.

At an order from the guide, Michael
Mushaha, the elephant caravan came to a
stop. The suffocating heat of midday was
beginning, when creatures of the vast nature
preserve rested. Life paused for a few hours
as the African earth became an inferno of
burning lava, and even the hyenas and
vultures sought the shade. Alexander Cold
and Nadia Santos were riding a wilful bull
elephant named Kobi. The animal had taken
a liking to Nadia, because during their time
together she had made an effort to learn the
basics of the elephants' language in order to
communicate with him. During their long
treks, she told him about her country, Brazil,
a distant land that had no creature as large
as he, other than some ancient, legendary
beasts hidden deep in the heart of South
America's mountains. Kobi appreciated
Nadia as much as he detested Alexander, and
he never lost an opportunity to demonstrate
both sentiments.

    Kobi's five tons of muscle and fat shivered
to a halt in a small oasis beneath dusty trees
kept alive by a pool of water the colour of
milky tea. Alexander had developed his own
style of jumping to the ground from his nine-
foot-high perch without mauling himself
too badly, since in the five days of their
safari he still had not gained the animal's ▶

If You Loved This *(continued)*

◀ cooperation. He was not aware that this time Kobi had positioned himself in such a way that when Alex jumped down, he landed in a puddle of water up to his knees. Boroba, Nadia's small black monkey, then jumped on top of him. As Alex struggled to pry the monkey off his head, he lost his balance and plopped down on his seat. He cursed to himself, shook off Boroba, and only with difficulty regained his footing because he couldn't see through his glasses, which were dripping filthy water. As he was looking for a clean corner of his T-shirt to wipe the lenses, the elephant thumped him on the back with his trunk, a blow that propelled him face first into the puddle. Kobi waited for Alex to pull himself up, then turned his monumental rear end and unleashed a Pantagruelian blast in his face. The other members of the safari greeted the prank with a chorus of guffaws.

Nadia was in no hurry to get down; she waited for Kobi to help her dismount in a more dignified manner. She stepped upon the knee he offered her, steadied herself on the trunk, and then leaped to the ground with the grace of a ballerina. The elephant was not that considerate with anyone else, not even Mushaha, for whom he had respect but not affection. Kobi was an elephant with clear principles. It was one thing to transport tourists on his back, a job like any other, for which he was rewarded with excellent food and mud baths. It was something entirely different to perform circus tricks for a handful of peanuts. He liked peanuts, he couldn't deny that, but he received much more pleasure from tormenting people like

Alexander. Why did the American get under his skin? The animal wasn't sure, it was a matter of chemistry. He didn't like the fact that Alex was always hanging around Nadia. There were thirteen elephants in the caravan, but he had to ride with the girl. It was very inconsiderate of Alex to get between Nadia and him that way. Didn't he realize that they needed privacy for their conversations? A good whack with the trunk and occasionally breaking wind in Alex's face were just what that young man deserved. Kobi trumpeted loudly once Nadia was down and had thanked him by planting a big kiss on his trunk. The girl had good manners; she would never humiliate him by offering him peanuts. ■

BOOKSHOP

Other titles by Isabel Allende available from Harper Perennial at **10%** off recommended retail price. *FREE postage and packing in the UK.*

Aphrodite
(ISBN: 0–00–720516–3)   £8.99
....

My Invented Country
(ISBN: 0–00–716310–X)   £7.99
....

City of the Beasts
(ISBN: 0–00–714637–X)   £7.99
....

Daughter of Fortune
(ISBN: 0–00–655232–3)   £7.99
....

Paula
(ISBN: 0–00–654856–3)   £7.99
....

Portrait in Sepia
(ISBN: 0–00–712301–9)   £6.99
....

The Infinite Plan
(ISBN: 0–00–654684–6)   £7.99
....

Total cost ....

10% discount ....

Final total ....

*To purchase by Visa/Mastercard/Switch
simply call **08707 871724** or fax on **08707 871725***

To pay by cheque, send a copy of this form with a cheque made payable to 'HarperCollins Publishers' to: Mail Order Dept (Ref: B0B4), HarperCollins Publishers, Westerhill Road, Bishopbriggs, G64 2QT, making sure to include your full name, postal address and phone number.

From time to time HarperCollins may wish to use your personal data to send you details of other HarperCollins publications and offers. If you wish to receive information on other HarperCollins publications and offers please tick this box ☐

Do not send cash or currency. Prices correct at time of press. Prices and availability are subject to change without notice. Delivery overseas and to Ireland incurs a £2 per book postage and packing charge.